1

Drop It

Tumble burst out of the bushes, clutching something ragged in his jaws. Something hairy. Something matted with what looked worryingly like blood.

Charlie assumed it was a dead rat or a rabbit. Tumble the Jack Russell often emerged from the undergrowth with such fragrant delights, all waggy and pleased with himself, like he was bringing you a thoughtfully chosen gift. What do you mean, you wanted aftershave, not a rotting rodent corpse that I found under a hedge?

As Charlie chased the hyperactively happy terrier around – ineffectually telling him to drop it while the other dogs milled about, making the task harder – he began to question if it was a dead animal after all. The texture looked artificial. It was less like a formerly living thing, more like one of those fluffy pencil cases that girls had at school, stuffed with rainbow gel pens, scented rubbers and novelty-shaped notelets to pass around in class.

Hang on, was that a fabric label sticking out of Tumble's mouth? Had he actually found some sort of strange fur hat? Or wait . . . was it . . . a wig? Maybe it had flown off in a strong gust of wind, like something from an old-fashioned farce.

Mildly amused, Charlie was pondering this possibility, picturing a Donald Trump type chasing his own hair through the trees, when Tumble's sibling Rough crashed out of the foliage with something remarkably similar in his mouth. This one was greyer and marginally less gore-encrusted but otherwise identical.

What was going on? To lose one toupée in high winds may be regarded as a misfortune. To lose two could be considered deeply bizarre. Or was someone running a wig shop back there? *Woodland Wigs. We care for the hair you wear. Discretion and mud stains guaranteed.*

The dogs worked each other into a state of bulging-eyed derangement and vanished back into the vegetation, which had acquired an orangey hue since October arrived. Cursing his luck and zipping up his parka, Charlie ploughed in after them. He just hoped they hadn't rolled in anything too gross. Tess, the long-suffering owner of Rough and Tumble, would pull a face and give him that 'not angry, just disappointed' look which always made Charlie feel hot-faced and guilty.

He pushed through the bushes, picking his way past all manner of detritus. Coffee cup lids, empty crisp packets, discarded vapes, fried chicken boxes, faeces of dubious origin. That was when Charlie saw him.

A man was sitting with his back to Charlie, slumped unmoving against a tree. He didn't appear to have noticed the surrounding cacophony of yapping dogs, rustling leaves and tutting dogwalkers.

That didn't ring alarm bells at first. Chancing across cottagers, crackheads or comatose 'gentlemen of the street' wasn't unusual in this part of Framstone Woods. Its proximity to both the seafront and the main road made it a hot spot

PENGUIN BOOKS

The Dogwalkers' Detective Agency

Michael Hogan is a writer and editor with a thirty-year career in journalism. He started out on teen magazines *More!* and *Just 17* before progressing to grown-up titles.

As a freelance writer for the past fifteen years, he's been TV critic for the *Telegraph* and written for the *Guardian*, BBC, *Observer*, *Independent*, *i Paper*, *Radio Times*, *Red*, *Q*, *Empire*, *Marie Claire*, *Grazia*, *Glamour*, *Heat*, *Esquire*, *GQ* and *You* magazine.

Michael now writes mainly about TV and pop culture, but also turns his hand to lifestyle pieces, topical comment, celebrity interviews and humorous articles. He occasionally writes and edits scripts for TV.

He lives in London with his family and a rescue dog called Ivy. To escape them all and get some work/procrastination done, he commutes to a shed at the bottom of his garden.

The Dogwalkers' Detective Agency is his debut novel.

The Dogwalkers' Detective Agency

MICHAEL HOGAN

PENGUIN BOOKS

PENGUIN BOOKS

UK | USA | Canada | Ireland | Australia
India | New Zealand | South Africa

Penguin Books is part of the Penguin Random House group of companies
whose addresses can be found at global.penguinrandomhouse.com

Penguin Random House UK
One Embassy Gardens, 8 Viaduct Gardens, London SW11 7BW

penguin.co.uk

First published 2025

001

Copyright © Michael Hogan, 2025

The moral right of the author has been asserted

Set in 12.4/15pt Garamond Premier Pro
Typeset by Six Red Marbles UK, Thetford, Norfolk
Printed and bound in Great Britain by Clays Ltd, Elcograf S.p.A.

The authorized representative in the EEA is Penguin Random House Ireland,
Morrison Chambers, 32 Nassau Street, Dublin D02 YH68

A CIP catalogue record for this book is available from the British Library

ISBN: 978-1-405-97795-1

Penguin Random House is committed to a sustainable future
for our business, our readers and our planet. This book is made from
Forest Stewardship Council® certified paper

For Roxie, Betty and Ivy
The goodest of girls

Dedicated to Alex, Kitty and the real Charlie, forever

for all manner of misbehaviour. Hell, Charlie himself had swigged cider, smoked cigarettes and snogged girls here as a teenager. Halcyon days.

Yet when he reached the tree in question and turned to face the slouched figure, he realized with a jolt that this was no dozing drunk. One side of his now bald head was gashed, which looked painful. Although not as painful as the deep knife wound in his chest.

As Charlie leaned in for a closer look, he half expected the man to open his eyes and prepared to jump back in fright, gabbling apologies, while offering to call an ambulance. However, he was disturbed to find the man's eyes already wide open. They were glassy and unseeing but somehow Charlie still felt like they were gazing straight into his soul. He glimpsed his own stricken reflection in them.

The man didn't appear to be breathing but something was moving under his torn shirt. Maggots. That was when the smell hit Charlie in a rancid wave. He wrinkled his nose, then turned and vomited against the nearest tree trunk.

Embarrassed, he wiped his mouth on his coat sleeve, spitting out some stringy bits in disgust, and shrugged sheepishly at the dogs. He'd only seen two dead bodies before. Both were his grandparents, laid peacefully in bedrooms that smelled of peppermints and stale biscuits. It was clear that this man's end had been far less peaceful. It certainly wasn't past-their-best Rich Teas that Charlie was whiffing. It was something meaty, eggy and vaguely fruity, like a food recycling bin that needed emptying.

As Charlie watched in fascinated horror, a fat bluebottle crawled out of the dead man's mouth and up his cheek. When it reached his staring but eerily lifeless eye, Charlie threw up again. The dogs sniffed tentatively at his vomit until he shooed them away.

Once he was confident there wasn't a third wave coming, he corralled them back on to their leads, fished out his phone and called Tess, followed by 999.

2

The Notorious W.I.G.

In terms of response time – and most things, come to think of it – Tess Cheong beat Framstone Police with ease. She found Charlie sitting on a bench, as close to his discovery as he could stomach. The dogs snuffled around his feet, occasionally pausing to peer up at him curiously, wondering why their walk had been interrupted and if there were any treats in it for them.

Alongside Tess's two tearaways, the aptly named Rough and Tumble, Charlie was accompanied by his own dog, Ruby. An ageing half-blind Staffy cross, brindle-coated with white paws, she was too creaky to get into much trouble herself these days, apart from when she followed her nose. As her eyesight faded, the stately old lady's sense of smell seemed to have gone off the charts.

Ruby had flumped to the ground for a rest but now hauled herself up to greet Tess with a wag as she hurried along the woodland path. Tess gave all three dogs a brief but fond fur ruffle, handed Charlie a strong white Americano from Coastal Coffee, and got straight down to business.

'Where's Wiggie Smalls then?'

Snapping out of his shell-shocked daze, Charlie took

a sip of nerve-steadying coffee before leading the way towards the bushes. For somewhere so close to the wind-swept seafront, Framstone's woodland was surprisingly dense. Thick and even slightly foreboding in certain light, it had been the prime spot for hide-and-seek when Charlie was growing up.

'How long did it take you to come up with that?' he asked as they shouldered their way through the autumnal undergrowth, which snapped and crackled loudly. *Enough to wake the dead*, thought Charlie grimly.

She shrugged. 'Just the two-minute walk here. I considered Badly Wiggins or Wiggo Mortensen, but Biggie's dead too, so it felt more fitting. Also known as the Notorious W.I.G. naturally.'

'Naturally.'

When he'd breathlessly given her the headlines down the phone, Tess had struggled to conceal her glee, concentrating hard on sounding sympathetic instead. In person there was no disguising it: her eyes shone and she was vibrating with excitement.

'Oof, mate. He honks,' was her considered verdict as they emerged into the small, almost perfectly circular clearing. It was less overgrown than the surrounding area. The leaves and grass here had been flattened, presumably by human feet.

Tess leaned in for a closer look, just like Charlie had. He felt a mix of disappointment and admiration when she didn't reel back and throw up.

'What do we reckon killed him?' she asked, glancing up at Charlie as he kept a respectful distance, feeling queasy again. 'Being whacked over the head or stabbed in the chest? And does he look vaguely familiar to you? Does to me. Buggered if I can place him, though. Or maybe old bald white blokes all look the same when they've carked it.'

'Not really, no, and we probably shouldn't disturb the crime scene,' said Charlie. 'I've watched enough detective dramas to know that.'

'You've already stomped all over it in your big size-tens,' Tess replied, her eyes flitting to his mud-caked Red Wing boots. 'A dainty visit from my tiny tootsies can't hurt. Besides, neither of us touched the body, right?'

'Right.' He hoped nobody would notice the two distinct splashes of vomit by a nearby tree.

Her curiosity with the cadaver sated, Tess did a slow lap of the tree, before broadening out to cover the entire clearing, peering down at the ground and studying foliage as she went. The ground was damp and spongy but annoyingly there was no sign of footprints.

'What are you actually looking for, Tess Marple?' asked Charlie as she snapped a few random pics with her phone. 'A dagger with a monogrammed handle? A recently fired revolver? A length of lead piping in the billiard room?'

'Clues, my dear Dr Flotsam, clues,' said Tess, her sights still trained on the ground. 'Aha!'

Charlie rolled his eyes. She'd reached the littered patch on the way into the clearing from the path and sank to her haunches, inspecting the tossed rubbish like an archaeologist who'd unearthed priceless ancient Roman remains.

'Coffee cup lids,' she called out, as if expecting Charlie to log it in some sort of ledger. 'None of them from Coastal Coffee, I might add. All from the McChains, the traitors. Empty crisp packets, obviously. Discarded vapes. The latest eco hazard. A fried chicken box . . . Get off, Rubes, you greedy guts.' She gently nudged away Ruby, who'd come sniffing over, lured by the lingering poultry aroma. 'Your bog-standard trash. Oh well. I was hoping for something that could be traced, like a bus ticket, shop receipt or casino chip.'

Casino chip? Charlie let that one slide. She'd clearly confused the flickering seaside illuminations of Framstone with the neon lights of Las Vegas. Easy mistake to make.

'I guess the big question is why two wigs?' said Tess. 'I mean, who needs more than one? Maybe apart from a drag queen and he doesn't look the type. Probably never sashayed or shantayed in his life. Now it's too late. He's literally slayed.'

Her rampant speculation was interrupted by wailing sirens and slamming car doors. 'The local plod have graced us with their presence at last,' said Tess. She adopted a cod-American drawl. 'Better get our stories straight, toots. Keep schtum and we'll be well looked after when we get out of the can.'

Charlie smiled wanly and turned to greet the new arrivals. He'd led a quiet life since returning to his home town from London the previous summer, and occasionally caught himself idly craving the excitement of his former life in the city. But corpses and cops? That was a bit too much excitement.

3

One of Ours

'Shit, he's one of ours,' said the first detective to arrive on the scene. 'Or at least, he used to be.'

As two uniformed officers grunted hellos and busied themselves with unfurling police tape, working out which trees to tie it round to cordon off the area, the male plain-clothes copper had walked straight past Charlie, Tess and the dogs. He marched purposefully into the bushes where the victim was sitting.

The female, who'd taken her time looking around, gave a start and strode in after her partner. 'That's Frank Courtney,' they heard her say. 'Ex-job. Decent copper. Retired a decade ago to run the Neptune pub on the seafront.'

'Landlord of the Neppy!' whispered Tess triumphantly. 'Knew I recognized him. Even dead and hairless, I never forget a face.'

Charlie was unsure how to respond. Congratulations didn't feel appropriate under the circumstances.

The detectives returned to the path, both talking into their radios. Charlie picked up phrases like 'deceased male', 'suspicious death' and 'send SOCO down here', aka scenes of crime officer or forensics. He knew those box sets he watched with his mum would come in handy some day.

'Are you the gentleman who found him?' the female detective called over.

'Yep, that's me,' said Charlie, pleasantly surprised to be called a gentleman.

As she came closer, she broke into a grin. 'Well, if it isn't Charlie Boardman.' She chuckled. 'Boardy Boy himself. I haven't seen you since sixth form.'

Wincing at a nickname he hadn't heard for years and not needing to look at Tess to sense her raised eyebrows, he asked, 'Anjali Sharma?'

'Detective Inspector Anjali Thompson, nowadays,' she said, shaking their hands. He'd taken a beat to recognize her. It had been twenty-odd years since school and she had longer, less business-like hair back then. 'And this is Detective Sergeant Craig Murdoch.'

She turned to her sidekick, who stared at Charlie suspiciously. He guessed it came with the job, especially near murdered bodies, but it still unnerved him.

'Craig, meet Charlie Boardman. One-time sporting hero of Framstone High. Captained every school team going and kept the trophy cabinet stocked pretty much single-handedly. Went off to university, then London to be a designer, I heard?'

Charlie nodded. 'Graphic designer, yeah. But now I'm back and discovering dead bodies, apparently.'

Nodding and noting it down, DS Murdoch turned to Tess. 'And you are?'

'Tess Cheong,' she said. 'Owner of Coastal Coffee, down the road. Charlie's a friend.' Murdoch glanced between them. 'Those two reprobates are my dogs. Strictly speaking, it's them who discovered the body.'

Murdoch didn't react. Clearly not one for friendly banter. Not at a murder scene anyway.

As DI Thompson turned back to Charlie, he thought he noticed a look which said 'You've only just met Murdoch. I have to work with the misery guts all day'. Although he might have been projecting. 'You mentioned something about wigs, Charlie?'

As he explained the chain of events, both detectives listened carefully and took notes. Anjali occasionally interjected to clarify a detail. Charlie could see why she'd done well in the force. She'd always been a good listener. Now she had a shrewdness and natural authority about her, too.

They'd run with different cliques at school – he'd strad-dled the sporty and party crowds, while Anjali was quieter, more of a swot – but he'd always liked her when their paths crossed. He seemed to recall her letting him copy her geography homework once or twice. Glaciation, was it? Oxbow lakes and truncated spurs rang a vague bell.

'I suppose it's a cliché for dogwalkers to find dead bodies, isn't it?' he said, snapping out of his nostalgic reverie as they closed their notebooks. 'You always hear about it on the news – "the body was discovered in parkland by a couple out walking their dog" – but it's never actually happened to anyone I know. A bit like being one of the hundred people surveyed on *Family Fortunes* or *The 1% Club*. Or being called up for jury service. Or catching swine flu or monkeypox or legionnaires' disease . . . Sorry, I'm waffling, aren't I?'

'Probably the shock.' Thompson smiled sympathetically. 'Statistics actually show that forty per cent of unexpected dead bodies are found by dogwalkers.'

'Quite a large proportion by joggers, too,' added Murdoch.

The senior detective turned to Tess. 'Didn't you say your shop's nearby? Maybe take Charlie for a sit-down and a sugary tea. He can come down to the station and make a formal statement when he's feeling more himself.'

'I might make it an Irish coffee,' Tess stage-whispered with a conspiratorial wink. She always kept a bottle under the counter for such eventualities.

As she led him back towards the high street, Tess chatted away to the dogs milling around their ankles, trying to act normal and take his mind off it.

Lost in his thoughts, Charlie barely noticed. Something was niggling away in a corner of his mind. Something wasn't quite right. And it wasn't just the fact that he'd stumbled upon a violently murdered man in a town he'd always considered so safe, it verged on sleepy.

4

It's Murder Out There

Charlie was still preoccupied the next morning. As he and Ruby made painstaking progress into town – stopping at every landmark to 'check her wee-mails' as Tess termed it – he puzzled over what was bothering him. It was like a splinter in his finger or a piece of food stuck between his teeth; he could feel it but couldn't quite prise it out.

As he waited yet again for her ladyship to fully inhale a lamp post's aromas, he looked around at his home town's curious mix of old and new. Once a thriving resort, Framstone had faded like an ageing beauty queen after everyone had their heads turned by sunnier holidays abroad. For most of Charlie's lifetime, it had reminded him of that mournful indie song from his student days. Something about a seaside town they forgot to shut down. Shops and businesses stood empty. Those that remained were frayed at the edges. The wind-battered seafront looked bleak and not just in winter any more. Its amusement arcades, promenade and pier were dowdy and dated, faintly echoing with the sounds of happy crowds long gone.

The past few years, though, had seen the green shoots of a miraculous renaissance. Only ninety minutes but half a world away on the train from London, Framstone had begun to attract commuters and work-from-homers. City-dwellers driven out of the capital by scandalous property prices suddenly found Framstone to be kitsch and ironically cool. A few relocated here for cheaper houses and fresh(ish) sea air. More arrived after the Covid lockdowns, only belatedly realizing that the mobile reception was patchy, the broadband was frustratingly slow and the pubs were just pubs, not gastro.

Yet their influence was being felt. Pockets of Framstone were slowly but surely gentrifying. Delis and boutiques had sprung up, much to the amusement of natives. Smug organic cafes stood next to defiant greasy spoons. Charlie had been able to pick up bits of freelance work, designing their menus and signage in typefaces carefully chosen to look like they hadn't tried too hard, even though they totally had.

Ruby didn't mind one bit. More middle-class shops meant more dog bowls placed outside for her to lap at, especially on warm days. Sometimes they kept jars of canine treats on the counter to lure in dogwalkers. Even better.

Yummy mummies, beardy hipster dads and shivering wild swimmers in Dryrobes (almost always the camo-and-pink colourway, he noticed) were being sighted at weekends, like something out of a broadsheet supplement. It was nice to see the old place stirring back into life. It was also fun to be cynical about it. Charlie didn't see them as mutually exclusive.

He arrived at Coastal Coffee to scoop up Rough and Tumble, only to find a tableful of humans and a veritable pack of hounds eagerly awaiting him. The dogwalker grapevine had clearly been humming.

Gathered round their usual table at the back of the cafe

were Tess's regular walking buddies, Viv, Sue and Malcolm. They'd been thick as thieves from way back but Charlie was still getting to know them since moving back here last year. However, what Charlie knew of the trio, he very much liked. Tess herself hovered nearby, ostensibly topping up drinks and dog bowls, but really just gossiping.

'Here's the man of the hour,' trilled retired solicitor Malcolm, as dapper as ever in a French chore jacket, chambray shirt and cravat. He looked anywhere between fifty and seventy, but if Charlie had to guess, he'd put him around halfway: early sixties but remarkably well preserved. Snoozing at his feet and complementing his outfit – Charlie suspected this was no accident – was his blue fawn rescue greyhound, Ted, a gentle soul who sprinted around at breakneck speed on his daily walk, before collapsing somewhere cosy and sleeping for the rest of the time. 'See what happens when you meet strange men in the woods? It's murder out there.'

Charlie laughed in spite of himself. 'It did cross my mind that you might've bored him to death, Malcolm.'

'Miaow,' said Malcolm. 'No offence, dogs.'

'Do stop flirting, boys,' said Viv with an eye-roll. 'Give us all the gory details, Detective Boardman of the Yard.'

Viv and Sue, partners in both work and life, were the only professionals present. Or at least, as professional as it got around here. Their dog-walking business was called Nuts About Mutts, even though Charlie and Tess (mainly Tess) had come up with countless other punning names. Hounds of Love, Top of the Pups, I Should Be So Licky, Muzzle Tov and Paw Things were favoured suggestions. Tess was a particular fan of Not That Kind of Dogging. Sue and Viv, not so much.

The inseparable pair drove a rackety old Volkswagen van and corralled a motley posse of hounds on behalf of their local punters. Their muddy-pawed pack had been known to reach double figures. Today just two of their regulars were in tow: goofy but lovable Labrador Humphrey, a one-pooch accident hot spot but an irresistibly waggy one, and grey-bearded terrier the Professor, a wise-looking 'dog on wheels' due to his arthritis-ridden back legs. Charlie always thought he would suit wearing a monocle and smoking a pipe. As he bent down to say hi, glad of the distraction, Ruby did likewise with sniffs and wags.

'Come on, spill the tea,' added Viv impatiently. Tess gave her a sideways look. 'Sorry, serve the fairtrade organic coffee.' She turned to Sue in mock exasperation. 'Put your knitting down, nanna. This is like those true-crime documentaries you're forever watching, only in 3D and right in front of you, rather than in redneck country.'

Since giving up smoking a few years ago, Charlie had gathered, Sue rarely sat down without picking up her knitting. Viv joked that she'd prised the cigarette out of her fingers and replaced it with a knitting needle. One addiction had supplanted another, although woolly jumpers were less likely to kill you. Sue always said that knitting helped her think. Viv usually scoffed at that claim, too.

'Better than the reality trash you keep rotting your brain with,' muttered Sue, glancing up from what looked worryingly like a novelty sweater for some unfortunate dog. '*Real Housewives Of Insert Location Here*. Who even says "housewife" any more? What is this, the fifties?'

Such affectionate bickering seemed to be their default mode. Tess reckoned the couple were never happier than when they were sniping at each other. Viv, all unruly curls and spectacles, was naturally the more gregarious of the pair. Sue tended to hide shyly beneath her greying bob but had a razor-sharp tongue when she needed it. Around Viv that was quite often.

'I can do better than tell you about it,' said Charlie. 'I can show you. Come on, the dogs need to stretch their legs anyway.'

Viv smiled. 'That's more like it.' She drained her coffee and purposefully zipped up her anorak. 'Lead on, Macduff.'

'That's a misquote,' chipped in Sue, stowing her knitting in her shoulder bag. 'Macbeth actually said "Lay on, Macduff."'

'I'll lay on *you* in a minute,' snapped Viv.

Now it was Malcolm's turn. 'Oh, do stop flirting, girls,' he said. 'Take us to the scene of the crime, Detective Boardman, and don't spare the horses. Or, indeed, the dogs.'

Charlie felt like he was running one of those Jack the Ripper walking tours of Whitechapel, only this ghost was much more recent – and his killer was still at large.

5

Can't See the Wood for the Trees

With the clearing taped off and a bored-looking uniformed officer standing guard, there wasn't much to see. That didn't stop Viv, Sue and Malcolm from playing amateur sleuth. 'Let's conduct a sweep of the perimeter,' said Sue, relishing a rare chance to parrot phrases from her true-crime consumption.

Viv sighed. 'She can't get to sleep without a murder podcast nowadays.'

Sue led them on a lap of the cordoned-off area while Rough, Tumble and Humphrey dashed around daftly, like the Keystone Cops. Ted trotted along, looking regally above it all. Ruby snuffled and the Professor squeaked along behind.

'There's too much rubbish in the bushes to know what might be significant and what isn't,' grumbled Viv.

Malcolm agreed. 'We literally can't see the wood for the trees.'

All five humans united in tutting disapprovingly at the dog owners who hadn't bagged and binned their pooches' business. At least they hadn't left any bulging poo bags dangling from the branches of trees, which everyone agreed was worse – like a Christmas tree decorated with aromatic brown baubles.

As they picked their way through the leaves and litter, Sue quizzed Charlie and Tess for extra detail.

'Did you hear anything?'

'Not above the noise of two furry nutters running around with wigs in their mouths,' said Charlie, his brow furrowing briefly. Had he heard something in the trees or was his memory playing tricks?

'Did you smell anything?'

'Not apart from rotting human flesh and dog poo,' said Tess with palpable relish.

'Did he say anything?'

'That would've been tricky, what with him being so dead there were flies on him,' said Charlie, pushing away a retrospective tingle of nausea.

'No flies on you, though,' said Tess. 'Am I right, Charlie?'

With their amateur CSI work yielding little of worth, conversation turned to the murder victim.

'You lot know the neighbourhood better than me nowadays,' said Charlie. 'What was the deal with Frank Courtney? Well, apart from the fact that he wore a wig. Or wigs.'

Fortunately Viv, Sue and Malcolm were a mine of local intel. Viv and Sue were both Framstone natives, born and bred, and Malcolm had had a holiday home here for years before moving down full-time upon retirement.

'Pretty popular bloke,' said Viv. 'In his police days he appeared to be one of the good guys. Knew everyone, streetwise, firm but fair, never used his cuffs or truncheon when a quiet word would do. Rose to the rank of sergeant but no further, partly because he wasn't one for sucking up to his superiors. Took early-ish retirement at fifty when he realized he was getting too long in the tooth for chasing muggers, bike thieves and shoplifters.'

'Frank nicked a lot of criminals over the years, obviously,

and a fair few got sent down,' said Sue. They were both loving the chance to play out their Helen Mirren-in-*Prime Suspect* fantasies. 'Didn't seem to make any major enemies, though.'

'He became landlord of the Neptune as soon as he got his gold watch, so it was always his retirement plan,' added Malcolm. 'Definitely one of the livelier venues in town. Always busy, rammed at weekends and attracts a younger crowd than the old soaks' pubs further inland. For the past decade, Frank's been a pillar of the community. Runs charity nights, does youth work, coaches football teams and boxing clubs. Well liked and well respected. And now, well, dead.'

'How about his private life?' asked the ever nosy Tess. 'Married? Kids?'

'Dogs even?' added Charlie. You could always tell something about a person from their dog.

'All of the above,' said Viv. 'His missus Jackie runs the pub with him. They've always looked pretty happy together. She's an *EastEnders* type with good hair and decent bone structure.' Sue shot her a look which might have been jealousy or just a warning. 'They've got a bulldog called Bobby – a sweetheart, despite his grumpy Churchill face – and three kids. Two girls and a boy. I forget their names but they're all in their twenties and moved out a few years ago.'

'They still go on holiday together every summer, though,' said Sue. 'Which I think is rather sweet in this day and age. They stay at a regular place on the Algarve, I believe.'

'Ah, I do love Portugal,' said Malcolm approvingly. 'The *vinho tinto*, the *pastel de nata*, the *bacalhau* . . .'

'The hot men,' added Tess.

'I couldn't possibly comment,' said Malcolm, faux-outraged. A growling Rough and Tumble were enjoying tug of war with a discarded wet wipe they'd found by a tree. The other dogs scurried over to join in or, in Ruby's case, have a tentative sniff of their fragrant find. Rough ran around with it stuck to her nose, resembling a manic Egyptian mummy.

Charlie looked on, amused by their goofy antics, until his eye was caught by a flash of movement. Alerted by an animal-like sense, somewhere between sight and sound, Charlie was suddenly on his guard. Had he imagined it or was something or someone rushing through the trees? The back of his neck prickled and he involuntarily raised a hand to touch it.

He turned to consult the others but nobody else had noticed. Tess and Malcolm were discussing her plans for new coffee blends and an expanded range of sandwiches. Viv and Sue were squabbling about whether DNA or fingerprints made better evidence. The only other one who seemed remotely perturbed was the Professor, who stared into the middle distance, head tilted and ears up.

He didn't want to appear paranoid, so Charlie said nothing and turned back to squint through the trees, now still and peaceful again. He glanced down at the Professor.

'You saw it too, Prof, didn't you?' he murmured. Perhaps that bored police officer wasn't the only one keeping watch.

6

When the Chips are Down

Talk of murder spread around town like a Mexican wave in a sold-out football stadium. After all, there hadn't been a suspected homicide in Framstone since five years ago, when a man was found dead on the promenade covered in small cuts.

Theories abounded, including an outlandish rumour about ninjas with swords and throwing stars, until the coroner ruled that he'd had a heart attack while scoffing a bag of chips. The cuts turned out to be from seagulls' beaks as a flock of the squawking scavengers greedily fought over the leftovers that had spilled down the poor bloke's front when he fell. The ketchup splashed everywhere had made the scene look extra-gruesome. For a while the local seagulls – with their dive-bombing, stamping feet and beady glares – had looked even more sinister than usual.

This time, the coroner came to a more obvious conclusion. Frank Courtney had been bludgeoned over the head by a large stick or plank of wood, judging by the splinters embedded in his skull. There had been a few hefty blows but the battle-hardened ex-cop appeared to have survived them, suffering non-fatal blunt force trauma. What killed him was the stab wound in his chest, likely administered by a mid-sized blade, possibly a kitchen knife, around twenty-five centimetres long and four centimetres wide – ten inches by an inch and a half in old money.

The angles of his wounds suggested that Frank had fallen to the ground while being repeatedly whacked over the head. The killer, presumably, had then stood over him as he slumped against the tree and pulled out a knife to finish him off. There were no signs of wrist restraints or drag marks, indicating that it had all happened where the body was found.

At least, this was what Charlie, Tess and the gang pieced together from local newspaper reports, the grapevine and a snatched chat with Anjali – sorry, DI Thompson. Charlie kept having to remind himself to call her that. He had run into her during another dog walk through the woods and managed to extract a few basic nuggets of intel before her professionalism drew the line. She'd been there in an official capacity to revisit the crime scene, after all.

'That's as much as you're getting from me, Boardy Boy,' she said, friendly but firm. 'More than my job's worth to go blabbing about an active investigation to random members of the public.'

'I'm not just a random,' protested Charlie, knowing it was probably futile. 'I'm the trusted old friend who found the body.'

'Trusted old friend now, is it?' Anjali smiled. 'You never call. You never write. Suddenly you can't stop sticking your oar in. Look, I'm grateful it was you that found him and it's been nice to see you again after all these years. But be a sweetheart – move along, beaky. Carry on walking these poor pooches and let me do my job.'

Charlie grinned. 'Yes, officer, sorry, officer.' He hauled

Ruby away from snuffling around Anjali's legs. He knew when he was beaten. He also knew it was a smart idea to keep her onside.

It had become common knowledge that Charlie had found the body and he was already bored of being interrogated by every dogwalker or coffee drinker he met. The community had clearly been shaken by a murder in their midst, let alone the murder of a widely known figure like Frank Courtney; it was all anyone could talk about. The gossipy, slightly ghoulish tone to the talk couldn't conceal that fact that it had got people spooked. The snoozy seaside town was the last place you'd expect a grisly killing. The victim was one of Framstone's own. Did that mean his killer was too?

Viv and Tess repeatedly reminded Charlie to engage everyone in conversation and see what he could glean. For the case, you understand, not just for their own morbid curiosity. He soon realized that the information went one way. They wanted gory details and mild reassurance, but had nothing to offer in return except headshakes, what's-the-world-coming-to sighs and wild conjecture.

As the rumour mill buzzed, Charlie's thoughts turned to the wigs. It was a detail that hadn't made the papers, so nobody apart from the dogwalkers and the police knew about it.

'Why two toupées?' he asked Tess when he dropped off Rough and Tumble, getting another free Americano for his trouble.

'That's easy for you to say,' she said. 'Besides, wasn't that the first thing I asked at the crime scene? Don't steal my line of enquiry.'

He laughed. 'We're a team, aren't we? Besides, it's been

bothering me. Who goes into the woods with two wigs? Wear one, take a spare? Doesn't add up.'

'You know what the obvious move is here? Taking me out for a drink or three.'

'Not this again,' said Charlie with an eye-roll. 'You're always trying to lure me out for drinks and, oh, look who's just happened to join us? It's yet another one of your single friends who apparently I've loads in common with. And guess what? You've suddenly got to go for some lame reason, leaving us alone with our stilted small talk and awkward silences.'

'Pardon me for trying to rescue you from a life of TV dinners with your aged mother.' She smirked. 'But point taken. This time it's different, though. I figured we might have a night out down the Neptune. See what we can find out.'

'Oh no,' groaned Charlie. 'That sounds even worse. Too late to swap it for some clumsy matchmaking, Cilla?'

'Sorry, partner,' said Tess. 'But trust me. We're going to find a lorra, lorra leads.'

7

A Regular Hector Poirot

Charlie suddenly felt very old. It was only a Thursday night, but the Neptune was rammed with a noisy young crowd. He didn't remember Framstone being this buzzy when he was a teenager. If it had been, he might not have left town at the first opportunity. OK, maybe he would, just not quite so rapidly.

There were about a dozen pubs, maybe fifteen, in Framstone but most people tended to stick to the same one or two. There were the livelier young person's pubs, like this one. There were the old man's pubs, which were quieter and cosier. Charlie and Tess tended to frequent the ones in between, where you could get a bowl of triple-cooked chips and a decent drink without feeling ancient or nodding off through boredom.

They had to lean in to hear each other at the corner table they'd managed to snag. Punters stood two deep at the bar and gathered in groups all over the pub. Rounds were bought. Trays of shots were manoeuvred carefully through the crowd. Whoops went up when they were downed. Cheers went up when someone dropped a glass. Flirtations and the odd snog were happening.

'Oh, to be young, free and nubile again.' Tess sighed faux-wistfully.

'Come on, you're still free,' said Charlie, getting a punched arm for his trouble. Tess was a few years younger than him, but they had a sibling-like bond which Charlie enjoyed. He'd never had a sister but he imagined this was roughly how it felt. Besides, she'd been good for him. After they first got chatting on a dog walk, she'd introduced him to people and made him feel welcome. Tess seemed to know everybody, either through Coastal Coffee or her insatiable pursuit of gossip. She became his handhold on Framstone society when he'd felt like a stranger in a no-longer-familiar land.

He wasn't quite sure what they were looking for. Still, there was plenty of people-watching to be done. Some of the drinkers looked suspiciously underage to Charlie's eyes. The atmosphere was upbeat, rather than respectfully in mourning, but apparently the Courtney family had let it be known it was business as usual.

'They want to celebrate Frank's life,' Malcolm had told them. 'Keep the pub that he loved packed out in tribute, that sort of thing. That's what the kids around here are saying anyway.' Charlie was intrigued by when Malcolm spoke to these so-called kids. He also didn't really want to know.

Drinks were half price all week between 7 p.m. and 8 p.m., according to posters in the windows, which certainly appeared to have lubricated the social wheels. More whoops went up as one group started a singalong to 'Sweet Caroline'. Charlie winced at the volume of the *ba-ba-ba*s.

Behind the bar was a well-preserved middle-aged woman who must be the newly widowed Jackie. Viv was right, she did have the vibe of a Cockney matriarch, all leopard print and red lippy.

She was joined by two young women who bore a definite resemblance, presumably the daughters. Both were serving drinks with practised efficiency. Collecting glasses, lugging crates and clearing up spillages was a gym-buffed boy-band type who could be their brother.

They looked close. Comfortable in each other's company. A well-drilled team from years of running a pub together. No obvious clues there.

'At least we're not the only oldies in here,' said Tess, nodding towards a bar stool where a ruddy-faced middle-aged man had taken up residence. He was drinking pints of lager with whisky chasers. Hardly in keeping with the rest of the punters, who were mainly on craft ale, Prosecco or cocktails.

'Looks like he's a regular, though,' said Charlie as the barmaid fetched him another pair of drinks, prompted only by a slight head tilt. Judging by the way the man was slumped bleary-eyed at the bar, he'd been here for several rounds already.

'Oh balls, I think he's rumbled us looking,' muttered Tess into her large glass of Malbec. 'Whatever you do, don't catch his eye.'

Charlie sighed quietly. 'Too late. I think he's coming over.'

'Champagne Charlie, is it not?' slurred the stranger as he lurched over, almost sloshing lager out of his glass. 'Not living up to your nickname drink-wise tonight?' He nodded at Charlie's pint glass and gave a lopsided grin.

'Nobody's called me that since we won the county football cup at school,' said Charlie with an uneasy smile. 'I managed to soak the headmaster in bubbly. He wasn't happy.'

'Do you two know each other?' asked Tess in surprise.

Charlie shot her a 'this is awkward' look before turning back to the man, who was gently swaying as he stood. 'I'm not sure, do we?'

'Not personally,' he replied. 'Only by reputation. I'm a copper, see? Poor old Frank is the talk of the station, not just the town. You found his body, right? I've seen you around, walking dogs, so put two and two together.' He tapped his nose unsteadily. 'Regular Hector Poirot, ain't I?'

'Hercule,' said Charlie, unable to help himself and immediately regretting it.

'Yeah, I heard you were a smartarse as well,' said the stranger, his rheumy red eyes flashing with anger. Charlie briefly feared they were about to come to blows over Agatha Christie, which wouldn't be a clever use of anyone's little grey cells.

'Let us buy you a drink,' interjected Tess – partly to keep the peace, partly planning to pump him for information.

'All right, cheers, pint, please,' he slurred, the words merging into one as he pulled up a stool and plonked himself down.

While Tess took what felt like an eternity fetching the drinks, Charlie attempted to make chit-chat. 'So was Frank a good mate of yours? Sorry for your loss, by the way.'

The man gave a mirthless laugh. 'That's funny. No, I wouldn't go as far as a friend. Let's say a former colleague. Very briefly anyway. Frank was . . . a character, put it that way. Fingers in pies. Everyone knew him, even if some didn't much like him.'

'How do you mean, *fingers in pies*?' asked Charlie, only for the question to fall on deaf ears as Tess returned from the bar and the man greedily grabbed his next pint.

'What were you boys talking about?' Tess asked, as he swigged it thirstily.

Charlie gave her a knowing look. 'Apparently Frank was quite a character,' he said. 'According to . . . Sorry, I didn't get your name.'

Before he could reply, a familiar figure burst through the door, quickly glanced around the pub and started making her way over to them.

'Isn't that . . . ?' asked Tess.

'Anjali, yeah,' said a confused Charlie.

The stranger turned to see her approaching. 'Well, well,' he scoffed, 'if it isn't my long-suffering lady wife, wielding the proverbial rolling pin.' He took a last gulp of his drink, somehow managing to drain it before she reached him.

'Wait, what?' asked Tess, failing to hide her surprise. 'You two are married?' The cool, calm detective and the shambling barfly weren't an obvious match.

Anjali greeted her husband with a tight smile. 'I thought you might be here. Time we were going. I see you've met Charlie and Tess.'

'Just thought I'd introduce myself, love,' he said, standing a little shakily. He extended a hand to Charlie. 'Rob Thompson. Sergeant Thompson when on duty, just Rob when not. We were just talking about our mutual friend Frank.' The words 'mutual friend' were spat out with as much sarcasm as he could muster through his booze haze.

'Well, whatever Rob said, don't believe a word of it,' said Anjali dismissively. 'Emotions are running high at HQ, aren't they?'

'Thanks for the drink,' Rob called over his shoulder as she hauled him away. 'We must do this again sometime.'

'Let's get you home before we go making any more social plans,' muttered Anjali, giving them a last look which was half apologetic, half annoyed.

As the pub door swung shut behind the Thompsons, Charlie and Tess turned to each other with puffed cheeks and raised eyebrows.

'Poor Anj,' said Charlie. 'She's got her hands full there.'

'Aggressive, volatile, connected to the victim, clearly bad blood.' Tess took a triumphant sip of her wine. 'We've also got our first murder suspect.'

8

Behind Closed Doors

Charlie had a mild hangover the next morning. As he soothed it with coffee at the dogwalkers' usual table, Tess was annoyingly bright-eyed. He was going to add 'bushy-tailed' but thought that might be disrespectful to the dogs flopped around their feet.

'Right then, Mulder and Scully,' said Malcolm impatiently, 'what did you learn from your stakeout?' Malcolm filled his days with voluntary work at a charity shop and a food bank. He clearly had places to go and good deeds to do.

Charlie sighed. 'I'd prefer Maddie and David from *Moonlighting* for future reference. And it wasn't so much of a stakeout as a couple of quiet drinks at –'

'A location of interest,' said Viv. 'And it was more than a couple by the look of you. You've got through two coffees in the time we've been here.'

'Three actually,' chipped in Tess unhelpfully. 'And he's had sugar in them. But let's say it was an enlightening evening's work.'

'Tell us everything,' said Malcolm, leaning forward in anticipation. 'Well, apart from whatever greasy takeaway monstrosity you bought on the way home. I don't think we could bear it, could we, Ted?' His greyhound looked up with soulful eyes, as if mourning the wasted calories.

Charlie was about to protest when he remembered that there had indeed been a swift stop-off at Framstone Kebabs. His stomach gurgled and he grimaced guiltily. At least Ruby wasn't judging when she'd gratefully scoffed the leftover doner meat for breakfast.

Tess recapped the entire evening in such detail that Charlie was a mixture of impressed and terrified. She described how rammed the Neptune pub had been and how the Courtneys had shown a united front behind the bar. The dogwalkers all gave sympathetic head nods. Sue even stopped knitting for a respectful few seconds.

Their interest was piqued when Tess moved on to their brush with off-duty (not to mention off-his-face) Sergeant Rob Thompson. There were murmurs of surprise when she got to him being escorted off the premises by the police. Who just happened to come in the form of his wife.

Viv tutted. 'Poor Anjali, stuck with that liability. I've seen him around town but didn't make the connection. Makes you wonder what goes on behind closed doors. I assume he wasn't such a mess when she married him.'

Charlie had pondered much the same thing. He guessed they'd met at work, but they still seemed an unlikely couple. Anjali was quiet and organized; Rob was loud and chaotic. He looked a decade older, although that might be the booze. Anjali had also carted off her husband home with such efficiency that Charlie figured it was by no means the first time. *She deserves better*, he thought.

'Is he really a suspect, though?' asked Sue, glancing up

from her clacking needles. 'Not only is he a copper but it doesn't sound like he's got the wherewithal.'

Again, Charlie was inclined to agree. He'd got the sense that if Rob had tried to punch him over the Poirot pedantry, he probably would have missed and ended up in an undignified heap on the sticky pub floor.

'Well, presumably he's not always multiple-pints-plus-chasers deep,' said Tess. 'From the way he spoke about Frank Courtney, there was clearly no love lost there.'

'Surely a policeman wouldn't commit murder in a public place,' chipped in Malcolm. 'Let alone go out of his way to get rat-arsed in front of the victim's family.'

'But what's that thing from your true-crime documentaries that you always say, babe?' asked Viv, turning to Sue. 'Some killers like to relive the moment?'

'That's right,' said Sue. 'If Rob really is the unsub –'

'Unidentified subject,' added Viv proudly. 'It's what the FBI call them.'

'He might well revisit the crime scene, insert himself into the investigation or befriend the bereaved family.'

'A bit awkward that his wife is leading the case,' said Tess. 'Makes pillow talk a minefield. Although last night, I'll bet he was banished to the sofa.'

'One thing's for sure,' said Malcolm decisively. 'We need to know more about this Rob.'

Charlie nodded. 'Particularly his beef with the deceased.'

'And why the hell Anjali is married to him?' added Viv. 'They remind me of this couple on *Married at First Sight* . . .'

'Now you're talking,' said Malcolm, suddenly not in such a rush and waving at Tess for a coffee top-up. 'UK, US or Australian?'

'Always Australian!' said Viv, warming to the subject.

Sue pulled a face and returned to her knitting.

His head beginning to throb, Charlie decided to leave them to their reality-TV natter and clear his head with a walk. 'Come on, Rubes,' he murmured. 'Let's have another snuffle around those woods.'

9

Something Gets You in the End

Approaching the crime scene, he'd been vaguely hoping to run into Anjali. As it happened, Charlie met another person of interest altogether. He took a moment to recognize her with her hair down and no make-up but as Ruby sniffed hello to a slavering but friendly bulldog, he realized its owner was Jackie Courtney.

Charlie was surprised to stumble upon Frank's widow but even through his fuzzy-headed fug, he knew the chance to chat was too good to pass up.

'That's it, Bobby, be nice,' cooed Jackie to her dog before looking up at Charlie. 'You were in the pub last night, weren't you? I never forget a face, especially if it belongs to a paying customer.'

'That's right,' he said, trying to hide his hangover and give his most sympathetic smile. 'Charlie Boardman. This is Ruby. She wasn't always this slow and blind, bless her.'

'I'm Jackie,' she said, 'and this drooling monster is Bobby. Before you ask, my husband named him after Moore and Charlton.' She rolled her eyes, presumably affectionately. 'Talking of names, where do I know yours from?'

'Ah,' said Charlie awkwardly. 'If I was flattering myself,

I'd say my school sporting career or my thriving graphic design business, but it's probably for much sadder reasons. I'm afraid I'm the dogwalker who found your poor Frank.'

'Oh!' said Jackie softly, like she'd seen a ghost. As she reached out to shake his hand, Charlie couldn't help glancing down at her rings. He was no expert but that sizeable diamond in her engagement ring didn't look cheap. 'Sorry you had to see that. It must've been a terrible shock.'

'Must have been a terrible shock to you and the family too,' he said.

'I suppose it was,' replied Jackie, her eyes somewhere in the middle distance. 'He was more complicated than he looked, my Frank. He did lots of good, especially for disadvantaged lads and youth charities, but he seemed to make a few enemies along the way. Something has to get you in the end, isn't that what they say?' She refocused and looked directly at Charlie. 'Listen to me, waffling on. I don't usually see you in the Neppy.'

'No, it's a bit lively for a man of my advanced years,' Charlie joked, glad of the chance to lighten the mood.

'Don't be daft,' she said, laughing. 'You must be, what, thirty-odd?'

'You flatter me,' said Charlie. 'I'd claim mid-thirties, others might say late thirties. I thought I'd pop in last night to pay my respects. I was going to say something but you looked so busy. I'm truly sorry for your loss.' He meant it sincerely but still felt a twinge of guilt for the white lie about the reason for their visit.

Jackie smiled. 'That's kind of you. Kindness is a precious commodity these days.' She briefly got a daydreamy look again, before snapping back to the present. 'Anyway, Charlie, tell me about you. How's the graphic design trade? Going well, I hope?'

'Not really,' he admitted sheepishly. 'I do bits and bobs for local businesses but it's pretty slow. A bit like Ruby, in fact. That's why I'm normally found wandering around with various mutts in tow. I take on the odd bit of paid dog walking while waiting for my main gig to take off.'

He decided to chance his arm and gave her his most charming smile. 'If the pub ever needs anything designed – posters, menus, websites, that kind of thing – I'm sure I could do you mates' rates.'

'Nice to know I count as a mate already,' she said with a laugh. 'We need all the friends we can get at the moment. Thanks, I'll bear it in mind.'

Strolling along, the dogs waddling contentedly behind, they completed a loop and ended up back near the entrance to the woods.

'I'd better be heading back.' Jackie sighed. 'Need to open up soon, play happy families again. It's been nice chatting to you, Charlie. Lovely to meet you too, sweetheart.'

She bent to give Ruby a stroke, before straightening up and lightly touching Charlie's arm. 'I'm glad it was you who found Frank. Even if you're not. Take care.'

'You too, Jackie. Sorry again for your loss.'

He watched her shudder and pull her sheepskin coat round herself as she left, Bobby panting at her heels, before walking on with Ruby. Was it his imagination – not to mention his male ego – or had she been very gently flirting with him? Probably just well-practised pub landlady patter. And what was all that cryptic stuff about her late husband and playing happy families? Viv was right. You never quite know what goes on behind closed doors.

Charlie was absent-mindedly musing on all this when something flashed in the corner of his eye. There it was again, that rapid movement among the trees. Ruby had sensed it too, her ears pricking, her near sightless eyes fixed in the same direction as Charlie's. This time he could've sworn it was a hooded figure beating a hasty retreat at their approach.

He recalled what Sue said about killers revisiting the scene. 'Unless I'm going mad, Rube,' he muttered, 'I might just have to give chase next time.'

She wagged her tail, which he took as a sign of agreement.

10

More Bodies than the Somme

'Haven't you heard?' said a wide-eyed and palpably excited Tess. Charlie had barely made it over the threshold of Coastal Coffee the next morning before she dashed over to share the news.

He was running later than usual to pick up Rough and Tumble. Charlie had slept in after a disturbed night dreaming of hooded figures in woods and breathless foot chases, like a mash-up of *Little Red Riding Hood*, *Don't Look Now* and *The Blair Witch Project*. Even his mum had remarked that he looked tired as he'd hurried out of the door with Ruby.

'Heard what?' he asked. 'And good morning, Tess, nice to see you. I'm well, thanks. And, no, since you ask, I haven't had my first coffee of the day yet.'

He looked knowingly at the espresso machine, refusing to say another word until caffeine was forthcoming. She sighed impatiently and busied herself, still talking over her shoulder.

'Our mate has been hospitalized,' said Tess above the sounds of hissing steam and frothing milk. 'Someone did a proper number on him last night – or maybe early this morning, I suppose.'

'You might need to be more specific,' he said, trying not

to look panicked while his mind raced with possibilities. 'Who exactly is our mate in this scenario?'

'Sergeant Rob,' explained Tess impatiently. 'You know, the drunken Poirot fan from the Neppy. Mr Anjali Thompson. Word is that he'll recover but the poor bloke got a right kicking.'

'Jeez, really?' Charlie said, taking a grateful sip from the cup she handed him. He was shocked by another violent incident so soon. Where had boring old Framstone gone? 'Do we know what happened?'

'Well,' said Tess, giving a quick glance both ways and leaning over the counter conspiratorially, as if this was top-secret data and enemy spies might be listening, 'not exactly no.'

'Typical,' said Charlie, rolling his eyes at Ruby. She looked back up at him lovingly, if fuzzily.

Tess shot Ruby a long-suffering look herself and continued. 'But he was found this morning in the woods by yummy mummies and their little darlings taking a shortcut on the school run. Apparently they thought it was another corpse at first and got the fright of their lives. Everyone's already on edge after the murder and now this, exactly a week later.'

'Framstone Woods are becoming quite the crime hot spot,' mused Charlie. 'More bodies than the Somme.'

'It wasn't until they rolled him over that they realized he was still breathing,' said Tess. 'They called 999 and he got whisked away in an ambulance about an hour ago, just after I'd opened up. Stretcher, oxygen, flashing blue lights, the lot. What do we think?'

'Not sure,' said Charlie. As he gave Ruby a thoughtful stroke, he remembered that this wasn't just a puzzle to solve.

There were real people involved. 'Actually, I do know what I think. I should call Anjali and see if she's OK.'

Tess grinned. 'I hoped you'd say that. Play the faux-concerned card while actually finding out all the gruesome details. Good thinking, sweetcheeks.'

'You're all heart, Tess Cheong,' said Charlie. 'But I'll have you know that I really am concerned.'

Tess snorted, turning to her next customer. 'Yep, yep, save it for someone who might remotely believe you. I'll alert the others. Keep us updated, OK?'

Charlie waited until he got to the woods and could let Ruby, Rough and Tumble off their leads. He gazed after them thoughtfully as they disappeared into the bushes, tails up and ears alert. The sight reminded him of the day he'd found the body and an icy lightning bolt shot down his spine.

He swigged his coffee, took a deep breath and dialled Anjali's number.

11

Something Personal

'Thanks for calling, Boardy Boy,' said Anjali. At least she used his main school nickname, unlike her hapless husband. Anjali must be about the only person left in town who knew him as Boardy Boy. Everyone else from Framstone High seemed to have left for the city or moved out to the suburbs. Or in a couple of embarrassing cases, changed so much since school that Charlie didn't recognize them until they introduced themselves.

They settled down on a bench and tried to ignore the aroma gently wafting from a nearby dog poo bin. 'Sorry I suggested meeting here. You must spend half your life in these woods.'

'No bother on either count.' Charlie smiled. 'I was worried about you. Both of you. Besides, I like the woods and Ruby's always happy with a bonus walk.'

He'd dropped Rough and Tumble back at Coastal, waving to Tess from the doorway. He'd have got the fourth degree again if he'd ventured any further in.

'Well, it's appreciated,' said Anjali with a weary exhalation. She looked like the weight of the world was on the shoulders of her smart camel coat. 'It's been a rough morning, as you can imagine, but I thought I'd kill two birds with one stone. I wanted to come and see where Rob was found anyway.'

'Where was it?'

'Just down the path,' said Anjali with an incline of her head. 'A couple of hundred yards from where you found Frank Courtney, luckily, or I'd have been even more concerned. Two separate attacks on retired or active police officers . . .' She frowned, anxiety flooding her face. 'Well, it's not good.'

'Do you think it's an anti-police thing?' Now it was Charlie's turn to look concerned. 'Not fearing for your own safety are you, Anj?'

'I wasn't until you said that,' she said, attempting a brave smile. 'No, not really. Hopefully it's just coincidence. Two violent crimes in quick succession has still got everyone rattled, though. The entire town seems jittery and who could blame them? It's been a scary week.'

'I'm sure it's just rotten luck,' said Charlie, trying to sound confident even if he didn't entirely believe it. 'How is Rob?'

'Well, he won't be winning any beauty contests.' She sighed. 'He's pretty banged up. Cuts, bruises, abrasions. A fat lip and a black eye. They think he might have broken his nose. Maybe a couple of ribs, too.'

'Ouch, poor him,' said Charlie. 'Is he conscious?'

'Yes, he came round earlier but he's resting again now. I took the chance to sneak out while he was asleep. I'll go back in a bit so I'm there when he wakes up.'

'Did he say what happened?' asked Charlie, as casually as he could manage.

'He wasn't making total sense,' said Anjali. 'I suspect he was still a bit drunk from last night to be honest. But he said he was on his way home from the pub when someone jumped him from behind and gave him a good shoeing.'

'Did he see who it was?' asked Charlie, suddenly aware that it was him who was sounding like the police officer here.

'No, frustratingly,' said Anjali. 'I don't imagine he could see straight even before he got flattened. You don't need me to tell you that Rob hits it pretty hard sometimes. OK, a lot of the time.' She suddenly looked sad and tired, as if burdened by her husband's problems.

Charlie reached out and squeezed her hand. 'Want to talk about it?' he asked gently. 'You don't have to, obviously.' He decided that quizzing Anjali for clues could wait. Right now she needed a friend.

'It's fine,' said Anjali. 'Probably do me good. I'm just not sure how much there is to tell. He wasn't always like this, you know. I wouldn't have married him if he was. But it's been getting worse for the last few years. Now the sober nights are rarer than the blind-drunk ones.'

'I'm sorry,' said Charlie. 'I know a bit of what that's like from my dad.'

'I know you do,' said Anjali. 'That's partly why I thought I could talk to you. That and the fact that you're not quite as much of a dick as you were at school.'

He laughed, despite himself. 'I'll take that as a compliment. Do you know why his drinking got worse? Did something happen to trigger it?'

'Nothing major.' She shrugged. 'At least, not that I'm aware of. Rob definitely found it hard when I was transferred to CID and he stayed in uniform. He'd served a few years longer than me and suddenly I was overtaking him. He found it even harder when I got promoted.'

'Bit of ego and pride maybe?' suggested Charlie.

'I guess. Of course, the lads down the station think it's hilarious to tease him about me being his superior and the main breadwinner. That doesn't exactly help.'

'I'll bet,' said Charlie sympathetically. 'Bloody lads and their lame banter.' The merciless locker-room chat was the one aspect of his sporting days that he didn't look back on fondly. 'Has he ever tried seeking help? Getting sober?'

'I've suggested it so many times,' said Anjali, her voice wobbling for a second. 'He doesn't seem to think he needs to. Thinks he can handle it and control himself. Yet he goes AWOL several times a week. I end up either worrying myself sick at home or going out looking for him. Well, you saw that in the Neppy. Sorry if I was arsey that night. I was embarrassed, I think, not that it's any excuse.'

'No need to apologize,' he reassured her. 'You were just fine. So do you think it was a mugging? Some opportunist thief saw him looking a bit unsteady and took advantage?'

'That's the thing,' said Anjali. 'I don't think so. Nothing was taken. He might have been lying there spark out for hours but he still had his phone, watch and wallet on him. I'm wondering if it was something more personal. Maybe he got into an argument in the pub.'

It wouldn't surprise me, thought Charlie, although he kept that to himself. 'Do we know which pubs he'd been in?'

'A few, by the sound of it,' said Anjali. 'His memory was a bit foggy, as you can imagine.'

'I can,' said Charlie. 'And did you find anything along the path?'

'Not a thing,' said Anjali. 'Just a flattened patch where he'd been lying all night. The usual litter in the bushes either side – coffee cups, vapes, food wrappers, even a couple of condoms – but nothing that looked recent or relevant.'

'You're starting to sound like a detective again now.' Charlie smiled. 'That's a good sign.' He gave her shoulders a supportive squeeze. 'Come on, let's get you back to the hospital.'

As they wandered towards the road, Ruby at their heels, Charlie gazed at the ground thoughtfully. He wasn't entirely sure why, but he found himself wondering if Rob Thompson had been in the Neptune again last night. Was that the pub from which he'd been reeling home when he was jumped? If so, why couldn't he keep away the Courtneys? The off-duty officer might have been digging for information, sure, but what if it was something more sinister?

12

Just Getting Juicy

'Who rings the doorbell at this time of night?' asked Polly Boardman, pausing the TV and looking over at her son, frowning with worry.

'Steady on, Mum, it's not that late,' said Charlie, glancing at his phone as he got up. 'It's not even ten o'clock yet.'

Creatures of habit, they'd been following their usual pattern. After Ruby's last walk of the day, they sat down to supper – lasagne and salad on laps in front of the TV, while Ruby noisily devoured her bowl of raw food in the kitchen – and sparked up a crime drama in front of the fire. This one was subtitled and Scandinavian, all moody detectives, chunky knits and designer lamps. A rich businessman had been murdered and it was just getting juicy.

Well into her seventies, retired midwife Polly was becoming 'a bit forgetful' – that's how she euphemistically put it, at least when she wasn't getting prickly and defensive – and a regular routine seemed to settle her. She and Ruby were similar in that way.

Charlie was only too happy to fit in with the two most important ladies in his life. He'd always hated the idea of her living alone since his dad left under a cloud during his teens.

This year, though, he'd really started to worry. First Polly had a fall. Only down the last few stairs and she'd played down her twisted ankle on the phone to Charlie, but he could tell she'd been shaken. He got the impression that she'd lost confidence and wasn't getting out and about like she used to.

A few weeks later, she'd left some soup boiling on the hob and wandered off to do some chores upstairs. Half an hour later, the saucepan had boiled dry and its base had burned to a cinder. It wasn't until smoke drifted up the stairs that Polly remembered what she'd been doing.

She increasingly needed someone to keep an eye on her. Charlie decided he was ready to leave London anyway. It seemed the obvious solution to head home and move in with her. He told himself it was temporary, but there was no sign of anything changing soon.

As he ambled to the front door, trying not to trip over Ruby as she also hauled herself to her feet, he wondered who'd come calling at this hour. He wasn't going to huff and puff about it like his dear old mum – Charlie was faintly paranoid that living with Polly would prematurely age him, so made a point of resisting it whenever possible – but it was definitely unusual. He found himself hoping it wasn't more bad news.

Charlie braced himself as he opened the door, only to find nobody there. He shivered in the frosty night air and glanced around, checking that some prankster wasn't about to spring out and surprise him. Nope, nobody. The front path was clear. The gate hadn't been closed properly but it rarely was, much to Polly's chagrin. He sometimes caught her bending the poor postman's ear about it and had to play peacemaker.

'It's OK, Mum,' he called over his shoulder. 'Nobody here. Maybe kids playing silly buggers. Or someone realized they'd got the wrong house.' He heard grumbling from the sitting room.

He was just closing the door when he saw it. Something was lying on the front step, probably left there by the phantom bell-ringer. As he leaned down to pick it up, Charlie realized what it was – a cuddly dog. One of those beanbag-type toys that you sometimes saw toddlers clutching in prams.

Charlie smiled. Who doesn't love a cuddly dog? Maybe it was a present for Ruby – well, she had many admirers – or an anonymous thank-you gift from someone whose pooch he'd walked. It was dark brown, so did bear a vague resemblance to brindle-coated Ruby, although it lacked her trademark white paws.

As he turned the toy over to look at its face, Charlie let out a soft gasp. It had no nose. Which sounded like the set-up for a corny old joke ('My dog's got no nose.' 'How does it smell?' 'Bloody terrible.'), but Charlie wasn't laughing.

The nose wasn't just missing, it had been violently torn off. There was a rough, jagged hole in the middle of the toy's face. Some stuffing was poking out, making it look sad, even slightly menacing.

Charlie liked to think he didn't scare easily but his pulse was suddenly pounding. A wave of dread undulated through his body. He hurried to the gate and looked both ways down the street but it was quiet and empty. The moonlight cast everything in black, white and shades of grey, making it resemble an old film noir. He looked down again at the disfigured dog and felt faintly sick.

The sense of threat he'd felt since finding Frank's body had suddenly come close to home. Somebody knew where he lived. Somebody was watching him. They might even be watching right now. Charlie swallowed down his fear, straightened his shoulders and did his best to look defiant before heading back inside. He leaned back against the closed door and tried to slow the thumping drumbeat in his chest.

13

Leave It to the Professionals

'You were right to call us,' said Anjali, sipping her tea and waving away Polly's latest offer of home-baked biscuits.

Next to her on the sofa, DS Craig Murdoch had no such qualms, tucking into what must have been his third or fourth. Charlie wondered where he was putting them all. Now they'd met again, he noticed that Murdoch wore his suits slightly too fitted, like an estate agent or a candidate on *The Apprentice*. His body was clearly gym-honed. Charlie suddenly felt old. He found himself breathing in and trying not to feel saggy by comparison.

He had hesitated before phoning Anjali. This was hardly an emergency; he wasn't even sure if it meant anything. He felt embarrassed, like he was probably wasting police time, so reluctantly tried Anjali's mobile direct. Calling the station or especially 999 would have made him feel even more ridiculous. He could imagine it now: 'Scramble a SWAT team and a chopper. We've got ourselves a cuddly code red.' Then the cops would fall about laughing at what an idiot he was.

The noseless toy was on the coffee table between them inside a plastic evidence bag. This looked oddly cruel, like leaving a dog in a car on a hot day.

'Do you think it might be a mix-up?' asked Charlie, keeping his tone as casual as he could. He didn't want Polly to fret any more than she was already. 'A kid's toy that got lost somehow?'

'In all honesty, no, I don't,' said Anjali matter-of-factly. 'You're known around the area as a dogwalker. This toy looks vaguely like Ruby and was left on your doorstep. It's too much of a coincidence.'

'You also happened to find a dead body just over a week ago,' chipped in Murdoch. He turned to Polly, who'd returned from fetching more refreshments. 'Lovely biscuits, by the way, Mrs Boardman. I'd say professional standard.' Polly shushed him modestly but looked thrilled.

'So you reckon it might be a message of some kind?' continued Charlie.

'Afraid so,' said Anjali. She and Murdoch exchanged a look. 'That's why I called Craig and came round on my night off.'

Charlie noticed now she wasn't quite as smartly dressed as usual. He felt even more guilty. With her husband still in hospital, Anjali probably had better things to do. Murdoch too, no doubt. They were both going above and beyond the call of duty. He appreciated their safe, solid presence. 'What could the message mean?'

'Unfortunately I think it's fairly obvious,' said Anjali, as her colleague nodded sombrely. 'It's telling you – and possibly Ruby as well – to keep your noses out.'

Charlie instinctively reached down to give Ruby a protective stroke. 'Keep our noses out of what?' he asked, even though he had a horrible feeling that he already knew the answer.

'The murder case,' said Murdoch.

Anjali nodded. 'We have to work on the assumption that it's connected. Again, it's too much of a coincidence not to be.'

'Right,' said Charlie, keeping his voice steady for his mum's benefit. 'So what now?'

'We'll send the dog off to the forensics lab,' said Murdoch. He glanced at Ruby, who stared back at him expectantly. 'Sorry, Ruby. The toy dog, I mean. I doubt they'll find anything on it but just to make sure.'

'We'll also make enquiries at toy and childrenswear shops around Framstone,' added Anjali. 'Just in case it was purchased locally in the last few days.'

'I'll do that tomorrow while you're at the hospital.' Murdoch nodded, making a note.

'Oh yes, how is Rob?' asked Charlie, glad to change the subject.

'On the mend, thanks,' she said gratefully, before getting back down to business. 'We'll make sure a patrol car passes by the house regularly and keeps an eye out for anything suspicious. In the meantime, I'd advise you to keep everything double-locked and to respect the wishes of . . . whoever.'

'Meaning?' asked Charlie. Polly had perched on the arm of the chair next to him. He patted her hand and attempted a reassuring smile.

'Meaning try not to worry and leave it to the professionals,' said Murdoch. 'Better and safer all round.'

'We'll keep you abreast of any developments,' said Anjali as they stood to leave. 'And thanks again for the tea, Mrs Boardman.'

'Especially the biscuits,' added Murdoch with a grin and a wink. 'Let me help you tidy away, Mrs B.'

She giggled, positively vibrating with pleasure as he scooped up plates and mugs. 'Oh, please, call me Polly.'

Charlie showed Anjali out. On the doorstep, she gave him a quick supportive smile and touched his arm. Murdoch, emerging from the kitchen to rejoin his boss, didn't appear to notice.

As soon as the front door was closed, Polly clapped her hands delightedly. Any concerns about doorstep deliveries were seemingly forgotten. 'That Anjali is a lovely girl,' she said. 'I've thought that since you were at school together.'

'Really, Mum?' Charlie smiled. 'I don't recall you ever mentioning it.'

'Well, I did,' she said firmly, straightening the sofa cushions where they'd sat. 'And DS Murdoch was such a nice young man too. Did you notice how much he loved my peanut butter cookies? I might make another batch tomorrow, just for him. And did you see how polished his shoes were? He smelled very freshly laundered too. Clearly takes care of himself.'

Standing there in his jeans, plaid shirt and battered desert boots, Charlie suddenly felt judged. *At least I don't dress like an estate agent*, he reassured himself. *Although maybe I should consider joining a gym.* He patted his stomach, aware that it wasn't as firm as it used to be.

As he helped Polly wash up, he wondered how the rest of the gang would like being told to keep their noses out. He didn't like it much himself. If they were being warned off, it meant they were on to something. So why had a chill settled over him?

Charlie went to lock the doors, trying to shake the feeling

that someone was still out there watching. The trees, cars and houses on the street created criss-crossing shadows for someone to hide in. Any number of threats could lurk in the faceless night. Hidden in the blackness, unseen but seeing. He hurriedly drew the curtains.

14

Lone Mavericks are More Fun

Charlie's suspicions were spot on. The dogwalkers didn't like it one bit. Gathered round their usual table the next day, there was an indignant caffeinated hubbub as they all spoke at once.

'If you ask me, it's just proof that we need to carry on,' said Viv defiantly. 'We're clearly getting somewhere.'

'I hate to admit it,' said Sue, wryly looking up from her knitting, 'but she's right.'

'Of course she is,' chimed in Tess. 'Giving up now would be cutting off our nose to spite our face. If that's not an insensitive turn of phrase under the circumstances.'

Charlie rolled his eyes. 'That's about the fourth nose-based pun we've had already this morning,' he said.

'I am as God made me.' The unrepentant Tess shrugged. 'It's as plain as the nose on my face.'

'I'm not intimidated easily,' added Malcolm. 'That's what decades of being out and proud teaches you. If I gave in to bullies, I'd probably be trapped in a loveless marriage right now, while looking longingly at Grindr in secret.'

'As opposed to looking longingly at Grindr in public?' Tess grinned.

'Saucer of milk for table twelve,' replied Malcolm, beckoning an imaginary waiter. 'Besides, it's hardly a horse's head in your bed, is it?'

'OK, OK,' said Charlie, sitting back and raising his hands in surrender. He might have been the relative newcomer but he was already feeling like part of the gang. 'Although, may I just point out that it's not your doorsteps that the threatening messages are being left on? It's mine. And more worryingly my mum's.'

She might have gone to bed happily enough, thanks to Anjali's visit and Murdoch's biscuit-based flattery, but Polly had woken today looking pinched and anxious.

'Polly's a tough old bird,' Viv reminded him. 'Everyone around here knows her, loves her and will keep an eye on her. She'll be fine. Besides, it's not her that's sticking her nose in and being threatened. It's you.'

'How reassuring,' said Charlie. 'So what's our next step?'

'I'm glad you asked,' said Viv, leaning forward eagerly. 'Me and Sue have been talking about this . . .'

Sue sighed. 'You've been talking *at* me, mainly, but yes.'

'Shush your complaining,' said Viv. 'As you're always saying, in the real world, crimes are best solved by teamwork and pooled knowledge, not lone mavericks.'

'Lone mavericks are more fun, though,' said Tess, who probably saw herself as one. Small business owner by day, crusading vigilante by night.

'As I was saying,' huffed Viv impatiently. 'We think it's all about the three Ws.'

'Worrell, Weekes and Walcott?' asked Charlie fauxinnocently. 'I didn't have you down as a fan of Caribbean cricket.'

'No, you numpty,' scoffed Sue. 'Woods, wigs and weapons.'

Viv elaborated. 'What was Frank Courtney doing in the woods? Why two wigs? Where are the murder weapons? Answer those three questions and we've pretty much cracked the case.'

'And how do we do that?' asked Malcolm sceptically.

'I don't know, do I?' snapped Viv exasperatedly. 'That's where I thought you lot might come in. Teamwork. Pooled knowledge. That kind of thing.'

'Surely we should also be asking what connects the two victims?' said Tess. 'Frank Courtney was attacked in the woods – fatally, unfortunately for him. Rob Thompson was attacked in the same woods shortly afterwards – not fatally, fortunately for him. That can't be random.'

'As far as I see it, there are two things they have in common,' said Charlie. 'First there's Framstone Police – one's an ex-copper, the other's a serving officer.'

'Yeah, but decades apart,' said Sue. 'Frank had probably already retired by the time Rob started.'

'Fair point,' said Charlie. 'But it's still a valid link worth exploring. Not like we've got loads else to go on, is it?'

They didn't look convinced, so Charlie made a mental note to pursue it himself.

'What's the other thing they have in common?' asked Malcolm.

'Oh yes,' said Charlie, almost losing his train of thought amid the worry about his mum. 'The Neptune. Frank was the landlord; Rob is a regular. The pub is what connects them.'

'I like it,' said Viv. She glanced at Sue, who nodded approvingly.

'So we have four lines of enquiry,' said Tess. 'The three Ws, plus the pub.'

'Five lines of enquiry,' Sue corrected her. 'You're forgetting our little noseless friend on Charlie's doorstep.'

'Well, that's handy,' said Charlie. 'Because there happens to be five of us.' He addressed the dogs flopped around their feet. 'Sorry, guys. Five humans. Let's take a line of enquiry each. I'll volunteer for the pub.' *And the police*, he told himself. *I trust my instincts, even if they don't yet.*

As the others started haggling over who wanted what, Charlie realized that he knew exactly where to start.

15

Some People are Just Trouble

It took him a couple of hours to manufacture a 'chance' meeting but Ruby didn't mind one bit. As they wandered up and down the seafront, she said sniffy hellos to all the fashionable Frenchies, dapper dachshunds and chic schnauzers being walked by yummy mummies. Ruby gave short shrift to the whippets, which Charlie noted with satisfaction. He found them a bit bony and spidery too. Less doggy, more Dobby.

They slowly strolled and snuffled in a methodical pattern, Charlie keeping a keen eye out, until he spotted them.

'There they are, Rubes,' he muttered with a mix of triumph and relief. 'Let's go and say hello.'

Jackie Courtney and Bobby the bulldog emerged from the Neptune and began perambulating slowly up the promenade. Their progress was interrupted by Bobby pausing to, put politely, make himself comfortable. Picking up the pace as Jackie bagged and binned it, Charlie and Ruby soon caught up.

'We've got to stop meeting like this,' teased Jackie. 'People will talk.' She gave him a cheeky wink before bending down to greet Ruby.

Charlie did the same with Bobby, massaging the folds of velvety skin on the back of his neck while he drooled happily.

'Let them talk,' said Charlie with what he hoped was a wolfish grin. 'How are you, Jackie?'

'Not too bad, considering,' she said with a brave smile. 'The pub and the arrangements for Frank's send-off are keeping us all busy. Well, when the coroner finally releases his body.'

'Oh really, does that take a while then?' asked Charlie, trying again to sound casual.

'It seems to,' said Jackie. 'It's been ten days now but they keep fobbing us off with excuses about further tests, waiting for lab results, that sort of thing. Police forensics have only just stopped swarming all over the pub, looking for God-knows-what. Sometimes it feels like Frank is a suspect, not the victim.'

Charlie nodded sympathetically, while mentally filing this away.

They walked on in thoughtful silence. As the crisp autumn wind whipped in off the sea and chapped their cheeks, the strings of light bulbs which passed for Framstone's illuminations swung back and forth. There was something about dog walking, Charlie always thought, which made people chatty. Perhaps because you walked side by side with no eye contact, you tended to open up. Dog walking often brought out the best in people. Made them freer. More relaxed. Plain nicer.

He waited until they'd safely passed some pedestrians heading the opposite way, then kept his tone light and gossipy. 'You heard about Sergeant Rob, I imagine?'

Jackie nodded, pulling her scarf round her. 'Terrible business. And so soon after Frank. What's the world coming to?'

She looked at Charlie, as if expecting a genuine answer to her rhetorical question. 'God knows,' he said. 'I understand

Rob was worse for wear but you'd expect a grown man to get home safely – and a policeman at that.'

'Oh, I don't know,' said Jackie. 'He was in a right old state that night.'

'You'd seen him?' asked Charlie, struggling to suppress the eagerness in his voice.

'Yes, more's the pity.' Jackie sighed. 'Rob's a regular of ours but I got the impression he'd been on a bit of a pub crawl. By the time he got to the Neptune, he was a liability, weaving about and shooting his mouth off like a loose cannon.' She shook her head and tutted. 'Nobody deserves that, though.'

'Shooting his mouth off about what?' asked Charlie.

Jackie gave him a sidelong look. 'You ask an awful lot of questions, Charlie Boardman,' she said. 'It's just as well I like you.'

'Sorry,' said Charlie sheepishly. 'Tell me to mind my own business if you like.'

'It's OK,' said Jackie. 'I know you mean well. It was hard to make sense of what Rob was saying. Slurring, mumbling, repeating himself. Mainly sounded like police-station politics. Self-pity and paranoia. You've seen what he's like, right?'

Charlie nodded sympathetically. 'Afraid so.'

'I do remember him having a bit of a row,' she continued. 'I noticed because they seemed like an unlikely pair. A drunk policeman in smart shirt and trousers, and a young guy in a hoodie, nose to nose, snarling at each other outside the gents.'

'What about?' asked Charlie, all too aware that he was asking questions again.

Jackie shrugged. 'God knows. Luke, our son – well, *my* son – kept an eye on them, just in case it kicked off, but

Rob wasn't in any fit state for fighting. He staggered out soon after that.'

'And the young guy . . .' Charlie left it hanging, hoping it didn't qualify as another question.

'Not sure who he was or where he went,' said Jackie vaguely, with a wave of her well-manicured hand. 'Why? You don't think he could have been the one who jumped Rob, do you?'

'Sounds like a distinct possibility,' said Charlie, trying to sound vague too. 'Hard to tell without knowing who he is or what the disagreement was about.'

Jackie turned to look at him. 'Some people are just trouble, Charlie,' she said. 'You learn that in the pub trade. Rob Thompson is one of them. It radiates off him. Hassle seems to follow him around. But, like I say, nobody deserves a kicking like that.'

'Did you tell the police about his little spat?' asked Charlie. 'Hoodie guy might be a suspect – for the attack on Rob, I mean.'

'I'm trying to stay out of it, to be honest,' said Jackie. 'Especially with what my family's going through. I'm sure the police will hear about it from someone else if it's significant. We can't go reporting every pub row. I just hope Rob's injuries aren't serious.'

'He's still in hospital but on the mend apparently,' said Charlie. 'Maybe a couple of minor broken bones, otherwise cuts and bruises.'

'You're remarkably well informed,' said Jackie with a twinkle.

'Not really,' said Charlie. 'I know his wife.'

'Oh yes, the lovely Anjali,' said Jackie. 'Good copper, that girl. Just not a great picker of husbands. But what woman is, eh? Love is blind, after all.'

He was pondering what this meant when Jackie veered off, back in the direction of the Neptune. 'See you next time, no doubt, Charlie,' she called over her shoulder, raising a hand in a regal wave. 'Bye, Ruby. Come on, Bobby.'

Charlie smiled as the slavering bulldog waddled devotedly after his mistress. Once again, he was struck by how upbeat Jackie was for a recent widow. She seemed relaxed. Relieved even. He liked her and felt disloyal for even thinking it, but . . . could she be a murder suspect too?

16

Mad About Murder

After an uneventful evening at home with Polly – no late-night doorbells, no sinister toy dogs, just a police patrol car cruising past every few hours – Charlie arrived at Coastal the next morning in good spirits. Although not quite as good as the rest of the dogwalkers, who could barely contain their excitement as they huddled round the table for a coffee-and-croissant-fuelled catch-up. Or a 'debrief', as Sue and Viv insisted on calling it.

Not for the first time, Charlie wondered if they'd missed their vocation. He could just imagine them as a proper detective duo, like a muddy-booted Cagney and Lacey. Or perhaps a pair of Veras.

They hadn't always been dogwalkers, of course. Tess had filled in Charlie when he first met them. Viv spent decades as a primary-school teaching assistant before exhaustion and plummeting morale (that's what round after round of government cuts will do) prompted her to jack it in for a quieter life. Dogs could be just as much trouble as children, Viv said, but they tended not to answer back or have pain-in-the-neck parents.

Apparently Sue had been all set to go to university until

her elder brother died in some sort of tragic accident. She didn't feel she could leave her bereft parents with an empty house, so she stayed in Framstone and became the local librarian. They'd met when Viv came in one day, asking for books on pet psychology. Bonding over their mutual love of dogs, they became an item and eventually set up Nuts About Mutts. Sue's parents had since passed away too, but in her relationship with Viv and friendship with the other dogwalkers, she'd found a sort of surrogate family. In fact, they all had.

The fleece-clad couple were currently so enthused that it wouldn't surprise Charlie if their next venture was a private investigation agency called Mad About Murder, Crazy About Crime or Dotty About Death. God, he was turning into Tess.

'Right, who wants to debrief first?' asked Viv, while Charlie and Tess exchanged a look, challenging each other not to giggle.

'I will,' volunteered Charlie. He told them about contriving an encounter with Jackie Courtney (which went down well), how Rob Thompson had been drunk and noisy in the Neptune on the night he was attacked, and his mysterious row. Everyone agreed that the hooded youth sounded like a potential suspect. They added working out who he was to their lengthening to-investigate list.

The women had rather less to report. Tess had looked into the noseless toy dog but being in the coffee shop all day meant her enquiries were largely limited to casual over-the-counter chats. She pretended she wanted to find a Ruby lookalike toy for her nephew but none of the local mums could suggest where to buy one. She fake-complained about doorstep pranksters and late-night bell-ringers to see if any potential names came up but again drew a blank. Everyone was too busy worrying that Framstone had turned into an epicentre of violent crime.

Sue and Viv had tackled two of the Ws – woods and weapons – and ended with more questions than answers. They'd struck up conversations with everyone they met in the woods, bemoaning this sudden crime wave, tutting about the state of the nation, then casually asking if anyone had seen Frank Courtney or Rob Thompson around. Both men had been sighted in the woods multiple times, but neither regularly nor suspiciously. Frank was usually walking Bobby. Rob tended to take short cuts to and from pubs.

The police had found neither weapon. Short of scouring the entire town, they'd limited their search area to Framstone Woods, hoping the killer might have thrown away any incriminating implements as they fled. Charlie had seen police combing the ground while walking Ruby.

At one point they'd even used a sniffer dog. When Ruby waddled over to say hello, Charlie got chatting to its handler. He'd admitted that locating a plank in a wood was nigh on impossible, even if it was smeared with blood. Too many other smells to mask it, he reckoned, especially with autumn taking grip and the ground getting wetter. Both weapons might still be in the woods somewhere. Everyone vowed to keep a keen eye out on their walks. The knife could be more easily spotted if it had been dumped somewhere nearby, but, again, no sign so far.

When it came to wigs, the third W, Malcolm had an interesting theory. 'Right, well, don't ask how I know this,' he said, which immediately made them want to ask how he knew this, 'but apparently wigs are a thing on dating apps.'

'Come again?' snorted Viv with laughter. 'You mean there are special niche apps for wig-wearers?'

'What are they called?' asked Tess, her wordplay synapses firing up. 'Love Is in the Hair? Sex, Rugs and Rock 'n' Roll? Toupée Is the First Day of the Rest of Your Life?'

'Don't be daft,' scoffed Malcolm. 'I mean on regular dating apps. You know how people often lie about their age, height or body shape? You turn up to meet a tall, handsome thirty-five-year-old only to find a short, chubby fifty-year-old with chronic halitosis?'

'I wouldn't know,' said Tess, Viv and Sue in almost perfect harmony, followed by a peal of laughter.

'Trust me, it happens all the time,' continued Malcolm patiently. 'People bend the truth, like on a CV. They use flattering old photos and tweak their stats. It's all a glorified sales game. The hotel is never as swanky and spacious as it looks in the brochure, right? Well, wigs are sometimes part of that too.'

'What, so bald men put wigs on for their profile pics and pretend they've got hair?' asked Charlie, more amused than anything.

'Exactly,' said Malcolm.

'How does that relate to Frank Courtney?' said Tess, equally baffled. 'Not only was he happily married but he had two wigs, not one.'

'Don't shoot the messenger,' said Malcolm. 'I'm just saying maybe his marriage wasn't so happy after all. He wouldn't be the first married man to go looking for a bit on the side on the apps. He could have been experimenting with different looks.'

Charlie silently pondered this. Perhaps it was why he'd

got the vague impression that Jackie Courtney was flirting with him. She was more than a decade older than Charlie but age gaps didn't mean as much as they used to. Maybe both Courtneys played away.

He also found himself musing on the hints that Jackie had dropped about playing at happy families. If Frank had been cheating, they could be looking at a crime of passion. Any lover would be a potential suspect, alongside Jackie herself. The plot – unlike Frank's hair – was thickening.

17

Off and Running

Charlie was still mulling over the significance of those wigs when he walked Ruby the next morning. After an amble along Framstone's pebbly beach in the mizzly October rain, wondering why the smattering of sea swimmers put themselves through the torture, they turned in the direction of the woods.

Having witnessed all four seasons since being back in Framstone, he'd learned how the local landscape subtly changed. Raindrops came down heavier here, rhythmically hitting his hood and dripping from the leaves all around. Fallen foliage was sodden and already turning to mulch. The spongy ground smelled fertile and peaty.

A rook – or was it a jackdaw? A crow? Charlie was never sure of the difference – looked down from a tree branch with a beady eye that made him shudder. Was it a warning of something? Or had he just watched too many Hitchcock films?

Ruby was in super-snuffly mood. She stopped at pretty much every trunk, bush or bench to savour the scents. Suddenly she raised her head and barked softly, almost to herself. This was followed by a disapproving snort from within her jowls. Ruby was the strong silent type. She rarely barked. Charlie couldn't see what was bothering her, so assumed she'd got wind of a squirrel or rat.

He was bending to give her a calming stroke when he saw it again – that sense of movement through the trees and an almost subliminal flash of a hooded figure. 'I said I'd give chase next time, didn't I, Rube?' he murmured, as she glanced up from her olfactory activities. No need to scare them off. He'd just casually head that way, like the harmless dogwalker he was.

Yet as soon as he took a step in the right direction, his target was off and running. Twigs snapped. Leaves crunched. Branches moved. Before he quite knew what he was doing, Charlie was running too.

After twenty metres, his lungs felt like bursting. He knew he was nowhere near as fit as in his sporting heyday, but he'd assumed all the dog walking had kept him in reasonable shape. Turns out that sauntering along with an ageing mutt is no substitute for actual sprinting. *Who knew?* he thought, as he barrelled through bushes and slalomed between trees. He hadn't got as far as working out what he'd do when he caught up, but a frisson of fear spurred him on. Fight or flight? This was sort of both. With a bit of fright for good measure.

He could have sworn he was gaining ground when he noticed that the only sounds of running were now his own. He slowed and stopped, gulping for air. He'd lost them. Charlie found himself blaming his muddy boots, hardly ideal running footwear on slippery ground, rather than the fact that he'd lost pace over the years.

He bent over, hands on his knees, and drew in big breaths as he looked around for signs of movement. Nothing. 'Hello?'

he called hesitantly, feeling foolish to be conversing with thin air.

As soon as the word escaped his mouth, another twig cracked. Charlie's head swivelled to where the noise came from. Whoever it was must've been waiting behind a tree, checking to see if they were still being pursued. Now they were on the move again. So was he.

Even more determined this time, he hurdled a log and swerved round a hedge. The runner ahead was getting closer. He could hear feet hitting the ground not far in front of him. Charlie really was gaining ground now. The thought spurred him forward, helping him ignore the burning in his lungs and legs. Sweat mixed with the raindrops on his face. He blinked it away.

As he emerged into a clearing, he expected to see someone's back mere metres away. Charlie visualized a few more strides before launching himself into a dive for their legs, like in his rugby full-back days. But there was nobody. The patch of ground was empty. Slowing to a halt and wincing in pain, he looked around, confused.

Hiding behind a tree again, huh? Two could play that game. Charlie stepped sideways, flattened his back against a gnarly old oak, kept still and listened. All he could hear was the rain, swaying trees and his own breath faintly rasping and rattling. He needed to get fit. He also needed to think clearly through the mild terror which was suddenly palpable now he'd stopped running.

That's when he heard it again: a branch splintering underfoot, much closer this time. Charlie's adrenaline surged. Someone was approaching from the other side of the oak. He squatted down and picked up the biggest stick within reach, trying to ignore his trembling hands and adjusting his grip until he was wielding it like a baseball bat. He waited for the next noise. *That's it, keep coming . . . Little bit closer . . . Now.*

He stepped out as swiftly and silently as he could, raising the stick. His muscles tensed and he was about to swing as a man stepped into view. 'There you are!' exclaimed a familiar voice. 'We were wondering if you'd fallen victim to the Framstone Woods weirdo, weren't we, Ruby?'

It was Malcolm, with Ted and Ruby trailing behind. Charlie exhaled, experiencing a rush of relief mixed with disappointment. Malcolm stopped when he saw the stick in Charlie's hands and looked at him enquiringly.

'Long story,' said Charlie sheepishly, dropping the weapon and crouching to greet the dogs.

'I'm sure it is, my forest-dwelling friend,' said Malcolm. 'We came across Ruby on the path and assumed you'd be around somewhere.'

'Sorry, Rube,' said Charlie. He massaged her silky ears the way she liked, while her tail wagged furiously. 'Thanks for looking after her, Ted.'

The greyhound looked back at him imperiously, as if to say he was right to be grateful. 'And you, of course.' Charlie smiled, straightening up and patting Malcolm's shoulder fondly. He felt a warm surge of friendship that he hadn't felt for a while.

'*De rien*, darling,' said Malcolm, already turning back towards the path. '*De rien*. But what's with the hiding place and deadly weapon?'

'Chasing shadows,' panted Charlie. 'Or maybe ghosts.'

Malcolm arched an eyebrow and carried on walking. As he followed, Charlie glanced back over his shoulder. Was

Frank Courtney's killer looking at them right now? Was Rob Thompson's attacker? Were they one and the same? He was probably just imagining it but Charlie hated the idea of someone out there still watching, laughing at him.

Fear was joined by simmering frustration. His physical prowess wasn't what it had been twenty years ago but his sporting competitiveness was still intact. Charlie hated losing. Especially when he didn't know who he was losing to.

18

Women, Money, the Usual

He'd say one thing for a fruitless chase through the forest – you certainly slept well afterwards. With his out-of-practice limbs creaking, Charlie had run himself a bath after supper. He'd made an undignified sequence of noises as he lowered himself in, relishing the feeling of piping-hot water soothing his aches and pains.

He'd stayed in for too long. The pages of his book were as wrinkled as his toes but he hadn't read more than a few pages. His mind had instead drifted to Frank Courtney's killer, to Rob Thompson's pub argument and to his own woodland adversary. Eventually Charlie began to feel faint and fuzzy with all the heat, so reluctantly hauled himself out. With his dressing gown still on and a towel round his neck, he'd fallen asleep almost as soon as he collapsed on to his bed.

He didn't stir again until one of his favourite aromas began drifting upstairs. A cooked breakfast. Maybe he should pursue phantom hooded figures more often.

'What's the occasion?' he asked Polly as he padded into the kitchen and sat down, wincing at his stiff legs. A pot of coffee was already steaming on the table. A basket of hot toast awaited. After she'd lifted griddle-striped bacon on to a plate and skilfully slid a wobbling fried egg next to it, his mother plopped it down in front of him.

'No occasion.' She smiled. 'Don't worry, you haven't forgotten my birthday or anything. It's just that you looked exhausted last night, so I hoped you'd sleep well and wake up famished.'

'You were correct on all counts,' said Charlie, tucking in hungrily. 'Not joining me?'

'Only for a cuppa,' she said, glancing at the kitchen clock and pouring herself a coffee. 'I had my breakfast a couple of hours ago. You lay in later than usual. Must've needed it.'

'I think I did.' Charlie grinned, buttering a piece of toast to mop up the egg yolk. 'Thanks, Mum. This is a treat. Really hitting the spot.'

Polly smoothed down his bed hair affectionately. 'My pleasure,' she said. 'What else are mothers for?' At times like this Charlie could temporarily forget Polly's growing physical and mental frailty. She seemed just like he'd always remembered.

'I'm so glad you've made good friends here again.' She smiled contentedly.

'So I was Billy No-Mates before, was I?' teased Charlie. 'Gee, thanks.'

'You know what I mean,' scoffed Polly. 'It took a while to find your feet back in Framstone, I think. Tess and the other dogwalkers seem to have helped.'

'I guess they have,' said Charlie, wiping brown sauce from his chin. He hadn't thought of it like that.

They blew on their hot drinks and sat quietly for a while, Radio 4 burbling away in the background, until Charlie voiced a thought that had been hovering at the back of his mind lately.

'Mum, can I ask you about Dad?'

She immediately looked worried. 'Of course you can, darling, anytime,' she said gently. 'Although you might not always like the answers. What about him?'

'Well, for starters, how bad did his drinking get before he left?'

'Pretty bad.' She sighed. 'You must remember some of it?'

Charlie had a jumbled patchwork of memories: long evenings without his father around; his mum's worried face. Anticipatory tension in the house when it got past pub closing time. Fearing what mood he'd be in; muttered swearing as a key scratched at the lock; the front door swinging open with a bang. The smell of stale booze and cigarettes. Slurring. Shouting. Crying. Self-loathing and apologies the morning after.

'Some, I suppose,' he said, giving her hand a squeeze. 'Did he lie about where he'd been?'

'Yes and no,' said Polly, sipping her coffee as she thought back. 'There was no strategy, it depended on his mood. Some nights he'd want to tell funny stories from the pub or gossip about a party. Other times, he wanted to hide how long he'd been out, where and who with. Partly to spare my feelings, I think, but partly because he had secrets.'

'What sort of secrets?' asked Charlie. 'Or do I not want to know?'

She chuckled wryly. 'Probably not. Women and money mainly. The usual. I knew them all deep down anyway.'

'How so?'

'Well, that's the thing with women in unhappy marriages to

men like your dad,' said Polly. 'You kid yourself. You pretend. You turn a blind eye. You don't want the truth because it will hurt. But the fact that you know it'll hurt means you already know the truth in your heart anyway. Does that make sense?'

'Sort of,' he said, squeezing her hand again. She gave a faraway smile. He didn't want to upset her or give her the fourth degree, so Charlie left it there and they listened to the news bulletin on the radio. Polly's hand shot to her mouth during a report on a grisly murder up north. Charlie was sure she wouldn't have been so shocked a fortnight ago. The attacks in the woods had affected everyone. That doorstep surprise brought it even closer to home.

As he showered, dressed and took Ruby out, he found himself thinking about husbands with secrets: what their wives knew or didn't know; what people put up with and how they decide that enough is enough; and how all this might apply to the Courtneys. Maybe the Thompsons too.

He arrived at Coastal Coffee to find Tess bubbling over with news. 'Haven't you heard?' she asked breathlessly as soon as Charlie appeared in the shop doorway.

He sighed and shot a look at Ruby. 'Not this old routine again. OK, I'll bite. What's happened this time?'

Ignoring his sarcasm, Tess said, 'The police have arrested someone for murder.'

19

It's a Hard-Knock Life

'What?' Charlie asked, stunned. 'When? Who?'

'Easy there, quizmaster,' said Tess, her eyes sparkling with excitement and cheeks dimpling as she smirked. She glanced around the busy cafe, which Charlie now noticed was positively buzzing with chatter, presumably about the arrest news. 'Not here. Let's walk and talk. I've wanted to say that ever since watching *The West Wing*.'

Tess unknotted her apron, ran her fingers through her long black hair and gestured to Leon – her part-time assistant was a local sixth-former she'd trained up as a barista over the summer holidays – to mind the shop, before rounding up Rough and Tumble. They joined Charlie and Ruby on the pavement outside.

All three dogs had picked up on their owners' animated mood – 'Your emotions radiate down the lead like an aerial,' Viv always said – and set off eagerly towards the woods, hauling their humans along behind them. Charlie and Tess felt like they were being dragged by a mismatched team of huskies.

'So what's with the uncharacteristic secrecy?' asked Charlie, once they'd let the dogs off their leads and watched them scamper ahead. Or waddle in Ruby's case. 'It's unlike you to be remotely discreet.'

Again, Tess ignored his sarcasm – a sure sign that something was afoot. 'My punters are edgy enough at the minute,' she said as they strolled. 'I didn't want to risk spooking them further by spreading rumours. Besides, it's a small town. You never know who might be listening – or connected to the suspect in question.'

'And who is the suspect in question? Come on, you big tease. Spill.'

'Do you know someone called Shane Carter?' she said. 'That's the name that keeps coming up among my customers.'

'Don't think so,' mused Charlie, scratching his stubbly cheek. 'Rings a vague bell but that might be because of Shawn Carter, aka Jay-Z, aka Mr Beyoncé.'

'Yeah, all right, hip-hop Roget.' Tess smirked. 'No relation – although this one does have quite a rap sheet, apparently. He's probably had a hard-knock life.'

'See what you did there. So who is he?'

'Local lad in his early twenties. Even if you don't know his name, you might know him by sight. Hangs around town a lot, getting up to God-knows-what. Usually wears a hoodie . . .' She glanced at Charlie, whose eyebrows raised knowingly, thinking of Rob Thompson's pub square-up. 'And a Framstone Rovers scarf.'

'Poor bloke,' quipped Charlie. 'No wonder he turned to a life of crime. Well, allegedly.'

Rovers were the beleaguered local football team and something of a running joke around Framstone. They'd done decently once upon a time but in recent decades their fortunes had declined in parallel with the town itself. Glories were far in the past. Crowds dwindled. The ground, with its red-and-yellow livery, looked increasingly tatty.

Charlie had turned out for Rovers' youth sides himself back in the day and perhaps could have progressed through the ranks if he'd stuck around. That all fell by the wayside when he went to university and discovered other pleasures like drink, dancing, girls and recreational drugs. Oh, and studying, of course. Let's not forget that. Ahem.

'I realize that a hoodie and a Framstone scarf aren't the most distinctive items around here,' said Tess with a shrug, 'but I bet you'd know Shane if you saw him.'

'Yeah, maybe,' mused Charlie, his mind elsewhere. As well as Sergeant Rob's squabbler from the Neptune, he was thinking about the hooded runner from the woods. He didn't think he'd glimpsed a Rovers scarf, though.

'Word is, Shane was taken into custody in the small hours this morning,' Tess continued breathlessly, pausing only to roll her eyes at Rough and Tumble running manically around Ruby, yapping as they went. 'The first customer I spoke to assumed it was for petty theft or drug-dealing – he's got a bit of a reputation, has our Shane – but when they mentioned that it was Anjali and Murdoch making the arrest, my spidey senses tingled. The grapevine now says it was on suspicion of murder.'

'Well, far be it from me to disagree with the Coastal rumour mill,' said Charlie. 'Fairtrade coffee with a side order of wild speculation.'

'That's our new slogan,' deadpanned Tess. 'I thought you might like to probe your police insider and get it from the horse's mouth, so to speak.'

'Sounds like Anjali might have her hands full, but I'll see

what I can do,' agreed Charlie. 'Although I'll leave out the bit where you called her "horsey".'

He felt like the wind had been taken out of his sails. He'd badly wanted to help find Frank Courtney's killer but it sounded like the case was already closed.

20

Something Fishy

Charlie was right. Anjali did have her hands full. Or at least, she wasn't answering her phone or replying to his text about meeting up. He decided not to push too hard. A murder investigation and a hospitalized husband were probably a good enough excuse for now.

In the meantime, he gleaned some intel from a surprise source. That evening, he knocked up a fish pie for supper. It was one of Polly's favourites, so he could almost make it with his eyes closed nowadays. As she pursued the last few peas around the plate with her fork, she asked what was happening with 'the police and that business in the woods'.

He told her about the arrest and she nodded thoughtfully but didn't seem terribly surprised. Charlie suspected she already knew. Like Tess, his mum was plugged in to the Framstone rumour mill. She didn't leave the house much nowadays but a few snatches of idle chit-chat with the postman, neighbours and local shopkeepers usually told her what she needed to know. It amused Charlie how a few well-placed, seemingly harmless questions from a canny old lady could elicit the juiciest gossip without anyone really noticing.

'Shane Carter, Shane Carter,' she repeated to herself, as

if searching her internal database. 'Do you know, I think I might have delivered him.'

Now it was Charlie's turn to not be terribly surprised. When you've worked for decades as a midwife and district nurse in a small town like Framstone, there aren't many families with whom you haven't crossed paths. Polly sometimes knew several generations of the same family by virtue of helping babies that she'd delivered, now grown up, have their own children.

'Oh yes?' He leaned down to ruffle Ruby's ears and hide his eager expression.

'If I'm thinking of the right one, his mother is Karen Carter,' continued Polly. 'Nice girl, if a bit chaotic. She had Shane very young.'

'I'm sure that's the right one, Mum,' said Charlie. 'How young?'

'Ooh, now,' she said, looking at the ceiling as if she hoped to find the answer written up there. 'She was certainly still in her teens. Fifteen maybe? Sixteen at the most. I remember thinking how Karen was barely older than you and your brother, carrying around this huge bump like she'd stuffed a cushion up her school uniform.'

'Was there a father on scene?'

'Not to speak of,' Polly said sadly, shaking her head. 'It had all the hallmarks of an accident after a fling. Karen was intent on keeping the baby, though, I remember that much. It seemed to be a matter of pride, even though she was clearly going to struggle.'

'Struggle how?'

'Well, she was young, had just left school, didn't have a job. Her parents disapproved and had their own problems, so she was on her own in a bedsit in town. But there was a fire in her, even at that age. Actually, this might tell you how young she was – she named her baby son after her favourite pop singer. One of those boyband ones. She told me she used to have his posters on her wall and that's where she got the name from.'

'Shane from Westlife, I'll bet,' said Charlie.

'You'd know better than me.' Polly smiled. 'I lost track after the Beatles and the Stones.'

Charlie laughed. 'No, you didn't. I remember you singing along with us to Wham! and Madonna on the radio before Dad came home.'

Polly smiled at the memory. 'Jitterbugging around the kitchen as we cleared up after dinner. We had some nice times, didn't we?'

'We still do, Mum,' Charlie assured her. 'Anyway, what happened with Karen and Shane?'

'The birth went fine,' recalled Polly. 'Karen was brave for such a young girl and Shane was a bouncy little boy. But things got harder for her after that.'

'Oh no. In what way?'

'Well, it's tough being a single parent without any support. She struggled for money. She wasn't sleeping well. I'm not sure the baby did either. Poor girl would turn up for postnatal clinics in a right state or miss appointments altogether. It was all a bit messy. Mother and baby both had health issues. I think there might have been drugs and bad influences involved. You know, nasty men taking advantage of a vulnerable young mum. We did what we could but . . .'

'I'm sure you did,' Charlie said gently.

'The upshot was that Karen couldn't cope. Eventually little

Shane got taken away by social services. He was a toddler by then if memory serves. It's heartbreaking when a child is separated from its mum. He was in and out of care for years, usually staying with Karen in between, but I'm not sure either of them were ever the same. And now this murder business.'

'Oh, Mum,' he said, patting her hand. 'We don't know yet if Shane was actually involved. There could be any number of reasons why he was arrested.'

Polly brightened. 'You're right, dear. I hope so. That poor family deserve a break. You will find out and let me know, won't you? Maybe you could ask that nice Anjali.'

Charlie smiled to himself. His mother was far more shrewd than she let on. Even now, it was like she could read his mind.

21

Back on the Mean Streets

As he sat waiting in the woods, Charlie watched a fellow dogwalker use one of those ball-launchers to propel a tennis ball down the path. His eager cockapoo scampered after it.

Ruby, now sprawled happily at his feet, had been a keen frisbee-catcher and ball-chaser once upon a time but he'd never been tempted by a plastic tool. Thanks to his sporting past, Charlie still had a strong throwing arm. He mixed it up by drop-kicking balls too, idly fantasizing that he was still on the rugby pitch as he did so. He was still a big kid at heart.

A whack on the ankles from Ruby's wagging tail snapped him out of his reverie. Anjali slumped down next to them with a groan and gratefully took the Coastal cup passed to her by Charlie. The usual strong white Americano for him, oat milk latte for her. Tess had approved of his double order this morning, knowing full well who it was for.

'Thanks, Boardy Boy.' Anjali smiled gratefully, taking a sip. 'I needed this.'

'Long night?' he asked innocently. Last time he'd seen Anjali, she'd been in civvies. Now she was back in her usual trouser suit and running a tired hand through her hair.

'You could say that. Me and Craig were interviewing a suspect until the wee small hours. This coffee is way better than the station machine's dirty brown dishwater, let me tell you. It's like a different genre of drink altogether.'

'I'll pass that on to Tess,' he said with a chuckle. 'She'll take compliments wherever she can get them. We're talking about Shane Carter, right?'

'Couldn't possibly comment,' stonewalled Anjali. 'But it's kind of immaterial now. We had to let him go this morning. Not enough evidence to charge.'

'Oh really?' said Charlie. 'That must be annoying.'

'Tell me about it.' She sighed. 'We were sure we'd got our man. Still are actually.'

'Why's that?' He was pushing his luck a bit, but Anjali's fatigue and evident frustration appeared to have let her guard down temporarily.

'He's got form for knife crime.' Charlie raised his eyebrows in surprise. 'Well, one previous conviction a few years back. We also know it was Carter who had a bust-up with Rob in the Neptune on the night he was beaten up. Several punters have corroborated that.'

'God bless the great British public,' said Charlie. 'What was the argument about?'

'That's another annoying thing.' She sighed. 'Neither of them will say. Rob waves it away like he can't quite remember. Which maybe he can't.' She looked at him knowingly. Charlie stopped short of making a drinky-drinky gesture. 'Shane just said it was a private matter, then started on the old "no comment" routine.'

'I feel your pain,' Charlie said sympathetically. 'That always drives me nuts on TV.'

Anjali rolled her eyes. 'People nowadays have watched enough crime dramas to know not to talk when they don't need to. How I long for the days when they'd blab away, incriminating themselves and half the town.'

Charlie felt a pang of guilt about wheedling out information while she was at a low ebb. He took a sip of his coffee in a bid to maintain the illusion of two friends casually chatting. 'He denies everything, I assume?'

'Of course. Frank's murder. Attacking Rob. Not me, guv, honest.'

'Does he have alibis for both?'

'You won't leave it alone, will you?' said Anjali, annoyed but smiling. 'You lot put the "dog" into "dogged".'

Charlie chuckled. 'Careful. With wordplay like that, you'll turn into Tess.'

'Oh, there are worse people to turn into,' said Anjali. 'Nope, no alibi. Nothing he'll share with us anyway – presumably because he either did it or was drug-dealing at the time. We even found a vape by the body which matched Carter's, but he insists it's not his. I checked and it's a fairly common type.'

'Goddammit,' said Charlie, channelling an NYPD cop in a bid to lighten the mood. 'So a potential violent perp is back on the mean streets of Framstone?'

'Don't give up the graphic design just yet,' she winced. 'I've said too much. You've caught me in a moment of weakness but thanks for listening all the same. And thank Tess for the coffee. If she ever fancies setting up a concession stand near the police station, tell her she'd do a roaring trade.'

'Will do,' said Charlie. 'Good luck, Anj. And get some rest.'

'Chance would be a fine thing,' she said wearily. 'Rob's still in hospital, so I'm shuttling between there and the station.

I seem to spend half my life walking down endless corridors or getting a sore backside on plastic chairs.'

'He'll be out soon and your load will lighten,' said Charlie, trying to sound hopeful. 'Keep your chin up.'

Anjali nodded, rolled her eyes again and turned back towards those mean streets. Charlie whiled away a few more minutes watching the cockapoo's game of fetch – it was showing no sign of tiring, unlike him and Ruby – before heading home himself. His mind wandered to what Polly said about Shane's tough start in life. A dogwalkers' debrief was required.

22

Agent Nuts and Agent Mutts

Framstone beach wouldn't win any awards for outstanding natural beauty. It was all pebbles, slate-grey sea and swimmers with goosebumps. No sign of sun-kissed models frolicking on tropical white sands. But Charlie and Ruby liked it as a dog-walk route when they fancied a change from the woods.

The North Sea wind was bracingly robust and the sky seemed to stretch on forever. The beach induced nostalgia pangs for his misspent youth, haunting the arcades on the pier or skinny-dipping as a dare after the pubs shut. He didn't share the latter memory with the gang. He'd never hear the end of it, especially from Tess and Malcolm.

As they strode along, buffeted by the breeze as their feet sank into the stones, Tess's twin terriers Rough and Tumble darted in and out of the water like damp dervishes, chasing the waves as they retreated, then fleeing from them as they came in. Ruby enjoyed getting her paws wet with a paddle. Humphrey the lunatic Labrador plunged into the surf like an overexcited toddler. Naturally Malcolm's graceful greyhound Ted and the Professor, the wise old terrier on wheels, were above it all, trotting and trundling along behind.

'I'm sure it's partly Pavlovian,' announced Tess. 'But I suddenly fancy a Flake ninety-nine or a bag of chips.'

'You'd be lucky at this time of year,' said Malcolm, gesturing at the shuttered shopfronts facing the prom. 'Anyway, don't keep us in suspense any longer. What's the latest, Boardman PI?'

Charlie filled them in about Polly's connection to the Carters, Karen's problems as a teen mum and Shane being taken into care. Everyone made sympathetic noises, especially Viv. Having worked in schools, she knew how single mothers could struggle and kids could fall through the cracks. So did Malcolm. During his decades as a solicitor, he'd always made a point of taking Legal Aid work.

Sue saw it in her library too. 'Some kids used it as a second home,' she said. 'I never minded. It was warm, quiet and safe, which their households probably weren't. I'd keep an eye on them and slip them the odd packet of sweets when nobody was looking.'

'I can vouch for that,' Malcolm said, chuckling. It was through the library that he'd first got to know Sue – and, via her, Viv. When he'd retired and moved to town on a permanent basis, Malcolm had become a daily fixture among the shelves and trolleys. If he wasn't reading the newspapers or borrowing old jazz records, he'd be looking up his latest home-improvement project in DIY manuals. YouTube did the job nowadays, but old habits die hard. Besides, he'd enjoyed the chance to swap gossip with Sue and her regulars.

Viv demanded a blow-by-blow, word-for-word rewind of Charlie's conversation with Anjali, occasionally interrupting with questions to which he generally didn't know the answers. That was always the trouble with briefing this lot.

They were even more nosy than him, so were rarely satisfied with the headline news. They wanted details that he didn't have.

'I can't say I'm surprised that Shane Carter's the prime suspect,' said Viv when Charlie had finished. 'A record of theft or drug-dealing, let alone knife crime, tends to put you in the frame for everything with the police around here.'

'I get that,' chipped in Sue, 'but it would be quite an escalation to suddenly start beating up coppers and stabbing publicans.'

'What is it they call it on your police shows?' said Viv. 'Criminal spin?'

'What's that?' asked Tess distractedly, still casting longing looks around for an ice-cream or chip van. 'Sounds kind of fun.'

'The process of someone's criminality worsening,' said Sue. 'If this guy Shane's crimes are escalating, it could be because he's covering something up in panic or an external factor has triggered it.'

'Maybe revenge, love or money,' mused Viv. 'The holy trinity of violent crime.'

'Whoa there, Agent Nuts and Agent Mutts,' interrupted Charlie. 'Before you get carried away with your FBI behavioural profiles, let's not forget that the police have let Shane Carter go already. Innocent until proven guilty and all that.'

'Just a procedural formality,' said Malcolm, his legal background lending him an air of effortless expertise. 'They're clearly still gathering evidence against him.'

'Not clearly, just probably,' said Charlie. 'Surely it's just as likely that he didn't do it than he did?'

'Hmm,' said Sue, the oracle of true crime. 'It sounds like any evidence is circumstantial. Even if he's admitted the pub row with Rob, he denies attacking him. He also denies stabbing Frank Courtney. And without the murder weapon . . .'

'Weapons, plural,' pointed out Viv. 'The bludgeon and the blade.'

'Sounds like the name of a dodgy pub,' said Malcolm.

'OK, weapons plural,' continued Sue. 'Without them, there's a reduced chance of DNA evidence. They're relying on his clothing, fingernails, any abrasions from a struggle, that kind of thing. Or physical proof found at the scene.'

'I can't take it any longer,' interjected Tess. 'All very interesting but my need for chips or ice cream is greater. I'll catch you up.' She strode off towards the promenade while the others ambled onwards.

'Sounds like what the police desperately need is hard evidence or a confession,' said Charlie. 'Oi, where are you lot going?'

Led by Rough, Tumble and a thoroughly soaked Humphrey, the dogs milled around a figure on the beach. Deep in their discussion, the dogwalkers hadn't noticed anyone else around. Not everyone is pleased to be accosted by stinking, wet, hyperactive hounds. Luckily this fellow didn't seem to mind. Quite the contrary.

'Sorry!' called Charlie as the dogwalkers hurried over, calling off their respective charges. 'They're overexcited and over-friendly.'

'Don't worry,' said the man, turning to face them. 'I'm always happy to meet dogs, even damp ones. Hello, aren't you gorgeous?'

Ruby arrived late on the scene and the stranger squatted to greet her. 'You're a wise old girl, aren't you?' He turned to

Ted and the Professor. 'You guys look pretty distinguished too.' As Rough, Tumble and Humphrey chased round his legs, he laughed. 'Not like you three goofs, eh?'

'The sea always gets them a bit frisky, I'm afraid,' explained Charlie apologetically, while Viv, Sue and Malcolm tried in vain to restore some semblance of order.

'I can see that.' The man grinned, ruffling various ears and rubbing proffered bellies. He even softly stroked Ruby along her head ridge right between her eyes, which she always adored. It sent her into a blissful semi-hypnotized stupor.

'O ye of little faith,' called a triumphant voice behind them. Tess returned from her supplies mission, proudly clutching an ice-cream cone with a chocolate flake, strawberry sauce and sprinkles. 'And before you ask, no, you can't have a lick. Oops, didn't realize we had company.' She looked surprised to see the normally introverted Charlie making small talk with a stranger. She looked even more surprised when she saw who it was.

'Don't mind me,' said the man. 'I'm more of a Cornetto guy.' He glanced round at the gang shyly. 'I'm Shane. Pleasure to meet you all.'

23

For My Sins

Everybody tried their best not to appear shocked. Charlie caught Tess giving him a knowing look, as if to say, 'Surely now you recognize him from around town?' He did indeed seem vaguely familiar.

'It's not Shane Carter, is it?' asked Charlie, consciously keeping his tone light. 'I think my mother delivered you, if that's not too weird a thing to say.' Face flushing, he hurriedly added, 'Sorry, that sounds like you're a parcel. Polly Boardman. The midwife. I'm her son Charlie.'

Shane smiled. 'I remember Polly. Not from delivering me obviously. But she used to look in on my mum from time to time. Always said hello if she saw us around. Nice lady.'

'That's her,' said Charlie, relieved that his unusual conversational gambit hadn't made the younger man run a mile.

'Well, tell her Shane Carter said hi,' he said. 'And thanks for bringing me into the world, for my sins.'

Now Charlie looked at him properly, Shane didn't resemble the monstrous career criminal they'd been led to expect. He was a regular young guy, wearing a hoodie, baggy jeans and Nike trainers. No football scarf today. Instead he had a safety-pin necklace round his neck. Short-haired, tattooed hands, tired but friendly face. The only sign of a troubled past was a mild hand tremor as he sucked on his vape, scars on his wrists which might have been caused by self-harm, and a reluctance to hold eye contact for long, which made him look slightly fearful and furtive.

'I don't think I've seen you on the Framstone Riviera before,' said Malcolm chattily after everyone had introduced themselves. 'It's usually just us dogwalkers and the odd swimmer who needs their head testing.'

If Shane felt like he was being interrogated all over again, he didn't show it. 'Nah, you're right,' he replied. 'But it was a long night. I thought some sea air might blow away the cobwebs.'

'And has it?' Malcolm smiled.

'It has actually,' said Shane. 'And meeting you lot has cheered me right up.'

Viv gave a surprised smile until Shane squatted down again. He'd clearly been referring to the dogs. She looked slightly sheepish, hoping that nobody had noticed. Fat chance. Tess and Malcolm smirked at each other, storing it up for later.

Shane made a fuss of the assorted pooches again. Ruby had taken a particular shine to him, rolling over to offer herself up for a tummy rub – not a privilege she granted any old human. She then gave his face a thorough licking. Shane laughed good-naturedly. 'After the night I had, I could do with a wash.'

Charlie raised his eyebrows meaningfully at the others. They'd accidentally got chatting to a potential prime suspect and needed to take advantage of the opportunity. Who knew if they'd get another?

'You've made some friends for life there,' said Viv approvingly. 'Are you a dog owner yourself?'

'Sadly not,' said Shane. 'I'd love it but I've never quite been in the position to take one on. Always waiting for the right time in the right home, you know?'

'I hear you,' said Sue. 'It's not something to take lightly. There are too many dogs in rescue shelters because the owners didn't think it through.'

'That's definitely where I'd go,' said Shane, massaging the back of Ruby's neck. 'We could rescue each other, couldn't we, darling?'

'Well, maybe the time will be right soon,' said Malcolm hopefully.

'Maybe,' replied Shane, not sounding terribly convinced.

'Haven't I seen you in the pubs around town?' asked Tess casually.

'I don't know, have you?' said Shane. It was with a smile but his guard was going up.

'The Neptune maybe?' added Tess. Charlie gave her a look. She was pushing it now.

Shane seemed to think so, too. After giving a last round of ear rubs, he straightened up. 'I could play with you lot all day but I was just heading home, as it goes. That wind's starting to bite and I'm not quite dressed for the weather.' He glanced round at the dogwalkers' anoraks and parkas. 'I need another layer. Couldn't even find my lucky scarf to put on.'

Charlie caught Tess looking at him knowingly again and did his best to ignore her. 'Well, it was nice meeting you, Shane,' he said. 'I'll pass your best along to my mum. Your canine fan club hopes to see you again soon.'

'I hope so, too,' said Shane with a wistful smile. He gave the wagging dogs a last wave and hurried back towards town, putting up his hood as he went.

24

Not Accused of
Murder Every Day

'Come on then, you lot,' said Charlie, as they grappled the dogs back on to their leads and turned for home. 'Say it. Go on. I know you're thinking it.'

'I haven't the foggiest idea what you mean,' said Malcolm with a glint in his eye. 'Do you, girls?'

'Nope,' chorused Tess, Viv and Sue.

Charlie chuckled and rolled his eyes. 'OK then, I'll say it. He's way too lovely with dogs to be a killer.'

'I doubt it would be a recognized deductive theory at the FBI Academy in Quantico,' said Sue. 'But you've got a point.'

'Much as it pains me to agree with the smug git, he does,' said Tess. 'I know we're biased, but dog people tend to be good people, right?'

'Right,' said Viv, nodding. 'It's not a foolproof personality test but it's not far off. Underneath the hoodie, tats and street swagger, he's obviously a great big softie.'

'The dogs certainly won't hear a word against him. Ain't that right, Rube?' Charlie said, smiling. As she looked up at him, Charlie was convinced he detected a nod of agreement.

'So what else did we glean, team?' asked Tess. 'There were hints at a chaotic life, which tallies with what Polly said about Shane's upbringing.'

'Troubled, for sure,' agreed Viv. 'The poor lad's never had a pet for lack of a stable home. He'd clearly been up all night at the cop shop, getting the third degree. It's not every day that you're accused of murder. Probably a bit shaken up, hence him needing to clear his head.'

'Did you notice his necklace?' asked Sue.

'Why?' asked Charlie.

'It was a safety pin on a chain,' explained Sue. 'Among others things, it can symbolize a past suicide bid. Young people wear them as a sort of promise not to attempt it again.'

'Oh, Sue, how sad,' said Tess.

'For what it's worth, I thought young Shane was a sweetheart,' said Malcolm. 'Rough around the edges, sure, but surely too gentle for the sort of violence we're talking about. To be honest, my gaydar was twitching a bit.'

Tess barked with laughter, briefly startling the dogs. 'Your gaydar is permanently twitching, Malcs. You're convinced that pretty much everyone is gay, bi, confused or closeted. It might be time for your gaydar's annual service. It's on the blink.'

'I get serviced regularly, thank you for asking,' Malcolm snapped back, pretending to be scandalized.

They walked on in silence, each replaying the encounter with Shane in their heads. For a while the only sound was canine panting and the Professor's back wheels squeaking.

'Did you pick up on the scarf thing, too?' asked Tess suddenly.

'I did,' said Viv, nodding. 'Said he'd lost his lucky scarf.

Unless he's disposed of it for some incriminating reason, of course.'

'Whoa there, DCI Vera Stanhope,' said Charlie. 'Not everything has a sinister explanation. I'm always losing scarves.'

'And gloves,' added Tess.

'And umbrellas,' added Sue.

'And the plot,' added Malcolm with a final flourish.

Charlie sighed. They already knew him well. Approaching the town centre, they prepared to go their separate ways. 'Anyway, he was nice about my mum and my dog,' concluded Charlie with a shrug. 'I can't ask much more than that. Shane Carter might be the police's prime suspect but he ain't mine.'

As he ambled home with Ruby, he began to wonder who might be his prime suspect instead – and what was the next step towards unmasking them. Charlie agreed with the others. Shane seemed far too benign to murder Frank Courtney. Even attacking Rob Thompson felt unlikely. Charlie didn't believe he was a mugger, let alone a killer.

Suddenly he and Ruby jumped out of their skins as a passing car honked its horn. What appeared to be a harmless old gent gestured furiously through the windscreen at a cyclist, who seemed taken aback by the driver's vitriolic reaction. Everyone in Framstone seemed jumpy at the moment.

As he soothingly told Ruby that it was OK, Charlie reminded himself not to make any assumptions. You never knew for certain what somebody else was capable of. Desperation, anger, fear – they could drive anyone to extremes.

25

Ordinary People, Extraordinary Lengths

Charlie was still mulling it all over the next day as he took Ruby for her morning perambulation around the woods. Over breakfast – just toast and cereal, no cooked treats today – he'd told Polly about running into Shane and how he'd asked Charlie to pass on his best wishes. She'd been quietly delighted.

'It's a funny job, midwifery,' she said thoughtfully. 'You briefly play a vital role in all these lives. You see people at their most raw and vulnerable. And then you're gone, on to the next one. It's nice to be remembered sometimes.'

'I bet you're remembered a lot, Mum,' said Charlie. 'Besides, it doesn't always stop with the birth, does it? Shane mentioned how you'd looked in on Karen afterwards and always stopped to chat if you saw her around.'

'Well, that's not just about being in the caring professions. It's about being kind and decent. I always tried to teach you and your brother that, too.'

'You did,' he said with a smile. 'Not sure how much of it we took in, mind you.'

She smiled back. 'Oh, I think enough. I don't know if it helped Karen Carter, though. Or Shane, by the sounds of it. He lived with his mother for periods, but after a while she'd struggle again and he'd get taken back into care. All those false starts and dashed hopes. It made Karen always seem lost somehow. A bit broken. I hope young Shane hasn't gone the same way.'

'Maybe a bit,' mused Charlie. 'But he's a nice enough lad. I don't reckon he's beyond repair.'

'So you don't think he's guilty?' asked Polly.

'My gut feeling is no,' Charlie reassured her. 'You never know for sure but Shane doesn't seem the violent type.'

'Then let's hope they find whoever was really responsible and justice is done,' Polly said with an air of finality. Charlie envisioned her banging a gavel on the breakfast table, sending toast crumbs into the air.

While Ruby snuffled along the leaf-strewn woodland paths, he wondered again if he was being naive. Just because Shane liked dogs and seemed fairly harmless, it didn't mean he wasn't capable of dark deeds – especially if provoked. Not every violent criminal was a psychopath. Some were just ordinary people driven to extraordinary lengths.

Charlie tutted, exasperated with himself. He was going round in circles now. And he didn't mean doing laps of the woods. He decided he needed caffeine – with a side order of mild snark to take his mind off things. He knew just the woman to expertly deliver both.

Ruby didn't need telling. Muscle memory steered her in the direction of Coastal Coffee, tugging Charlie along behind.

Her tail began to wag as she waddled through the door. Charlie half expected to see the full dogwalker contingent at their usual table. Instead he found Tess in deep conversation with someone else.

They looked up as Charlie and Ruby came over. 'Talk of the devil and he shall appear.' Tess smirked to her companion. 'And look who else came in for the finest coffee this side of Framstone High Street.'

Anjali grinned. 'Hello, Boardy Boy. You've got me dangerously addicted to Tess's oat lattes. Were your ears burning?'

Charlie was just opening his mouth to reply when there was an almighty bang. It was like a clap of thunder directly behind him, as if the air itself had split open with a deafening crack. He instinctively crouched down and clutched Ruby protectively.

Everything seemed to slow down as shards of glass flew through the air, hitting Charlie's back and skittering on the floor all around them, sparkling like snow in the sunshine. There was a steady ringing sound in his head. Anjali and Tess rose to their feet, chairs tipping backwards as they ducked for cover. It was like a bomb had gone off.

26

Something Explosive

It didn't take Charlie long to realize that a bomb hadn't gone off. This was Framstone, not the front line of the war on terror. But that's not to say something explosive hadn't occurred.

Once he'd got his bearings and glanced around to check nobody was hurt – Ruby gave a brave wag, Tess and Anjali looked shaken but unscathed – Charlie clocked what had happened. A missile had been sent straight through the front window of Coastal Coffee. And judging by the way it had sent shattered glass in all directions, it had been propelled with some force.

He ran out of the door, Anjali close behind. Her professional instinct had kicked in and she leaped into action. They looked both ways but whoever was responsible had long gone. The only sound was a car engine receding into the distance. The high street was otherwise quiet, as it usually was on a weekday morning in the off season.

Luckily – well, if there was anything lucky here – they had a police detective as a witness. Anjali would doubtless ensure that passers-by and neighbouring businesses would be asked if they'd seen anything. That wasn't Charlie's job. With one last glare in each direction, he went back inside.

Tess, in spite of her shock, was already getting busy with a broom, clearing up glass while warning humans and dogs to mind where they stepped. Her assistant Leon was making complimentary coffees for the handful of customers who'd got the fright of their lives – and possibly some sharp splinters in their cups.

Meanwhile, Anjali borrowed some disposable latex gloves from the sink behind Leon's counter. She snapped them on, took a few phone pictures of the missile on the floor, then bent to examine it. Peering over her shoulder, Charlie was expecting to see a brick – the traditional object to get thrown through windows. This one, however, was a hefty-looking chunk of wood.

'Are you thinking what I'm thinking?' Anjali said, straightening up and turning to Charlie, her brow furrowing.

'I suspect so,' replied Charlie with a gathering sense of dread.

'Exactly the kind of plank that was used on Frank Courtney's head,' said Anjali. 'Similar size, weight, the lot. As far as I can tell until forensics examine it anyway.'

'Wait, you mean it's one of the murder weapons?' asked Tess, looking up from her sweeping.

'I very much doubt it,' said Anjali, frowning as she considered it. 'Nobody would be daft enough to present an incriminating item like that to the police, gift-wrapped and placed at their best detective's feet. Besides, there's no blood or impact marks. I reckon it's just a lookalike. Even so, it sends a message.'

'What message is that?' asked Charlie. He was getting used to asking this question and didn't much like it.

'Presumably it's telling you dogwalkers to back off again,'

said Anjali. 'This is Tess's place of business. It's where you all meet. And this seems to be direct communication from the killer.'

Charlie and Tess caught each other's eyes and gulped in unison.

'Don't worry too much,' said Anjali, clocking their exchanged look. 'I'd guess it was intended to get your attention, not to hurt anyone. Vandalism rather than violence. Now if you'll excuse me, I need to call it in.'

As Anjali phoned the police station, appraising them of the situation with clipped efficiency, Charlie turned to look through the yawning gap where the window used to be. Until a glazier arrived, Coastal Coffee would be open to the elements. He felt a cold wave ripple through his body. And it wasn't all down to the autumn climes.

He went over and enveloped Tess in a tight hug. They both knew it was as much for Charlie's benefit as hers.

27

Partners in Amateur Crime

'Mate, I'm so sorry,' said Viv, hurrying through the door and taking over hugging duties from Charlie. Not far behind was Sue, with the customary dog pack in tow and an equally concerned look on her face.

As soon as she saw them both, Tess's usual bravado fell away. Her face crumpled and her bottom lip wobbled. Charlie had never seen her so upset and his heart ached to see it. Her business had just been attacked, after all. It must suddenly feel personal.

Tess buried her face in Viv's shoulder. Charlie imagined she was shedding a few tears but was too proud to show it. By the time she emerged from the cuddle, Tess had dried her eyes and the set of her mouth was determined again. She gave them all a brave look and mouthed thank-yous which were waved away.

Closing her notebook, Anjali stood and put on her coat, brushing it down for glass fragments and gesturing to the uniformed officers who'd just arrived.

'Sorry for the bad timing but I've got to scram. Me and Murdoch are seeing the CPS to see if our suspect passes the evidence threshold.' She sighed. 'I suspect it'll be a no but it's the sort of meeting I can't put off, what with the pressure to make progress in the case. Tess, I'll pop back afterwards and finish off here.'

'Well, good luck and keep me updated,' said Charlie. 'As much as you can anyway.'

'Your partner in amateur crime already got enough out of me for one day,' said Anjali, glancing back at Tess, who adopted her best innocent face. Normal business was resumed. 'I'll leave her to fill you in. Bye for now. And be careful.'

Charlie watched her hurry out of the door before turning to Tess, whose expression had by now switched to smug.

'Am I good or am I good?' She smiled, a quick sniff the only thing betraying her recent wobble. 'Consider our police contact pumped for intel, all for the price of two lattes and a cinnamon roll. Plus a new window, I suppose.'

Charlie laughed. 'You're insufferable. Besides, it's a criminal offence to bribe a police officer, even if it's with Nordic buns. But go on, what did you find out? And are you sure you're OK, by the way?'

'I'm fine, promise,' said Tess, giving him a reassuring smile. 'I'm made of sterner stuff than to give in to vandals. It's nothing a pane of glass and a wee dram from under the counter won't fix.'

Charlie smiled. 'That's the spirit.'

'Quite literally,' said Tess. She leaned forward on her broom conspiratorially, beckoning Viv and Sue to huddle round too. She clearly wanted a distraction, so the others put their concern aside for the moment and indulged her. 'For a start, Sergeant Rob gets home from hospital today, which might rock the boat of marital bliss. I got the vibe that Anjali is a mixture of relieved and slightly dreading it.'

'Hmm, it probably won't make her life any easier,' replied Charlie. 'Taking care of him and trying to keep him off the sauce while he recovers. What else?'

'This is the good bit,' said Tess with relish. 'Turns out that now he's dried out, Rob's magically dredged up some memories of the night he got battered. Apparently the argument in the Neppy was about Shane dealing drugs on pub premises. Rob spotted him palming baggies to a couple of punters.'

'Baggies of what?' asked Sue. 'Weed? Pills? Powder?'

Tess chuckled. 'Steady on, Miami Vice. She didn't specify. She was spilling trade secrets already, so I didn't want to ask superfluous questions.'

'Fair enough,' said Charlie. 'Although I bet you found it hard to bite your tongue.'

'We'll have less of your cheek,' said Tess. 'Especially when I'm unearthing gold here. Any dealing must have been pretty unsubtle for Sergeant Soak to spot it through his booze goggles. Apparently Shane denied everything and told Rob to back off.'

'Not least because he was drunk and off duty,' said Charlie, finding himself siding with the younger man. 'How did Rob react?'

'We've seen his flashes of temper after a few drinks,' said Tess. 'Apparently he threatened to search Shane, drag him down the station, all sorts. That's when it got heated and Luke Courtney stepped in to break it up.'

'So Rob reckons what?' asked Charlie. 'Shane waited outside and roughed him up in the woods to make a point?'

'Doesn't sound very likely,' said Viv doubtfully.

'No, it doesn't,' agreed Tess. 'But Rob thinks so. Anjali and Murdoch seem to agree.'

'Typical police,' muttered Sue. 'Sticking together and closing ranks.'

'I think Shane's just a convenient scapegoat,' said Charlie. 'They're keen to nab someone for both crimes – Frank's murder and Rob's assault – and he fits the bill.'

'Afraid so,' said Tess. 'Luckily they lack enough firm evidence for either. And here's where it gets even more interesting.' She paused for dramatic effect.

'Don't be a tease,' said Viv impatiently. 'Pray continue.'

Tess leaned forward again. Most of her customers had started to drift away now that the free coffees had run out but Tess was enjoying the amateur theatrics. 'Anjali even seems to think Shane got rid of his football scarf deliberately, so forensics can't match it to either crime scene. Red fibres were found at one of them apparently.'

'She divulged a lot of information,' said Sue. 'Did you have her in thumbscrews or something?'

'I know, right?' Tess chuckled. 'I got the vibe it was a quid pro quo. Anjali wants us to keep our eyes peeled for the discarded scarf on our dog walks. Sounds like it could be the key to the case, so she's desperate to find it.'

'Again, Shane binning it doesn't sound very likely to me,' said Charlie doubtfully. 'He's hardly a calculating criminal mastermind. Even supposing he was guilty, disposing of potentially incriminating evidence probably wouldn't occur to him. Besides, he seemed genuinely sad about losing his lucky scarf.'

'You boys and your sporting superstitions,' said Tess with an eye-roll. 'I once dated a bloke who wore the same old threadbare pair of pants every Saturday afternoon. I still can't see onions in a mesh bag without shuddering.'

'Thanks for that image,' Viv said, grinning. 'Any other nuggets?'

'The rumour is that the police have put Shane under surveillance while they try to find some actual evidence,' said Tess. 'I've heard his usual turf is Framstone Rec. That's where he deals from during the day.'

She looked down at Ruby knowingly. The Staffy perked up and gave a tentative tail wag. 'Charlie, I thought you and Rube might fancy a change of scene for your next walk.'

28

Too Dangerous a Game

It never ceased to amaze Charlie how Tess could charm and cajole him into doing pretty much whatever she wanted. It was like witchcraft. He was still marvelling at it the next day as he and Ruby strolled around Framstone Rec.

Further inland than the woods, Framstone Recreation Ground was an unpretty but perfectly serviceable public park. A pair of muddy football pitches, a children's playground that had seen better days, a few benches and a scattering of trees. It lacked the sense of untamed nature that the overgrown woods possessed and wasn't as good for dogs, especially an ageing mutt like Ruby. Now her days of endlessly chasing balls and frisbees across flat terrain were over, the rambling woodland offered a richer variety of sounds and smells.

The Rec was, however, another favoured hangout of teenagers, even more so after dark. Charlie had spent some long naughty nights here himself once upon a time. Sitting on the swings, swigging illicit booze, trying to look cool with a cigarette, occasionally snogging. As they sauntered along, he both grimaced and grinned at the memories.

The intel that Tess had gleaned from Anjali was accurate.

Charlie had growing suspicions that his old friend was deliberately drip-feeding them leads. Quid pro quo, as Tess put it. Anjali had never been guileless, not even at school. When he'd borrowed her homework, she'd always asked for something in exchange.

He'd wager that Tess only wheedled out of Anjali what she was willing to share. The police seemed short of manpower and resources. Anjali was smart enough to realize the dog-walkers could help. It was a two-way street. The amateurs got their curiosity sated, the professional got to hear about anything they discovered.

At a picnic bench, as predicted, two youths sat opposite each other. There was a complicated handshake, which might have involved them passing something to one another. Charlie was too far away to tell. One of them departed, leaving Shane sitting alone, hood up, neck still scarf-free.

Ruby recognized him immediately and waddled over, tail wagging eagerly. 'Hello you!' Shane laughed. 'It's my old mate from the beach. I mean her, not you,' he added, looking up at Charlie shyly. 'I wasn't calling you old, honest.'

'Wouldn't mind if you did,' Charlie reassured him. 'I'm all dog walks and quiet nights in front of the telly nowadays. Might as well admit defeat and start claiming my pension.'

Shane gave a shy laugh and made a fuss of Ruby, more comfortable looking at her than meeting Charlie's eye. Ruby lapped up the attention. Every time Shane stopped, she'd nudge against him for more. She seemed especially taken with his aroma, burying her snout deep in his clothing as he fondled her velvety ears.

In front of Shane on the picnic bench were his mobile

phone and vape. Charlie made a mental note of the vape's bottle shape and purple colour, wondering if it matched any of those littered around where he'd found Frank's body. The police had probably bagged and tagged anything significant, but next time he was in the woods he'd have a hunt around anyway. A vape was hardly a fingerprint or a DNA trace but it was something.

'I passed on your message to my mum,' said Charlie. 'She said hi and sent her best wishes back.'

Shane smiled. 'That's nice. Cheers for that. Good old Polly.'

'No worries,' said Charlie. 'Now she's retired, she loves any chance to reminisce.'

'Wait up, there they go again,' said Shane, nodding towards the road, where a black SUV was driving slowly past the park.

'Who's they?'

'The police,' said Shane resentfully. 'Unmarked cars keep doing laps every fifteen minutes or so. I guess they think I won't notice but I've got a good mind to report them for harassment.'

'I imagine they'd call it surveillance rather than harassment,' said Charlie. 'Although it kind of amounts to the same thing.'

'Too right it does,' agreed Shane. 'They arrest me, accuse me of two crimes, keep me all night, give me the fourth degree – and now this.'

'For what it's worth, I don't think you did any of it,' said Charlie. 'And they've clearly got bugger all to prove otherwise.'

'Thanks, man, I appreciate that,' said Shane, looking Charlie in the eye for once. 'When you've got a record and a bit of a reputation, you get used to everyone thinking the worst.'

'Well, you've got a friend in Ruby at least.' Charlie laughed as she gave Shane's face an enthusiastic slurp and rolled over for more tummy rubs, her eyes closing with pleasure.

There was the beep of a message alert. Shane wiped the dog drool off his cheek, fished a mobile out of his hoodie pocket and quickly read it. Charlie glanced over at the other phone, which was still on the picnic bench. It seemed he carried two.

Shane noticed him looking and shrugged. 'Occupational hazard,' he said sheepishly. 'One for personal, one for business.'

Charlie nodded. 'I know the score. I used to work in London. Around Soho, all the local dealers carried two phones. Sometimes three or four. God knows how they kept track. I have my hands full keeping up with WhatsApps on one.'

Shane laughed. 'Yeah, it can get confusing.'

Charlie was pleasantly surprised by Shane's honesty. It reinforced his feeling that this was no criminal mastermind. He seemed too open, lacking the in-built wariness of a hardened crook. Either way, Charlie seemed to have won his trust, so he risked a question. 'What did your supplier make of you being arrested? Must've made them edgy.'

'They know I'd never grass,' said Shane. 'Too dangerous a game. There'd be consequences.'

'Reprisals?'

'Yep, they've made that pretty clear.' He gave a hollow laugh. 'Besides, there's not much to tell. I don't actually know who my bosses are, believe it or not. Everything is done by text on burners.'

He waved the second phone vaguely in Charlie's direction. It was a basic pay-as-you-go Nokia. 'We even use code names. Besides, I doubt they even know about me being pinched.'

'Oh, they'll know about it,' said Charlie.

'How come?'

'Maybe heard it on the grapevine,' Charlie explained. 'Suppliers often have insiders on the police force, too. Tip them off, feed them intel, help protect their business. For a modest fee, of course. I wonder if that's the case in Framstone, too.'

'You seem to know a lot about it.' Shane smirked. 'Something you want to share?'

'My shady Soho past,' said Charlie with a chuckle. 'Let's say I had a bit of a party lifestyle for a while back there.'

Shane winked. 'Don't worry. I won't tell anyone if you don't.'

'Appreciate it,' said Charlie, laughing. 'Wouldn't want to scandalize the dog-walking circuit. Talking of which, didn't I see you in the woods the other day?'

'Not guilty,' said Shane. 'I rarely go down there. Why?'

'I've just seen someone in a similar hoodie a few times. Sorry, I'm probably starting to sound like the police.'

'Trust me, you're much more friendly,' said Shane, smiling. 'And your sniffer dog's way cuter.'

As he made a last fuss of Ruby before they parted ways, Charlie's cogs were already whirring. If it wasn't Shane, who was the woodland lurker? Could it be the same culprit who'd left the toy dog on Charlie's doorstep and hurled a missile through Coastal Coffee's window?

Just a fortnight ago, Framstone seemed like just another sleepy small town. Now there seemed to be hidden dangers and looming darkness around every corner.

29

Be Careful Out There

Its front window might have been as good as new but Charlie wasn't sure Coastal Coffee's proprietor was. Once the adrenaline had worn off, even the nerveless Tess seemed affected by the events of recent days. Her hospitable smile wasn't quite as convincing as usual. Charlie noticed her eyes darting towards the door when people went past on the pavement.

Some edginess was inevitable so soon after such a shock. It would likely wear off with time. He resolved to keep an eye on his friend. She'd kept watch over Charlie when he'd first moved back home, taking him under her wing and introducing her to the others. It was time to repay the favour.

These caffeinated debriefs were becoming a regular routine. Charlie found himself looking forward to them. Walking Ruby and caring for Polly aside, his time often felt unstructured, especially when design work was quiet. Sitdowns with the gang gave his days shape and purpose. It was probably the closest the dogwalkers would ever come to one of those roll-call meetings in TV police procedurals. Charlie was always tempted to sign off with 'And, hey, let's be careful out there'.

While the assorted animals flopped, snuffled and snored

around their feet, he filled everyone in on his latest encounter with Shane.

'Did you believe him when he said he hadn't been lurking in the woods?' asked Sue, sipping her black filter coffee sagely, like a Mafia consigliere.

'I did actually,' said Charlie. 'He was quite matter-of-fact about rarely going to the woods. And why would he? He does his business at the Rec during the day and around town by night. It's not like Shane's got a dog to walk, as much as he'd love one.'

'Still sweet on Rube, was he?' said Malcolm, bending down to give her a stroke. 'Who could blame him with those big brown eyes?'

'Are you talking about Ruby or her dashing owner?' teased Viv. 'You did say your gaydar twitched last time. Tell us again about the drug-dealing stuff, Charlie.'

'Well, Shane definitely seemed to be selling from the picnic benches,' he recapped. 'Although I didn't see exactly what and it was pretty low-key, presumably because the police were keeping an eye. He had two phones, one of them a burner for business. He said everything was done by text. He'd never even met the people higher up the food chain. He was surprisingly forthcoming, in fact, which only makes him look less guilty to me.'

'And again, you believed him?' asked Sue.

'No reason not to,' said Charlie. 'His guard was down. He seems to trust me and we were just chatting like mates. Whether he's met them or not, he seemed pretty intimidated by his suppliers. Shane said he'd never grass for fear of reprisals.'

'What about that bit about an inside man?' chimed in Viv.

'That was fairly throwaway,' said Charlie. 'He wasn't sure his bosses would even know about him being hauled in for questioning. I said they probably would. Partly the grapevine – I mean, even we heard about it, right?' He looked over at Tess, who nodded. 'I also mentioned that drug gangs often have a copper on the payroll to help them stay in business.'

'Nice,' said Sue approvingly. 'How did he react to that?'

'Not sure,' mused Charlie. 'He gave the impression that it had never occurred to him.'

'You know who the inside man could be, don't you?' said Tess, looking pleased with herself.

'The late Frank Courtney?' offered Viv. 'He seems a likely candidate, except he retired years ago.'

'With respect, he's also now dead,' said Tess. 'No, I mean Sergeant Rob. It might explain their Neptune ruckus.'

'Rob reckoned that was about Shane indiscreetly dealing in the pub,' said Charlie. 'Although maybe he said that to misdirect his wife.'

'Rather than a stern warning from a straight copper, maybe it was advice from a bent colleague,' reasoned Tess.

'Shane's the silent type,' said Malcolm. 'Surely Gobby Robbie's more likely to be the indiscreet one?'

'Good point,' acknowledged Viv. 'Maybe his drunken prattling was spooking the drug gang, so Shane – or whoever – attacked him later that night as a warning. A cautionary kicking to keep their tame copper in line.'

Charlie considered this possibility. 'The occasional kicking aside – which probably comes with the territory – being married to the lead detective would put Rob in the ideal position to watch his back. If he is a bent copper, even a killer, he'd be perfectly placed to cast suspicion elsewhere.'

'Maybe the boozy loudmouth act is misdirection too,' added Sue thoughtfully.

'Either way, we still don't believe Shane killed Frank,' said Charlie. 'Agreed?'

There were murmurs and nods of assent round the table. If Ruby could speak, she would doubtless have concurred.

'So let's do whatever we can to help clear his name,' concluded Charlie, a note of steel creeping into his voice. 'And maybe we'll find the real murderer in the process.'

'Yes, chief,' said Tess. She already seemed to be brightening. Nothing like a spot of amateur sleuthing to take your mind off a vandalized window. 'So what's our next move?'

'Well, I'm going to start by searching the woods for vapes and deadly weapons. And you're going to help me, Rube, aren't you?' This time, her ears pricking up, Ruby definitely did concur.

30

Nose to the Ground

Charlie gave an involuntary shudder as he plunged into the undergrowth near the murder scene. The last time he'd pushed his way through this patch of foliage, there was a fly-covered corpse waiting for him. Was it psychosomatic or could he taste acidic vomit rising in his throat again? He suppressed such thoughts and got on with the job at hand.

The area was still cordoned off but a constable hadn't been stationed here on watch for the past week. Charlie waited until he was sure the coast was clear – pardon the seaside pun – and ducked under the police tape, which was now fraying and fluttering in the wind.

'Come on, Ruby,' he muttered to his faithful shadow. 'Let's get this over with.'

The rubbish strewn around the forest floor was much as he remembered it. Coffee cups and lids – none of them from Coastal, much to Tess's chagrin. Because the sort of endorsement you really want is your shop's branded packaging to be found near a stabbed and bludgeoned cadaver.

The ground beneath the tree where he'd found Frank's body was noticeably clearer. Presumably forensics had collected any debris directly around him as potential evidence.

But even a few metres away, where the clearing faded into the footpath, it was the familiar mess. Maybe their search area was restricted by limited resources. The labs couldn't test a whole woodland full of litter, after all. Or maybe they'd found whatever they were looking for and called off the hunt.

Charlie poked around with his foot. Crisp packets. Bunched-up tissues and napkins. Balls of chewed-up gum. Discarded vapes. He remembered Tess remarking on how they were bad for the environment and here they were, loads of the confounded things. *Bring back proper cigarettes*, he thought. *Worse for you but better for the woods. Also: way cooler.*

He scoured the ground for a bottle-shaped vape to match the one he'd seen on Shane's picnic bench and the one he'd been sucking on at the beach. A flash of purple would likely catch Charlie's eye amid the autumnal shades but he found nothing. As if further confirmation was needed, Ruby's super-sensitive snout arrived on the scene. She had a good long snuffle around to no avail. If she'd recognized the whiff of her mate Shane, she would surely have reacted.

Charlie kept on searching, inch by inch, in a widening circle. The police had already combed the area for weapons but they might have missed something.

Several times he thought he'd struck gold. Hang on, did that hunk of timber resemble the missile hurled through Coastal's window? No, it was too short, too flimsy or so woodworm-ridden it crumbled to the touch. Wait, was that the metallic glint of a knife blade? No, it was a beer bottle top or a foil wrapper.

Charlie smiled. He truly hoped Shane was innocent and was gratified not to find evidence of his guilt.

Eventually he straightened up and spoke aloud, partly

to Ruby and partly to himself. 'Wonder what the Coastal crew will make of this, Rube? Probably time for a catch-up with Anjali, too.'

Just as Charlie thought of Anjali, something made him stop in his tracks. The sound of a damp twig splintering was followed by a rustle in the bushes. With a surge of panic, Charlie suddenly remembered that he was behind police tape, intruding on a crime scene. Someone was coming. He was about to be caught. This wouldn't look good.

He took a step back, his eyes fixed on the spot where he'd heard the noise. Ever loyal, Ruby took a step back too, before looking up at Charlie inquisitively. His breath quickened as the branches trembled. The noise got louder. There was a blinding flash of white.

Charlie almost leaped out of his skin as the foliage appeared to detonate in a hail of feathers. He felt a waft of air from flapping wings as he reared back to let them past. Pesky seagulls. The Framstone plague. Charlie exhaled as they squawked away above the treeline. He'd never been more pleased to see the irksome things.

'Come on, Rube,' he said with relief. 'Best consider that a warning. Let's get out of here before something non-avian spots us.'

As they rejoined the path and turned for the gate, Charlie saw a familiar figure in the middle distance. Not his hooded nemesis for once. This one was wrapped up in a faux-fur coat and had a bulldog waddling along behind her.

As if she'd sensed Charlie looking at her, Jackie Courtney turned her head, spotted him and gave a wave. *Quite a cheery wave for a widow*, thought Charlie. Surely her being here was a coincidence. Well, wasn't it?

31

Oh No, Not Again

'Oh no,' said Tess as she and Charlie walked the dogs along the beach. 'Not again.'

The next morning, Viv, Sue and Malcolm had all been busy for once. Nuts About Mutts were driving a vanload of hounds inland to the countryside for their weekly extra-long walk. Malcolm had texted on the group chat that he also 'had his hands full'. Nobody dared ask with what.

A walk with just Tess was fine by Charlie. That's how they'd first become friends, after all. Caught short in the woods, Tess had sheepishly asked the passing Charlie if she could borrow a dog poo bag. He'd joked that he was happy for it to be a permanent loan and he definitely didn't want it back. She'd laughed and they'd strolled on together, chatting away while Ruby bonded with Rough and Tumble.

Before Charlie knew it, they'd become regular walking buddies. He was usually happier alone but it was his first experience of Tess's magical ability to get what she wanted. She was determined they'd be friends and he'd been power-less to resist. Soon he was a fixture at Coastal Coffee. She'd introduced him to three regulars who often joined her for dog walks. The rest was history. Recent investigations had only tightened their bond. Dogs had a funny way of bringing people together like that.

Since it was her who'd done the whole Miss Marple routine at the murder scene, it felt appropriate to tell Tess first what he'd found upon revisiting. She didn't recall seeing a purple vape either. Then again, Tess pointed out, she hadn't been looking for anything specific, so might well have not noticed one.

She was also intrigued by his latest sighting of Jackie Courtney near the scene. Her hints at an unhappy marriage and Frank keeping secrets certainly put her in the frame. Jackie would by no means be the first spouse to commit a crime of passion. It was a tale as old as time. Charlie always felt somehow disloyal for suspecting Jackie of her husband's murder, but, as Tess pointed out, she did have a habit of popping up at inopportune moments.

'Don't let gallantry get in the way of logic, my knight in shining armour,' Tess teased as they walked into a stiff sea breeze. 'Jackie's just as much of a suspect as Rob, Shane or anyone else.'

It was when they hopped over a seaweed-draped break-water that they saw it. A figure was lying motionless and face down on the shore twenty metres ahead. Charlie and Tess looked at each other, their faces a mix of concern, fear and – for Charlie, at least – sudden queasiness.

'Not Sergeant Rob again?' said Tess, as if reading Charlie's mind. He'd been found like this before. Fresh out of hospital, he could've celebrated with one of his self-destructive benders and got himself into trouble again. Except he didn't look so fortunate this time.

As they got closer, they saw that the waves were lapping

gently against the man's head and spreadeagled hands as he lay there, his feet facing inland. If he was unconscious or in a drunken stupor, the icy water surely would have woken him up. Instead he was unmoving, which only made Charlie's background hum of dread grow louder.

Rough and Tumble had seen him too and scampered forward to investigate, Ruby huffing along behind. Their humans didn't need to communicate, instinctively knowing what to do. As the wind fluttered her hair across her face, Tess glanced at Charlie, then called the dogs back. She wrestled them on to leads while Charlie reluctantly walked over to the figure. A sense of foreboding seemed to weigh him down. He felt like he was moving at half speed.

He bent down when he reached the prostrate figure. Apparently male. Definitely not moving. Not even breathing, as far as Charlie could tell. He tentatively grabbed the nearest shoulder and tried to turn the man over but he was heavier than he looked and barely budged.

He glanced back at Tess, who gave an encouraging nod. Charlie tried again, putting more heft into it this time. As he grunted with effort, the body finally turned over. Charlie had involuntarily screwed up his eyes for a moment, afraid of what he might see. Now he took a deep breath and opened them.

He gasped with surprise. He'd been fully expecting to see Rob Thompson's face – stubbly, ruddy, a little lived-in, still with some healing grazes and fading bruises from the attack. Charlie had shuddered at the prospect of telling Anjali that he'd chanced upon another corpse – and that this time it was her husband's.

However, what greeted him was a very different face. A younger one. Shane Carter.

In the little time he'd spent with Shane, Charlie was used to seeing him jumpy and jangly with nervous energy – wary of the police's eyes on him, of the walls closing in. At least he looked relatively peaceful now. How tragic that it took death – at such a young age, in such a public place, after such a brief but turbulent life – to finally bring Shane some calm.

Charlie's guts flipped and seemed to plummet towards his feet. He staggered back a couple of steps in shock and turned towards Tess, trying to call to her. No words came out.

She rushed over, looked down and gasped. A sob rose to her throat and she clutched a hand to her mouth in horror. All three dogs sniffed tentatively at Shane's outstretched arm. Ruby's slow deep snuffles seemed especially mournful. Tess put her arm round Charlie and buried her face in his chest. Her support and the dogs' reassuring presence gave him the strength to look down properly at poor Shane.

Unlike the last time Charlie had found a body, Shane had no obvious visible injuries. He genuinely did look tranquil and untroubled. Charlie briefly wondered if he'd taken his own life, hence the sense of repose that seemed to hang over him. The self-harm scars and safety-pin necklace suggested he'd tried it before. Was it the stress of police surveillance or fear of reprisals from his drug bosses that had caused Shane to snap? Or had guilt at killing Frank finally tipped him over the edge?

With a start, Charlie realized that Shane was also wearing his mysterious missing Framstone Rovers scarf. Charlie sighed, suddenly ineffably sad. It seemed the scarf wasn't so lucky after all.

32

Deadly Déjà Vu

Charlie was definitely experiencing déjà vu. Normally it happened with mundane occurrences – an eerie tingle, like he'd been in a certain building or met a stranger before. Now it came as he was waiting for the police to arrive at a murder scene. Once could be regarded as a misfortune. Twice looks like a pattern.

They were too far from Coastal for Tess to rustle up consoling coffees this time. Ever resourceful, she left Charlie standing guard and came back with a pair of what she called 'Irish teas': Styrofoam cuppas from the nearest greasy spoon, topped up with whisky miniatures from the off-licence next door.

Charlie didn't normally drink tea – or, indeed, cheap blended whisky – but right now he wasn't complaining. Needs must. He sensed that Tess was more shaken up by their discovery than she was letting on. She'd needed the distraction of fetching drinks. It meant she could avoid spending more time with Shane's body than necessary.

Charlie gave her a reassuring back rub. They stood to one side, holding back the dogs, as the circus arrived. Ambulances, police cars, even the local coastguard, all with blue lights flashing. Finally an unmarked saloon from which Anjali and Murdoch stepped out.

They glanced over at Charlie and Tess – Anjali with a sympathetic expression, Murdoch with an appraising stare – before heading over to where forensics were in the process of putting on hazmat suits and erecting a white tent round Shane's body. Meanwhile, uniformed officers cordoned off a stretch of the beach and promenade.

Charlie and Tess sipped their drinks and waited. Soon enough the two detectives came over.

'We've got to stop meeting like this,' said Anjali, her tone laced with stress.

'We really, really have.' Charlie sighed. He was glad to see her friendly face, despite the circumstances.

He and Tess knew the drill by now. They explained what they'd been doing on the beach and how they'd chanced upon the body, while Anjali and Murdoch took notes. When they got to the part where Charlie turned Shane over, that's when things got tricky.

'Tell me exactly why and how you turned him over again,' said Anjali, now in serious official mode.

'I wanted to check he wasn't still alive,' replied Charlie. 'He might have needed first aid or an ambulance. I didn't immediately assume it was a dead body.'

'Despite this being the second one you've found in quick succession?' asked Murdoch. There was an arch to his eyebrow which suggested this was just black humour. A cop's version of a bedside manner.

Charlie turned to him, resisting the temptation to get defensive. 'No, I didn't,' he said, fighting to keep his voice level. 'It might have been a rough sleeper or a drunk who'd passed out. Even an asylum seeker who'd swum to shore from a boat. I just figured it was worth checking.'

'You should know never to touch anything at a crime scene,' said Anjali.

'That's what Charlie's trying to tell you,' said Tess, backing him up. 'At that point we didn't know it was a crime scene.'

'Couldn't you tell from looking at him that he was dead?' asked Murdoch.

'Rob – I mean, Anjali's husb— sorry, Sergeant Thompson was found lying face down and motionless recently too,' pointed out Charlie. 'He wasn't dead.' He glanced at Anjali. 'Thank goodness.'

'Maybe not but it was still a crime scene,' said Murdoch stubbornly. Anjali always said he was a determined detective. Charlie and Tess were beginning to agree. If they'd been asked for a dog analogy, they'd say he was tenacious and stubborn like a Jack Russell. Charlie found himself smiling inwardly at an image of Murdoch careering around the woods with a wig in his mouth. Just the idea of it made Charlie warm to him.

'Mate, he was lying face down on the pebbles with the sea lapping around him,' argued Tess. 'It was hardly a sterile environment.'

'OK, that'll do,' interjected Anjali. 'Thanks, DS Murdoch. Can you start asking nearby shopkeepers if they saw anything please? I'll join you in a moment.'

Murdoch gave Charlie and Tess a last sceptical look, before stomping away over the shingle.

'I suppose I can't blame him for being suspicious,' admitted Charlie. 'I have developed an unhappy knack for stumbling across corpses.'

'Both of which you reported to the police immediately,

before waiting around to give a detailed statement,' said Tess. 'Anyone would think he didn't want the public's help.'

'Look, he's just doing his job,' said Anjali. 'Murdoch is a solid copper. Maybe the best on the Framstone force – except yours truly, of course. I'd rather have Craig by my side when the going gets tough than most of the pen-pushers and clock-watchers around here.'

'What was that you said about forty per cent of unexpected dead bodies being found by dogwalkers?' asked Charlie, trying to lighten the mood. 'Presumably that percentage just crept up a bit.'

'Let's hope it doesn't go any higher,' said Anjali. 'Just between us, we're up against it here. We were already under pressure to solve two cases. Now there's a third. What's more, with Shane dead, we've got no living suspects for the first two. It's tough times.'

'We get it,' Tess told her. 'Anything we can do to help.'

Their conversation was curtailed by a kerfuffle behind the police cordon. A hysterical woman was trying to get through to the beach but being held back by a uniformed constable.

'I've got a feeling that's the mother of the deceased.' Anjali sighed. 'Better go and have a word.'

As she hurried away, Charlie's heart sank even lower. From what Polly had told him about Karen Carter, she didn't need any more pain in her life. She was about to experience the worst moment of her life, the loss of her only child.

Charlie looked away, blinking back tears. He couldn't bear to watch. The case, for him, had just become even more personal.

33

Emergency Protocols Activated

The mood at Coastal Coffee was sombre. As the gang gathered round their usual table the next morning, the dogs seemed to have picked up on the mood, sighing mournfully and snoring quietly at their feet. Customers seemed thinner on the ground too. Charlie hoped people weren't steering clear since the smashed window. He thought better of mentioning this to Tess.

'It's tragic,' muttered Malcolm. They were all keeping their voices low out of respect. Even Sue's knitting needles were clacking more softly than usual. 'That poor young man. Raised in care. Victimized by the police. What chance did he have?'

'Absolutely,' said Viv. 'I used to see it all the time at school. I bet you did in the legal trade, too. The die is often cast for kids like that.'

'So what do we think?' asked Sue, looking up from her knitting with a sorrowful frown and damp eyes. 'Cause-of-death-wise, I mean.'

'Tactfully put, babe.' Viv smiled ruefully, patting Sue's hand.

'We genuinely have no idea,' said Charlie, glancing at

Tess for confirmation. She nodded. 'There were no visible wounds nor other signs, as far as we could tell. Not like Frank Courtney, that's for sure.'

'The water wasn't deep enough for him to drown in,' said Tess. 'Not when we found him anyway. I guess it depends on the tide and how long he'd been lying there.'

'God knows if Shane could swim,' said Charlie. 'It wouldn't surprise me if he couldn't, with no parent around a lot of the time to teach him.'

'And patchy attendance at school presumably,' added Malcolm.

'Do we think, well, that Shane could have taken his own life?' asked Sue. 'Sorry if that sounds insensitive.'

'It's OK,' said Charlie, trying to sound consoling. 'Our minds went there, too. He didn't seem like a suicide risk when we spoke, but we know he was troubled, so I wouldn't rule it out.'

'Or maybe an accidental overdose of something,' said Tess sadly. 'You have no idea what's going on in people's heads, do you?'

'If he was murdered . . .' said Viv, before hesitating. 'Sorry, I know it's too soon but we've got to consider that possibility. I guess his drug contacts would be in the frame, especially as he'd just been questioned at length by the police.'

'He insisted that he didn't even know who they were,' replied Charlie. 'And he wouldn't have grassed if he did.'

'Sure, but they might not have believed that,' said Viv. 'So are we looking at whoever murdered Frank for this too? And maybe whoever attacked Mr Anjali?'

'Maybe so, maybe not,' mused Charlie. 'Different locations

and different causes of death might mean different killers. But you know who suddenly looks even more suspicious, right?'

'Apart from you?' said Tess, the impish glint coming back to her eye.

Charlie was pleased to see it. 'Apart from me,' he conceded. 'It's Rob Thompson. He might have been the second victim of the three but it's some coincidence that he was released from hospital yesterday – right before Shane, who many suspect put him there, is found dead.'

'Keep your voice down, Foghorn Leghorn,' whispered Malcolm, glancing around at the smattering of coffee shop customers. 'Everyone's badly shaken already, without us loudly connecting the dots.'

'I know.' Tess sighed. 'A second death. Maybe a second murder. It's all anyone's talking about. Most people assumed it was Shane who'd killed Frank. Nobody knows what to think now. I even heard one punter mention a serial killer. In Framstone. Imagine.'

'They probably said that about John Wayne Gacy and Jeffrey Dahmer,' pointed out Sue.

Charlie remembered being tempted to say 'And, hey, let's be careful out there' at the end of their conflabs. Sadly it didn't need saying out loud any more. The entire community was now on high alert.

'I guess the main thing we can do, the most useful thing, is help the police collar whoever did it,' he said. 'So let's redouble our efforts, shall we?'

'I'll drink to that,' said Tess. She went to the counter and came back with a bottle of Laphroaig, the one she kept for Irish coffees, and five glasses. 'Emergency protocols have been activated,' she said, setting it down on the table and pouring them each a generous measure.

'To Shane,' said Charlie, raising a toast. 'And if foul play was indeed involved, to catching his killer.' He slugged down the single malt with fire in his belly and a grimly determined look on his face.

34

Victim or Criminal

Perhaps he shouldn't have been, but Charlie was surprised by how affected Polly seemed by the news of Shane's death. While they cooked supper that evening – spaghetti and meatballs, one of Charlie's go-to dishes – the latest tragedy was all his mother could talk about.

'It seems so unfair,' she said. 'And terribly sad. So soon after Frank Courtney, too.'

Charlie sighed. 'I know, Mum, I know. I mean, even if Shane wasn't murdered, you've got to assume the two corpses are connected in some way. It's too much of a coincidence otherwise. No dead bodies found in Framstone for years, then two in a matter of weeks.'

'Do you think the town has changed?' she asked anxiously. 'Is that what we are now? Some sort of crime hot spot?'

'It must feel like that right now, Mum, but I honestly don't think so,' said Charlie. 'Crimes can happen anywhere. It's just Framstone's turn at the moment. Soon it will be somewhere else on the news, trust me. Somewhere further away.'

'I hope you're right, son.' She sighed. 'I'd hate to live somewhere scary.'

'You've got nothing to be afraid of, Mum,' said Charlie. 'Besides, me and Ruby are here to protect you.' At the mention of her name Ruby wagged her tail in her basket.

Charlie felt a little disingenuous mollifying Polly like this, especially after his doorstep gift and woodland stalker, but it was for the best. As she got older, he'd watched his mum become increasingly confused and frightened by modern life. For someone who'd always been such a pivotal part of the community, it felt all the more acute.

When Charlie's dad left – and his brother Danny ultimately followed – Polly retreated into herself. Since she retired, then became slightly forgetful and frail, the process had hastened. It caused him a twinge of sadness to think about how much her world had shrunk.

'Perhaps it's because I brought him into the world,' said Polly. 'And now he's left it far too early. But I feel so sad for Shane. And for Karen too. It's such an unfathomable thing for a mother to lose a child. I'm not sure Karen's emotionally equipped for it. Maybe nobody is.'

Charlie frowned, as he warmed some olive oil in a pan. 'Me too. I feel devastated for both of them – the dead and the living, left alone to face it. Call me naive but Shane always struck me as more victim than criminal.'

'I don't think that's naive, son,' said Polly. 'I think it's empathetic. People can be so judgemental about the poor. They don't realize the precariousness of living in poverty. The constant worry. It's so draining and stressful. The odds are stacked against them. Dealing with people like Karen and little Shane used to break my heart.'

She sniffed and pressed the back of her hand against her eyes. She was chopping onions but Charlie thought she might be shedding a tear too. He gently patted her back as he passed her on his way to the kettle.

'Speaking of Karen, I wonder how she is,' added Polly.

'Not good, I'm afraid,' said Charlie. 'I saw her briefly at the beach. She was in a right old state at the police cordon. To be expected, I guess, but still awful to witness. My heart went out to her, Mum, it really did.'

'Oh my,' said Polly. 'It doesn't bear thinking about. I can only imagine how I'd feel if that was you lying there.'

'That's a cheery thought,' said Charlie, experiencing a mild shudder but attempting to keep it light.

'Sorry, love, but that's how the mind of a mother works,' she said. 'Your brain doesn't want to go there but you can't help it.'

'I know, I know,' he said, dropping the meatballs into the pan with a sizzle. 'Try not to dwell on it.'

'I might send Karen a card or some flowers,' said Polly. 'And I'll look out for her around town. Take her for a cup of tea and a chat if I see her. She must be feeling very lonely and lost right now.'

'You're a good 'un, Mum,' said Charlie, smiling as he swirled the spaghetti in the boiling water. As it bubbled, his mind went to Shane face down on the shore, and whether someone had left him lying there like that. *Don't worry, mate*, he thought. *We'll help catch them for you.* He looked over at Ruby in her basket. She'd be with him all the way, he was sure.

35

What a Way to Go

'It's been quite a week,' said Tess. 'I needed this.' At her insti-
gation, as always, she and Charlie were at the Neptune again.
As well as relishing a nerve-steadying drink, the pair were
on a mission.

They hoped to see two of their prime suspects in one
place: Jackie Courtney behind the bar and Rob Thompson
propping it up. Engage them both in conversation. See what
they could glean.

If the opportunity arose, Charlie also wanted to ask around
about Shane Carter. They knew he sometimes dealt drugs
at the Neptune. People were unlikely to volunteer anything
which might incriminate themselves, of course. Drug-related
crime thrived in silence and shadows, Charlie knew that,
but he wasn't about to give up on another line of enquiry.

It was a relatively quiet weeknight and unlike their last
visit, they could hear themselves talk above the music and
hubbub. Tess chinked her wine glass against Charlie's pint.

'First the whisky at work and now this,' he joked. 'People
will think you're dangerously off the rails.'

'Maybe I am.' She shrugged. 'All this death puts things in
perspective, doesn't it? Life is for living and all that.'

'Talking of which, it's my round,' said Charlie. 'Same again?'

'Now you're talking, partner.'

While Charlie waited at the bar, he looked around for Jackie Courtney, but there was no sign of her. He was disappointed but not surprised. Tess had heard that the police had finally released Frank's body, so a funeral date had been set at last. Jackie was probably busy making arrangements and ringing round relatives.

As he got served by one of her daughters, a familiar voice piped up behind Charlie. 'If you're buying, Boardy Boy, I wouldn't say no.'

He turned to see Rob Thompson giving him a wonky grin. Charlie was intrigued to note that he looked less dishevelled and, well, less drunk than usual. Apart from a few cuts still healing on his face, he looked as good as new. He even seemed to have had a shave and combed his hair like a functioning human.

'Rob!' said Charlie, feigning pleasure at running into him. 'Of course, my shout. What are you having?'

'Pint of lager, please,' came the answer. No chasers this time thankfully. 'Cheers, Charlie. I'll go and keep your lady company.'

Charlie laughed. 'Tess would definitely object to being called "my lady", but feel free. I'll bring the drinks over.'

By the time he got back to the table, Tess and Rob were chatting away. As Charlie passed Tess her wine, she gave him a raised eyebrow as if to say, 'This is unexpected but let's go with it.' Knowing Tess, she was about to squeeze him for intel about the murder inquiries. Luckily Rob the Gob was rather less discreet and professional than his wife.

'I'm celebrating being back in the land of the living,' said

Rob. 'Um, if that's not an insensitive phrase after recent events.' He took a swig of his pint to cover his embarrassment, wincing slightly as it stung his split lip. The pain was apparently not enough to stop him drinking.

'You knew poor Shane, didn't you?' asked Charlie, watching Rob's reaction intently.

Rob nodded. 'A bit. Police stations are like pubs. You get to know your regulars and their ways. Decent enough lad but he took a few wrong turns.' Charlie studied his face for signs of guilt.

'Hadn't you fallen out?' asked Tess, guessing that tricky questions might sound better in a female voice. She was right.

'You're referring to our little discussion in here on the night I was jumped?' Rob smiled. 'Something of nothing really. I just warned him not to take the piss by blatantly dealing in public. Shane gave me some grief to save face but he got the message.'

'So you don't think it was him who jumped you?' probed Tess.

'Who knows?' Rob shrugged, not entirely convincingly. 'Either way, it's in the past now. I wouldn't want to speak ill of the dead, especially after what happened to him.'

Two pairs of ears pricked up. 'So you know how he died?' asked Tess.

'Drowned, sadly,' said Rob. 'Sometime in the wee small hours, it seems. He'd been there a while before you found him. The tide had gone out in the meantime.'

It was Charlie's turn to ask the questions. 'Was it an accident or deliberate?'

Still not a flinch from Rob. He looked around and leaned in conspiratorially. 'This didn't come from me, obviously, but deliberate.'

'Shane drowned himself?' said Charlie aghast. 'Oh no, that's awful.'

'Nope, it's worse than that,' said Rob. 'When I say "deliberate", I don't mean by his own hand. Considering the bruising and him being fully clothed – plus the fact that his phone and wallet had been taken – we're working on the assumption that he was forcibly drowned.'

On that bombshell he drained his pint, studied the empty glass and looked at them expectantly, waiting for someone to refill it for him. 'What a way to go, eh? Your round, Tess, I think.'

Charlie was aghast. What a way to go indeed. Beneath his horror, a flame of fury had been lit inside him.

36

Amateur Hour

When Rob wobbled off to the gents after he'd rinsed them for a third pint – his last of the night, he claimed, which Charlie and Tess would believe when they saw it – they breathed a sigh of relief and had a hurried debrief before he returned.

'Forcibly drowned,' muttered Charlie bitterly. 'I can't stop thinking about it.'

'I know.' Tess nodded. 'Poor Shane. I guess it was impossible to see the signs when we found him.'

'Yeah,' said Charlie sadly. 'According to Sergeant Blabbermouth of Scotland Yard, the bruising was on his upper arms and round his neck. Both of which were covered by his clothing.'

'I wondered if the football scarf was deliberately put round his neck to cover the marks,' said Tess. 'I mean, it was missing, then suddenly it wasn't.'

'It's a possibility,' agreed Charlie. 'I must say, I was surprised by Rob's tone. He talked about murder like it was a jokey bit of gossip. He'd only spoken to Shane, what, a week ago? You'd think he'd show more feeling. Unless, of course . . .' He left the sentence unfinished but his train of thought definitely wasn't.

'I know, right?' said Tess. 'Maybe it's gallows humour or blokey bravado. And how about Shane's wallet and phone being taken?'

'Phones plural,' Charlie pointed out. 'He had an extra burner for drug deals, remember? I suppose taking them could make it look like a mugging. Or the killer had something to hide and didn't want to leave an evidence trail.'

'Rob's being very free and easy with the info, isn't he?' said Tess. 'Forthcoming doesn't cover it. Why is he giving so much away, do you reckon?'

Charlie nodded. 'I've been wondering that too. Trying to make himself look innocent maybe. But if you ask me, right now it's making him seem even more suspicious.'

'Hold the line, caller,' whispered Tess urgently. 'He's coming back.'

'What have I missed?' asked Rob as he sat down. It was as if he knew what they'd been talking about.

'Oh, nothing of note,' fibbed Charlie. 'We were just talking about our dogs, as it happens.'

'One thing I did want to ask you, though,' said Tess, 'is what about the police surveillance? Your guys were keeping an eye on Shane, right? Shouldn't they have seen something?'

'Ah, yes,' replied Rob. 'I was hoping you wouldn't ask that, to be honest. Apparently Shane gave them the slip when it got dark. They lost him when he left Framstone Rec. It wasn't until you found him on the beach that we had any idea where he'd got to.'

'For heaven's sake,' snapped Charlie before he could stop himself. 'What is this, amateur hour? If they'd done their job, this might never have happened.'

Beneath the table, Tess put her hand on his knee to restrain him but it was too late.

Rob flashed with anger. 'Watch it, Boardy,' he snapped. 'That's my colleagues you're talking about. They feel pretty shitty about what happened. We didn't have the resources for round-the-clock surveillance anyway. If Shane really wanted to shake it, he could.'

'OK, OK,' said Charlie, holding up his hands. 'I'm just upset about Shane, that's all.'

'Well, mind your tone,' said Rob, which was a bit rich coming from him. He stood up, drained his pint and slammed the glass down, still scowling. 'Right, that's my three drinks. Cheers for those. See you around.'

As he headed sulkily for the exit, Tess said, 'Well, that was a lot. Something tells me that three pints won't be his limit. Bet he's off to another pub.'

'I probably shouldn't have said anything.' Charlie sighed. 'We might've lost a valuable source there. Maybe spooked a potential suspect. But his attitude to both murders doesn't sit well with me. Not at all.'

'Don't beat yourself up, babe,' said Tess sympathetically. 'It needed saying. Besides, next time he wants free drinks, he'll be sweetness and light again.'

'Fingers crossed,' said Charlie. 'Hope he doesn't tell Anjali.'

'Something tells me they don't communicate that well. Besides, he'd have to admit to discussing the case with us over a few tongue-loosening beers. I doubt he'd risk her wrath.'

'I wouldn't either to be fair.' Charlie grinned, cheered up already.

'Looks like you're wanted, Mr Popular,' said Tess, looking

over his shoulder. Jackie Courtney was behind the bar, beckoning Charlie over.

'Be right back,' he said.

Tess smirked. 'No rush. Come back bearing intel. And maybe a complimentary drink for the road.'

He made his way across the pub. 'Hello, Jackie. How are you?'

'Hi, Charlie,' she said, smiling. 'Not bad, thanks, considering. Did I just see our friendly neighbourhood policeman leaving in high dudgeon?'

'You did indeed,' he said. 'My fault, I'm afraid.'

She shrugged. 'Don't worry. Rob's always getting the hump about something or other. Probably a bit jealous of you and Anjali as well, I shouldn't wonder.'

'No need,' said Charlie, his cheeks reddening slightly. 'We're just old friends.'

'Sure you are, darling,' she said with a twinkle. 'Now then, sorry to interrupt. I just wanted to let you know about Frank's wake and wondered if you'd like to come.'

Charlie was taken aback. 'Really? I mean, thank you. Are you sure?'

'Course I am,' she said. 'I consider you a friend of the family. You found him, after all. The funeral itself is at full capacity with family, friends, his old police colleagues and people he met through his community work. Probably not your scene anyway. But we're having a few drinks and a little buffet here afterwards. Nothing fancy but I thought you might like to pop in.'

'That's very kind of you,' said Charlie. 'I'd love to.'

'Good, that's sorted then,' said Jackie, giving him a last smile before turning to serve another customer.

Charlie stood there a moment, mulling it over. He didn't exactly relish the prospect but who knows what he might find out? Jackie's demeanour wasn't half cheery for a widow ahead of her husband's funeral.

Charlie wondered why she'd invited him along. He was keeping an eye on Jackie. Maybe she was keeping an eye on him in return. Keep your friends close and your enemies closer. It was getting harder to tell which was which.

37

Widowhood Becomes Her

'Right, dimples,' said Tess. 'Keep your eyes peeled and your ears open.'

'I'm not sure I'm anatomically capable of closing my ears, but sure,' muttered Charlie.

He had taken Tess along for moral support. Not to mention the fact that she'd insisted. As Charlie approached the Neptune, feeling self-conscious in a suit and tie, he reminded her, 'We're also here to pay our respects. Try not to turn it into a murder-mystery weekend.'

'That's exactly what it is,' she replied. 'We're on an intel-gathering trip, so let's mingle with intent.'

As Charlie pushed open the pub door, they were hit by a different noise to usual. No pumping music or excited chatter today. Just the low hum of respectful murmuring and clinking glasses.

If Charlie was self-conscious before, he suddenly felt even more so. As he and Tess looked around at the mourners, he realized he hardly knew anyone. He recognized Jackie and her children, of course. There was a huddle of off-duty coppers in the corner, come to give their former colleague a send-off. Otherwise it was a sea of unfamiliar faces.

'Drink?' he asked Tess.

'Hell yeah,' she said. 'I think we're going to need it.'

As they weaved their way to the bar, issuing polite apologies as they squeezed past, Jackie Courtney peeled away from a group of guests to greet them.

She smiled, leaning in for an air-kiss. 'I'm glad you came, Charlie. You too, Tess.'

Being a widow suited her, thought Charlie. She looked chic in her black dress. Her hair had been freshly blow-dried. Maybe it was recent tears but her eyes sparkled. Jackie was positively glowing.

'I wouldn't have missed it, Jackie,' he said. 'So sorry again for your loss. Looks like a good turnout, though.'

'Not too bad, is it?' she said, glancing around at the busy pub. 'Say what you like about my Frank but he had several chapters to his story and picked up plenty of friends along the way.'

'I can see that,' said Charlie. 'It must be a source of comfort for you all.'

'Some of the lads here were helped by Frank's youth work,' said Jackie proudly. 'He changed a lot of lives.'

'Did the service go OK?' asked Tess.

'It was lovely, dear, considering,' said Jackie. 'Now, we're in a pub but you're both dry, which simply won't do. Let's get you a drink.'

She turned to her son, who was hovering nearby. 'Luke, darling, would you do the honours? Pint of lager and glass of red, is it?'

'Of course, Mum.' He smiled, turning to Charlie and Tess. 'I've seen you both in the pub, but I don't think we've met properly. I'm Luke Courtney, as you might have guessed. I'll be back with those drinks before you know it.'

'Nice to meet you, Luke, and cheers,' said Charlie, raising an eyebrow at Tess. 'You must have lots of people to meet, Jackie. Don't let us keep you.'

'See you in the woods again soon, no doubt,' said Jackie as she glided away to circulate.

'What's with the eyebrow?' Tess asked Charlie innocently. 'I didn't even notice how tall and handsome he was. That would be inappropriate on this day of all days.'

'Don't kid a kidder,' replied Charlie. 'He must be, what?' He did some mental arithmetic. 'Fifteen years younger than you?'

'Charming,' said Tess. 'Jackie must be fifteen years older than you, but it doesn't stop you two flirting.'

'Behave yourself,' said Charlie. 'Blimey, that really was quick.'

Luke handed them their drinks. 'Everyone needs a bit of Dutch courage at times like this,' he said. 'Thanks so much for coming. It means a lot to my mother. Talking of whom, I can see her beckoning me over. Excuse me. Anything else, just ask.'

Tess waited a polite few seconds after he left before turning eagerly to Charlie. 'Did you spot his bandaged fingers?'

'I did, yeah,' said Charlie. 'What of it? He works in a pub. Probably gets glass cuts all the time.'

'Or he hurt them some other way,' replied Tess. 'Maybe sustained an injury in a struggle with Shane.'

'The simplest explanation is often the right one,' said Charlie. 'Occam's razor, philosophers call it. But I can tell by your face that you're not going to let this go, so feel free to add it to your spreadsheet.'

'Notice anything else about him?' she asked knowingly.

'Apart from the square jaw and bulging biceps?'

'Oh, come now,' she said. 'He was noticeably better-spoken than Jackie, don't you think?'

'Now you mention it, I suppose he was,' replied Charlie. 'But that's often the way with working-class families who've done well. The next generation are upwardly mobile.'

'Spoilsport,' huffed Tess. 'Sociology as well as philosophy, huh? Much as it pains me, Luke the looker is going on my list of suspects. Hang on, from beauty to the beast.'

Charlie turned to see who she was referring to and saw Rob Thompson making his way through the crowd – towards the bar naturally.

'Hello, Boardy Boy,' he said by way of greeting. 'Didn't expect to see you here.'

'Likewise, Rob, but good to see you all the same,' said Charlie, bristling but trying not to show it. 'Jackie invited me as a friend of the family.'

'Did she indeed?' snorted Rob. 'Well, be careful what you wish for.'

'How about you?' asked Charlie, shrugging off Rob's snide tone. 'I thought there was no love lost between you and the deceased.'

'Don't know where you got that idea,' protested Rob, convincing nobody. He nodded towards the corner. 'A few of us from the station came to pay our respects. Always do when we lose somebody who served on the force, even if they left long ago. Once a copper, always a copper and all that.'

Charlie wondered what the local plods were doing here en masse, drinking the day away, rather than being out there trying to catch a killer. Maybe they didn't see Shane's murder as high priority – he was a known drug dealer and convicted criminal, after all – but surely Frank's was?

'Quite right too,' said Charlie, trying to sound offhand as he added, 'Anjali didn't join the delegation?'

'She popped in early doors with Craig Murdoch out of politeness,' said Rob. 'Showed her face, then left. Didn't think it was right to stay, what with the ongoing inquiry. She's spinning lots of plates.' Again, Charlie's mind whirred. If Framstone Police were so low on resources, why hadn't Rob been drafted into the investigation?

'Fair enough,' said Charlie. 'I just thought she might fancy some people-watching.'

Rob grinned. 'You're not as daft as you look, mate. They've retreated to a safe distance to keep an eye on comings and goings from their car. You never know what you might see at a murdered man's funeral.'

'I'll bet,' chipped in Tess.

'Mum's the word, Sarge,' said Charlie, tapping his nose knowingly.

Rob nodded and continued bar-wards. For once he was right. You never knew what you might see at a murdered man's funeral. And what better place for a murderer to hide in plain sight?

38

Charlie Has His Chips

Charlie and Ruby weren't usually in the habit of taking late-night walks, but after Frank's wake he needed to clear his head.

Several drinks hadn't helped. They'd stayed in the Neptune for a couple of hours, making small talk with various guests. Despite the persistence of terrier-like Tess – dogs really do resemble their owners, in behaviour if not appearance – they failed to learn much more of value.

Every conversation seemed to follow similar lines: how did you know Frank, so sad, sorry for your loss, what's the world coming to, great turnout, lovely spread, I'd recommend the sausage rolls, egg mayo sandwiches are underrated in my book, Jackie's done him proud, nice to meet you, bye.

It struck Charlie that in a small town like Framstone, a local pub landlord knew his punters' business. He kept their secrets. He saw through their lies. Had Frank been killed to keep something hidden?

When he'd got home and changed out of his suit, Charlie had nodded off for a while on his bed and woken up groggy, hence hauling Ruby out for a stroll. She was always happy for a snuffle around, whatever the hour. They found themselves heading for the beach. Some salty air should blow away the fuzziness. He could take home a bag of chips to share with Polly as a surprise treat.

Under cover of darkness, Framstone beach looked very different. Wilder somehow. Moonlight flickered off the shimmering North Sea. The still night air made the crashing waves seem that much louder. The so-called 'seaside illuminations' – the optimistic local term for the odd string of coloured light bulbs wrapped round lamp posts and strung along the prom – lit the way inland. Facing out to sea, though, the view felt timeless. You could easily convince yourself it was centuries ago.

Charlie was doing just that when he saw it. Torchlight flashing on and off, a little way offshore, rising and falling with the waves. Surely it was too dark for fishing. Ruby had sensed it too. She gazed out to sea, her soft suede-like ears rippling in the breeze.

He heard voices and turned towards the road. A car facing out to sea was flashing its headlights. Was it signalling to the boat? Charlie wished he could remember the Morse code he'd learned when he was a boy scout. Like how to tie obscure knots, it was lost in the mists of time.

The boat was coming closer to shore and the voices got louder. As his eyes adjusted to the darkness, Charlie could see it was a small-ish dinghy with an outboard motor, now switched off. Two silhouetted figures were on board, one of them rowing while the other flashed a torch.

Charlie suddenly realized the beam could alight on him and Ruby. He instinctively took a step back into the shadows. The shouting grew louder and more urgent. There was a wet, stony whoosh as the dinghy landed at the water's edge. Both figures hopped off and began to run up the beach.

'Oh balls, Rube, I think they've spotted us,' he whispered, as much to himself as anything. His heart was racing. Hearing his own voice in the dark was somehow reassuring. He shuffled sideways and dropped behind a breakwater, bending low and pulling Ruby with him. She gave a surprised grunt, then a wag as he ducked down to her level, thinking it was some sort of game.

'Ssh, easy, girl,' said Charlie as she gave his cheek a loving lick. Peering over the mossy stone barrier, he was pretty sure they couldn't be seen in the gloom.

He needn't have worried. The two dark outlines had appeared to aim straight for him and Ruby but it was just coincidence. They scuttled past, heading towards the parked car. The driver got out, as if to greet them.

Charlie squinted through the darkness, trying to make out who they were, even what age or gender, but they were just shadows. He strained to hear what was being said. All he could hear was garbled noises, any detail blown away by the wind.

Before he knew it, the interaction was over. The two figures ran back down the beach, dragged the boat into shallow water and began rowing out to sea again. Charlie turned back to the coast road, just in time to see the car pulling away and roaring off. A black or navy BMW, he thought, although he could be mistaken. In the distance he heard the outboard motor fire up and gradually fade away.

The beach fell quiet again. The only sounds were the swish of waves and the squawk of seagulls. 'Looks like the show's over,' he said to Ruby, straightening up and brushing shingle from his knees.

Charlie's pulse rate gradually returned to normal. For a

tense moment he'd been convinced the maritime mystery men were coming for them. The image of Shane's body – so still, so lifeless, so final – had flashed through his mind.

He blew out his cheeks with relief, patted Ruby and turned towards the late-night takeaway. He thought he'd had his chips. Instead he and Polly were going to enjoy some. The evocative smell of salt and vinegar tickled his nostrils. Ruby inhaled deeply too.

As they headed towards the fish and chip shop's flickering sign, with its kitschy cartoon of a grinning haddock, Charlie considered the significance of what he'd seen. Like the sea, Framstone looked innocuous enough but it had dangerous depths. Charlie fought down an unsettling sense that the threat to his home town was escalating.

39

Imposter, She Wrote

'Plenty to chew on there,' said Viv. She looked down at the dogs. 'A bit like you lot with a bone, eh?'

It might have been the full Coastal Coffee crew but for once they weren't huddled round their usual table. In fact, they weren't in the coffee shop at all. Malcolm had imperiously insisted that if they required his presence today, they'd need to come to his allotment. He was busy planting garlic and harvesting pumpkins apparently.

Along with Ted, the allotment was Malcolm's pride and joy. On a patch of land behind Framstone Rec were forty plots, each around the size of a tennis court. They were cheaply rented out by the council and lovingly tended by tenants keen to grow their own fruit and veg. With their furrowed soil and rows of plants stretching into the distance, it was like a little bit of the countryside in the middle of town.

The rural vibes were only enhanced by the abundant animal life. The insects seemed more plumptious and more plentiful than anywhere else in Framstone. Some of Malcolm's neighbouring gardeners kept chickens, bees or rabbits in hutches. One even had a caged ferret, which immediately flung Charlie back three decades.

It was his first time here with the dogwalkers, but as they'd arrived, vivid memories had come flooding back. He recalled a short-lived stint in childhood when his dad had bagged a plot. Boardman Snr soon lost interest and sloped back to the local pubs, but for a few months Charlie and Danny had been press-ganged into coming down to 'help'. This mainly involved weeding, digging, lugging around sacks and wheelbarrows, or ineffectually rubbing their itchy stinging nettle rashes with dock leaves. One time, Charlie had failed to heed everyone's warnings about the ferret and poked his finger through the wire of its cage to see what would happen. What happened was lots of blood and a patch of skin on one fingertip that never quite fully healed. He sometimes rubbed it absent-mindedly while trying to think.

He and Danny had complained non-stop, naturally, while their father insisted it was character-building. *Funny how age changes your perspective*, thought Charlie. Back then it had felt like horticultural torture. Now it seemed wholesome and bucolic here. An oasis of calm. A mini holiday from the hustle-bustle of modern life.

Malcolm's plot was nettle-free, ferret-free and typically pleasing to the eye. Well-cultivated crops had a patchwork informality which recalled an old-fashioned kitchen garden. Colours were vibrant, beds were marked out with repurposed timber and brick. Even his potting shed was chic: Farrow & Ball-painted with a caravan-style curved roof.

This was where the dogwalkers were holed up now, sitting on folding chairs and sheltering from the rain, which pit-pattered on to the corrugated iron above their heads. The shed smelled of tomato plants, creosote and compost. On a dinky portable stove Malcolm made a round of brews in enamel mugs. The stream rising off the five hot drinks seemed to merge into one cloud of homeliness. Crammed in, their knees almost touching, made it all the more cosy.

The dogs loved it down here too, although it was a full-time task to stop them bothering the rabbits or their inquisitive noses suffering the same ferret-y fate as Charlie's fingertip. Their snoozy sighs sounded like a mixture of contentment and annoyance that rain had stopped play.

Charlie and Tess had plenty to share. They'd given the others a rundown of events at Frank Courtney's wake – as usual, Tess's version was considerably more detailed than Charlie's – before he recounted his late-night near miss.

'Sounds like Jackie Courtney's blooming,' said Viv, earning herself a look from Sue. 'I'm not sure if that makes her more or less of a suspect.'

'Me neither,' agreed Malcolm. 'Is she blooming out of blessed release from an unhappy marriage? Or relief that she hasn't been caught for murder?'

'Yet,' added Sue. 'Hasn't been caught *yet*. There's still time.'

'Although you'd think that if she was guilty, the stress of hiding it might take a toll,' said Viv. 'Maybe she wouldn't be looking quite so well.'

'Sounds like this Luke could also be a person of interest,' said Malcolm with a twinkle. 'In more ways than one.'

'Don't you start.' Charlie sighed. 'I had enough of Tess drooling into her Merlot yesterday. Most unseemly, it was.'

'I will not be shamed for being a warm-blooded woman,' she said defiantly. 'Talking of blood, any thoughts on Hot Son's bandaged hand?'

'Charlie's right, I'm afraid,' said Sue. 'Law of probability says it's more likely he cut it on a knife or broken pint glass than it being defence wounds from Shane. Although obviously we can't rule it out.'

'Hmph,' grunted Tess. She'd expected everyone to side with her.

'For the sake of argument let's say it was from a scuffle with Shane,' said Charlie, trying to avoid the triumphant look in Tess's eye. 'Are we suggesting a revenge attack on the man who Luke thought had killed his father?'

'Payback is a powerful motive,' Sue said, nodding.

'That's why I still prefer Rob as a suspect,' said Charlie. 'He thought Shane had jumped him, so as soon as he got out of hospital, Rob went looking for revenge. Maybe he just planned to give Shane a taste of his own medicine, but it escalated and Rob accidentally drowned him somehow.'

'What about Luke being noticeably posher than his parents?' chipped in Tess. 'Could he be adopted or something? Maybe he's not even their real son but an imposter.'

Malcolm laughed. 'Steady on, Jessica Fletcher. Let's keep things loosely within the realms of possibility. I'll ask around, though. See if there's any gossip there.' He gave Tess a knowing wink.

'And how about the shady sailors?' said Charlie. 'Heard anything on the gossip circuit about that? It looked like a well-drilled operation, so I wondered if it was a regular occurrence.'

'Drug traffickers is the obvious answer,' said Malcolm, and everyone murmured in agreement.

'Really? I knew imported drugs were big business in London but I assumed it wasn't such a problem around here.'

'There's more of a Framstone drug scene than you might think,' said Viv knowledgeably. 'It's fairly easy to buy anything

162

around here nowadays. I wouldn't say the town is awash with the stuff but it's definitely fairly flush.'

'Ask your mate Anjali,' added Sue. 'Drug-related crime is probably the bane of her life.'

'Well I never,' said Charlie, shaking his head in disbelief. 'Dear old Framstone, a hotbed of narcotics. Who'd have thought it?'

'Pretty much everyone except you,' said Tess with a chuckle. 'Did you really think Shane, God rest his soul, was the only one dealing around here?'

'I hadn't thought of it like that,' said Charlie, suddenly feeling naive. 'So the boat people were bringing in the gear and the car people were buying?'

'Sounds suspiciously like it,' said Sue. 'I'll wager there's a holdall of something swapped for a cash-stuffed envelope at a regular time and place.'

'Well, I'm glad I didn't get in the way of free enterprise,' said Charlie. 'They probably wouldn't have taken kindly to a surprise guest.'

'Probably not,' said Malcolm. 'Wrong time, wrong place. It can be dangerous. Is that what we think happened to Shane?'

'Well, it was a stretch of beach not far from where he was found,' admitted Charlie. Having been spooked there himself, he felt another surge of empathy for Shane.

'Yes, but he was in the business too,' said Tess. 'Honour among thieves and all that. Why would they suddenly turn on one of their own?'

'Unless it was a deal gone wrong,' suggested Viv. 'Maybe Shane got in over his head. Out of his depth. Sorry, every phrase I try sounds tactless.'

'Don't worry, we know what you mean,' said Tess. 'It's certainly a working theory.'

'But what about Frank and Rob?' asked Charlie. 'Even if Shane's murder was down to a drug deal gone bad, that doesn't explain the attacks on them.'

Everyone fell silent, lost in thought. Judging by the jowly snorts down by their feet, even the dogs seemed deflated. The sooner the rain eased off and they could get out to harass the rabbits, the better. Meanwhile, theories in Charlie's mind were germinating and blooming like Malcolm's prize produce.

40

Murderous Whack-a-Mole

One step forward, two steps back. That's how Charlie was feeling. Thankfully not literally. Dog walks would take even longer than they did already.

Once the rain eased off, he accompanied Ruby back to the woods. She was happy enough, as always, but it was really for his benefit. He wanted to have a think away from all the horticultural chat and huffing dogs.

'Except you, Rube,' he murmured. 'You can snore, snuffle and sigh on me whenever you like.'

Every time they thought they were getting somewhere with one case, questions arose with another. It was like playing a murderous game of whack-a-mole. There must be something that connected it all: Frank's stabbing, Rob's assault, Shane's drowning. Charlie might have been imagining it but the answer felt tantalizingly close, as if it were hovering just out of reach. Every time he grabbed for it, it slipped through his fingers.

Or maybe the cases weren't linked at all. Life was only that neat in the movies, all tied up with a bow. It could be coincidence that the three crimes had happened so close together, both geographically and chronologically. No master criminal or fiendish scheme, just random.

He was tying himself in knots, so Charlie tried to think back over it all, right from the start. As they walked, stopping every few yards for Ruby to catch an interesting scent or the sound of something rustling in the bushes, he mentally rewound the past four weeks.

He'd discovered Frank's body and as a result, become reacquainted with Anjali. He'd chased and tracked a hooded figure through the woods. He'd met Frank's widow Jackie and Anjali's husband Rob, who was then assaulted and hospitalized. A threatening toy dog had been left on Charlie and Polly's doorstep. Shane was arrested, then forcibly drowned. He'd attended Frank's wake and witnessed some alleged drug smuggling on the beach. All within less than a month. It had been eventful, that's for sure.

As he ambled along, Charlie found his mind straying back to details that still puzzled him. He was bothered by that football scarf. Shane was superstitious about wearing it. It seemed important to him yet he'd lost it. When he died, though, it had mysteriously reappeared round his neck.

Charlie was reminded of how he'd been similarly bothered by the wigs found around Frank's corpse. Neither sat right with him and he couldn't quite work out why. But these weren't the main things intruding on the periphery of his brain. Something else bugged him about the day he found Frank's body.

Charlie breathed slowly and rhythmically, attempting to unclutter his brain. He deliberately tried to not think about it, hoping that his mind would subconsciously guide him back to the right place.

The trees rippled and rustled. Rainwater dripped from russet leaves. The woods smelled fresh with the tang of wet earth. Watery sun peeped through the trees, perhaps its last appearance before popping on its out-of-office and going on sabbatical until spring. Ruby padded along, obliviously dog-like, happily enjoying nature. As Charlie felt tranquillity descend over him, an idea began to emerge.

The thought came into focus and gradually took shape . . . Could it be . . . ? Yes, that was it. It was the fact that no one seemed terribly taken aback by Frank's demise.

That's what had been niggling at him. Charlie gasped with sheer relief that he'd finally put his finger on it.

Not Anjali and Murdoch, when they arrived on the scene and saw who it was. Not Jackie Courtney, when her husband had been brutally murdered down the road. Not Rob Thompson, a fellow police officer. Not even Luke Courtney, who seemed to have taken his father's violent death in his stride.

A local publican and former policeman had been bludgeoned, stabbed and left for dead in the woods, but somehow nobody was remotely surprised.

41

A Non-Accident Waiting to Happen

'Interesting,' said Tess. 'Very interesting. Good work, partner.' She sat back happily in the Boardmans' creaky kitchen chair, pondering this new angle.

At Polly's insistence she'd been invited round for afternoon tea. 'I know Tess is a good friend, maybe even your best friend nowadays, but I rarely see her,' Polly had told Charlie. 'I pop my head into her cafe sometimes but she's always so busy; we rarely get a chance to chat.'

'She'd probably say that it's a coffee shop, Mum, not a cafe,' said Charlie. 'And why she'd want to come for tea and cake when that's literally what she serves all day is beyond me.'

'OK, smarty-pants,' Polly said with a smile. 'Just ask her, please, would you? Indulge your aged mother for once.' He could hardly say no to that.

So it was that the three of them were now sitting round the well-worn pine table with a pot of tea, some of Polly's home-made brownies and a freshly baked caramel-and-walnut sponge. Polly hadn't gone all out to impress, Charlie noted with relief – there were no lacy doilies and she'd used her second-best china, not the poshest set – but it still made him feel slightly awkward to have two of the main ladies in his life ganging up on him. Three, if you included Ruby, who was looking on contentedly from her basket and occasionally waddling over to check the floor for cake crumbs.

Tess and Polly had already bonded over local gossip. Conversation soon turned to Charlie and how Polly 'despaired of him sometimes'. When's he going to get a proper job, rather than scraps of graphic design and dog walking? When's he going to meet a nice girl and settle down? When's he going to get a haircut and have a shave? You know, make the best of himself. He's not a bad-looking boy underneath the scruffiness.

'You do realize I'm sitting right here, don't you?' he'd said more than once, as his looks and his life were deconstructed.

'We've only got your best interests at heart, Charlie,' teased Tess, who was enjoying this far too much for his liking. 'Or is it "Charles"?' she asked, turning back to Polly with her best guileless look.

'Well, yes,' said Polly, taking the bait, 'Charles and Daniel are my two boys, but everyone calls them "Charlie" and "Danny". Always did really. Although now we've got a King Charles, maybe he should revert to his full name. More regal and majestic.'

'Don't suppose we know any nice girls called Camilla?' quipped Tess.

The two women found this hilarious. Charles, sorry, Charlie rather less so.

Eventually Polly had decided that Tess absolutely needed to see some childhood photos – *When will this torture stop?*

thought Charlie – and scurried off to find the family album. He and Tess took the opportunity for a quick catch-up.

'Look, I know it's not evidential in any way . . .' he said after telling Tess about his moment of epiphany in the woods.

'Evidential?' she repeated. 'You've been hanging out with Viv and Sue too much.'

'Yeah, yeah,' he continued, glancing at the door to check Polly wasn't returning yet. 'But do you agree? Am I on to something?'

'I reckon you might be,' mused Tess. 'I know what you mean about Anjali and Murdoch's reaction at the first crime scene. They were matter-of-fact about it, rather than shocked or horrified. Almost like they were half expecting it.'

'Exactly,' said Charlie, relieved he wasn't going mad. 'What about Jackie and Luke's reactions?'

'You know Jackie better than me,' said Tess. 'I've not spoken to her enough to judge. With Luke, I was too busy gazing up at him in awe, like you would a statue of a Greek god.'

Charlie sighed impatiently. 'Yes, but he was pretty smooth and relaxed, considering it was his dad's funeral, right?'

'I suppose so,' conceded Tess. 'That might just be boys, though. Shoulders back, chest out, upper lip stiff. What did you expect? Tears, wailing and rending of garments?'

'Obviously not, but at least some sense of sadness,' said Charlie. 'He was all charm and chit-chat. More like he was schmoozing at a cocktail party than mourning a parent, let alone a violently murdered one.'

'Perhaps,' said Tess thoughtfully. 'I'm more intrigued by the police response. I must say, it makes me wonder if Frank was dodgy in some way. Maybe the cops had him down as a suspected criminal. Maybe he was risking his safety by running with some shady people and it was a matter of time before he came a cropper. That might explain Anjali and Murdoch's reaction. A bit like when Shane turned up dead, I suppose. An occupational hazard.'

'A non-accident waiting to happen,' agreed Charlie.

'So what's our next move?' asked Tess, eagerly sitting forward again.

'I reckon we all do some digging around Frank Courtney's possible dodginess,' said. 'Was he a bent copper? Or just a bent ex-copper?'

Tess nodded. 'I'll send something round on the group chat when I leave.'

Charlie was just getting his hopes up that she was set to depart when Tess looked up at the doorway and smiled. 'Ah, here she is,' she said gleefully. 'Blimey, Polly, they're big photo albums.'

Charlie groaned. It was going to be a long afternoon.

42

It's Hardly a Crime

Two days since being given their Frank-focused mission by Drill Sergeant Tess, the dogwalkers assembled in Coastal, keen to report back. Small talk round the table was slightly strained, so eager was everyone to get down to business.

There were more hounds than ever flopped around their feet. Alongside Ruby, Ted, Rough and Tumble were four of Nuts About Mutts' canine clients. If Tess hadn't been the coffee shop's owner, they'd probably have been politely asked to leave. Eight dogs was a bit excessive. It's hardly like the furry octet were spending money. They were merely taking up floor space. And because they were hiding from the relentless autumn rain again, the place smelled of damp fur.

Tess took her time getting everyone set up with drinks and snacks, including the animals. A bowl of water and some of her home-made peanut-butter dog biscuits were laid on, before she finally sat down and looked round at her impatient pals. Charlie suppressed a smirk. He could've sworn she was doing it on purpose to build up the drama.

'Frank Courtney, then,' she said eventually in an expectant tone. 'Who's managed to find anything out?'

Several mouths opened and began talking at once. 'One

at a time,' said both Viv and Malcolm – ironically at the same time. You could tell they once worked in school classrooms and legal chambers respectively. It was a wonder they didn't go for 'Care to come down to the front and share the joke with the rest of us?' or 'Order, order! Silence in court'.

'After you, ladies,' insisted Malcolm gallantly, gesturing to Viv and Sue that the floor was theirs.

'Right, well, we've solved the mystery of Courtney Junior's posh accent,' said Viv proudly. 'And, like so many things in life, it comes down to education.'

The teaching assistant, the librarian and the solicitor all nodded sagely, like those wobbly-headed dogs you see in car windows. Suddenly intrigued, Charlie made a mental note to find out their academic qualifications some day. He idly wondered who had the best grades.

'Meaning?' asked Tess. Now it was her turn to be impatient.

'Meaning that it turns out that little lord Luke went to private school,' said Sue. 'His two older sisters went to Framstone High, the local comprehensive, hence their more salt-of-the-earth accents.'

'That breeding ground for reprobates and ne'er-do-wells?' said Tess, glancing sideways at Charlie. 'The poor lambs.'

'But the prodigal son is an alumnus of the illustrious St Jude's,' continued Sue.

Charlie knew of it. St Jude's was the nearest fee-paying school to Framstone. About ten miles out of town in the countryside, it was all rolling grounds, gravel driveways and distinctive blazers. Framstone High often played them at sport. He'd always taken pleasure in putting one over the poshos.

'How did you find that out, dynamic duo?' he asked.

'One of our posher clients – owners of Humphrey, in fact – has a son who went there,' said Viv proudly. 'He's now at university. Anyway, when we let ourselves in to collect daft old Humph the other day, there was a framed picture of the 2021 St Jude's rugby first fifteen in the hall. Sue spotted Luke just behind their son.'

'Top sleuthing skills, Sue,' said Charlie admiringly.

'Aww, shucks,' she said, busying herself with knitting to disguise how pleased she was.

'Bit unusual, isn't it?' asked Tess. 'Don't parents usually make a point of sending their kids to the same school? So they're kept together and to make it fair?'

'Not always,' said Malcolm. 'It can depend on the individual kids. Sometimes the parents' situation changes too.'

'Well, they should,' said Tess decisively. 'It seems sort of Victorian that the boy gets the silver-spoon treatment, while the girls get what they're given.'

'Point taken, Emmeline Pankhurst,' said Malcolm. 'Now is it my turn? Good. Well, I made some enquiries with my contacts in Portugal.'

'Contacts?' Tess laughed. 'That's what you call your old flames and holiday flings, is it?'

'I shall glide gracefully past that outrageous insinuation,' said Malcolm. 'Anyway, you know how the Courtneys go to the Algarve each summer? Well, they don't hire the same villa every year. They own it.'

'*Qué?*' asked Viv, hastily adding, 'Yes, I know that's Spanish.'

'They keep it pretty quiet apparently,' said Malcolm. 'It took lots of asking around. They rent it out most of the year via a holiday-lets website and just take a fortnight there themselves each summer, plus the odd long weekend.'

'Wonder why they keep it secret?' asked Tess. 'It's hardly a crime to have a holiday home.'

'Overseas property. Private-school fees. Frank Courtney was clearly doing all right for himself,' said Charlie.

'He does sound unusually affluent for a policeman-turned-publican, does he not?' agreed Malcolm.

'You're thinking what we're thinking, right?' said Viv. 'That a pub and a police pension wouldn't make you that loaded.'

'He presumably had another income stream,' agreed Charlie.

'Seems like he might have been dodgy after all,' said Sue. 'Maybe that was enough to get him killed.'

'So do we reckon he was a bent copper?' asked Charlie. 'Or did his shady dealings start after he'd left?'

'Good question,' said Tess. 'If only we knew someone on the force with a loose tongue that we could ply with drinks and ask.'

43

Don't Get Too Involved

'This is getting to be a habit, Charlie,' said Rob Thompson in the Neptune that night. 'Does my darling wife need to worry about your drinking, too?'

Anjali certainly needed to worry about Rob's. Still not signed off by doctors to return to work, he'd clearly been filling his time in pubs instead. Anjali had hoped him being hospitalized would be a wake-up call. A chance to dry out and change his ways. By the look of it, though, he'd relapsed completely. Rob had the sickly pallor of someone who'd only seen pub light for the past few days. Any colour in his face came from booze-flush.

Charlie felt deeply uneasy about buying Rob drinks but figured that if he didn't, someone else would. He hoped Anjali wouldn't blame him for enabling her husband's boozing. Besides, over Rob's shoulder he could see Tess, tilting her head to encourage him.

Once the three of them sat down at a table, Charlie and Tess led some idle chit-chat, just to warm him up. After exchanging looks with Charlie, Tess dived in.

'You know everything that goes on in Framstone, right, Rob?' He shrugged modestly but was clearly flattered. 'You might be able to satisfy my curiosity. We'd heard rumours that Frank Courtney was Mr Moneybags. Holiday homes, school fees, that sort of thing.'

'Heard about all that, have you?' said Rob, relishing a chance to gossip. 'Well, yeah. He kept it quiet, but Frank was pretty flush.'

'How come?' asked Charlie, as innocently as he could manage. 'I wouldn't have thought the pub was that much of an earner.'

'You'd be surprised,' said Rob, sipping his drink and looking knowledgeable.

'We just idly wondered if he might have another income source,' said Tess.

'How do you mean?' asked Rob.

'Oh, like an inheritance or something,' she said, keeping it vague.

'Not that I know of,' said Rob. 'His parents were pretty humble. In fact, Frank had quite a poor upbringing. He'd refer to it sometimes. You know, "In my day we wore paper shoes and shared a pair of trousers between six of us", that kind of thing.'

'Right,' said Charlie. 'So do you reckon he could have been . . . how do I put this . . . on the take somehow? You know, when he was still on the force?'

Rob's mood suddenly changed. He sat up straighter, an alert expression on his hitherto bleary face. 'Whoa there, Boardy Boy,' he said. 'That's a serious accusation to make.'

'Sorry, I didn't mean any offence,' said Charlie quickly. 'Just thought I'd ask. We were speculating whether someone might have been out to get him because of something financial.'

Rob seemed to relax a little. 'Well, I wouldn't know

anyway,' he said. 'We barely overlapped in the force, to be honest. Frank was retiring just as I was starting out.'

'Of course, of course,' said Charlie. 'But you never heard any talk?'

'Nope,' said Rob firmly, bringing the conversation to a close. 'And I'd change the subject if I were you, look.'

Tess and Charlie turned round to see Luke Courtney behind the nearest end of the bar. He was half-heartedly drying pint glasses with a tea towel while glaring straight at them.

Charlie turned back to the table but could feel Luke's eyes boring two holes into his back like laser beams. 'My round, isn't it?'

'Nah, you're all right,' said Rob, even though his glass was empty. 'I've just seen someone I know over there.' He hurried across the pub to greet two of his fellow regulars.

'Well, I'll get one more for us,' he said to Tess. 'It would look a bit blatant if we left the minute we'd finished milking him for info.'

'Agreed,' she said. 'Although I'm not sure how much useful stuff we got.'

'Yeah, I can't work out if it made minted Frank or shifty Rob look more suspicious,' agreed Charlie.

Avoiding Luke, who still wasn't looking terribly welcoming, he headed over to where Jackie Courtney was holding court behind the bar.

She smiled. 'Ah, it's my woodland-walkies friend. Same again?'

'Yes, please, Jackie.' He grinned back. 'How are you all?'

'Not too bad, considering,' she replied, glancing up at him as she poured Tess's glass of red. 'I see you were as thick as thieves with Rob Thompson again. You want to be careful, Charlie.'

'How do you mean?'

She set their drinks down on the bar and said quietly, 'I wouldn't get too involved if I were you.'

'In Rob and Anjali's marriage, you mean?' he said, momentarily confused.

'In anything, Charlie,' said Jackie, the smile gone from her face. 'In anything.'

As he carried the drinks back to Tess, Charlie wondered if he'd just been threatened. If so, did that mean they were one step closer to the truth?

44

Just as Spooked as You Are

One drink turned into two as they dissected the chats with both Rob and Jackie. This time, Charlie made sure to keep their voices low. He didn't want to rile the Courtneys again.

When they left the Neptune, he gave Jackie and Luke a cheery wave. In return he got a tight smile from Jackie and was pretty much blanked by her son.

As he and Tess said their goodbyes on the pavement outside, they heard a groan and a splat, followed by a hacking cough.

'Oh dear,' said Tess. 'That didn't sound too healthy.'

They peered round the corner to see Rob Thompson, one hand braced against a wall, throwing up over the kerb.

Charlie winced. He suddenly felt nauseous himself, as if it were contagious. 'Should we go over and check he's OK?' he whispered.

'I don't fancy it, do you?' replied Tess. 'Besides, I imagine he's used to it. All part of another night out on the tiles. At least it might sober him up a bit before going home to Anjali.'

'Poor her,' said Charlie with a sorrowful shake of the head. 'Let's hope he's got it all out for her sake.'

'Why, fine sir, you're such a gentleman,' said Tess with a chuckle, giving him a goodnight peck on the cheek. She tottered off, pausing only to grimace at Charlie when another unsavoury sound echoed from round the corner.

Charlie pulled a face back, before turning for home. It was a crisp, clear night, so he decided to take a short cut through the woods. Like a less inebriated version of Rob, it might help clear his head before bed too.

As he strolled down those familiar paths, he thought back over the evening's events. They'd had it confirmed that Frank Courtney had mysteriously deep pockets but been stone-walled when it came to whether he'd once been a corrupt copper. Rob Thompson was prickly and defensive on that point. Something to hide himself potentially. And possibly related to the above, he'd got a dirty look and a dark warning from Luke and Jackie respectively. Quite the evening's work.

The Framstone night felt expansive and silent. The air was still. Stars glimmered from a clear sky. As Charlie walked, he felt a calm descend over him – until he heard it.

His train of thought was derailed by a noise on the path behind him and a prickle at the nape of his neck. Someone was approaching from the rear. Charlie didn't stop walking but stepped more lightly and held his breath, straining to listen. Yes, there were audible footsteps behind him.

He told himself he was being daft. Probably a fellow pub-goer on their way home or even a late-night dogwalker. He looked back over his shoulder, peering into the gloom. There was definite movement in the darkness but he couldn't make out more. He wished the moon would come out from behind a cloud and illuminate the scene, but it wasn't playing ball.

This is silly, he thought, coming to a halt. *Just say hello. Bet they're just as spooked as you are.*

'Hello?' Charlie called out tentatively, suddenly

self-conscious of his small voice in the endless night. 'Lovely night for a stroll, isn't it?'

The silence that came back was deafening. Now he really was on edge. He started walking again, picking up the pace. His breath grew louder but it was accompanied by another sound. The footsteps were quickening, hitting the ground more heavily and closing in fast. Someone was rushing up behind him.

Charlie realized he was on the same stretch of path where Rob Thompson had been jumped. Not wanting to suffer the same fate, he glanced around. Courtesy of a misspent youth and countless dog walks, he knew these woods intimately. Every thicket and clearing, every nook and cranny.

There was a hollowed-out tree trunk just ahead and to the right. He used to conceal himself in it during childhood games of hide-and-seek. Later, during his teens, he'd occasionally smoked or kissed a girl there. It offered a rare bit of shelter and privacy in the great outdoors.

He peeled off the path and sped straight for it. The tree was long dead but its trunk still stood, half eaten away, forming a crescent-shaped natural alcove. Charlie tucked himself inside, flattening against the knotty, gnarly wood. He inhaled, held it and listened.

The footsteps stopped, before seeming to go round in a circle. Whoever it was, they were prowling around, wondering where the hell he'd got to. Hand in his pocket, Charlie put his mobile phone on silent and thumbed its camera into life. If he got a chance to take a photo, he would. It was a long shot in the gloom but he might be able to zoom in later and find some kind of clue.

He heard panting, followed by a frustrated grunt as his

pursuer realized they'd lost him. The footsteps retreated the way they'd come, back towards town.

Charlie waited a few seconds before leaving his bolt-hole and stepping back on to the path. He stared into the darkness, feeling a surge of relief that he was unscathed, mixed with frustration that he didn't get a look at who it was.

Had it been Rob Thompson, who was known to take this route after pub closing time and had taken exception to Charlie's questions? Luke Courtney, who'd been giving him evils earlier this evening? Charlie's hooded woodland stalker? Or whoever attacked Rob on this very spot?

Suddenly he heard another sound behind him and sensed motion in his peripheral vision. Perhaps he hadn't shaken them off after all. His heart thumped in his chest.

As the moon finally emerged from its cloud cover and the path lit up, a fox stared back at him. Its russet fur looked healthy in the lunar glow. Its ears were pricked and its wild eyes pierced the night. After what felt like a meaningful pause, it turned and casually trotted away. Charlie realized he'd been holding his breath again.

He gave an embarrassed snort and suddenly felt freezing cold. The chase might have been a narrow escape but it had done the trick at clearing his head. He shoved his hands deep into his pockets, knuckles tight with tension, and hurried home.

45

Dream Witness

'It was right here,' he said the next day. 'This exact spot. I know because I hid in that hollow tree.'

'Well, aren't you the dream witness?' said Anjali. 'You know times, you know places, you describe the incident in vivid detail. Except for the fact that nothing actually happened and you didn't see anyone anyway.'

He smiled in spite of himself. 'Annoying, huh? I realize I must sound paranoid, but it definitely happened. Someone followed me into the woods and was about to jump me. I figured that after Rob was attacked here in exactly the same way, I should let you know.'

He'd phoned Anjali, a little sheepishly, as soon as he woke up. They'd arranged to meet in the woods an hour later. Anjali walked up and down the path one last time, looking around, before admitting defeat. Charlie's mystery predator hadn't dropped anything obvious. Any footprints had been wiped away by the weather or other walkers.

'Sorry, mate,' she said. 'There's nothing more I can do. But thanks for the call. You never know. Sometimes these things are significant – if not at the time, then later.'

'Thanks for indulging me,' he said. 'And apologies again for dragging you down here first thing in the morning.'

Charlie – and Ruby, of course – fell in step alongside her as she headed back towards the road. 'So how's the case going? Or is it cases, plural?'

'A bit of both.' She sighed. 'Two murder inquiries, one case of grievous bodily harm, all possibly connected, all currently unsolved. The press are getting restless. To say my superiors are getting impatient would be an understatement. They're breathing down my neck on a daily basis.'

'I'm sorry,' he said. 'Surely they realize how tricky these investigations are?'

'They just want results, preferably yesterday,' said Anjali, her shoulders slumping. 'It's a month since Frank Courtney was killed, nearly a fortnight since Shane Carter, and I'm not sure we're much further forward. Me and Craig are exploring all avenues, but we badly need leads.'

'We'll help however we can,' promised Charlie. 'Talk of the devil, how is the charming Mr Murdoch?'

'Craig's been great actually,' said Anjali, suddenly serious. 'Supportive, diligent, really putting the hours in. I know you've rubbed each other up the wrong way a few times but if you stopped locking horns like two macho stags, you'd get on well. He's got a soft spot for your mum for a start.'

'He was very good with her the other week,' conceded Charlie. 'She thinks the sun shines out of his jacket vents.'

Anjali laughed. 'Craig was mainly raised by his granny, which might explain it,' she said. 'His parents died in a car crash when he was a boy. Tragic but it means he's great with old dears. If ever we need to interview a witness over sixty, I delegate it to him.'

'How magnanimous of you,' said Charlie with a raised eyebrow.

'He also loves sport and the odd pint. You've got more in common than you think.'

Charlie scratched his stubbly cheek. 'I'll take your word for it.'

'You should,' said Anjali. 'I don't know what I would've done without him lately.'

'Well, I'm glad he's got your back,' he said. 'It can't be easy working under pressure like that. No progress at all?'

'Not much, to be honest,' she replied. 'We've looked for people with potential grudges against Frank Courtney. Any debtors, suppliers he was in dispute with, disgruntled ex-employees.'

'And?' said Charlie, trying to sound hopeful.

'Nothing of note,' said Anjali in a defeated tone. 'Nothing worth killing over, at least. Although we have traced what we think is Shane's burner phone. It was disconnected the night he died and hasn't been switched back on since.'

'So how did you trace it?' asked Charlie. 'Or is that an embarrassingly dumb question?'

'Not for a civilian, I suppose,' she said with a laugh. He was pleased to see her smile again. 'By triangulating the signal from his known movements before that. He was under surveillance, remember? Anyway, we've requested his call log and text transcripts from the service provider, so we'll see.'

'I'll keep my fingers crossed,' said Charlie. 'It's time you caught a break.'

'Detective work isn't all glamour and car chases,' she said, sounding jaded. 'Sometimes it's boring techie stuff. Combing through reams of mobile data, while trying not to despair that there's still a killer, or even two killers, out there somewhere. Oh, and just to make it even more glamorous, there's the vomit,' added Anjali.

'Vomit?' asked Charlie.

'Forensics found three puddles of sick near Frank's body,' she said. 'Sadly it's nigh on impossible to harvest DNA from them.'

'I didn't even know there was DNA in vomit,' said Charlie, trying to disguise the note of worry in his voice.

'Yep, it contains traces from the vomiter,' explained Anjali. 'But the digestive process tends to degrade it. In the open air it degrades even quicker. It's also mixed up with any DNA from food in the stomach, just to confuse matters.'

'If only they'd had the decency to be sick into an evidence bag, then seal and refrigerate it,' he joked, relieved that he wasn't about to be exposed as a squeamish wuss who contaminated crime scenes.

Charlie knew that two of the puddles of vomit were his. Whose was the third? He couldn't help picturing Rob Thompson throwing up the night before. As Tess said, it clearly wasn't a one-off. Had Rob also lost his stomach after killing Frank?

He glanced guiltily at Anjali. If the murderer she was desperately hunting down turned out to be her own husband and a serving police officer . . . It almost didn't bear thinking about.

46

Scare You Off, Shut You Up

Brows were furrowed round the Coastal Coffee table later that day. Tess kept making sure that Charlie was fully fortified with caffeine. Malcolm and Viv looked concerned. Sue even put down her knitting to give him an anxious look. Charlie might have been imagining it but even the dogs had flattened ears and sad eyes.

'Sorry you got pursued, pal,' said Viv. 'Must have been scary.'

'Only a bit,' said Charlie, putting on a brave face. 'But I guess it's like that toy dog on our doorstep. It must mean we're making progress.'

'Yes, but it's not worth risking your personal safety for,' said Malcolm. 'Imagine if you'd ended up in hospital like Rob Thompson. We'd feel terrible. Not least because we'd have to do more of our own dog walks.'

That lightened the mood.

Charlie laughed. 'Thanks for your concern. I'm truly touched. Anyway, what do we make of the latest developments?'

'Shane's mobile data might be interesting,' offered Viv. 'Less sure about the vomit.'

'Yes, that doesn't exactly throw up any clues,' said Tess, never one to miss a punning opportunity.

'The phone records might mean police can trace his drug contacts,' said Sue, glossing over the queasy wordplay.

'Just depends if Anjali spews up their contents to you,' added Tess. 'Sorry not sorry.'

'And what about my attempted assailant?' asked Charlie. 'Any thoughts?'

'Well, you'd just been in the Neptune, asking questions about Frank Courtney,' said Malcolm. 'Let's assume it was related.'

Charlie nodded. 'Maybe Rob Thompson was on the take with him. Maybe some other copper was. Maybe they wanted to scare me off and shut me up.'

'I've got another theory,' said Tess. She'd stopped punning at last and leaned forward eagerly. 'What if Frank did have dodgy deals going on, hence him splashing the cash? Might they not keep it in the family after his death? Luke Courtney could have taken over his dad's shady business.'

'It might explain the dirty looks from behind the bar,' conceded Charlie.

'Maybe his hand injury too,' said Tess.

'In possibly related news,' added Malcolm, 'I've had it confirmed by my younger friends around town – no wisecracks, thank you – that drugs are routinely sold in the Neptune. The night of Shane's confrontation with Rob was by no means a rarity. Somebody deals in there pretty much daily. It's partly why the pub's always so busy.'

'Makes sense,' Charlie said, nodding. 'Presumably also why it attracts a younger crowd than most Framstone boozers. The atmosphere does often seem quite, um, lively.'

'So it's plausible that Frank and now Luke could be part of

that,' said Viv. 'Turning a blind eye in return for a cut of the proceeds perhaps. Or even involved in the supply somehow.'

'He's also a strapping lad,' said Charlie. 'Right, Tess?'

'I hadn't noticed his height or his muscles at all,' she deadpanned. 'But what's that got to do with it?'

'Just that he's an imposing figure,' explained Charlie. 'A rugby forward, I'll wager, from that framed photo at Humphrey's house.'

Tess giggled. '*Humphrey's House* sounds like a kids' TV show. And if it's not, it should be. Sorry, we're getting off the point.'

'No change there, then,' said Charlie. 'All I meant was that Luke is physically intimidating enough that buyers or suppliers would think twice about messing with him. You meet some unsavoury characters in the drugs world. It helps if you can look after yourself.'

He noticed Tess and Malcolm giving him a curious look. 'I should imagine,' he hurriedly added. 'Look, let's not get too carried away with the whole druggy angle. We don't know yet if the Courtney menfolk really are Framstone's answer to Tony Montana.'

'*Scarface* reference, nice,' said Sue without looking up from her knitting.

'Let alone how that could connect to the murders,' continued Charlie. 'But it's worth exploring, right?'

There were murmurs of agreement round the table.

'Say hello to my little friend,' said Tess in her best Cuban accent. She bent down and scooped up a Jack Russell. 'He's called Tumble.'

47

A Crime But Not Murder

Charlie pretty much did the next day's dog walk on auto-pilot. He'd made breakfast for Polly who was having a forgetful morning. She told him the same things several times and at one point called him by his brother Danny's name. This always unnerved him but he'd managed to stay patient, making sure she was settled with a cup of tea, Radio 4 and the newspaper before heading out with Ruby.

Her nose, as usual, led them straight to the woods. Charlie let her off her lead and watched fondly as Ruby sniffed the air and gazed off in various directions. Her head cocked to one side and her velveteen ears moved with a will of their own. Birds, rats, squirrels, who knows what else – she was monitoring them all without even moving. Who needed wildlife documentary cameras when you had a Staffy with heightened senses?

As the pair of them padded off down the path, Charlie tried to take his mind off worrying about Polly, which wouldn't do much good. Instead he reflected on the latest revelations.

Malcolm's intel about sanctioned drug-dealing at the Neptune had cast the pub – and the Courtney family – in a whole new light. The odd deal on the odd night for personal use was one thing. A dealer permanently on the premises surely meant the licensees were in on it. He wondered if Frank had become embroiled while he was still a serving police officer, or whether it only became his sideline when he swapped blues for booze.

Could Luke Courtney really have taken over the family business already? Was Jackie complicit? How about her daughters and the other Neptune staff? Just how big and how organized was this drug operation? Could it be connected to the boat and car rendezvous he'd witnessed at the beach?

Framstone's underbelly was more grubby than Charlie had assumed but it was still conjecture. Gossip and hearsay from a handful of nosy dogwalkers in a coffee shop. They lacked anything resembling evidence. They hadn't established any meaningful connection to Frank and Shane's deaths, or indeed the attack on Rob Thompson. Drug-dealing might be a crime but it wasn't murder.

Then came the threats closer to home. The hooded figure who kept reappearing near where he'd found Frank's body. The nocturnal version who'd followed him into the woods and been poised to jump him from behind. Was it the same stalker or someone else entirely? Not forgetting the menacing Ruby-lookalike toy left on his and Polly's doorstep with its nose ripped off. Thinking about it still made him shudder.

Charlie glanced back over his shoulder, fully expecting to see the comforting shape of the real Ruby padding along loyally like his ever-present shadow. But the ground was empty.

She must have fallen behind or strayed off the path on

the trail of a particularly irresistible scent. Whiffs often made Ruby wander off, so Charlie didn't think much of it. She rarely got very far. He retraced his steps, glancing from side to side. He assumed he'd find her poking around in the bushes or staring up a tree at a squirrel she could sense but not quite see.

No sign. He stood stock-still for a moment, his ears straining for the telltale sounds of Ruby snuffling and rustling around in the leaves. Nope, nothing. Where had the daft old girl got to?

He gave a low whistle and called out 'Rube!' At this point she'd usually emerge from the undergrowth, pleased to see him and wondering what the fuss was about. When she didn't, Charlie began to worry.

'Ruby!' he called again, louder this time. He jangled her lead and crinkled the bag of treats in his coat pocket.

Appealing to her appetite usually did the trick. Still she didn't appear. Charlie broke into a jog, first one way, then the other, calling her name and whistling as he did so. He tried slapping his thighs with both hands, the gesture that had beckoned Ruby since she was a puppy. Nothing.

Charlie noticed his heart rate was hammering. Blood rushed in his ears and around his head. His face felt flushed. He told himself not to get hysterical. There was a perfectly logical explanation and she'd be somewhere nearby. Any minute now, she'd waddle happily into view as if nothing had happened.

Half walking, half running, he searched in a widening circle. He parted bushes, circled trees and peered through foliage. Charlie was annoyed at himself. He hadn't been paying attention. While he had daydreamed, Ruby had got herself lost. Or, he thought with a sickening lurch of the stomach, she'd been taken.

He'd been trying not to think the worst. Now he entertained the possibility, Charlie somehow knew it was true. Panic flooded his body. Bullets of sweat sprang to his brow. His head began to spin. *Oh, Ruby*, his racing mind repeated over and over, *what have they done to you?*

48

Something Dog-Shaped

Charlie was getting frantic. Dogs got stolen sometimes, sure, but usually puppies, sought-after breeds or pricey pedigree pooches. An ageing Staffy was the canine equivalent of a rust-bucket car with flat tyres and a broken headlight. Hardly a magnet for thieves.

But of course Ruby wasn't just any dog. She was Charlie's dog, inseparably by his side. They'd both been sniffing around not one but two murders. She'd been specifically targeted because of Charlie. First her safety had been threatened via that doorstep toy. Now came the next escalation. Charlie hadn't heeded the warning and this was the result.

He told himself to slow down and stay methodical. He took some deep breaths, working out what to do. He'd start again. Walk a full circuit of the woods round the outer path, then move towards the centre, searching as he went. He'd keep whistling, keep calling her name, keep rattling the bag of treats. Ruby would turn up sooner or later. She had to, right?

If by some miracle she didn't, he'd move to phase two. He'd ring Tess and Polly. Keep it light, being careful not to panic Polly especially, and find out if Ruby had somehow come home or turned up at Coastal Coffee.

If the unthinkable happened and he still came up empty-handed, he'd call the police and local animal-rescue centres. Ruby was microchipped, as well as having Charlie's name and mobile number on her tag. If somebody found her, she'd be identified and returned to him. He latched on to this reassuring thought, trying to suppress his sense of foreboding.

He commenced his circumnavigation of the woods, seeking as he went and asking everybody he passed if they'd seen her. Most of the other dogwalkers knew Ruby. They expressed concern and assured him they'd keep an eye out. People were kind and keen to help. Right now, this wasn't much consolation. He just wanted to find her.

Charlie's sense of dread mounted with each fruitless minute. When he called Ruby's name, his voice sounded weak and wobbly to his ears. He tried to push panic from his mind and keep the faith.

As his circuits spiralled in towards the middle of the woods, Charlie realized that he was nearing the scene of Frank Courtney's murder. Right now, he'd swap today for that day in a heartbeat. Even Rough and Tumble's wig-based antics would be welcome relief. Ruby would be back by his side and all would be well with the world, even if it very much wasn't for poor old Frank.

A glimmer of optimism flickered in his mind and Charlie clung to it as he approached the exact spot. Ruby had been here before. Maybe something had led her back here. Or someone had.

He emerged into the familiar small circular clearing, his spirits lifting in expectation. His eyes immediately alighted on something dog-shaped but it was far smaller than what he'd hoped to see. Instead of Ruby, he found something else. Something that made his heart plunge down to his feet.

Against the base of the tree where he'd found Frank was another cuddly toy dog. Its nose was hacked off again. Only this time, Charlie saw with a jolt as he picked it up, its belly was slashed and spilling out stuffing. It was the same Ruby-resembling russet brown but this one was even more butchered.

Charlie's worst fears were confirmed. Somebody had taken Ruby and left this unmistakable message to taunt him. He felt like being sick again.

49

Here Come the Canine Cavalry

He'd only phoned Tess but the whole crew arrived in record time, complete with dogs. It was the canine cavalry. Charlie just prayed it wasn't too late for them to ride to the rescue.

Having closed Coastal Coffee – a rare event, which proved how seriously she was taking this – Tess was pulled along the path by Rough and Tumble, tugging at their leashes like tiny demented huskies. Malcolm walked behind with Ted, both looking somehow leisurely and chic, even though they were clearly hurrying too.

Bringing up the rear were Viv and Sue with a ragtag pack from Nuts About Mutts. Humphrey the endearingly loopy Labrador and dog-on-wheels the Professor were joined by various wire-haired terriers, snorting pugs and fluffy cross-breeds that Charlie vaguely recognized. In different circumstances, he would have laughed at the comical sight of them all. The Professor looked like Charles Xavier leading the X-Men into battle, even if the squad was a bit overstaffed with Wolverines. Seeing his fellow dogwalkers with their own furry friends just made him more anxious to find Ruby.

After giving Charlie a tight hug, Tess took charge. She was clearly alarmed too but hid it beneath brisk efficiency. Waving her arms around like she was directing traffic, Tess split the woods into three sections. She, Charlie, Rough and Tumble would search the first segment. Malcolm, Ted and half the other dogs would search the second. Sue, Viv and the remaining dogs would search the third.

Like Charlie, they'd ask any passers-by if they'd seen Ruby. They'd all keep their phones to hand in case they needed to communicate any sightings. Otherwise they'd rendezvous back at the entrance in half an hour. The hounds were their secret weapon, Tess promised Charlie. Either they'd sniff out Ruby or vice versa.

Malcolm, Viv and Sue gave him supportive squeezes of the arm before heading off. They were all dog lovers, all adored Ruby, and were all anxious too. They tried not to show it but their worried faces revealed the truth. Ruby's disappearance had rocked them all.

Keeping busy made Charlie feel useful, at least. As he and Tess methodically combed their section, she did her best to keep his morale up with a stream of optimistic chit-chat. When it became clear that Charlie was too preoccupied to respond, Tess got the message. They continued in companionable silence.

Charlie began to dread what they might find. If Ruby was still alive and in the woods somewhere, she'd surely have been found by now. He took the toy out of his coat pocket and looked at it again. Was it a warning of what might happen to her? Or a foreshadowing of what already had? He involuntarily pictured Ruby lying dead somewhere.

Charlie's chest tightened and he gulped for breath as if he was drowning.

Without saying a word, Tess came up from behind, took the hand holding the toy and gently guided it back into his pocket.

They carried on searching. Charlie looked at his phone every few minutes – it felt like that but might have been even more frequent – in case he'd missed a call or text. As much as he stared at the screen, willing it to light up with good news, none came.

Half an hour later, the search party met back at the entrance to the woods. Nothing much needed saying. As each group arrived, you could tell from their downcast expressions and regretful shakes of the head that they'd found nothing. Charlie was so downcast that he barely noticed that their number had been swelled.

'Look who we ran into,' said Malcolm. He gestured at the newcomer, a slightly shy-looking DS Craig Murdoch. Malcolm raised his eyebrows behind Murdoch's back as if to say, 'I know, right?'

'Hi, all,' said Murdoch. 'I was just passing through the woods and Malcolm told me what had happened. I'm sorry, Charlie. You must be worried sick.'

Charlie could barely bring himself to nod in agreement.

'We did our best but nothing, I'm afraid,' added Murdoch with a sorrowful sigh. It was as if he'd realized this was another investigation without any progress.

'Well, thanks for trying anyway,' said Tess, realizing that Charlie was too distracted to show much gratitude. Murdoch mumbled that it was no problem, wished them luck and went on his way.

'Oh, Rubes,' muttered Charlie, feeling like he might cry. 'Where are you?'

Tess put her hand on his arm. 'Do you reckon it's time to call home?' He looked back at her, feeling like a little boy. She nodded, answering for him.

Charlie walked away from the group and rang Polly. When she picked up the phone, her tone of voice was bright. For a brief moment Charlie thought it was going to be good news.

'Hi, Mum, it's Charlie,' he said, forcing his voice to sound as normal as possible.

'Hello, love,' said Polly, pleased to hear from him.

'Strange question, but I don't suppose Ruby has turned up at home, has she?' He closed his eyes and silently prayed. He wasn't even sure who to.

'Ruby?' she asked, suddenly bewildered. 'No, I . . . Why? Isn't she with you?'

'That's the thing, Mum,' Charlie said, struggling to sound jovial, like this was an amusing muddle they'd laugh about later. 'She wandered off in the woods and I can't find her. I was hoping she might have found her way home.'

'Oh no,' gasped Polly. Charlie could picture her hand going to her mouth. 'No, dear. I was just in the front garden and there was no sign of her.'

'Has anyone called round or phoned?'

'Nobody, love, apart from you.' Polly sounded upset.

Charlie's heart broke all over again. 'OK,' he said gently now. 'Try not to worry, Mum. I'm sure it's some kind of mix-up and she'll turn up soon.'

'This is awful,' said Polly, her voice wavering. 'Charlie, what should we do?'

'Put the kettle on, that's what you should do,' said Charlie decisively. 'I'll come straight home and be there by the time it's boiled.'

As he hung up, Charlie thought he heard a quiet sob at the other end of the line.

50

Famous Nostrils

He should have foreseen the effect this would have on Polly. After Charlie had said his hurried goodbyes in the woods and rushed straight home – Ruby's lead was still in his pocket, he realized, which made a breath catch in his throat – he arrived to find his mum pacing the house, wringing her hands with worry.

He and Ruby had become the twin cornerstones of Polly's life. The constants amid her growing confusion. No wonder she was sent into a tailspin by one of them suddenly being snatched away.

Comforting his mum at least took his mind off his own anxiety for a while. They had a long tearful hug in the hallway, before Charlie made a fresh pot of tea, sat Polly down at the kitchen table and held her hand.

'I'm sorry, love.' She sighed. 'Don't know what's come over me. I can't work out what to do with myself.'

'It's the shock,' he reassured her. 'I feel it too.'

'Poor Ruby,' said Polly, dabbing at her eyes with a hankie. 'What do you think has happened?'

'I honestly don't know, Mum,' he admitted. 'She's wandered off before, especially in the woods when she gets a scent in those famous nostrils.' Polly smiled, which was encouraging. 'But she normally turns up again within minutes. It's been a couple of hours now. We searched the woods from top to bottom. I'm pretty sure she's not there. She must have left the woods somehow. Or someone found her, thought she was lost or stray, and took her somewhere.'

'What do you mean?' asked Polly, confused. 'Where would they take her?'

'I guess the police station or a rescue centre,' said Charlie. 'Sue and Viv are ringing round for me. Ruby is microchipped and my phone number's on her collar, so they'll be able to get in touch.'

'Oh good,' said Polly vaguely. He sensed that she was too worried to listen to his words but hoped the steady tone of his voice would calm her.

'Or maybe a kind person has taken her home and will put up "dog found" posters. If they do, I'm sure we'll see them and have her home in no time.'

He couldn't bear to tell Polly about the latest threatening toy dog. Not yet, maybe not ever. It would terrify her. Charlie was torn between feeling protective and feeling guilty about giving her false hope.

'I hope so, Charlie, love, I really do,' she said, her voice trembling with emotion. 'I keep thinking about her big brown eyes and her putting her white paw on me when she wanted attention.'

They often joked that Ruby's paws looked like she was wearing white-lace gloves, like a demure lady in a period drama. With her aversion to mud and rain, they called her 'Princess Tippy-Toes' as she daintily skirted around puddles, as if reluctant to soil her pristine gloves.

'I know, Mum,' he said, squeezing her arm. 'I'm sure she'll be pawing you for attention again soon. Not to mention making you tut at muddy footprints on the tiles.'

'It's the not knowing that I can't stand,' said Polly. 'I must admit, it's taking me back to your father.'

'But Dad left, didn't he?' asked Charlie, his brow furrowing. 'He didn't disappear.'

Polly flapped her hands, flustered. 'Yes, yes, of course,' she said. 'I meant feeling the absence of him. Daydreaming about where he was and whether he was OK.'

Charlie looked at her, wondering if there was more to the story of his father's departure than he'd always been led to believe. His memories were so vague and the stories so euphemistic that it was like peering through the mist at a blurry figure.

Still, there was no point in dredging up the past now and upsetting Polly even more. Besides, he had Ruby to worry about. She was the priority. Her safety was everything.

'Come on,' he said, standing up. 'Let's take our minds off it by making supper. You never know, maybe the cooking smells will lure her home.'

Polly gave a brave smile and Charlie smiled back. But inside he felt like doing anything other than smiling.

51

Ghost Sightings,
Phantom Sounds

There didn't seem much more to be said, so they ate their supper in front of the TV as usual, both lost inside their worried minds. From muscle memory Charlie had knocked up one of his midweek staples – a veggie chilli with brown rice, part of his ongoing attempt to get five-a-day into Polly and keep her healthy. It wouldn't do him any harm either.

Without needing to say it aloud, they'd opted against their usual choice of a detective drama on TV. Deaths and disappearances were the last thing either of them wanted to watch tonight. Instead they whiled away an hour with a double bill of quiz shows. They called out the odd answer but their hearts weren't in it. Mother and son were both too distracted. Ruby would normally be curled up in her usual half-moon shape, like a fox in a garden, dozing happily. Without her, Charlie realized how much he relied on to her constant consoling presence.

He kept peering out of the window and looking at his phone. Every time the screen lit up, he leaped to grab it. It was invariably one of his fellow dogwalkers asking if there was any news. Even DS Murdoch checked in, which was good of him. Charlie knew everyone meant well but he soon wished they'd stop. The surges of hope, then typing the same replies, was becoming depressing.

Meanwhile, Polly fussed around, as if preparing for Ruby's grand homecoming. She washed her food and water bowls, then the bone-shaped mat they stood on. She rearranged the blankets in her basket several times. She kept leaning out of her armchair and looking around on the floor, as if Ruby was going to magically materialize. Watching his mother made Charlie's spirits sink.

Polly was keen to stay up with him but eventually Charlie persuaded her to get ready for bed. 'No point both of us waiting in the dark and making ourselves exhausted, Mum,' he said, straining to keep his tone jovial.

Polly went upstairs but he could hear her still pottering around. He decided to wash the dishes and clean up the kitchen to keep busy. Anything to stop him alternating between the window and his phone screen.

As he scrubbed away at the stock pot, trying to dislodge chunks of welded-on chilli from the base, Charlie suddenly stopped. He thought he'd heard something. This wasn't terribly surprising. Ever since Ruby had gone missing, he'd been driving himself mad with ghost sightings and phantom sounds. He kept thinking he'd glimpsed a brindle shape in the corner of the room or heard her collar tinkling against her food bowl as she ravenously gobbled her supper.

Charlie put the scouring sponge and saucepan down and listened. Polly was still moving around upstairs. Seagulls squawked in the distance. He heard a car door slam somewhere down the street. There was a hooting that might have been an owl. Just the noises of Framstone at night.

He sighed and picked up the sponge again, ready to resume scrubbing. But before he did so, he heard it again. A soft sound that could have been a bark. It might have been wishful thinking but it seemed to be coming from the front of the house.

He strode down the hall, trying not to get his hopes up, and took a deep breath before opening the door. This time, he didn't find a cuddly dog on the doormat. He found a real one.

'Rube!' he exclaimed in delight. Brown eyes shining in the moonlight, she wagged back. He'd never been more thrilled to see that familiar tail thwacking back and forth. As he bent down to greet her, Charlie got an enthusiastic face-licking in response. He hugged her tight, feeling the warmth of her body and her grunting breath in his ear. It felt like coming home – for both of them.

Realizing they were out in the bitter night air, Charlie stood up and stepped aside, allowing Ruby to trot over the threshold and him to close the door. 'Welcome home, gorgeous,' he said, grinning. Now she was in the warm light of the house, he looked her over. She seemed healthy, happy and was back safely where she belonged. Regardless of how she got there, that was all that mattered.

Charlie was elated with relief yet somewhere at the back of his mind, a desire for answers remained. Whoever had taken Ruby was still out there. And he wouldn't rest until he knew who.

52

Never Again, Lady

'What's all this fuss?' he heard Polly call out. 'Is it who I hope it is?'

Alerted by the sound of the front door closing, she hurried downstairs in her nightwear to find Charlie and Ruby still clutched in a joyous mess on the hall floor.

'Darling girl!' she cried out. Ruby writhed out of Charlie's arms, loped over and buried her face in the folds of Polly's dressing gown, her tail wagging so hard it looked like it might fly off. As they embraced, Polly looked up at Charlie, her eyes moist and smile beaming. Like him, she was experiencing a heady cocktail of joy and relief. Hopefully without the hunger for revenge that lurked beneath.

'I'll pop the kettle on,' said Charlie, giving them both a loving pat as he headed for the kitchen. The roller coaster of emotion meant they weren't likely to sleep for an hour or two at least. Might as well get cosy and savour having Ruby back where she belonged. As he made yet another pot of tea, he typed a quick text to the dogwalkers group chat, sharing the good news of Ruby's return. Their rejoicing replies showed they were almost as relieved as he was.

Once they were settled on the sofa with steaming mugs,

Ruby – allowed to sit up on the squishy cushions with them as a special treat – flumped contentedly in the middle, alternating her head between their laps as if being scrupulously fair to both her humans.

Polly turned to Charlie. 'I can't tell you how pleased I am to have her back,' she said.

'Me too, Mum, me too,' he said, giving Ruby's ears a ruffle. 'Never do that to us again, lady, do you hear?'

'What do you think happened?' asked Polly.

Charlie still thought it best not to mention the toy dog and his fears that Ruby had been taken as a warning. Polly wouldn't sleep if she knew.

'I reckon she wandered off in the woods like we thought,' he fibbed. 'Maybe found her own way out or fell asleep somewhere we couldn't see her.'

'And how did you find your way home, clever girl?' asked Polly, addressing the question to the now dozing Ruby.

'I guess that sense of smell came in handy,' said Charlie. 'It's her superpower. She knows her way around town by scent, so could presumably retrace her steps using her nose. You see stories like that in the news sometimes, don't you?'

Polly seemed suitably convinced. 'All the excitement has fair worn me out,' she said, giving Ruby a last stroke. 'I think I'll go up. I'll have much sweeter dreams knowing she's safe and sound. Night-night, you two.' She kissed them both gently on the head as she went.

As Charlie sat with Ruby a bit longer, finishing his tea and enjoying the reassuring sound of her snoring next to him, he'd almost convinced himself there had been nothing unusual about her disappearance, too. Ruby wandering off and getting lost sounded all too plausible. So did sniffing her way home. Maybe the toy in the woods was merely a coincidence.

Delirious with sudden exhaustion, that's what Charlie told himself anyway. He stood up, stretched and yawned. 'You've worn us both out, Rube,' he said.

She rolled over on the sofa and looked at him through half-asleep eyes, relishing a rare chance to make herself comfortable on the sofa. 'You stay there tonight if you want,' added Charlie. 'Just don't get used to it. Back in your basket tomorrow, OK?'

Picking up the empty mugs, he padded around and switched off the two standard lamps in the sitting room. But as he turned for the door, Charlie let out an involuntary gasp. Ruby was glowing in the dark.

At least, part of her was. Using phosphorescent paint or marker pen, someone had crudely circled her nose and drawn a dotted line down her belly. Charlie realized with a shudder that the markings were an exact recreation of the slits in the toy he'd found in the woods.

Ruby going missing *had* been a message after all. Not only had someone dognapped her but they'd returned her home with an unmistakable visual vow that she wouldn't be unharmed next time. Charlie stood in the darkness, his mind spiralling, staring at his snoring dog in horror.

53

Literally Close to Home

The Coastal Coffee crew were in giddy mood, hailing Ruby like the homecoming queen that she was. She seemed bemused by all the fuss but wasn't complaining about the extra treats – especially when Tess busted out the peanut-butter dog biscuits in celebration.

'You must be more relieved than the Framstone relief road,' said Tess as the dogs munched away happily under the table.

'Of course,' said Charlie. 'But also seriously spooked.'

He filled everyone in about Polly's dog-induced discombobulation, Ruby's late-night reappearance on the doorstep and what he'd seen when he turned off the lights.

He'd stayed up an extra hour after the sinister discovery, gently washing Ruby with soapy water in a bid to remove the markings before Polly saw them. It was small consolation but since they were only visible in the dark, he could finish the job later today. As Ruby had rolled and wriggled, thinking it was some fun new snout-fondling and tummy-tickling game, he hadn't managed to remove every trace.

'OMFG,' said Malcolm, setting down his coffee cup, aghast. 'If you'll excuse my F. What a sick stunt to pull.'

'I'll never understand people being cruel to dogs,' added Sue. 'Or forgive it.'

'I know, right?' said Charlie. 'Poor Rube must've wondered what the hell was going on. Lured out of the woods somehow, kept who-knows-where for a few hours, daubed with glowing paint, then dropped off home in the dead of night.'

'At least she's happy and unharmed,' said Tess, fondly watching Ruby compete good-naturedly with Rough and Tumble for the last few biscuit crumbs. 'Let's count our blessings. It could have been much worse.'

'True,' admitted Charlie. 'But it's certainly made me think.'

'And what do you think, Charlie?' asked Viv. 'About potential culprits, I mean. Methods and motivations.'

Charlie sighed and rubbed his bleary eyes. He'd been through the wringer in the last twenty-four hours. 'To be honest, I haven't been able to process it very logically. But I reckon the message is pretty clear.'

'And the message is?' asked Malcolm.

'It's another warning to mind my own business,' said Charlie. 'Only this time, a much more serious one.'

'Presumably it was someone who knows Ruby, at least by sight,' said Viv. 'Someone who knew how to tempt her into going off with them happily.'

'Someone who knew how much Charlie adored her and how to hurt the most,' added Malcolm.

Charlie had thought much the same but was disquieted to hear it said out loud. Danger suddenly seemed nearer than ever.

'And someone who knew the exact site of Frank's murder,' added Tess.

'Probably because they did it,' said Viv.

'Girls, girls, I'm not sure Charlie's in the sleuthing mood,' said Sue, putting down her knitting and laying her hand over his. 'Are you OK, mate? It must have shaken you up – first Ruby going missing, then this business with the markings.'

Charlie smiled at her, glad of some respite from the theorizing. 'It has wobbled me, Sue, I must admit,' he said quietly. 'It's all getting a bit too close to home for my liking.'

'Literally close to home.' Tess nodded. 'Sorry, partner.'

'That's OK,' he said. 'But I've decided it's time I heeded the warnings. Back to the quiet life for me, I think. No more investigations or enquiries. From now on, I'm leaving all that to the police. I quit.'

Everyone was stunned into silence, even the dogs.

54

Handing in His Badge

'Sorry for rattling on,' said Viv, breaking the tense silence. 'I momentarily forgot that it wasn't just a puzzle to work out and there were people at the centre of it. Let alone people I care about.'

'Me too,' chorused Tess and Malcolm, with matching contrite faces.

'Honestly, it's fine,' said Charlie. 'But Sue's spot on, as usual. I'm not in the sleuthing mood. Frankly I can't see myself being in the mood anytime soon.'

'You've had a couple of terrible shocks,' said Malcolm gently. 'No wonder you've lost the stomach for it today. But let's not be too hasty.'

'He's right,' added Viv. 'We shouldn't give up just as we're getting somewhere.'

'I've got to think about Mum and Ruby,' said Charlie. 'Their safety comes first. Ruby's been snatched and threatened. Twice they've come to my mum's doorstep. It's far too close for comfort. I'd never forgive myself if anything happened to them because of me blundering about, thinking I'm Father Brown.'

'Father Ted, more like,' said Tess, unable to resist a wise-crack even now.

'Making threats and silencing people,' said Malcolm. 'That's how bullies operate. You can't let them win.'

'Yes, actually I can,' replied Charlie. He realized Malcolm was likely speaking from experience but Charlie stuck to his guns. 'On this occasion anyway. Sorry, but my mind's made up. Carry on investigating if you want, obviously, but I'm afraid it'll be without me.'

'OK,' said Tess reluctantly. 'We understand. We'll keep you abreast of any developments and –'

Charlie interrupted her. 'No need, honestly. It's not my business any more. Now if you'll excuse us, me and Ruby are off to get some fresh air. Take care, everyone.' He peeked beneath the table and grinned. 'And you, dogs. See you around.'

After he left Coastal, the remaining dogwalkers looked at each other, unsure what to do or say. Not only had the investigation and near daily debriefs over coffee brought the four of them even closer together, it had cemented Charlie's place as the latest member of the crew. They weren't just losing their natural leader. They were losing their new friend.

Eventually Viv broke the silence again. 'Well, what do we think? Give up too or keep going?'

'Keep going,' said Malcolm firmly. 'For Charlie, Polly and Ruby, if nothing else.'

'And for poor Shane too,' added Sue.

'So that's decided, team,' said Tess. 'I'll get us a refill, then we can discuss how to proceed without Charlie.'

By the time she came back with a fresh round of coffees, a consensus had already been reached.

'We've conferred and we're all in agreement,' said Malcolm

as Tess handed him his espresso. 'You're the obvious choice to take the lead in Charlie's absence. Even the dogs think so.'

'Not least because you've been his closest confidante,' added Viv. 'If that's OK with you, of course.'

Tess nodded, not-so-secretly flattered. 'Sure. Hopefully it's only on a temporary basis. Just until Charlie's back to being his usual annoying self.'

'I'll say it this time –' Sue smiled over her knitting – 'so that's decided, team.'

'What next, new leader?' asked Malcolm.

'I've been thinking about Rob Thompson,' said Tess. 'Ruby was dognapped shortly after he came out of hospital and got back on his feet.'

'And soon after the two of you asked him about possible police corruption at the pub,' said Viv. 'You're right, Tess. It could be too convenient to be coincidence.'

'Also, you know how we've been focusing on Frank Courtney's money?' Tess continued, clearly warming to her new role. 'Well, Rob's finances don't add up either. How come he can afford so many benders on a police salary? It's not like he's some high-flying plain-clothes detective.'

'Unlike his wife,' said Malcolm. 'Anjali is higher up in the force, so presumably on more money. Yet it's Rob who seems to be the big spender. Anjali doesn't seem the type who'd let her husband waste her hard-earned wages on booze.'

'You think he could be in debt?' asked Sue. 'Or bent and taking backhanders?'

'It's worth considering,' said Tess. 'Or maybe the Neptune gives him free drinks in return for services rendered. Shady services.'

'I like it,' said Viv, who always enjoyed a conspiracy theory.

'Why does he hit the bottle so hard anyway?' asked Tess. 'We've never got to the bottom of that. Maybe he's feeling guilty about something.'

'Sounds like we should do some digging into the suspicious Sarge,' said Malcolm. 'His drinking, his money and just how dodgy he might be.'

'Exactly,' said Tess. 'I also think we should meet for two daily debriefs from now on, not just one. Maybe at the start and end of each day?'

They all made positive noises. A good gossip over complimentary coffees wasn't much of a hardship.

'Oh, and one last suggestion,' added Tess as the others got ready to leave. 'Let's all promise to keep an eye on Charlie, yeah? Polly and Ruby, too. I've never seen him this shaken up. It's all become a bit personal. The more of us watching his back, the better.'

Viv, Sue and Malcolm nodded in agreement. Charlie might have handed in his gun and his badge, metaphorically speaking, but he was still their friend. And the best way of proving their friendship would be to bring the culprit to justice. It was down to them now.

55

Downright Dangerous

He wasn't sure he could bear the woods. Not yet anyway. Charlie and Ruby took a walk along the beach instead, refreshing his senses by inhaling the briny smell of seawater and washed-up kelp.

As he tramped across the pebbles at Ruby's pace – she snuffled at every glistening stone or piece of seaweed, interspersed with tentatively getting her paws wet like the dainty dowager she was – Charlie had plenty of time to think.

He was convinced he'd done the right thing. Apart from his unfortunate habit of finding dead bodies, he had no business sticking his beak into the two murder inquiries. It was becoming downright dangerous to do so. Whoever was responsible for the killings clearly knew Charlie was getting involved in the investigation – and they didn't like it one bit.

They also knew where he lived, where he walked Ruby and how to seriously scare him. It was time to leave police work to the professionals before somebody he loved got hurt.

He would miss it, though. He already was missing it, truth be told. The case had given him purpose, something to occupy his mind on dog walks and while trying to drum up design work. It had made him feel like part of a proper gang for the first time in years. Without anything to investigate, Charlie already felt listless and aimless. He caught himself daydreaming about what the others were up to.

Charlie also pondered what had happened to his home town. For as long as he could remember, Framstone had been a quiet place. Nothing much happened here, just the waves washing in and out as the locals went about their business. Now that was changing. Framstone was enjoying something of an overdue resurgence. People were moving in, rather than moving out. Had that brought a crimewave in its wake? There were two unsolved murders, one violent attack and a vandalized shop window. Drugs were being smuggled ashore and sold around town. Shady figures were lurking in the woods. And now these threats.

No wonder there was palpable tension. After years of slumber, the peace had been disturbed by an ominous hum. The streets seemed emptier and more fearful, especially late at night. People were startled by noises and looked suspiciously at strangers. They seemed to expect bad news now, not good. It was like the darkness of urban life was somehow spreading to the provinces.

Charlie was still mulling over this as he and Ruby headed home. 'Hi, Mum, only us!' he called as they came through the front door. As she trotted off happily down the hall, he was reminded of the sheer relief of having Ruby home.

'Hello, loves!' responded Polly, her voice carrying from the kitchen. 'A letter came for you, Charlie. Handwritten envelope by the looks of it. I found it on the doormat. And no stamp, so it must have been personally delivered. It's on the hall table.'

Her voice was matter-of-fact but Charlie was immediately

on edge. Handwritten and hand-delivered would once have felt full of romantic intrigue. Now it sounded sinister. The last thing he needed was more trouble arriving on their doorstep.

He picked up the envelope and turned it over in his hands. *To Charlie Boardman* was all it said in black ink. The pen strokes were slightly shaky. Perhaps the sender had tried to disguise their handwriting.

Charlie realized his fingers were trembling. Not another warning. He'd already backed off but maybe it was too soon for the message to have got through.

He took a deep breath and opened it. He was fully expecting some sort of hate mail or menacing message. Instead what he found inside was an invitation to Shane Carter's funeral.

Charlie exhaled with relief. He'd never been so happy to receive something so sad.

56

You're Nicked, Son

The last time Charlie had worn his suit had been at Frank Courtney's wake a fortnight ago. This was getting to be an unfortunate habit. *I'd better wear it for a wedding or some other happy event soon*, he thought, *otherwise it will become my death uniform, like a Mafia widow's black veil.*

He fished it out of the wardrobe to check it wouldn't need dry-cleaning before Shane's funeral in two days' time. As he did so, Charlie could hear Tess's voice mocking him for only owning one smart suit. Weddings, funerals, bar mitzvahs, court appearances. This one did the lot.

Apart from the odd bit of fluff or strand of hair – a couple of Tess's and a single blonde one, presumably from Jackie – the suit looked fine for another outing. As Charlie brushed it down, he felt something stiff in the inside jacket pocket. It was the order of service from Frank's send-off, which he'd picked up in the Neptune and pocketed, doubtless on Detective Tess's instructions.

He sat down on the bed to read it. It had been dark by the time they left the pub, so he hadn't looked at it properly.

He smiled at himself for instinctively judging its typefaces and layout but it was nicely done. Classy white card, simple black font. Not as stylishly designed as he would have done, of course, but not a bad job. The usual mix of church service terminology – *rites, liturgy, committal, homily* and so on – alongside more personal readings, poems and hymn lyrics.

At the back were a few pages of photographs from throughout Frank's life. A nice touch. A reminder of the man's life, rather than his death. Charlie absent-mindedly studied them. There he was marrying Jackie in quintessentially seventies outfits. A moustachioed Frank wore a suit with big lapels, a paisley tie and flared trousers. Jackie looked every inch the glamour puss with beehive hair and a white-lace gown.

There he was, arms round his wife and three children in a soft-focus family portrait. There he was, posing with the youth football teams and boxing clubs he coached – teenage lads with their benevolent mentor and the cup they'd just won. And there he was, standing proudly outside the Neptune – presumably on the day he took over as licensee. The pub looked far scruffier than it did today. Amazing what a difference a bit of money and a lick of paint could make.

Among the other snaps of charity functions, sporting events and foreign holidays, one black-and-white pic caught Charlie's eye. A group of men were having celebratory drinks in a pub. It might even have been a pre-gentrified Neptune. Judging by Frank's age in the pic and what might have been uniformed officers in their shirt sleeves at the bar behind, it must have been a Framstone Police night out – perhaps toasting a colleague's promotion or retirement.

The details were so dated, it was like a time capsule. Pints in dimpled glasses and crystal tumblers of whisky littered the tables. Smoking seemed virtually compulsory. Swirly carpets, a vinyl jukebox and long defunct beer adverts made it resemble a retro cop drama. You could almost hear them bellowing 'You're nicked, son!' There wasn't a single woman in the shot. This was a time before female officers became commonplace, especially in Framstone. He could imagine Anjali rolling her eyes at the sheer patriarchy of it all.

Charlie's eyes slid over the men's faces. There was Frank at the front. A proper man's man, out with the lads, in his element. Charlie didn't recognize any of the others, he didn't think, although it was hard to tell under all the perms, mullets and facial fuzz.

Wait, was that a young Rob Thompson next to Frank? He was partially turned away from the camera, seemingly laughing at a joke. He looked fresh-faced with carefully coiffed collar-length hair. Very different to now (blame age and booze), but, yes, it was definitely him. Frank's right arm was hardly visible but now Charlie looked closely it was flung warmly round Rob's shoulder.

It appeared that Rob Thompson and Frank Courtney were much closer colleagues than Rob had claimed. Despite himself, Charlie was getting drawn in again. Why did Rob lie? What exactly did he have to hide?

57

Bang Bang

For a horrible moment Charlie thought another missile had been thrown through another window. Startled awake by a loud bang, he sprang out of bed, all senses firing, before he knew where he was and what was happening.

A beat later, he realized with relief he was in his bedroom at home. It also dawned on Charlie that the bang which had rudely awakened him wasn't an isolated noise. Another came, then another. No missiles this time. It was someone thumping on the front door, loudly and insistently. Even a little rudely.

He'd been deep in slumber, dreaming about sepia-tinted policemen, so maybe they'd been knocking a while. He hoped the racket hadn't frightened poor Polly. Talking of whom, where was his mum and why hadn't she answered the door already?

With relief he remembered Polly saying she had a doctor's appointment first thing this morning. 'Just a check-up,' she assured Charlie when he'd looked worried. 'You get them every few months at my age. Enjoy your youth while you can, son. Before you know it, medical stuff will be the main thing in your diary.'

Bristling slightly, Charlie pulled on jeans and a T-shirt, then hurried downstairs to see what the fuss was about. Ruby was standing in the hall, her head tilted and one ear up, clearly wondering the same.

As he opened the front door, it seemed to take DS Craig Murdoch by surprise. He was just bringing his hand forward to bang again. When there was suddenly no door there, his arm flopped forward in almost farcical fashion and he briefly lost his balance.

'Aha, there you are,' said Murdoch sheepishly.

'About time,' added DI Anjali Thompson, one eyebrow arching in amusement. 'We guessed you were still in bed. Not even Craig's best copper's knock could rouse you from your beauty sleep.'

'Well, it did eventually,' mumbled Charlie. Now it was his turn to be embarrassed. 'Gave me a bit of a fright, to be honest. But now I'm here, how can I help?'

In unison, as if they'd been rehearsing, both detectives' faces rearranged themselves into serious expressions.

'We have a few questions to ask you actually,' said Anjali in an official tone. 'If you'd like to accompany us to the station?'

Charlie almost laughed at how preposterously clichéd this sounded but managed to stop himself in time. As he did so, a thought popped fully formed into his half-asleep brain: *Hang on, am I being arrested?*

58

Criminal Brief on Speed Dial

The police station corridors smelled of industrial bleach with a top note of stale vomit, like someone had recently mopped up a puddle of sick. Strip lighting lent everyone a harsh, unhealthy pallor. Plastic chairs were slightly too small to be comfortable. It all reminded Charlie of school.

He was tempted to remark upon this to Anjali, his fellow Framstone High alumnus, but figured this wasn't the appropriate time for nostalgic whimsy. He was too busy trying to stay calm and not get carried away by his galloping mind.

Besides, Anjali was subtly different inside the station, Charlie noticed. She projected an air of steely authority. A don't-mess-with-me toughness. He imagined that she'd had to develop this protective shell in such an unreconstructed workplace. His mind returned to that female-free photo of a police function. Talk about a sausage party.

After having his fingerprints and a DNA swab taken – all routine, all voluntary, Charlie was assured by DS Murdoch – he was allowed a phone call. His immediate instinct was to ring Polly, who would likely be back from the GP's surgery by now, but that would only send her into a flap. Then he realized exactly who he should call.

'I'm a bit out of practice and rarely practised criminal law,' said Malcolm down the phone. 'Employment, property and divorce were more my fields. But, of course, lovely boy, happy to help. Better it's me than some dozy duty solicitor. In fact, it would be an honour.'

By the time he arrived at the station, Malcolm properly looked the part. He'd swapped his usual chore jacket for something more suity and had enjoyed a rare opportunity to raid his tie collection. Charlie hoped this didn't make him look like a hardened crook with his 'brief' on speed dial.

'Thanks for this, Malcs.' He smiled ruefully. 'It's all a bit surreal, but you seemed like the man for the job.'

'Not at all,' replied Malcolm smoothly, already shifting into professional mode. He turned to the bemused Anjali and Murdoch. 'I'll be representing Mr Boardman,' he told them. 'If I can consult in private with my client, we'll be with you shortly.'

In a soulless side room, Malcolm promised Charlie they could laugh about this later but the first priority was to get him through the interview and out of there. He advised Charlie to answer their questions truthfully but as briefly as possible.

'Rambling on with extraneous detail is where people tend to trip themselves up,' he said with a worldly wise tap of the nose. 'They get nervous and talk themselves into trouble. Remember, it's just a formality. They've already got your statement from both crime scenes. This is probably a matter of getting your account formally on record and making sure it's consistent. If it was more serious, they'd have arrested you. Instead you're here on a voluntary basis. It's a fishing expedition because they don't have many proper suspects.'

They both thought it was best not to mention that one of the prime suspects, to the dogwalkers' minds at least, happened to be the lead detective's husband.

So reassuring was Malcolm's presence at Charlie's side that by the time they sat down in the interview suite, he felt strangely calm. Even having his rights read to him under caution and the ominous beep of the recording device, all so familiar from cop shows, didn't put him on edge. Charlie felt detached somehow, like he was watching himself on TV.

They eased him in gently with questions confirming his name, address and occupation before gradually focusing on the recent crimes. First they got him to retell the stories about finding Frank Courtney's and Shane Carter's bodies.

'I've already told you all this,' Charlie reminded Anjali.

Murdoch fielded that one. 'Just one more time, please, for the recording.'

They made a point of double-checking Charlie's whereabouts the night before both discoveries, zoning in on the windows of time when the murders took place. Both times, Charlie's answer was the same. He was at home with Polly and Ruby, like he was most nights. He sounded a bit boring, he realized. Malcolm didn't have to intervene much. It was all factual stuff.

They grilled him about the night of the attack on Sergeant Rob Thompson. Anjali was in official mode and didn't acknowledge in any way that he was her husband. Again, Charlie explained that he'd been at home that night. Forget 'a bit boring', he'd now moved into the 'deeply dull' category.

Then things got trickier. With Murdoch leading the questioning, they probed his relationship with both victims. Charlie had nothing to hide but still felt himself tensing up.

'I didn't have a relationship with Frank,' said Charlie. 'The first time I ever clapped eyes on him was that day when I found him in the woods.'

'You'd never been in the Neptune pub?' asked Murdoch, holding his gaze. 'Not seen Mr Courtney and –' he checked a file in front of him – 'his bulldog Bobby out on walks?'

'Nope,' said Charlie.

Murdoch turned and looked at Anjali, as if they didn't believe him, but they moved on to Shane. Anjali sat forward now, suddenly more interested. Charlie inferred from this that Shane was still prime suspect for Frank's murder, regardless of his own subsequent death.

'I met Shane twice, I think,' said Charlie. 'Ran into him on walks a couple of times. He was a real dog lover and always made a big fuss of Ruby. Nice lad.'

More exchanged looks. Malcolm noticed and didn't like it. 'Where are you going with this?' he asked politely but firmly. 'My client has found two bodies, yes, but he reported both immediately. Since then he has cooperated fully with your enquiries.'

Murdoch acknowledged this with an inscrutable nod, before turning back to Charlie. 'It's just that as a relative newcomer to the community –' Anjali gave Charlie an almost imperceptible smile, acknowledging the irony – 'you'd already be a person of interest. Throw in the fact that you discovered both murder victims and it would be remiss of us not to ask questions.'

Here we go, Charlie thought. *Now they're getting to it*. He swallowed and bit the inside of his lower lip. He didn't think either detective had noticed but it still made him self-conscious.

'Sure,' said Charlie. 'I get that. I do seem to have a knack for finding corpses, but, trust me, it's a knack I'd rather not have.'

'Just keep finding yourself in the wrong place at the wrong time?' said Murdoch as if he sympathized.

'It seems so,' said Charlie.

'You only arrived in town last summer, is that correct?' asked Murdoch.

'That's right,' said Charlie, nodding.

'What brought you back here?'

'My mum mainly,' said Charlie. 'She was getting doddery and forgetful. Needed keeping an eye on. And I was ready to leave London anyway.'

'Why was that?' asked Murdoch. 'Much more exciting than sleepy old Framstone, isn't it?'

Charlie smiled. 'A bit too exciting sometimes, I'd say.'

'Were there specific reasons why you left?' pressed Murdoch.

Charlie thought of something his mum had said. 'Oh, you know,' he repeated. 'Women, money, the usual.'

In unison, like before, Anjali and Murdoch both raised an eyebrow.

'Exactly how is all this relevant?' butted in Malcolm. It seemed a reasonable question.

'Just trying to get a rounded picture,' said Murdoch, looking appraisingly at Charlie. 'Let's move on. Do you have any idea how many murdered bodies are reported to the police by the perpetrator, Charlie?'

Malcolm started to object again but not before Charlie

could say, 'No, I don't.' He fidgeted in his seat and immediately regretted it.

'Well, it's a lot,' said Murdoch. 'I guess they think that it
will make them look innocent.'

'Except I actually am innocent,' said Charlie.

He was rattled now but still self-aware enough to realize
this was exactly what Murdoch wanted. Charlie took a breath
and glanced at Malcolm.

'I think that's a good place to stop, don't you?' said Malcolm
in a business-like tone. 'I assume you've asked everything
you wanted to ask?'

'For now,' said Murdoch in that unreadable manner. 'Thanks
for your cooperation, Mr Boardman.' Anjali gave him a nod
and Murdoch switched off the recording device. Charlie
tried not to show how relieved he was. Something about all
this was making him feel guilty for things he hadn't done.

Anjali said goodbye but stayed seated, poring over her
files, leaving it to the junior officer to show them out of the
interview suite and back to reception. Now the tape wasn't
running and his boss wasn't present, Murdoch was suddenly
charm personified, ushering them through doors and making
polite small talk.

'No hard feelings, I hope?' he said to Charlie with a
sheepish smile.

'Not at all,' replied Charlie. 'You're just doing your jobs.
I only hope it was helpful. I want this killer caught as much
as you do.'

'Say hello to your mum for me,' said Murdoch with a
smile. 'Tell her that applications for *The Great British Bake
Off* are still open.'

Charlie smiled back – both at Murdoch's clear fondness

for Polly and the prospect of her and Ruby waiting for him at home. 'I'll pass it on,' he said.

As he and Malcolm pushed through the swing doors into the fresh air, he was grateful to escape the pervading smell of bleach. Walking across the car park, Charlie was certain of two things. He did indeed want to catch the killer as much as the police did. He was also baffled why Rob Thompson wasn't on their radar for both murders. Was Anjali too blinded by loyalty to see it?

59

Someone So Young

Polly insisted on coming to the funeral the next day. 'I want to, love,' she told Charlie firmly. 'I helped bring Shane into this world. It feels only right to say goodbye as he leaves it, God rest his soul.'

She'd been through a lot recently but there was no arguing with her. Polly had as much right to attend as he did, maybe more. Charlie worried it might be too much for her, but in light of recent events he was also feeling protective. Keeping Polly by his side was a way of ensuring her safety. So it was that mother and son stood in the hallway that morning, checking their reflections in the mirror before leaving. Polly tutted and adjusted Charlie's collar and tie, propelling him right back to childhood. She'd done the same most mornings before he left for school.

The funeral was a far more modest affair than Frank's. Rather than at the old church in the centre of Framstone, it took place at a slightly soulless modern one on the outskirts of town. There was no posh printed order of service for Shane, just a flimsy sheet of A4 paper with hymn lyrics printed on it. Rather than at a packed pub, the wake would be held at a shabby-looking hall opposite the church.

Charlie and Polly slipped quietly into the service and took seats near the back of the sparse congregation. There couldn't have been more than twenty people in attendance. This only made it more poignant. Charlie was soon passing his sniffly mum tissues, while a bored-looking priest went through the motions. His eulogy didn't feel remotely personal. You could tell he hadn't known Shane at all.

Up ahead on the front row, Charlie recognized Shane's mother Karen from the police cordon at the beach. She'd been inconsolable then and still looked that way today. Her shoulders shook throughout the service. Every now and again came a heart-rending sob.

When the priest asked 'the mother of the deceased' (*How sensitive of him*, thought Charlie) to come up and say a few words, Karen tottered up the steps, clutching a piece of pastel-coloured notepaper in her trembling hand. When she opened her mouth to speak, a grief-stricken keening noise came out instead. It was painful to witness. As she wept, she shook her head apologetically at the front row. Someone hurried over and led her back to her seat.

It was over mercifully quickly. Charlie slowly led Polly out of the church. She held on to his arm with one hand, dabbing at her eyes with the other.

Glad of the fresh air, he turned to his mother. 'Well, that was tough.' He sighed heavily. Down the road, he spotted Anjali and Murdoch in their unmarked car, maintaining a discreet distance but keeping an eye on proceedings, just like at Frank's wake. He was somehow pleased that Shane got the same police treatment.

Polly nodded. 'I know. The older you get, the more used to funerals you become, but that was a particularly sad one.

It's always awful when it's someone so young, let alone with such a low turnout. I wish he'd been more loved.'

Charlie turned to head home but realized that Polly wasn't moving. Instead she was watching the paltry congregation sombrely make their way across the road to the wake.

'I didn't think you'd want to intrude,' he said. 'Come on, let's get you home.'

Polly had that determined expression again. 'No, I'd like to pay my respects,' she said. 'And perhaps have a quick word with poor Karen if she's up to it.'

Her mind was made up. Charlie sighed, loosened his tie and held out his arm again.

60

Bad People, Bad Things

The hall was the sort of place where jumble sales and AA meetings took place, with stackable chairs and an ancient tea urn. They helped themselves to a cup each. Charlie stirred two sugars into his, thinking he might need it. There was a platter of sandwiches too but they were still covered in cling film and nobody wanted to be the first one to peel it off.

Karen Carter seemed more together now she was out of the church. The sight of Shane's coffin wouldn't have helped. She stood in the centre of the room while people came up, murmured a few words, then hugged her or patted her arm. It was like the tragic equivalent of a wedding line-up.

Charlie and Polly waited their turn. With so few people in attendance, it didn't take long. Karen turned to them as they approached. You could still see the schoolgirl in her delicate, doll-like features, but her face also showed signs of a hard life. She looked bone-tired, with eyes sore and red from crying.

'Hello, Karen,' said Polly gently. 'Polly Boardman, I'm not sure if you . . .'

'Of course I remember,' said Karen, attempting a smile.

'You were so kind to me when Shane . . .' She tailed off, as if the memory was too much to bear.

'I'm truly sorry for your loss,' said Polly, reaching out and holding her hand. 'You've been in my thoughts since we heard. I can't begin to imagine how you feel.'

'Thank you, Polly,' she said, glancing at Charlie. 'It's been hard, I won't lie. No mother should have to bury her child.'

'Oh, Karen, I know,' said Polly. 'Sorry, how rude of me. This is my son, Charlie.'

'Hello, Karen,' said Charlie. 'I'm so sorry. Shane was a lovely lad.'

'He was.' Karen nodded proudly. 'And I must thank you too, Charlie. I understand you're the one who found him . . .' She tailed off again before collecting herself. 'Shane said you'd chatted a few times. He mentioned your beautiful pooch and how nice to him you were. That means a lot, especially now.'

'Well, it's no more than he deserved,' said Charlie. 'I just can't believe what happened.'

'I know,' said Karen, sniffing. 'I blame myself for a lot of it.'

'Karen, you mustn't,' said Polly, squeezing her hand. 'You've got nothing to feel guilty about.'

'Not about his death,' replied Karen. 'I mean for Shane's start in life. I was only fifteen when I fell pregnant, as you know. I was in no position to be a good parent, not on my own. I named him after the bloke from Westlife, for goodness' sake.' She gave a short laugh. 'Looking back, I made some bad decisions, but it still broke me when my little boy was taken away.'

'It must have been very difficult,' said Polly, nodding. 'But social services thought it was for the best at the time.'

'I know,' said Karen, nodding. 'I'm just not sure it was.

Not for Shane. Getting taken into care . . . It didn't care for him, if you know what I mean. I let other people raise my boy and they weren't always good people. He met some bad characters, learned some bad things.' Her chin suddenly wobbled. 'And I'm pretty sure he was . . . well, abused.'

She glanced around to check nobody else could hear. She didn't want to start any gossip, not today, but Karen was clearly in turmoil. 'Sorry, I just needed to say it. It's horrible but it's been on my mind . . .'

'Oh no, how awful,' said Polly, her brow furrowing with concern. 'Do you know what happened?'

Karen sighed again. 'Not in any detail. Just from certain things he said. Hints he dropped. Shane came to stay with me when he was in and out of care but he always clammed up if I asked about what he'd been through. He'd freeze and go all distant. Whatever happened, it changed him. My Shane was never quite the same. First I lost him to the care system, then I lost him to a life of crime.' Her hand flew to her mouth and her voice went all fluttery. 'Now I've lost him full stop.'

As Polly comforted Karen, Charlie wondered whether her suspicions were correct. He feared they might well be. Shane had seemed damaged somehow. A predator might see that too and take advantage. Abuse tended to thrive in the hidden corners of society. The care system, sadly, was one of those.

'I've seen too many young people get on that path,' said Polly, reaching out to rub Karen's arm. 'It's hard to get them off it again.'

'You know he once thought about going into social work?' said Karen. 'Inspired by people like you, Polly. People who liked to help. Or working with animals. That was his dream.'

'Our dog Ruby adored him,' said Charlie, smiling. 'Shane was great with animals.'

'He always was,' said Karen. 'I encouraged him to volunteer, but after a while it was hard to get him interested in anything but drink and drugs.'

'And supporting Framstone Rovers,' said Charlie in a bid to lighten the mood. 'We used to see him around town wearing his scarf, didn't we, Mum?'

'Only ever on match days, though,' said Karen, brightening at the memory.

'Oh really?' asked Charlie. 'I thought he never took it off.'

'Lots of people did.' Karen shrugged. 'But it was only once or twice per week. It was his superstition from childhood. Rovers won on the day he first wore it, so Shane kept up the tradition. He thought it was bad luck to wear it on days when they weren't playing. Silly really.'

'Not silly at all,' said Charlie. 'Us sports fans are a superstitious bunch.'

He noticed a few people hovering nearby, waiting to share their condolences. 'It was lovely to meet you, Karen,' he said. 'Deepest condolences again.'

'Take care, Karen,' added Polly. 'If there's ever anything we can do, please just ask.'

'Thanks for coming, both of you,' said Karen. 'And thanks for your kindness to Shane.'

As she turned to the other mourners, Charlie was still thinking about that scarf.

61

Coffee Couldn't Hurt

Charlie and Polly couldn't wait to change out of their funeral clothes. It was partly comfort, partly what they represented. Almost as soon as they got through the front door to be welcomed by a wagging Ruby – she'd missed them but had doubtless dozed through their entire absence – both went upstairs to slip into something more cosy.

Once he'd swapped his suit for jeans and a sweatshirt, Charlie did what he'd been meaning to do ever since their conversation with Karen Carter. He checked the Framstone Rovers FC fixture list.

There were three dates he wanted to look up. First, Frank Courtney's murder. He ran his finger down the list of matches. Bingo. Rovers had neither played on the day Charlie found his body nor the day before. If what Karen had said was true – and there was no reason to doubt her – then Shane wouldn't have been wearing his lucky scarf.

Charlie realized he'd been holding his breath. Now he let it out with relief. The mysterious red fibres must have come from something, or someone, else. OK, it wasn't enough to posthumously exonerate Shane but it definitely didn't incriminate him either.

Next, he looked up the day that Rob Thompson was attacked. Again, no Framstone Rovers match. That made sense. It was a weeknight so if they had been playing, it would have been an evening fixture. Instead of attending a match, Shane was free to be in the Neptune, dealing drugs and getting into an argument with Rob.

Lastly, with a heavy heart, Charlie checked the day when he and Tess had stumbled across Shane's body on the beach. Charlie frowned. Rovers hadn't played then either. Maybe Shane had been lying there since the night before but again, no Framstone fixture. Why had superstitious Shane been wearing his scarf when they found him? According to Karen, he thought it was bad luck.

Charlie had taken Ruby on a long walk before leaving her alone in the house for the funeral. It was probably time for another stroll, even if it was just a mooch around the block. As she followed her nose through the neighbourhood, Charlie mulled over his discoveries.

He wasn't entirely sure what they meant but there were four people he should probably share them with. He'd promised himself it wasn't his business any more, but a coffee with friends couldn't hurt, could it? Neither had he yet told them about the old photo of Frank Courtney looking as thick as thieves with Rob.

With two juicy pieces of intel to impart, Charlie felt like both were burning to be told. One weakened the case against Shane for Frank's murder. The other strengthened the case against Rob. He wasn't quite sure where Shane's potential abuse in care fitted in, not yet, but there was something significant about it. He'd soon work out what.

He looked down at Ruby, as if for reassurance. She looked

back up at him, seeming to understand. He could've sworn she nodded encouragingly. Charlie tapped his phone and brought up the dogwalkers' group chat. He found multiple messages from Tess, Viv and Sue, asking why he'd been taken in for questioning and checking he was OK.

These had been met with a reply from Malcolm, promising that all would be revealed in Coastal Coffee soon, followed by a zipped-mouth emoji. The big tease. After a nerve-shredding few days – first down the station, then at the funeral – Charlie didn't mind his brief building up his part. He also had to remind himself that the case wasn't his business any more.

62

All Quiet on the Framstone Front

Charlie and Ruby got a hero's welcome in Coastal Coffee the next morning. He was slightly sheepish about all the fuss but Ruby relished it. Attention. Ear rubs. Dog biscuits. She was in canine heaven. She sniffed every inch of the proffered hands, squirming and licking with joy. It had only been a week since they'd all seen each other, but for Ruby it felt like a reunion with her long-lost family.

As Charlie fondly greeted the other dogs, Tess sprang into action and swiftly put a freshly made Americano in front of him. He smiled through the steam at the friendly faces round the table.

'Well, this is lovely,' he said. 'Just don't let me get used to it. I'll expect bunting and ticker tape every time I pop in for the best coffee in town.'

Tess grinned. 'I've trained you well. Welcome back, pal.'

'Thanks,' he replied. 'Although don't go getting any ideas about me being back on the case, so to speak. I've just come to tell you about my police interview and share some intel. Do with it what you will.'

'Understood,' Viv said with a nod. 'Malcolm might already

have spilled about your little adventures at the cop shop, though. He couldn't help himself.'

Charlie laughed. 'Well, that emoji didn't stay zipped for long.'

'I couldn't bear the torture any longer.' Malcolm shrugged. 'Sorry not sorry. How are you all, by the way? You, Polly and Ruby. No more trouble, we hope?'

'All quiet on the Framstone front,' said Charlie. 'And I intend to keep it that way, so I'm keeping my head down.'

'Fair play,' said Sue. 'Take as long as you like. Do what you've got to do. Family comes first.'

'Although we do like to think of ourselves as your second family,' chipped in Malcolm with a mischievous glint in his eye. 'I'm the devilishly attractive uncle obviously.'

'Well, I really am grateful for you coming out of legal retirement, Uncle Malcs,' said Charlie. 'How can I repay you? Try to keep the answer clean.'

'No need, dear boy,' said Malcolm.

'I insist,' said Charlie. 'There must be something I can do for you. And again, keep it clean.'

'A day's labouring on my allotment would come in handy, I suppose,' admitted Malcolm.

'Consider it a date,' said Charlie. He liked it down there and would do it gladly. Hopefully with fewer nettle stings and finger bites this time.

'When you've quite finished, Monty and Don,' said Tess. 'What have you got for us, Charlie?'

He filled them in on recent events. The dogwalkers listened keenly, letting him speak and not interjecting as much as usual. They were clearly on best behaviour. Tess even took notes on her phone, which made Charlie smile. In his absence she'd clearly been taking unofficial leadership seriously.

'That's what mystifies me about Rob Thompson evading suspicion, at least as far as the police are concerned,' explained Charlie. 'From the photo you'd think he was Frank's right-hand man. Literally.'

'So why lie about it?' asked Tess.

'Exactly,' said Charlie. 'Unless you were trying to distance yourself from a murder victim because you've got something to hide.'

Viv frowned. 'Surely Murdoch and Anjali are aware of the link, though?'

'They're both younger than Rob,' pointed out Charlie. 'It was before their time in the force.'

'But if they're so short of suspects that they're hauling you in for questioning, they must be looking at Rob too,' offered Sue.

'Honestly, he was barely mentioned in the interview, was he, Malcs?' said Charlie. 'And when he was, Anjali brushed over it as if they weren't even acquainted, let alone married.'

'Probably just what she has to do at work,' said Tess. 'Keep it purely professional to minimize gossip.'

'OK, but I don't get the impression they're even entertaining the idea of Rob as a suspect, even though he had beef with both murder victims. He's clearly volatile and unstable. He clearly keeps secrets from his wife. Yet they still seemed fixated on poor Shane.'

'That does seem blinkered,' agreed Malcolm. 'Any thoughts on why?'

Charlie sighed. 'I don't know. It just seems like they're closing ranks and not even considering one of their own as a suspect. It might be down to us – well, you guys – to pursue that line of enquiry as impartial outsiders.'

Eyebrows were raised about that 'us' slip-up. Charlie skipped over it and continued relaying his recent discoveries. When he got to the bit about Shane's lucky scarf, Tess's note-taking intensified.

'Forgive my ignorance of football matters,' said Malcolm, 'so he never wore his Framstone scarf on days when they weren't playing?'

'That's what his mum told me,' confirmed Charlie. 'Karen was certain about it. And Rovers didn't play on any of the three dates I checked – Frank's murder, Rob's attack or Shane's own death.'

'Meaning he wouldn't have been wearing his scarf,' said Viv. 'So the red fibres found at the scene of Frank's murder weren't from Shane.'

'They *probably* weren't,' Sue corrected her. 'Just because they didn't come from that particular scarf doesn't mean they didn't come from something else he was wearing.'

'Did you ever see him wearing red?' asked Viv, enjoying the chance to bicker with a broader purpose. 'I didn't. He was usually in black. Navy or grey at a push. That scarf was probably the only brightly coloured thing he owned.'

'OK, OK,' said Tess, holding up her hands for calm. 'Let's assume Shane was innocent of killing Frank – and probably attacking Rob, too. Which is what our gut feeling said anyway after we met him. How does this help us?'

'Because he was wearing his lucky scarf when he was found dead,' said Charlie, unable to resist chipping in. 'But according to the Framstone Rovers fixture list, he shouldn't have been.'

'So not only was it not remotely lucky,' said Malcolm. 'It made no sense that he was wearing it at all.'

'Precisely,' said Charlie, relieved he didn't have to go over it again. Sometimes talking to people who didn't like sport was exhausting.

'What if it was planted on him, then?' asked Sue. 'Maybe Shane's killer put it round his neck, either pre- or post-mortem.'

'Before or after he died,' translated Viv unnecessarily. Everyone nodded impatiently.

'Why would the killer do that?' asked Malcolm. 'They wouldn't have cared about him getting cold or looking well accessorized.'

'To frame Shane for the other murder,' said Sue in a triumphant tone.

'I see where you're going with this,' said Viv. 'The killer tried to incriminate him but got it wrong.'

Sue nodded. 'Exactly. They knew Shane was recognizable for wearing a Framstone scarf. But they didn't know the match-day detail, which gives it away.'

Everyone sat back looking impressed, while Sue picked up her knitting again smugly.

'One other thing occurred to me,' said Charlie.

Heads turned from Sue to him.

'As well as the scarf stuff, Shane's mum mentioned possible abuse, right?'

'I was just thinking about that too,' said Viv. 'Was she fairly sure that something happened?'

Charlie nodded. 'She didn't know any details but she was convinced. She believes it happened when Shane was in and out of care. And I was thinking, well, could that have been connected somehow to Frank Courtney? I mean, he worked a lot with troubled lads at sports clubs, youth charities and the like.'

'Hmm,' mused Malcolm. 'It's a lot of dots to join but . . .'

'It might give someone a motive to kill him,' said Charlie.

63

Something Fishy

Charlie had sworn he wouldn't get involved. He'd tried to push it all from his mind. Yet no matter how hard he tried, his thoughts kept straying back to the case he'd vowed to drop.

Tired of fighting a mental battle, he decided to give himself a break. A double murder didn't often happen in towns like Framstone. He was only preoccupied with it like the rest of the local population. When the unthinkable happened, it was perfectly natural to think about it.

He and Ruby had left the others to their cogitations. Before they departed, Tess had pressed a takeaway coffee into his hand and given him a brief hug.

'Thanks, Charlie.' She'd smiled up at him. 'And I mean that for once.'

'What for?' he said. 'Coming down here, drinking free coffee and spreading unsubstantiated gossip?'

She laughed. 'Well, yeah. Although it wasn't entirely unsubstantiated. I know it must have taken a lot to get involved again. You've been worried about Ruby and Polly, understandably, so to come and indulge us is appreciated. By all of us. Even Malcs.'

'Well, I got payment in kind,' said Charlie, holding up

a carrier bag which Ruby sniffed inquisitively. 'Now stop it before you make me blush.'

She put her hand on his arm as he turned to leave. 'I'm going to make you blush even more now,' said Tess. 'Forget the case for a minute. We've missed you as a friend, too.'

Charlie was surprised to find a lump in his throat. 'I've missed you, too,' he said, trying and probably failing to conceal how touched he was. 'All of you. Even Malcs.'

Tess laughed. 'Well, look at that,' she said. 'A rare flash of sincerity from us both. Let's not make a habit of it. Take care of yourselves. All three of you.' She bent to tickle Ruby's chin. 'That includes you, gorgeous.'

While he made supper that night – Malcolm had given him two fresh plaice fillets 'from a fishmonger friend of mine' (he didn't ask), so he pan-fried them with butter, lemon and capers – Charlie gave it some more thought. He still believed it was right to step back after Ruby had been snatched and threatened. But the mystery of the murders, especially Shane's, had burrowed under his skin.

'This is a treat,' said Polly when they sat down to eat. 'We haven't had fresh fish in ages.'

'Seems strange in a seaside town, doesn't it?' said Charlie. 'All that food swimming around out there but we head inland to the supermarket instead.'

'Well, you must thank Malcolm for me,' Polly said with a smile. 'And his fishy friend, whoever that may be. Delicious.'

Charlie chuckled. 'I suspect Malcs has many fishy friends. But I will.'

'The other person I wanted to thank was Karen Carter,' said Polly. 'She's been on my mind a lot. It's always hard after a funeral. You've been building up to it, but afterwards you're left alone with your grief.'

'Yes, I can see that,' said Charlie. 'It keeps you busy, then suddenly there's time to dwell on things.'

'Exactly,' said Polly, patting his hand. 'I knew you'd understand. I thought I might send a card to thank her for having us and to show we're still thinking of her. Would that be a good idea, do you think?'

Charlie smiled, patting her hand back. 'It's a lovely thought, Mum.'

'Good, that's decided,' said Polly brightly. 'I'll do it tomorrow.'

'Talking of poor Shane's funeral,' said Charlie. 'There was something I wanted to ask you.'

'Of course, love, anything,' said Polly, putting down her knife and fork.

'What did you make of Karen saying Shane had been abused in care? Did that ring true to you?'

'I regret to say it, but, yes, it did.' Polly sighed. 'All kinds of horrible things can happen to children in care. Good things come out of it too, of course, but you hear so many sad stories. It's partly why there's such a pipeline from social care to mental health services and prison.'

'So something might have happened to Shane?'

Polly nodded. 'Quite possibly. Troubled kids – either in the care system or young offenders' institutions – can be vulnerable. Neglected. Treated cruelly. Manipulated and exploited by nasty people. They're away from their parents, if they've got any, so a predator can step in and fill the gap.'

'They're supposed to be under the protection of the

authorities,' said Charlie sadly. 'It sounds like they're taken out of one bad situation and put somewhere worse.'

'I know, love,' she said. 'But resources are stretched. Things get covered up. Sometimes there's nobody to spot the signs. And who'd believe them anyway?'

'It's tragic,' said Charlie. 'Did you ever see this stuff happening?'

'I was aware of it. I worked alongside social workers a lot. And don't forget, I was a nurse as well as a midwife. I met all sorts of people in all sorts of situations. You'd be surprised what goes on in the places where society isn't looking.'

Charlie let that sink in. It dawned on him that his dear old mum had seen a lot more during her career than he'd imagined. While his heart went out to Shane, Charlie's head whirred with questions about how this might factor into his murder.

64

A Name of Interest

'It's been a while, Boardy Boy,' said Anjali from the park bench, smiling. She'd texted Charlie, asking to meet for a coffee and a catch-up. *I'll even go to those precious woods you love so much*, she'd said in her message.

In return, he brought the coffees. Ordering them had caused Tess's nose to twitch, naturally, but when Charlie dodged her questions, she got the message.

'Too long,' he agreed, passing Anjali her oat milk latte and sitting down. 'Although I think I glimpsed you from afar the other day, lurking outside Shane Carter's funeral.'

'Our surveillance wasn't quite covert enough, eh?' She smirked. 'Guilty as charged. We didn't want to intrude but you never know what might happen at a murder victim's funeral.'

Charlie chuckled. 'You know, your husband said something uncannily similar at Frank Courtney's wake. Have you two been comparing notes?'

'Maybe that's what happens when two coppers marry.' She shrugged. 'You end up thinking and talking the same.'

'Not exactly the same,' said Charlie. 'This chat wouldn't be half as pleasant for a start.'

She punched him on the arm. 'Oh, you smoothie. I'm better company than my spiky, frequently sloshed and slightly jealous husband, am I? High praise indeed.'

'Jealous of what? Of me? Of us?'

'All of the above probably,' said Anjali, waving the thought away. She took a sip to cover her embarrassment. 'Thanks for coming down to the station for that interview, by the way. Hope it wasn't too boring.' She looked at him sideways, as if gauging his reaction.

'Not boring at all,' he said. 'The opposite of boring, in fact. It was interesting to see you both in good cop, bad cop mode. And, like I said to your glamorous assistant Mr Murdoch, you're just doing your jobs.'

'Which was I?' she asked, raising an eyebrow. 'Good cop or bad cop?'

He smiled. 'An alluring blend of both.'

She laughed. 'I'll take that. Anyway, enough of your charm and chit-chat. I just thought I'd update you about what we found on Shane Carter's burner phone, since we spoke about it before.'

'Ah yes, about that,' said Charlie. 'I've decided to leave detecting to the professionals. Not before time, you might well say.'

'My glamorous assistant certainly would. He often bends my ear about how you and your canine cronies should keep your snouts out of police business.'

'Murdoch's been full of surprises lately,' admitted Charlie. 'He even helped me look for Ruby recently when she got lost.'

He'd decided not to tell Anjali about the more sinister aspects of Ruby's disappearance. There probably wasn't much she could do. Besides, he was trying to keep his nose clean. Whoever had been warning him off didn't need any more provocation.

'See?' said Anjali triumphantly. 'I knew you'd warm to him.'

'I wouldn't call it the bromance of the century just yet,' said Charlie. 'But I have come to the conclusion that Murdoch's right. Investigating is best left to the pros. So thanks for the offer, but I'll politely put my fingers in my ears if you don't mind.'

'Sure,' said Anjali, clearly unconvinced. 'But indulge me for a minute. Sharing is caring. Besides, I think you'll find it interesting.'

The Coastal crew, especially Tess and Viv, would never forgive him if he passed up a golden opportunity to glean some police intel. Against his better judgement, Charlie gave in. 'OK, OK, I guess you can use me as a sounding board. Consider it payback for all that borrowed geography homework.'

'Attaboy,' said Anjali, grinning. 'And attagirl, too.' She bent over and rubbed Ruby's neck as she wagged enthusiastically.

Anjali's got Ruby wrapped round her little finger, thought Charlie ruefully. *A bit like me.*

'Well, there's the stuff you'd expect on there,' said Anjali. 'Football banter, texts to his mum, texts to his punters, drug code that's not particularly subtle. Yadda yadda yadda. But then a name of interest popped up.'

Charlie's interest was piqued. 'Go on, you tease,' he said, admitting defeat.

'It seems that Shane and Frank Courtney were surprisingly well acquainted,' she said, arching an eyebrow. 'And I don't just mean across the Neptune bar.'

'Acquainted in what way?' asked Charlie, silently cursing his own curiosity.

'In a consenting adults kind of way,' said Anjali. 'They'd been anonymously flirting, both via burners. If the content of their messages didn't shock you, the grammar and spelling certainly would.'

Charlie's interest was no longer piqued, it was fully activated. 'You're kidding?'

'Nope,' she said. 'They'd exchanged multiple texts in the days leading up to Frank's murder. From what we can glean they met online, probably on an app, before swapping numbers and moving to text.'

'Well I never,' muttered Charlie, shaking his head in disbelief. 'I'd never have put that pair together, not least because Frank was a married man. It just goes to show.'

'That's not all,' continued Anjali, clearly enjoying dropping bombshells. 'Here's the kicker. They'd agreed to rendezvous in the woods the night before you found Frank's body.'

Charlie sat back on the bench, his head swimming. Football scarf or no football scarf, it seemed fairly damning. Shane Carter was firmly in the frame for killing Frank Courtney after all. However, he had an airtight alibi for his own murder. Even if the dogwalkers' instincts had been wrong and Shane was guilty, it still meant there was another killer on the loose. Charlie's nerves jangled and his mouth tasted metallic. Who was to say the death toll wouldn't rise again?

Riddle of the Two Toupées

After bidding farewell to Anjali, they embarked on a lap of
the woods before heading home. As Ruby nosed around tree
trunks and had to be stopped from scoffing a discarded burger
in the bushes (*Who throws away an entire burger without
even taking a bite?*), Charlie digested this latest revelation.

Frank and Shane's tryst was a curveball he hadn't seen
coming. Had one or both of them been catfishing? Was one
trying to entrap the other? Or should it be taken at face
value – just two small-town residents, craving a connection
and seeking a convenient hook-up away from prying eyes?
Charlie recalled Malcolm's comment about his gaydar twitching around Shane. From what he knew of Frank Courtney,
however, his sexuality was more surprising.

He also wondered how calculating Anjali had been by
telling him. Had she deliberately dropped such a bombshell,
knowing full well it would cause ripples among the dogwalkers and hoping to see if anything bubbled up as a result?

As he strolled and Ruby snuffled, Charlie heard noises in
the bushes again. He snapped out of his reverie and listened.
Ruby cocked her head to one side, too. Charlie's belly churned
with nerves and his mind raced. Could it be the phantom

hooded lurker who he'd chased? Or the attempted post-pub attacker he'd hidden from?

As the noises got louder and nearer – twigs cracking underfoot, branches being pushed aside, leaves rustling – he found his muscles tensing and adrenaline surging. Bring it on. He was ready.

Suddenly a blurred shape came hurtling out of the trees. It was moving fast and heading straight for them. Instinctively Charlie leaped aside and dodged it. Ruby wasn't so lucky.

Heart in his mouth, he turned to see her clutched in a waggy embrace with Ted the greyhound. As they wrestled, pawed and sniffed at one another like long-lost friends, Charlie breathed a sigh of relief. He bent down to say hello. 'You've got to stop blindsiding me like that, Ted,' he muttered, fondly stroking his elegant silvery head. 'Nearly gave me a coronary.'

'You seem jumpy,' said a voice behind him. 'Can't an innocent greyhound barrel out of the bushes at thirty miles per hour any more?'

He turned to see Malcolm, dapper as ever in a peacoat and cable-knit cardigan, smiling warmly but with a concerned look in his eyes.

'Ted took me by surprise, that's all,' said Charlie. 'I was miles away.'

'You often are, darling boy,' said Malcolm. 'It's only to be expected that you're on edge after recent events. Sorry if we spooked you.'

'All forgotten,' Charlie said, as they fell into step and strolled down the path together, the dogs capering up ahead.

'I'm glad I ran into you, even if you're not,' said Malcolm.

'Don't be daft,' scoffed Charlie. 'Always a pleasure to see my hotshot lawyer. Why are you glad?'

'Well, there was something I thought might interest you. I heard from my sources over in *República Portuguesa* again last night.'

Charlie knew better than to ask him to define 'sources'.

'They bore intriguing news,' Malcolm continued. 'It seems the Courtneys – or Frank, to be specific – didn't just buy their villa in the Algarve outright. They bought it in cash.'

'How on earth did you find that out?' asked Charlie, impressed.

'It caused quite the ripple on the local property market,' said Malcolm. 'An Englishman turning up with a briefcase full of used currency? No mortgage, no chain? It's an estate agent's dream. No wonder it got gossiped about.'

'I see what you mean,' said Charlie. 'All a bit Costa del Crime, isn't it?'

'It also begs questions,' said Malcolm. 'How did Frank accrue such a hefty lump sum? And why pay in cash?'

'Presumably he wanted no paper trail,' suggested Charlie. 'Probably cheaper, too. Puts him in a strong negotiating position and avoids all sorts of fees. That's basically money laundering, right?'

'I'll wager the taxman wasn't told either,' said Malcolm.

'Regardless of the admin,' said Charlie, 'it definitely makes Frank look even dodgier.'

'Maybe his dodginess got him killed,' added Malcolm.

'Funny you should say that,' said Charlie, stopping to let the dogs play and turning to face Malcolm. 'I've got Frank Courtney news of my own.'

He filled in Malcolm about Shane's phone log and their planned assignation in the woods.

Malcolm could hardly conceal his glee. 'I told you my

gaydar beeped at Shane, didn't I?' he exclaimed delightedly. 'It's rarely wrong. Never, in fact.'

Charlie laughed. 'I find that hard to believe, but, yes, you did call it first. Anyway, it was Frank's proclivities that flabbergasted me.'

'Well, he wouldn't be the first married man to be bi or in the closet,' said Malcolm. 'Certainly not the last. You'd be shocked how many men on the gay scene have ring marks on their fingers and a wife waiting at home.'

'Really?' asked Charlie. 'Even in the twenty-first century?'

'Afraid so,' said Malcolm. 'Besides, Frank came from a different generation. Back in the bad old days, a blokey bloke like that might struggle with being out and proud. It sounds like he grew up in a rufty-tufty kind of environment, which won't have helped.'

'Married with three children, though,' said Charlie. 'That's quite a cover.'

'Maybe he felt like he needed to create a perfect family,' said Malcolm, gazing thoughtfully into the trees as they walked. 'That was the facade he maintained to hide behind.'

'I can see that,' said Charlie. 'I guess attitudes in the police weren't terribly tolerant either.'

'Well, quite,' said Malcolm. 'The boys in blue were hardly enlightened when it came to things like race or sexuality, especially in the era when Frank was rising through the ranks. I saw it when I was a solicitor. There were some right knuckle-draggers in the force. It probably made Frank bury his true self even more.'

'How grim.' Charlie sighed. 'I wonder if Jackie knew.'

'I'm just insulted he never showed any interest in yours truly,' said Malcolm with a twinkle.

'You're out of his league, Malcs,' said Charlie.

'I didn't like to say so,' said Malcolm, 'but yes. And it all fits with the wig business. If a wig-wearer's on the apps, he might swap for a fuller, less grey number to take a few years off.'

'Gotcha,' said Charlie. 'And because he probably switched them secretly, he could well have been carrying the spare with him when he died.'

'Eureka!' Malcolm grinned. 'The riddle of the two toupées is solved.'

Maybe so, but Charlie still wasn't satisfied. Surely such a deception wouldn't have been enough to provoke Shane – or another illicit hook-up – into killing Frank? And even if it did, who killed Shane?

Every time they got an answer, it seemed to prompt more questions. Charlie looked at Ruby and Ted chasing each other around in circles. It felt like he was doing the same.

66

Ulterior Motives

Tess didn't often insist upon coming along on dog walks like this. She had a coffee shop to run, so was usually more than happy to let Charlie do the honours with Rough and Tumble in return for a gratis drink or two. Not today, though.

'This is nice,' she said as they tramped through the woods. 'Reminds me of when we first met.'

'All right, don't get too misty-eyed,' said Charlie, chuckling. 'You'll be whipping out a framed poo bag and striking up a string quartet next.'

'But it's the poo bag that brought us together,' said Tess melodramatically. 'Don't deny its historical importance. It's like the Bayeux Tapestry or the Rosetta Stone. But, you know, made of compostable corn starch and filled with turds.'

'Stop, I'm welling up,' said Charlie. 'But seriously, to what do Ruby and I owe the pleasure?' He did air quotes round the word 'pleasure', just to hammer home the point.

Tess tutted. 'Can't a girl and her two furry friends hang out with her best mate and his brindle diva without an ulterior motive?'

'Well, yes,' said Charlie. 'But you've normally got latte

art to create and customers to pump for information. What gives?'

'Is it that obvious? I thought I was being subtle.'

'You're about as subtle as an XL bully in a china shop,' said Charlie. 'So 'fess up.'

'I've just been worried about you,' said Tess. 'And about her ladyship here.' She stooped to massage Ruby's jowls, while her eyes closed with pleasure.

'That's kind of you,' admitted Charlie. 'But we've been just fine. No alarms, no surprises.'

'I know a song about that,' said Tess. 'Glad to hear it.'

'Something tells me that's not all, though,' he said, narrowing his eyes. 'I see you, Tess Cheong.'

She sighed. 'Dammit. Busted. Malcolm also mentioned how he'd run into you the other day – delicious intel on Shane's phone, by the way, my compliments to the chef – and you'd been a bit jittery. I just thought I might accompany you on more dog walks for a while, that's all. Is that so very wrong?'

Charlie smiled. 'Not at all. But no need, honestly. Especially now I've backed off a bit from the sticky-beaking and amateur sleuthing.'

'Just allow me to watch your back until all this blows over,' insisted Tess. 'At least until a murderer or two gets caught. Agreed?'

'As if I have any choice in the matter.' Charlie laughed. 'OK, agreed. You can be my bodyguard and I can be your long-lost pal.'

'I know a song about that too,' said Tess, satisfied. 'That's decided then.'

They walked on a while, catching up on all the latest

gossip. Not just about Shane, Frank and shady Portuguese property deals, but the travails of Malcolm's love life, Sue's latest woolly masterpiece and how Viv was hatching a plan to have them all round for dinner.

'Oh, please, no,' groaned Charlie. 'Not again. My blood sugar levels have only just rebalanced from last time.' As a relative latecomer to the gang, he'd only once experienced Viv's chronic lack of portion control. Among the others, it was a long-standing joke.

'She sure does like to over-cater,' said Tess, laughing. 'Just thought I'd warn you so you can starve yourself in advance.'

'Thanks for the heads-up,' he said. 'I'll commence my training regimen forthwith. Cabbage soup and fresh air for dinner it is.'

'Hang on, look who it is,' whispered Tess. Rounding the bend and heading towards them was a familiar figure with a bulldog panting along beside her. 'It's Jackie the black widow.'

'Just the woman I was hoping to bump into,' muttered Charlie. 'We'll say hello, then you make your excuses and leave. I'll see what I can find out about money and sex.'

'Steady on,' said Tess. 'You'll get me excited. Are you sure? What with everything I was just saying about having your back?'

'I'm sure,' Charlie reassured her. 'Besides, what's she going to do, set her slavering devil dog on me to lick me to death?'

67

Extracurricular Activity

Once Tess had made her excuse about a milk-frother emergency at Coastal Coffee, hurrying away with a disappointed-looking Rough and Tumble in tow – it both impressed and worried Charlie how accomplished she was at lying – he was left alone with Jackie and the dogs.

'We were planning on another circuit of the woods,' he said. 'Mind if we walk with you and Bobby?'

'Not at all, Charlie,' Jackie said, smiling. 'Nice to have some company. Isn't it, Bob?' The bulldog and the Staffy were getting along well. With Bobby's short legs and Ruby's aged creaking ones, they were a good match pace-wise. Neither would be competing with Ted for the title of fastest dog in Framstone.

Considering that the last time Charlie had seen Jackie, she'd warned him darkly about getting too involved, today she was warmth personified. She made a fuss of Ruby, enquired about Charlie's graphic design business and asked after his mum. Charlie was relieved Jackie was back to her usual friendly, faintly flirtatious self. Maybe him stepping back from the dogwalkers' investigations was a factor in her thawing towards him.

'And how about your family, Jackie?' he asked in return. 'How are you and the kids coping?'

'Oh, not too bad,' she said. 'What's it called? "The new normal"? We're adjusting to life without Frank slowly but surely.'

'It must be tough,' he said. 'I imagine he was a big presence around the pub and your home. That must leave a hole.'

'Well, yes and no.' She sighed, gazing off down the path. 'Frank was a big personality for sure. But he wasn't around all the time. He always seemed to have several lives happening at once.'

'How do you mean?' asked Charlie, probing but trying not to put her on the defensive. 'Too busy with all his community work?'

She nodded. 'Yes, that and other stuff. He even had a second phone. That's how much his life was compartmentalized.'

'Oh, I see,' said Charlie. 'You mean . . .'

'Yes, I mean what you probably think I mean,' she said, suddenly sounding world-weary. 'Frank called it his "extra-curriculars". I got used to it a long time ago and didn't ask many questions.'

'That must have been hard for you and the children, though,' said Charlie gently. 'Him having affairs.'

'Oh, I wouldn't even call them affairs as such,' said Jackie with a dismissive gesture. 'He was a restless soul, was my Frank. He had a hard upbringing, you know. I think that's partly why he joined the police. To bring some order to his life, some rules. But it still affected him. Made him –' she groped for the right word – 'reckless. Yes, reckless.'

'That sounds like it could have been dangerous,' said Charlie.

Jackie shrugged. 'As long as he didn't bring any trouble

to our door and provided well for the family, I turned a blind eye. He stuck to that, on the whole. And Frank never forgot his roots. He was so good with boys from bad backgrounds.'

That 'on the whole' begged some questions but Charlie sympathized. 'My own dad wasn't dissimilar,' he said. 'He had a whole other life too. Eventually it eclipsed the main one.'

'I'm sorry, Charlie,' said Jackie, giving his arm a rub. 'But you've turned out all right, which is a mercy. It gives me hope for our three.'

Now they'd found common ground, Charlie decided to be bold. Talk of Frank having two phones reminded him of Shane.

'Might Frank's extracurriculars also have included, well, drugs?' he asked her outright. 'You sometimes hear rumours that the Neptune is the place to go for that stuff.'

Jackie bridled briefly but gathered herself. 'I wouldn't know,' she said vaguely. 'Not my generation. I'm old school. That sort of thing isn't really on my radar.'

Charlie wasn't sure he bought Jackie's innocent act but he nodded and kept quiet, hoping she'd fill the silence. She did indeed keep talking.

'It wouldn't completely surprise me, though. Frank had his fingers in all sorts of pies. He was determined to give our kids a better start in life than his.'

'That's understandable,' said Charlie. 'A noble aim even.'

What he didn't say was that Frank Courtney appeared to have resorted to police corruption, drug supplying and all manner of other dodgy dealings to achieve it.

'It is, I suppose,' said Jackie, looking pleased. She patted his arm again. 'See, I knew you'd understand. I always feel better after talking to you, Charlie. You've got a good 'un there, Ruby.'

There was more he wanted to ask but Charlie was keen to keep Jackie onside, so that would do. For now anyway. He looked at their dogs waddling along happily. Sometimes slow and steady wins the race.

68

A Tragic Cycle

'You've barely said a word all evening,' said Polly softly, putting her hand on his shoulder. 'Something on your mind, love?'

Charlie realized with a start that his mum was right. He'd done his domestic chores and made them a risotto supper almost on autopilot, lost in contemplation. Maybe it was because he wasn't having daily debriefs with the dogwalkers and was left to work through his thoughts on his own.

Still, it wasn't fair on poor old Polly. He put down his fork and turned to her. 'Sorry, Mum.' He smiled at her. 'I was just thinking about a conversation I had earlier today. You might be able to help actually.'

'Oh yes?' said Polly, perking up. 'I can try.'

'Do you reckon troubled boys can be drawn to joining the police force?' asked Charlie, opting against going into specifics. 'I guess as a way of regaining some control over their lives?'

'I think it happens quite a bit,' said Polly. 'I worked alongside the police occasionally. My social worker friends often did. A lot of the coppers we met had issues, shall we say? Sexist, racist bullies or worse.'

Charlie hated the idea of his mum being exposed to such unsavoury characters. 'What attracted them to the job, do you reckon?'

'It can be about self-preservation,' said Polly. 'If you've spent most of your life feeling scared, it's a way of making yourself feel safer. Policing attracts alpha males, of course. Men who want power and authority. But it also attracts beta males, who hide behind the uniform and use it to make up for their own shortcomings.'

Charlie nodded, while idly wondering where she'd picked up terms like 'beta male'. Radio 4 maybe. His mum was always surprising him. 'And in your experience can policemen with dark pasts exploit their position? Perhaps become abusers themselves?'

'It happens, sadly,' said Polly. 'It's a tragic cycle. Childhood victims become adult abusers. Prey becomes predator. Sufferers become perpetrators. They'll come across plenty of vulnerable people to take advantage of. And they're even less likely to speak out against a policeman.'

'I get that,' said Charlie, nodding. He was beginning to form a picture of what might have happened with Frank Courtney.

'What's all this about anyway?' she asked, her brow furrowing. 'Do I need to worry?'

'Not at all,' he reassured her. 'It's a long story. Just a debate I was having with Tess. There's another couple of spoonfuls of risotto in the pan. Want to help me finish it?'

'It would be a shame to waste it,' she said, holding out her plate. 'By the way, did I tell you that I'm meeting Karen Carter for a cup of tea later this week?'

Charlie had just been thinking about Shane. It was like

she'd read his mind. 'No, you didn't, but I'm pleased. How did that come about?'

'I sent her that card after the funeral, like we talked about,' explained Polly. 'I put my phone number at the bottom, just in case she ever needed anything. She rang this afternoon and I suggested meeting up.'

'That's a nice thing to do, Mum,' he said. 'I'm sure she needs a friend at the moment.'

'That's what I thought,' said Polly. 'A cuppa, a cake and a chat never did any harm, did it?'

Charlie smiled. His mum's mind might be getting foggy but her heart remained in the right place.

As he divided the remaining risotto between their plates, his smile melted away. Charlie pictured the two murder victims again. That woodland assignation aside, what did Frank Courtney and Shane Carter have in common? Maybe more crucially, *who* did they have in common?

As Charlie returned to the table with second helpings, he couldn't shift the photo of Frank with his arm round Rob Thompson from his mind.

69

A Whole Secret Second Life

Charlie decided it was time to meet some friends of his own for a hot beverage. Happily he knew just the place.

It was a strange feeling rejoining that familiar table at Coastal Coffee but by no means an unpleasant one. It rather reminded Charlie of coming home from university during the holidays. He felt like he belonged and didn't belong at the same time.

As far as the others were concerned, he definitely belonged. The welcome was just as effusive as last time. He greeted the humans first, then the dogs – the correct pecking order, tempting as it was to reverse it – before settling down with a fresh Americano, courtesy of the extra-attentive Tess, for a status report.

After summarizing his conversations with Jackie and Polly, Charlie laid out his latest idea.

'Let's assume Frank Courtney ran a whole secret life from that second phone,' he said, 'because, well, why else would he have one? I'll bet that meant both his illicit sex life and a drug operation. Texting the likes of Shane on burners under code names and allowing dealing to happen on Neptune premises, while hooking up with the odd man on the side.'

'What was the word Jackie used?' asked Viv. 'Reckless? Sounds like his thrill-seeking led him into trouble.'

Malcolm nodded. 'It can be dangerous out there on the app scene. People are so desperate for intimacy they throw caution to the wind and end up in all sorts of risky situations.'

'I doubt Frank was totally reckless,' said Charlie, thinking aloud. 'He wasn't just an ex-copper but he had too much to lose. I'd guess he was just a deeply closeted man who sought company every now and again.'

'I'm inclined to agree with my client here,' said Malcolm, nodding. 'If it was more habitual, chances are I'd have heard about it.'

'I can't see Jackie putting up with that either,' added Viv.

'True,' said Charlie. 'It's kind of tragic. A man born out of time, who felt he couldn't be his true self.'

'Yes, but what about the alleged abuse?' asked Tess. 'How would that tie in?'

'Well, we keep hearing how Frank had a rough start in life,' said Charlie. 'Potentially involving abuse, be it sexual or physical. That likely became one of his motivations for joining the police – partly to right wrongs, partly for self-protection. After a chaotic childhood, the structure and routine probably appealed too.'

'Yet you think he became a predator himself?' asked Sue, frowning.

'Hard to know for sure but it would explain a lot,' replied Charlie. 'His devotion to youth work for one. Between that and his police day job, Frank would've come across a lot of vulnerable boys, often at their most vulnerable moments. It's not hard to see how he might've taken advantage. That and his criminal activity could even have fed off each other.'

'How do you mean?' asked Tess.

'He could leverage his position of power to coerce young lads into all sorts,' said Charlie. 'Not just sex but dealing, smuggling, stealing, other dodgy stuff. A corrupt copper with – as both Jackie and Rob have put it – his fingers in many pies.'

'Maybe he left the force because it was getting tricky to juggle with his ever-growing side hustles,' suggested Viv.

'And he bought a Portuguese villa with his dirty money,' said Malcolm.

'As well as doing up the run-down pub and sending his son to St Jude's, which doesn't come cheap,' added Charlie.

'That still bothers me,' said Tess. 'The son getting an elite education while the daughters had to make do.' She glanced at their fellow Framstone High alumnus. 'No offence, Charlie.'

'None taken,' he said, laughing. 'So how do we reckon this all relates to Frank and Shane's murders? Not forgetting the assault on Rob either.' Charlie remained convinced that Rob Thompson was involved somehow. He just couldn't work out where Rob being attacked himself fitted in.

'I've got a hypothesis here,' said Sue, putting her knitting aside and her elbows on the table. 'May I?'

Everyone nodded eagerly. Normally the quiet one, she was enjoying a rare chance to take centre stage.

'Let's say, for the sake of argument, that one of the boys abused by Frank – or at least horribly exploited – was young Shane when he was in care.'

'It's a depressing thought,' said Charlie. 'But one I've had, too.'

'Then, because Framstone is a small world, imagine that they unwittingly hooked up on a dating app,' continued Sue.

'Frank turned up in a thicker, less grey wig in a bid to look younger. But all Shane saw was the Frank Courtney he'd known and feared in his youth.'

'The wig swap backfired and Shane realized it was his abuser?' said Charlie. 'Wow. It's possible, I suppose. He'd suppressed the memory but it all came flooding back.'

'And how do we picture Shane reacting to this realization?' asked Sue. 'First, he might've thrown up – sickened, from sheer shock or because of all that repressed trauma suddenly resurfacing.'

'Hence those pools of vomit found at the crime scene,' said Charlie. *The third one anyway.*

'And what might Shane have done after that?' asked Sue.

Viv looked at her proudly as Sue took a sip of black coffee, picked up her knitting again and sat back smugly.

Malcolm gasped. 'Hit him.'

It was a seductive enough story, thought Charlie. But could the Shane he'd met really have hit Frank Courtney that hard and that repeatedly, before pulling a knife and stabbing him? And even if it was true, who killed Shane?

Charlie couldn't shrug off the feeling that there was something they were all missing.

70

Hardly a Smoking Gun

As Charlie headed home with Ruby, he turned it all over in his mind. It was a compelling theory which ticked a lot of boxes. Yet it still didn't sit right with him. He debated whether he should share it with Anjali. But what would that gain at this stage? It was all hearsay and speculation. They had little to no actual evidence.

Sure, they'd heard that the Neptune was a hotbed of drug-dealing, but if that was true, one would hope the police were already aware. Frank Courtney was secretly flush, with a holiday home and a private-schooled son, but without proof of how he got the money, this wasn't exactly a crime.

Karen Carter – a bereaved mother whose son Shane had been taken away from her, on and off, throughout his childhood – thinks he was abused in care. Frank might well have been among his abusers but so could any number of nasty people. Courtney Snr had likely been a corrupt copper too, potentially even a crime kingpin, but throwing such accusations around could land someone in serious trouble.

As for the woodland hook-up, it was Anjali herself who'd

uncovered it via Shane's phone records. All the dogwalkers had to add was some supposition about wigs and vomit, which was hardly a smoking gun.

Charlie imagined the look on Anjali's face at how deranged he'd sound if he told her all this. He also pictured Murdoch rolling his eyes about busybody civilians. Worst of all, he pictured Rob Thompson laughing and raising a glass to his idiocy. He'd be tickled pink that they were chasing shadows rather than investigating Rob himself – the only man left standing out of the Frank–Rob–Shane triumvirate of trouble. No, better to sit on it all for now. Wait until the time was right and they had something more concrete.

Charlie and his faithful four-legged friend arrived home to find Polly in an effervescent mood, keen to tell Charlie all about her cuppa with Karen. After he'd heard the key details – English Breakfast and millionaire's shortbread for Karen, Earl Grey and a slice of lemon drizzle cake for Polly, who picked up the bill – Charlie asked how Karen was coping.

'Not well, to be honest, but I suppose that's to be expected. She looked like she hadn't been sleeping well. Her eyes were puffy from crying. She's just buried her child, which is something no mother should have to do.'

'I know, Mum. I know,' said Charlie with a mystified shake of his head.

'Poor Karen feels terribly guilty,' continued Polly. 'I think she's been going over and over it in her mind. All the mistakes she made. The things she could have done to help Shane. Whether she could have straightened herself out sooner and stopped him being taken into care so much. I told her that she shouldn't torture herself, but that's easier said than done, I suppose.'

'That's rough,' said Charlie. 'I'm sure she did her best under difficult circumstances.'

'Well, quite,' said Polly. 'It doesn't help that detectives have been asking Karen all sorts of intrusive questions about Shane's love life.'

'Ah yes.' Charlie sighed. 'Apparently his phone records threw up some interesting leads, let's say.'

'Well, they should follow those leads, rather than harassing a grieving mother,' said Polly firmly. 'They're still convinced Shane killed Frank Courtney, it seems, which is upsetting Karen terribly. She doesn't seem to be able to get through to them that he's innocent.'

'The mobile data does put him firmly in the frame unfortunately,' pointed out Charlie.

'That's the thing,' said Polly, 'Karen was quite insistent that Shane couldn't have done it.'

'Why?' Charlie asked hopefully. 'Can she give him an alibi?'

'No, nothing like that sadly. She says Shane was out at all hours, all over town. She rarely knew his whereabouts.'

'Why can't he have done it then?'

'Because he wasn't capable,' said Polly. 'Karen says he'd never been violent in his life. The only time he came close was years ago. Some business with a knife but that was in self-defence.'

'Maybe so, but he was charged back then,' said Charlie. 'Now there's been another knife crime and Shane had a record for it. From the police viewpoint, this does just sound like a mother standing by her son.'

'According to Karen, violence always sickened him,' said Polly. 'Couldn't stomach it, ever since he was a little boy.

Never got into a fight at school. Never lashed out in anger. He didn't even like violence in films or on telly. So you see, he couldn't have killed Frank, no matter what the police say. Karen has told them this until she's blue in the face, but Anjali and DS Murdoch won't listen.'

As Polly busied herself pottering around the sink, Charlie idly watched her. His mum becoming emotionally involved was understandable, he supposed, considering her personal connection to the Carters. It was almost like Polly was defending Shane on Karen's behalf.

He'd noticed her tendency with age to latch on to things. Sometimes it was a story in the news. Other times it was something mundane like bin collections or parcel deliveries. He figured it was a symptom of her fading mind. Fixation was a way of clinging on.

Polly was invested in Frank and Shane's murders, that's for sure. Charlie just hoped she wouldn't be disappointed if the case went in a direction she didn't expect.

Sitting there in the cosy kitchen, he also let what Karen Carter had said sink in. Instinct had told him that Shane wasn't a killer. Looking at Polly and Ruby, the two things he loved most, Charlie desperately hoped it was true – not just for his own mother's sake but for Shane's memory, for Karen and for justice to be done.

71

People Are Weird

'This betrayal is like a dagger to my heart,' she said. 'If that's not too insensitive a phrase nowadays.'

Lord knows how but Tess had tracked down Charlie to Monty's on the seafront. In his youth it had been a burger bar with Formica tables and shiny smooth plastic seats. A popular destination for teenagers after school. You could order a milkshake, share a portion of 'fries' (so much cooler than chips) and see how long you could hang out in there before being shooed out by Monty himself or his uniformed waitresses. Its sea views and diner-style fittings gave it a sheen of retro glamour.

In recent years, though, Monty's had gradually gentrified. Well, to an extent. The furniture was now mismatched wood with splashes of colour. The menu was big on all-day brunches, salads, smoothies and sandwiches. It was a decent spot to grab a bite and gaze out to sea, while getting misty-eyed over one's misspent youth.

Every now and again, Charlie resolved to spend more time down at the seafront. Sometimes, particularly in town, you could briefly forget that Framstone was on the coast. Then you'd reach the crest of a hill and the sight of the glittering ocean laid out before you would take your breath away.

He was pootling away on a graphic design project – the logo and branding for a local landscape gardening business – and had decided to squat on Monty's Wi-Fi for a change of scene. His go-to destination would usually be Coastal but since stepping back from the investigation, he'd headed elsewhere so things didn't get awkward.

His concession to loyalty was that he didn't order a coffee, instead slurping on a fresh orange and pineapple juice. Well, the vitamins couldn't hurt. He hoped Tess had noted this gesture of solidarity as she plonked herself next to Charlie at his window seat. While Ruby, Rough and Tumble got re-acquainted, she ordered a turmeric and ginger shot for herself.

'Look at us,' said Charlie with a raised eyebrow. 'We're like a couple of wellness influencers.'

'Steady on, Gwyneth Paltrow,' Tess said with a smirk. 'You'll be shoving candles in your ears and jade eggs somewhere unmentionable next.'

'Who's to say I haven't already?' deadpanned Charlie.

'I thought I could hear something clanking,' fired back Tess. 'So you cheating on me with old Monty aside, what gives?'

Charlie chuckled at her brazenly fishing for gossip but it was a treat to see her. He told Tess about Karen Carter's utter certainty that Shane couldn't be a killer and his aversion to violence.

'Hmm,' said Tess sceptically. 'Don't let your bleeding heart get in the way of your brain.'

'What's that supposed to mean?'

'It means that you're too nice for your own good sometimes,' said Tess, smiling at him indulgently. 'I refer you to the fact that you can't say no to dog owners when they ask for favours and often end up walking a pack of random hounds for free.'

'That's not an inaccurate summary,' he admitted. 'But what's it got to do with the murders?'

'You think the best of people,' said Tess. 'You're too forgiving. Too trusting. Don't get me wrong, it's a lovely quality a lot of the time. Just maybe not in this scenario.'

'You think emotion has clouded my judgement?'

'It's a suspected murderer's mum protesting his innocence,' she said. 'Just like they always do. After all, you don't see many mothers on the news, saying, "Yep, I always knew my little darling was a total wrong 'un. He definitely committed this heinous crime. Lock up the psychopathic little numpty and throw away the key." Well, do you?'

'OK, point taken,' said Charlie, chuckling.

'Come on then,' said Tess. 'Let's take these three lunatics for a stroll while we chat.' Still in protective lioness mode, Tess remained determined to join Charlie on as many dog walks as possible. He knew from bitter experience that resistance was futile. Once they'd drained their juices and settled up, they headed for the woods.

As Ruby, Rough and Tumble scampered off ahead, Charlie fell into step alongside Tess. 'For what it's worth, I do believe Karen Carter,' he said. 'We only know one example of Shane being violent in his entire life and that was in self-defence. Other than that, nothing. For a drug dealer and repeat offender, he was a gentle soul.'

'I agree to an extent,' said Tess. 'But that sole example was with a knife, don't forget.'

'I know, I know,' said Charlie. 'But even if Shane did kill Frank, that doesn't explain who killed Shane. As for him bludgeoning Frank, then stabbing him? I just don't buy it.'

'And as if by magic, here we are,' said Tess.

Absorbed in his murderous musings, Charlie hadn't been paying attention to their surroundings. He now realized Tess was right. They were approaching the spot where he'd found Frank Courtney's corpse. In some ways it felt like a long time ago. Charlie could also picture it so vividly, it was like yesterday. In reality, just over a month had passed. Five weeks since Framstone's innocence had been shattered. Charlie wondered if his home town would ever feel the same again.

They glanced around the clearing. Apart from the leaves being a bit browner and even more litter strewn around, it was unchanged. So were the dogs.

Hearing growling, they turned to see Rough and Tumble playing an enthusiastic tug of war with something they'd found on the ground. Ruby circled them, almost like she was refereeing the match. Charlie felt a shudder of déjà vu.

'Not again,' he said. 'Do you remember the day after I found Frank? We brought Viv, Sue and Malcs here on a ghoulish guided tour. These two idiots did exactly the same that day. Fighting over a discarded wet wipe like it was some precious find.'

Tess grimaced. 'Ugh. If one of them swallows the pesky thing, it could obstruct their airway.'

She bent down to take it off them, which proved easier said than done. Assuming it was part of the game, Rough and Tumble began scurrying back and forth, still connected by the wet wipe locked in their jaws. The more exasperated Tess became, the harder Charlie laughed.

'Drop!' commanded Tess, managing to grab the wipe.

'Drop it!' She only succeeded in joining the tug of war herself, only this time it was one human against two dogs.

Eventually Charlie took pity on her. He crinkled the bag of treats in his coat pocket. All three dogs immediately forgot what they were doing and trotted over.

As he made them sit and gave them each a treat, he glanced over at Tess. She was sniffing the wet wipe tentatively.

'Careful,' he said. 'You don't know where it's been.'

'I thought I'd be a good citizen and find a bin for it,' she said. 'Stop some other demented dog swallowing it and making itself sick. It isn't actually a wet wipe, you know. It's one of those fabric-conditioning sheets.'

'Those what now?'

'You put them in the washing machine or tumble dryer,' explained Tess patiently. 'They're supposed to soften and freshen up your laundry.'

'You learn something new every day,' said Charlie.

'God knows how it got here,' said Tess, tutting. 'A wet wipe you could understand. Probably dropped by a yummy mummy after cleaning their kid's face – or worse. But a tumble dryer sheet? People are weird.'

Charlie frowned. Why was this ringing a distant bell?

72

Framstone's
Own Professor Moriarty

'At last,' said Viv. 'We thought you'd deserted your post and were about to report you for dereliction of duty.'

'Who exactly would you report me to?' asked Tess.

'I dunno.' Viv shrugged cheerfully. 'The Coffee Shop Complaints Bureau? Is that a thing?'

All these chaperoned dog walks were eating into Tess's time at Coastal Coffee. They hurried straight back so she could take over from her caffeine protégé Leon.

Here they found Viv, Sue and a couple of their 'regulars': Humphrey the one-dog disaster zone and the altogether more dignified Professor. No sign of Malcolm because it was his day volunteering at the food bank.

Everyone was pleased to see them but only the humans bore news. Well, unless you counted the Professor having new tyres. He seemed terribly proud of them and rightly so. All the better for tackling tricky terrain on walks.

Once everyone had said or sniffed hello (delete according to species), Viv was eager to share their latest discovery. As phlegmatic as ever, Sue didn't deem it worth missing a stitch for and carried on knitting – although Charlie could tell she was listening by how the sound of needles clacking slowed down during the juicy bits.

'Remember how Humphrey here has quite posh owners?' began Viv. 'It was at their house that we saw the framed photo of the St Jude's rugby team.'

'Of course,' said Tess. 'With Little Lord Luke Courtney pride of place, while his sisters languished at the local comp.'

'Steady on,' said Charlie. 'That comp has produced some illustrious, successful alumni. And also me.'

'Yesterday the lady of the house offered us a drink when we dropped off Humph,' continued Viv.

'We'd normally politely decline, of course,' chipped in Sue. 'Seeing as we accept no substitute for the best coffee in town.'

'Your loyalty is appreciated,' said Tess, looking askance at Charlie. It might be a while before he was forgiven for Monty's.

'But just this once, we figured we could grill her while we were chit-chatting,' said Viv, keen to get back to the point, 'so she sat us down for a good gossip.'

'I bet you hated that,' deadpanned Charlie. 'The sacrifices you make, Viv, honestly.'

'The sacrifice was worth it,' said Viv, refusing to rise to the bait. 'We thought it was unusual for the Courtneys to send only one of their three kids to private school, right? Well, we found out why they did it.'

'Don't leave us in suspense,' said Charlie.

'Yeah, I can't wait to hear this twisted logic,' added Tess. 'Something to do with the patriarchy and unequal opportunities, was it?'

'Not really,' said Viv. 'Much as I'd love to join you on the barricades. Apparently little Luke – he hadn't had his growth spurt back then – was being badly bullied at Framstone High.'

'Oh,' said Tess. 'That's taken the wind out of my feminist sails.'

'It must've been bad to make them uproot him,' said Charlie.

'It was fairly brutal, apparently,' said Viv. 'And get this: it was because he had a policeman for a father. A few rough kids started picking on him, likely encouraged by their criminally inclined parents, and it escalated from there. It became pretty much a daily occurrence by the end.'

'Word is, Courtney Senior tried to have a word with some of the culprits at a school sports day,' added Sue, putting air quotes round "have a word" and giving a knowing look. 'Their parents waded in as well. By all accounts, it became quite the altercation.'

'Poor Luke.' Tess frowned sympathetically. 'It wasn't his fault what his dad did for a living. I realize this was years ago but I wonder if he needs a shoulder to cry on.'

'I'm sure if he does, he'll find one belonging to someone his own age,' said Charlie. 'Sending Luke to St Jude's seems like an extreme solution, though. Plenty of kids get bullied at one time or another. You can't move schools whenever it happens. It's not practical.'

'No, but we were thinking,' said Viv, glancing at Sue, who nodded in agreement, 'what if this was one of the motivating factors for Frank being on the take? He suddenly had expensive school fees to pay for his son. I guess he also felt guilty that the bullying was partly his fault.'

'Makes sense,' said Charlie. 'It would certainly put financial pressure on the Courtneys. Emotional pressure, too. You can imagine Jackie wanting to protect her boy. Maybe Luke himself was keen to move schools and make a fresh start.'

'So dodgy dad stepped in, waving his grubby cheque-book,' said Tess.

'Jackie reckons Frank wanted his children to have a better upbringing than he had,' said Charlie. 'This could have been part of it.'

'I get that,' said Tess. 'It's just that he paid for it with dirty money. He exploited less fortunate boys to bankroll his little darling.'

'Put like that, it sounds even more unsavoury,' conceded Charlie.

'Anyway, does this mean you're back on the case?' Sue asked with a hopeful smile. 'Is the squad at full strength again?'

Charlie sat back and considered her question. He'd been so drawn in by Frank Courtney's double life and protestations of Shane Carter's innocence that he'd temporarily forgotten his pledge to back off.

'Not quite,' he said. 'Call me a consultant. A bit like Sherlock Holmes unofficially helping out Inspector Lestrade. My priority is still Mum and this one.' He reached down and gently rubbed the groove between Ruby's eyes like she'd always enjoyed.

'Fair play,' said Viv. 'Let's try to unmask Framstone's own Professor Moriarty, then.'

As Charlie nodded and sipped his coffee, he was still ruminating on the Courtneys' ill-gotten gains, as well as the wet wipe that wasn't. Despite what he told the others – and indeed told himself – he wasn't done with this case after all.

73

A Woolly Breakthrough

This was becoming a habit, Charlie realized, but one that he rather enjoyed. The following day, he met Anjali on their usual bench, handing her the usual coffee. He might have cheekily described them as an old married couple if, well, she wasn't married to someone else.

As well as Ruby, he had Humphrey, Rough and Tumble in tow. Walking Humphrey was a favour for Sue and Viv. And quite a sizeable favour, considering the trouble Humphrey tended to get into. Rough and Tumble was the price he paid for a round of takeaway coffees. Tess had needed some convincing not to come with him but the fact that he was meeting an officer of the law did the trick.

'This has probably become an irritating question, but what news on the case?' he asked as they watched the four canines caper around like loons.

Anjali gave a hollow laugh. 'Too right it's become irritating. My superiors ask me several times per day. I'm running out of different ways of saying "Actively pursuing multiple lines of enquiry, sir".'

Charlie was desperate to help her out. Maybe give her some new leads. However, everything they had was still based on supposition. Right now, Anjali wouldn't thank him for sharing idle gossip.

'Surely Shane's phone data was progress?' he said.

'Yes and no.' She sighed. 'It puts Shane at the scene, or at least near it, but it's not enough. We're lacking little things like motive, a murder weapon, actual physical evidence.'

'Weren't there some red fibres?'

'You sound like your new mate Murdoch,' she said with a smile. 'He's obsessed with those pesky fibres. Turns out they're quite a common type of merino wool. Craig's off making more red-yarn-related enquiries right now actually.'

'Shouldn't you be riding shotgun?' asked Charlie. 'The dream team on the trail of a woolly breakthrough?'

'Thrilling as that sounds, I've got wifely duties to attend to.'

'I'm not sure I like the sound of that,' said Charlie.

She laughed. 'Oi, don't be rude. I'm taking Rob to the dentist.'

'What? Is he eight years old? Does he get a lollipop afterwards?'

'Something like that,' she said with a long-suffering expression. 'He's terrified of the dentist. Always has been. He reckons it's a genuine phobia. I suspect he's just a wuss.'

'I couldn't possibly comment,' said Charlie. 'What's he having done? Turkey teeth installed? Dazzling white veneers for full C-list celebrity effect?'

'He's just getting the damage from the attack fixed, finally,' she said. 'Didn't you notice him looking a bit snaggle-toothed lately?'

'I did think he had a bit of a crooked grin,' said Charlie. 'But I tried not to look too closely. Didn't want to make him self-conscious.'

'Well, that's why,' she said. 'A couple of his front teeth got chipped when he was beaten up.'

'Ouch,' said Charlie. 'Poor Rob. Sounds painful.'

'Now the rest of his wounds are healed, we figured it was time to get his gnashers restored to their former glory. Talking of which, it's time I got going.'

'Don't forget to buy him a comic to read in the waiting room,' said Charlie. 'Brave little soldiers deserve a treat.'

'Well, you can't say "Anjali" without saying "aah".' She grinned, getting up to leave.

Once she was out of sight, Charlie stayed seated for a moment. Punching Rob viciously enough to chip multiple teeth must have been a hefty blow. Once again, he couldn't picture Shane Carter hitting anyone that hard, even if his blood was up from their pub set-to.

It was all too tempting to deduce that Shane attacked Rob, who then murdered Shane in revenge when he got out of hospital. For Charlie, that story still didn't stack up. He briefly wondered if Tess was right and emotion was blinding him to the truth.

Charlie hadn't punched anyone for years but he did remember that it tended to hurt both parties. Taking a chunk out of someone's teeth must have damaged the fist-thrower's knuckles. His mind went to Luke Courtney's bandaged hand at his father's wake. Could he have been Rob's attacker? If so, why?

Tess had floated the possibility of Luke taking over his dad's dodgy business. Maybe Rob wanted a piece of the action, too. After all, there was that old photo of him and Frank looking cosy. Perhaps he saw himself as the rightful heir. Charlie wondered if Luke and Rob had fallen out over who took control of the drugs operation. If a power struggle had come to blows, there was only one winner. And it wasn't the one about to hop reluctantly into the dentist's chair.

Charlie's quiet contemplation was interrupted by a right old racket. Barks, growls and scrabbling sounds were coming from directly beneath his feet. What in dog's name were those bothersome hounds up to now?

74

Let the Dog See the Rabbit

The dogs were digging. None of them were usually big diggers, especially not during walks. A bone buried in their own garden was a different matter, but in the great outdoors? Never. Charlie wondered what had got into them.

Humphrey was leading the way, his front legs already an unseemly shade of brown as he scrabbled at the ground, sending dirt flying. Rough and Tumble joined in from the sides, occasionally darting in for a flurry of excavation activity, then retreating to a safe distance and barking excitedly. Ruby milled around at the back, occasionally lending an ineffectual paw but mainly on supervisory duties.

Charlie looked on amused as they pawed and raked frenziedly behind the bench. He guessed they'd smelled some sort of meaty goodies or animal remains.

He tried heading off down the path, calling them to follow, but the doggy diggers were having none of it. Whatever was below ground was clearly far more interesting than a boring old walk. Charlie admitted defeat and strolled back for a look. Between them, the muddy-furred quartet had already burrowed a hole several inches deep. As Charlie peered into it, he glimpsed something being slowly uncovered.

For a horrible moment he had images of a human hand or even a skull. He shuddered. The last thing anyone needed was more dead people. Thankfully this didn't appear to be organic matter. It looked like plastic.

He leaned over the dogs for a better look. It resembled the corner of a transparent bag peeping out of the earth. As more soil got removed, he got the impression there was something inside the bag. He wasn't sure why but he had a spike of adrenaline.

'Come on, you lot,' he said, nudging the mutts out of the way and joining them on all fours, which they only found even more exciting. 'Let the dog see the rabbit, so to speak.'

He reached into the hole and grabbed the corner that was poking out. It was definitely a plastic bag – and there was definitely something solid inside. He decided to speed up the process before the dogs did any damage to it.

'Stand clear,' he said, suddenly self-conscious that he was talking aloud to them, like a first responder addressing a crowd of bystanders.

He tugged. It budged a bit but not much. He pushed away a few more handfuls of dirt and tried again. More movement. By now the dogs were milling around frantically. Charlie gritted his teeth, heaved away a huge handful of mud and pulled at the same time.

It gave way so quickly it surprised him. He toppled over with the momentum, ending up on his back, the plastic bag clutched in his hand, while the overexcited dogtectives jostled to lick his face.

He struggled to get up but eventually pushed himself into a sitting position, parting what seemed like a sea of filthy fur and wagging tails. Finally he could see what all the fuss was about.

It was a mid-sized knife, maybe a kitchen one, sealed in a ziplock bag. And the knife had blood on it. If Charlie were a betting man, he'd wager that his canine companions had just found the missing murder weapon.

75

An Uncanny Knack

This took Charlie right back. Once again, he was in the woods, surrounded by police. Uniformed officers busied themselves, cordoning off the bench with crime scene tape. DS Craig Murdoch paced around, pointing and issuing instructions.

This time, thankfully, Charlie wasn't feeling nearly as sick. His first phone call had been to Anjali. She was still en route to cajoling Rob into the dentist's chair, but told Charlie she'd dispatch Murdoch to the scene immediately and join him as soon as she could.

Eventually Murdoch came over, a quizzical expression on his face. Charlie really did have an uncanny knack of turning up at crime scenes. If he was DS Murdoch, he'd probably suspect himself too.

'Here we are again,' said Murdoch with a wry grin. Well, that was an improvement at least. 'You know the drill by now. Can you talk me through what happened, please, Charlie?'

He described how he'd been sitting on the bench when he noticed the dogs suddenly going nuts and digging. How he'd assumed it was a bone until he glimpsed the corner of plastic. How he'd pulled it out, taken one look at it and phoned Anjali. Sorry, DI Thompson.

Murdoch finished taking notes and looked up at him. 'Do you mind clarifying why you thought it was so important?'

'Well, there was a fatal stabbing nearby recently,' said Charlie. 'I don't believe the murder weapon was ever found. And I thought the knife had blood on it.'

Murdoch nodded. 'Forensics will establish that. Which reminds me . . .' He beckoned over a constable.

'Make sure forensics take prints and swabs from the bench please,' said Murdoch. 'It's exposed to the elements in a public place and dozens of people have probably sat on it since, but you never know.'

The officer hurried off to do as he asked.

'I think that's all for now,' said Murdoch, pocketing his notebook. 'Thank you. And thanks to you lot as well.'

He bent down and patted the heads of all four dogs in turn. They looked thrilled, as if they'd received a police commendation apiece.

'Reckon it'll be useful?' asked Charlie.

'You never know, it could yield something,' said Murdoch. 'Especially if that blood turns out to be Frank Courtney's.'

'Hopefully it'll keep your bosses off your back for a while,' said Charlie. 'I get the impression they're keen for a result.'

'Aren't they always?' said Murdoch with a roll of the eyes.

'I meant to thank you,' said Charlie. 'For helping us look for Ruby the other day. That was kind of you. I forgot to say so in the midst of all the interview excitement.'

'Pleasure,' said Murdoch modestly. 'Policing comes in many forms. I'm just glad she's safe and sound.' He glanced down at Ruby with a smile, nodded to Charlie and went back to work.

As he led the mud-spattered mutts out of the woods, Charlie mulled over their discovery. Had the knife been there, under their noses – particularly the dogs' noses – all along? And why was it bagged up like that? How oddly thoughtful of the killer to preserve any fingerprints or DNA. It was almost like they wanted it to be found.

76

Corpsefinder General

Sometimes only the seaside will do. With part of the woods still cordoned off and memories of blood-spattered blades still fresh, Charlie decided to switch things up for the next day's walk.

He also fancied a quieter one, so just he and Ruby – no deranged terriers, loopy labs or inveterate diggers – headed for the beach. If a greasy paper wrapper of vinegar-splashed, super-salty chips happened to fall into his lap for lunch, all the better.

As they strolled along the shore, the air damp with imminent rain and the wind rippling Charlie's hair, he looked around. Unlike the town centre, where the slow process of gentrification was beginning to take grip, Framstone seafront had remained relatively unchanged since his childhood. The amusement arcades still looked alluring in a dated way. All flashing lights and retro fonts, like a provincial 1980s British version of Vegas glamour, where lots had been lost in translation during the trip across the Atlantic.

Shops along here were even more stuck in a time warp. Outside each was the compulsory display of buckets, spades and inflatables. Often a rotating rack of postcards or sticks of rock with 'Framstone' written all the way through in blurry upper case. The seagulls, with their dazzling white feathers and bright yellow beaks, were the only things that hadn't faded.

The same old Framstone. Charlie found it all strangely comforting. Ruby was equally pleased, sniffing inquisitively at every tangle of seaweed or interestingly shaped shell.

In the middle distance, Charlie noticed a male figure standing stock-still on the pebbles, hands in his coat pockets, staring out to sea. As he and Ruby got closer, Charlie recognized him.

'I'd say it was a lovely day for it,' he called out. 'But it's not really, is it?' He tried to stay relaxed and sound natural but felt his heart rate quicken at running into a prime suspect for murder.

'No, it's not,' said Rob Thompson, turning to face them. 'I wish I'd worn my thermals. And it's going to chuck it down any minute.'

'So what brings you down here?' asked Charlie, stopping as he drew level with Rob. 'It can't be the tropical climes.'

Rob looked down briefly at Ruby, as she gave his shoes a sniff, then pootled on. 'Much the same as you, I expect,' he said. Was Charlie imagining it or was his tone slightly defensive? Hostile even? 'Fresh air, change of scene and so forth.'

'The air's fresh all right.' Charlie rubbed his hands together to keep warm. He turned to look out to sea, curious about what Rob had been gazing at. There was nothing, except slate grey waves and the outline of a few ships in the foggy distance.

'I hear you made another of your dark discoveries yesterday,' said Rob. 'Charlie Boardman: corpsefinder general. Now does weaponry too.'

'It wasn't me who found the knife, not really,' said Charlie. 'It was Ruby and her furry friends.'

'Right, sure,' said Rob impatiently. 'I must say, I did wonder if where it was buried was significant in some way.'

'How do you mean?' asked Charlie, puzzled.

'Wasn't it right beneath the bench where you and my lovely wife often meet for your little chats?' said Rob, his voice laced with sarcasm. Charlie feared a flash of temper, like the first time they'd met in the Neptune.

'Yeah, but I still don't see what you're getting at,' said Charlie, although he had a sneaking suspicion he did.

'Maybe whoever buried it there was trying to tell you something, that's all,' said Rob.

'Tell me what?' asked Charlie, tiring of his cryptic pronouncements and truculent tone.

Rob shrugged. 'God knows. Stop talking to the police maybe? Just a thought. Anyway, I need to be getting back. Shift starts soon. I'll leave you two to it. Bye, Ruby. See you around, Charlie.'

As he stomped off across the shingle, Charlie looked down at Ruby and rolled his eyes. 'Sounds to me like the surly sarge might have something to hide, Rube,' he muttered. She wagged her tail in agreement.

As Charlie watched him walk away, back towards town, he clocked something. Rob paused briefly by a bench on the promenade where a young man in a tracksuit and baseball cap was sitting, distractedly tapping at his phone. From a distance it looked like the pair exchanged words before a curt handshake. The young man nodded. Rob said something else, then continued on his way.

As he did so, he seemed to sense he was being watched. He glanced back over his shoulder and just for an instant met Charlie's gaze. Rob let his eyes slide off Charlie, as if he could have been looking anywhere, but Charlie was convinced that Rob knew he'd been spotted.

As Rob rounded the corner and vanished from view, Charlie wondered what he'd just witnessed – and the possible consequences of Rob rumbling him.

He had an uneasy feeling that he couldn't shake for the rest of the dog walk. As they meandered on, Charlie mulled over what Rob had said. It hadn't occurred to him that the knife's location could be some sort of warning. Why had Rob made that leap of logic? Because it was him who'd buried it there? Charlie's cogs began to whirr. Could Rob have killed Frank, hence having the murder weapon? Could he have killed Shane after their pub row and the woodland attack? Did he kill both and might he strike again? If so, Charlie himself could even be the next target.

He tried not to dwell on that and thought back over all the red flags about Rob. The vomit at the crime scene and him throwing up outside the pub. The mood swings which verged on instability. The fact that he couldn't stay away from the Neptune. The reason behind his booze binges. The disconnect between his animosity towards Frank and that photo of them looking like best buds. Now he was looking distinctly shifty about being caught in cahoots with a random youth.

Was Sergeant Rob Thompson a bent copper too? Had

he taken over the dead man's drug operation, making an enemy of Luke Courtney in the process? Rob might have been staring out to sea for any number of reasons, but was it related to Shane's murder? Or the drug traffickers? And what better way to avoid suspicion and stay one step ahead than being married to the investigating detective?

Charlie's stomach churned. He suddenly didn't fancy those chips after all.

77

Six Letters and a Punctuation Mark

After being blown and buffeted on the beach, then thoroughly rained on during the walk home, Charlie couldn't wait to get into the warm – but what he found there chilled him to the bone.

'Only us!' he called, closing the front door behind Ruby, unclipping her lead and watching her trot off towards the kitchen, ever-hopeful of food.

'Through here!' came Polly's voice in reply.

Charlie took off his coat, hung up Ruby's lead and followed her through the house. Polly was sitting at the kitchen table, a piece of paper in her hand, staring at it uncomprehendingly but calmly enough.

'Hello, love,' she said, smiling. 'I was hoping you might be able to make sense of this for me.'

'Of course, Mum,' he said, flicking the switch on the kettle. 'What is it?'

As Polly's faculties slowly faded, she seemed increasingly worried by things that arrived in the mail. With her permission, Charlie had taken to opening her post, binning most of it and dealing with any admin himself. He talked his mother through anything important or urgent. Otherwise he didn't bother her with it. He assumed this was more junk mail. Perhaps a confusing bill or something from the bank. Charlie silently wished that he'd got to it before Polly.

'I'm not sure what it is, to be honest,' she said. 'It was waiting on the doormat just now in a plain envelope. Not even a stamp on it but there's a handwritten note inside.'

Charlie's stomach rolled again, like it just had on the beach. As Polly passed him the sheet of A4 and as he reached out to take it, Charlie noticed his fingers tremble. He hoped Polly hadn't noticed too.

'I wondered if it might be a computer password or a meter reading or something,' continued Polly. 'It seems to be written in code. Maybe someone playing a prank?'

Charlie glanced down at what she meant. He was confused at first, his brow furrowing. Who sends a letter like this? And what does it mean? He heard the kitchen clock ticking loudly, like it was inside his head. His mouth went powdery dry as the realization hit.

He felt like he was made of plastic. His muscles weren't working properly. His fingers seemed to lose their grip on reality. He dropped the paper on the kitchen table and felt dizzy, like he might keel over.

Charlie took a beat and regulated his breathing. He picked the note up and looked at it again, trying to ignore the fact that his vision was swimming. With an effort, he brought the note's contents back into focus. Written in black pen in the middle of the paper were just six letters and one punctuation mark – but he was poleaxed by them.

The note read:

FC
SC
PB?

'Any ideas?' asked Polly.

In a voice that sounded weak and far away, Charlie said, 'Yes. I think I should phone the police.'

78

Not Subtle But Effective

'What do you think it means?' asked DS Craig Murdoch, picking up the note – now in an evidence bag – from the table in front of him and reading it again.

FC
SC
PB?

'Surely it's pretty self-explanatory,' said Charlie, trying to keep the exasperation out of his voice. 'It is to me anyway.'

'Enlighten us, please,' said DI Anjali Thompson, playing peacemaker. 'Tell us in your own words how you interpret the text.'

'Well,' said Charlie, 'it's the initials of the two recent murder victims, Frank Courtney and Shane Carter, followed by my mum's initials. Not exactly subtle, but effective in that it's shaken me right up.'

He glanced at the sitting-room door, checking that Polly was still busying herself in the kitchen, making tea and rustling up biscuits. He hadn't spelled this out to his mother, deciding that he wouldn't unless he had to. No need to panic her if it could be avoided. He'd merely told her that he thought it was connected to the recent crimes, hence phoning the police.

They'd been gratifyingly swift to respond. Within ten minutes of his call Anjali and Murdoch were sitting on the sofa, asking him to state the obvious.

'So you think . . .' said Anjali, leaving him to fill in the blanks.

'It's implying that my mum might be the next victim,' said Charlie, hoping the tremor of fear in his voice wasn't too audible. 'It's clearly yet another threat.'

'Wait, how many have there been?' asked Murdoch. 'The only one we have a record of is that toy on your doorstep. Plus the coffee-shop window, if we're counting that.'

Charlie checked the door again. Hearing the familiar sound of Polly still pottering about in the kitchen, he quickly explained about Ruby's disappearance from the woods, which Murdoch already knew about. What they didn't know about was the second toy dog, Ruby's mysterious late-night return and her phosphorescent markings. At the mention of her name Ruby tottered over expectantly. Charlie absent-mindedly fondled her silken ears and she lay down by his feet with a satisfied sigh.

'Why didn't you report this to us at the time?' asked Anjali.

Charlie couldn't tell if the look on her face was puzzlement or disappointment. Maybe both.

'I was reluctant to,' he said. 'I took it as another warning to keep my nose out. Rather than calling you, I thought I'd do as they asked.'

'So what's changed now?' asked Murdoch.

'First I wondered if the location of the buried knife in the woods was significant,' explained Charlie. 'You must have realized, Anjali, that it was right under the bench where we sometimes meet for a catch-up?'

She nodded. 'That had occurred to me.'

'And then this note arrived,' continued Charlie. 'The previous warnings have been to keep my nose out, whereas this seems like . . . something else.'

He meant something far more serious but managed to avoid saying so just as Polly entered the room with a laden tray.

'Here we are,' she said proudly, setting it down on the coffee table. 'A pot of tea and two types of home-made biscuits. These ones are Viennese whirls and those are double-chocolate cookies.'

'You're a marvel, Mrs Boardman,' said Murdoch with a charming smile. 'Paul Hollywood would be proud of those.'

While he helped himself, Polly looking on happily, Anjali asked more questions about the note – when and how it arrived, if they'd seen or heard anything, whether they recognized the paper, envelope or handwriting. Nothing more about its actual contents in front of Polly, which Charlie appreciated.

Once she was satisfied, Anjali put her notebook away. 'We'll send the letter to forensics, see if they can get anything from it,' she said. 'We'll arrange for a patrol car to pass by the house every hour. One of our officers will check in with you every morning and every evening, just to make sure everything is OK. I'd also advise you to keep everything double-locked and not to go out alone until this blows over.'

Charlie nodded along, even though he'd heard all this before. Fat lot of good it did last time. He walked them to the front door, Ruby padding along behind.

'Try not to worry,' said Murdoch, turning to Charlie as they reached the doorstep. 'Just stay close to your mum, which I'm sure you were planning to do anyway.'

'We'll try to do our bit by cracking this confounded case,'

said Anjali. 'The note and the knife give us more to go on, at least.'

She gave Charlie what was supposed to be an encouraging smile but looked about as convinced as he felt.

As he watched them pull away, their car headlights swept across the house, briefly illuminating Ruby's eyes in the darkness. Charlie frowned, trying to work out what had just jogged his memory.

'Come on, Rube,' he muttered. 'Let's see if I'm allowed one of those chocolate cookies or if they're for VIP guests only.'

As he headed back towards the kitchen, Charlie's face clouded over, conflicted with worry. His first instinct was to fight. To try to help catch the killer before anyone else was in danger. But the stakes had just been raised. Now the people most precious to him were being used as pawns, did he really want to play this deadly game?

79

Nothing to See

Although he was sceptical about exactly how much help the police would be, Charlie did follow one piece of Murdoch's advice by staying close to his mum for the next few days.

As well as bringing him some peace of mind, it would have the added benefit of keeping him away from the Coastal Coffee gang, not to mention avoiding any impromptu chats in the woods or on the beach. If someone was watching for signs of sleuthing or snooping, Charlie would give them nothing to see.

He tried to do some bits and bobs of work on his laptop at the kitchen table, idly musing on why his home-made coffee didn't taste nearly as good as Tess's. Polly chatted away as she busied herself with domestic chores.

'DS Murdoch does enjoy my baking, doesn't he?' she said. 'He virtually polished off that plate of biscuits on his own.'

'Hmm?' replied Charlie, only half paying attention. 'Oh, yes, he does. Who can blame him, Mum? The one you let me have was delicious.'

Probably wisely, Polly ignored his sarcasm. 'I suppose they don't get a chance to stop for proper meals,' she continued.

'Detectives seem to be always on the go. Spend half their lives in a car. No wonder he's permanently peckish, the poor thing.'

Charlie couldn't summon up an opinion about the vagaries of Murdoch's diet, so he made a non-committal noise.

'And what about your friend Anjali? I thought she looked tired, bless her.'

'It wouldn't surprise me,' said Charlie. 'She's under pressure to solve these murders. Really putting the hours in. But I thought she looked just fine.'

'Of course you did, dear,' teased Polly. 'You've always had a soft spot for her, ever since school.'

He rolled his eyes. How would his mum even know? He was sure she said this stuff just to wind him up.

'I just hope they catch someone soon.' Polly sighed, as she unfolded the ironing board. 'Karen can't rest until Shane's name gets cleared. She's upset about the police ignoring her but I've reassured her that you're on the case.'

As she came back into the kitchen with her arms full of laundry, Charlie looked on absent-mindedly. He felt for both Karen and Anjali. He hadn't detected physical signs of fatigue like his hawk-eyed mother, but between the high-profile cases and her handful of a husband, he'd bet she was indeed knackered.

Polly began expertly folding the clean clothes and piling them tidily into a laundry basket, ready for ironing. She'd always insisted that she enjoyed doing the washing. Said she found it therapeutic, especially with the radio burbling away in the background.

Charlie smiled to himself. Whenever he'd been responsible for his own laundry, it did his head in. Changing bed linen or ironing shirts was his idea of hell. How Polly made it look so effortless and smell so fresh was a mystery.

As he watched her, something began to shake loose in his memory. The last time that Anjali and Murdoch had been here, sipping Polly's tea and scoffing her baked goods, she'd remarked on how crisply laundered the detective sergeant smelled. Charlie remembered taking it as a dig at his own lack of personal neatness.

In turn, he was reminded of Rough and Tumble fighting over that fabric-conditioning sheet in Framstone Woods. Such fripperies felt like the sort of gimmicky product that a well-groomed young bloke like Murdoch might fall for.

Charlie's mental cogs began to turn. Could the tumble dryer sheet have come from the detective? Might it have become stuck in Murdoch's clothing due to static, then fallen out in the woods without him noticing? It was possible, like putting on a clean jumper and finding a rogue sock in the sleeve.

If so, why did the dogs keep finding them so close to where Charlie had discovered Frank Courtney's body? It was the uniformed officers' job to keep watch over crime scenes, not the plain-clothes detectives'. The chances of Murdoch being in the woods long enough to drop not one but two tumble dryer sheets seemed remote.

Hang on. Unless it was him who kept lurking among the trees and running away when spotted? Could Craig Murdoch be another suspect?

Charlie scoffed at the idea, aware that the death threat had made him paranoid. His imagination was running away with him. Yet the idea of Murdoch being Anjali's ever-present, all-seeing sidekick suddenly started to make him feel uneasy.

80

Curiosity Didn't Kill the Cat

'Dog-walking wingwoman, reporting for duty,' announced Tess on the doorstep.

After receiving the threatening note, Charlie had asked her for a favour. While he stayed home for a couple of days to keep a protective eye on Polly, could Tess pick up Ruby for the odd walk? She'd agreed without hesitation. After all, as Tess pointed out, she probably owed him several hundred dog walks. And he owed her several hundred coffees, he admitted. The pair were probably about quits.

Without being asked, Tess said she'd take Rough, Tumble and Ruby somewhere other than the woods. Either the beach or Framstone Rec. Somewhere with wide-open spaces where she could keep an eye on Ruby at all times. No more wandering off into the trees and disappearing.

Charlie appreciated her understanding. Beneath the puns, repartee and nosiness, Tess was a kind soul with a big heart.

The house seemed oddly empty without Ruby's presence, snoring in a corner or padding around happily. With a shiver, it reminded Charlie of the night she went missing. It was like those twee fridge magnets you saw: *A home without a dog is just a house.*

He couldn't relax until Tess brought her back safely. He breathed a sigh of relief when, an hour or so later, the doorbell rang and she reappeared on the doorstep with all three hounds happily in tow. Ruby looked almost as relieved to be reunited. She wasn't used to walks without Charlie either.

Polly persuaded Tess to come in for a warming drink before she headed off. 'Tea, I think,' she said, smiling. 'I know we can't compete with you on coffee, Tess, but I hope we make a decent cuppa.'

As Polly busied herself – Charlie secretly hoped those biscuits would make an appearance again – he told Tess about his laundry-sheet idea.

'I hope I'm getting some credit here,' she said. 'Without my expertise, you'd have still thought it was a baby wipe.'

'I'll make sure you're mentioned in the speech when I collect my medal,' he replied drily. 'Anyway, what do you think?'

'I like it,' said Tess. 'You're right, clean-cut Mr Murdoch is exactly the uptight type who'd use fabric-conditioner sheets. And they do get stuck in clothing sometimes due to static.'

'I knew it,' said Charlie triumphantly. 'So he might well have been loitering in the woods.'

'I guess the problem is it proves nothing,' added Tess. 'Two tumble dryer sheets in such a large area as Framstone Woods is hardly rock-solid. And it's not like they'd be trace-able back to him. It's a line of enquiry, I reckon, rather than actual evidence.'

Charlie felt deflated. He knew it wasn't a magic bullet but he'd convinced himself it was a breakthrough that put Murdoch firmly in the frame. Since that not-so-cryptic letter plopped on to their doormat, he was clutching at any possibility.

He took a consoling bite of double-chocolate cookie, which Polly had indeed brought back out in honour of Tess's presence. They were clearly for important visitors only, not the second-class citizens who actually lived there.

'I remember what I meant to mention,' said Polly suddenly. 'You left Frank Courtney's funeral order of service lying around and I couldn't help taking a look.'

Tess grinned. 'A woman after my own heart, Polly. Some would say "nosy", I would say "naturally inquisitive".'

'I agree,' said Polly. 'Nothing wrong with a bit of curiosity, as long as it doesn't kill the cat.'

'Cover your ears, you lot,' Tess told the three dogs around their feet.

'So what was it, Mum?' asked Charlie, trying to steer her back on track.

'Oh yes,' said Polly. 'Well, I think I recognized some of the men in one of the old photos. Look.'

She turned to the worktop, retrieved the order of service and put it down in front of Charlie and Tess. 'Here,' said Polly, pointing her finger at the black-and-white photo of police officers in a pub. 'I know that's Frank Courtney in the middle. But I also encountered these two back in my working days.'

They leaned in for a closer inspection. Either side of Rob Thompson and Frank were a pair of bruiser types, all cigarette smoke, chest hair, broken boxers' noses and beady eyes.

'Me and my social worker friends dreaded working with those two,' said Polly. 'Horrible, they were. Always making inappropriate remarks or being mean to clients. They gave us the creeps.'

'Sound like a right couple of charmers,' muttered Charlie, confused about how this helped them.

'Wait, do you see what I see?' said Tess, struggling to contain her excitement.

'No, what?' asked Charlie.

'I spy someone else too,' she said, indicating the top left-hand corner of the photo. Slightly out of focus and only visible in profile, carrying a tray of drinks back from the bar, was a baby-faced junior officer who resembled a young Craig Murdoch.

81

Knowns and Unknowns

'Of course you can go out for a few hours,' insisted Polly. 'Don't be silly. No need to nursemaid me. I'll be just fine on my own.'

Charlie supposed that she knew a thing or two about nursemaiding. It was the night of the supper at Viv and Sue's house. He'd been worried about leaving his mum alone in the house for a few hours – and secretly relished having an excuse to cry off – but Polly was having none of it.

'You deserve an evening off,' she told him. 'You'll be back before you know it. Besides, I've got Ruby to look after me. We'll have a girls' night in, Rube, won't we?'

Ruby wagged happily, as if planning a night of face packs, wine, chocolate and romcoms. Charlie realized he was fighting a losing battle.

He dressed semi-smartly (meaning a clean shirt and the least muddy of his various pairs of boots), kissed Polly goodbye, told her for the umpteenth time to phone if she needed him and reluctantly headed off to the dogwalkers' dinner. Dress code: unspecified, except Tess had predicted Malcolm would dazzle in something new and dapper. Bring: an empty stomach and a bottle or two but no furry friends. This was a night of play, not work.

He rang the doorbell and was ushered into their lived-in but cosy house. Books, vases and mementos lined the walls. Their dining table, normally for two, had its extensions unfolded and had been moved into the front room. Candles and fairy lights twinkled. Mouth-watering smells wafted through from the kitchen as Viv fussed around fetching drinks and Sue pleaded with her to relax, knowing full well she wouldn't.

It was rare to see everyone without dogs. They all looked a little like they had a limb missing. Tess had asked her Coastal assistant Leon to look in on Rough and Tumble, just to make sure they hadn't entirely destroyed her flat. Malcolm had left Ted snoring happily at home. Viv and Sue did pet-sit sometimes when their regular clients went on holiday but, on the whole, Nuts About Mutts were doggy daycare only.

Viv had gone for a Spanish theme, which meant a comically giant pan of paella, not one but two *tortillas española*, a bubbling bowl of meatballs, a vat of *patatas bravas*, plus assorted plates of croquettes, anchovies, prawns, calamari, chorizo, salads, olives and cheeses. There were even some surprisingly delicious side dishes based around beetroot and spinach from Malcolm's allotment. It was more like a buffet for a crowd than a supper for five.

Charlie and Tess had, on several occasions, attempted to psychoanalyse why Viv so loved to feed everyone up round a noisy table. Maybe it harked back to her childhood in a large rackety farming family in the countryside. Maybe it reminded her of her old school canteen, making sure everyone was eating their vegetables and her favourite kids got extra helpings. Maybe she was even one of those fetish 'feeders' you saw on lurid late-night documentaries. Either way, the table was groaning under the weight of it.

It didn't take long for conversation to turn to the case. Charlie and Tess filled everyone in on recent developments: the scarf fibres, chipped teeth and cut knuckles, the dogs digging up the bloodied knife, the warning note, Charlie's hypothesis about the tumble dryer sheet and Murdoch's presence in the background of that old police photo.

For a short time there was silence round the table – partly while everyone mulled over the latest intel, partly while they quietly groaned and loosened their belts.

'Hmm,' said Viv finally. 'It seems to me we have a rogues' gallery of suspects. For Frank Courtney's murder, the police still seem convinced it was Shane Carter. Alternatively it might have been someone connected with Frank's dodgy dealings or the various woodland lurkers. Rob Thompson is in the frame after lying about his relationship to Frank and his possible involvement in police corruption. We've also got our suspicions about the Courtney family and now Craig Murdoch, right?'

'Right,' everyone agreed. Frankly they were relieved to hear her speaking without an offer of more food.

'And for Shane's murder, who knows?' continued Viv. 'Most of the same suspects, bar Shane, of course, but with an added druggy dimension.'

'Don't forget Rob Thompson's attacker,' chipped in Malcolm. 'And whoever tried to ambush Charlie in the woods.'

Charlie smiled. 'Thanks, Malcs. There was me thinking that nobody cared. There's also the Coastal Coffee missile-thrower, of course.' He glanced over at a vengeful-looking Tess.

'Plus the anonymous stalker who's been leaving doorstep toys, dognapping poor Ruby and sending you threatening notes,' added Tess, returning the favour.

'Although lots of these could be the same culprit obviously,' Sue pointed out.

'I can feel one of my migraines coming on,' muttered Malcolm. As Tess had predicted, he was sporting a box-fresh shirt beneath his fine-gauge cardigan.

It went quiet again as everyone agonized over what they knew and didn't know.

Eventually Charlie broke the silence. 'What are we missing? I feel like the answers are all here but we can't see Framstone Woods for the trees.'

'I might be able to help with that,' said Sue. She self-consciously brushed aside a strand of grey-blonde hair and gave a shy smile as all eyes turned to her.

82

Murder Map

As they watched, Sue stood up. She slowly walked to the head of the table, appearing to relish the theatre of it all, pausing only to tuck her familiar knitting bag out of sight. It had been on the floor behind her chair and now she nudged it under the sideboard with her foot. Whatever she was about to do clearly needed some space.

There was a hush of anticipation until Viv muttered, 'What the actual hell, love?'

'Don't worry, I'm not about to confess.' Sue giggled. 'But maybe I can help us root out someone who will.'

Charlie found himself breathing a sigh of relief and relaxed in his chair again.

'I just thought a visual aid might help,' said Sue, popping round the corner and swiftly re-emerging with the cork board from the kitchen wall. 'An evidence board, if you like.'

'I knew all those true-crime documentaries would come in handy some day,' said Viv proudly.

'No, you didn't,' said Sue with a chuckle, swiftly clearing the board of takeaway menus, holiday snaps and business cards. The librarian in her was suddenly apparent again. 'You're always demanding to watch some brain-rotting reality show instead. But they might just come into their own here.'

The board was now empty. As everyone watched and chipped in suggestions, Sue began to construct a visualization of everything they knew.

In the absence of crime-scene photos or mugshots, Malcolm drew rudimentary portraits on paper napkins and handed them over. Tess went back through the notes on her phone, calling out dates, times and places that seemed significant, while Viv jotted them on Post-it notes. Charlie deployed his graphic designer's eye by sketching rough maps and still lives of objects like the wigs, bloodied knife, toy dogs, vape, football scarf and tumble dryer sheet.

Sue stuck it all on the cork board with drawing pins, then joined the dots with different coloured offcuts of wool. By the time she'd finished and stepped back to admire her handiwork, it genuinely looked like something from a crime thriller – albeit with hand-drawn pictures and a lack of newspaper cuttings, like you usually saw in the movies.

'Whoa,' said Tess without a trace of irony for once. 'Great work, Sue. I feel like an FBI agent who's about to blow the biggest case of her career wide open, catch who assassinated the president and get a commendation.'

'That's my girl,' said Viv.

'The Professor couldn't have done a better job, Sue,' said Charlie. 'Not least due to a lack of working back legs and opposable thumbs.'

'Colour me impressed too,' said Malcolm. 'But what now?'

'I was hoping you wouldn't ask me that.' Sue shrugged. 'I guess it's a makeshift murder map. We need to study it and work out the right direction to take.'

They all sipped their drinks and stared at the collage of places and faces, events and incidents, connections and conjecture. In some ways it made things even more confusing. In other ways it clarified them.

As a graphic designer – not to mention an inveterate daydreamer – thinking visually was Charlie's superpower. He let his eye roam slowly across the material, trying to clear his mind, shut out external noise and focus. He found himself rubbing that ferret-scarred patch of skin on his finger, which always seemed to aid his concentration. Slowly but surely the mists began to clear. A mental picture began to form. He closed his eyes to fully concentrate on it.

He held his breath. So did everyone else.

'I don't want to speak too soon,' said Charlie, opening his eyes to see everyone staring back at him expectantly. 'But I reckon I know who the killer is.'

83

Prepared to Kill for It

There was stunned silence round the table. You could have heard a pin drop, let alone a knitting needle. Everyone looked at Charlie, then at the impromptu evidence board, then back to Charlie. He took a nerve-steadying sip of Rioja and licked his lips.

'Oh, for goodness' sake,' said Malcolm impatiently. 'The drama! This is like one of those long pauses before they announce the winner of a T V talent show.'

'Yes, come on,' said Viv. 'Cough up, my dear Holmes. After all this cooking, you owe me that much.'

Charlie chuckled. 'I do indeed. I suspect a full stomach is what fuelled my brain.'

Just like Sue had done a short while ago, Charlie pushed his chair back, stood up and walked slowly round to the pinboard. He studied it again and nodded to himself. Quietly confident that he was right, he turned to his friends. You could sense the anticipation and impatience in the room.

'We're pretty sure Frank Courtney was a bent copper, right? He likely had links to the drug trade, hence allowing dealing in his pub. That's how he could purchase a Portuguese villa in cash, do up the pub, buy Jackie a bling engagement ring and pay private-school fees.'

There were murmurs of agreement.

'And we thought that either Sergeant Rob Thompson – Frank's one-time sidekick but now his sworn enemy – or Frank's son Luke might have taken over his operation when Frank was killed. Maybe they even fought for it.'

More affirmative noises.

'But what if someone else was hell-bent on taking over Frank's criminal empire? And what if they were prepared to kill for it?'

'I suppose that sounds pretty plausible,' admitted Viv. 'But who?' She looked at the evidence board herself, then round at Sue, frowning like she was none the wiser.

'I've got a good idea of who you mean,' announced Tess out of the blue. Everyone's heads swivelled in her direction, like meerkats sensing danger.

Charlie grinned at her. 'I thought you might. Go on then, who?'

Tess cleared her throat and smiled triumphantly, savouring the moment. She'd always loved being right. She looked round the table, then back at Charlie. 'It's Craig Murdoch. Am I right?'

'As we all know, Tess Cheong is rarely wrong,' said Charlie. 'Detective Sergeant Craig Murdoch. Not just a corrupt copper but a double murderer. And now . . .'

He paused for effect again, partly just to press Malcolm's buttons.

'All we need to do is prove it.'

84

One Fateful Night

There were intakes of breath round the table. Viv sensed that fortification was needed and topped up everyone's glasses. It really was a delicious Rioja. Malcolm's choice, Charlie suspected. He took pride in knowing his wine. Charlie wanted to be like that when he grew up.

'OK,' Sue said once everyone had taken a sip. 'Tell us how and why.'

'Maybe take us back to the beginning,' added Viv.

'Sure,' said Charlie, pulling up the chair nearest the evidence board. 'I'm thinking out loud here, so don't sue me if I miss anything out. And feel free to chip in. Not that you normally need any invitation, Tess.'

She looked faux-outraged and did a 'my lips are sealed' gesture, which nobody quite believed.

Charlie pointed at his sketchy recreation of the order-of-service photo from Frank Courtney's funeral.

'Right,' he began. 'We know that Murdoch overlapped with Frank in Framstone Police. Judging from this photo and their relative ages, when Murdoch joined as a probationary constable, Frank was approaching retirement. He had a whole criminal empire by this point, very likely exploiting – and in some cases, we think, abusing – the vulnerable young men he encountered through his police and community work.'

'What a scumbag,' muttered Sue. Without her kitting to occupy her hands, she was shelling pistachios, popping them into her mouth and nibbling pensively.

'Well, quite,' continued Charlie. 'Frank was always on the lookout for young men to join his network. He spotted naive new blood in Murdoch and recruited him to be a gofer in his drug operation.'

'Do we think Frank abused him, too?' asked Viv, her brow furrowing with concern.

'I honestly don't know,' admitted Charlie. 'I'd guess it was often his way of asserting control, so it's possible. Abuse is often about power more than sex. Then again, abusing a fellow officer might be too risky. What we do know is that Murdoch grew up without parents and was raised by his grandmother instead. It might well be that Frank found that out and inveigled his way in as a surrogate father figure. But what I'm more sure about is that over the years, Murdoch became Frank's deputy and partner in crime.'

'Frank then left the force, though, right?' asked Malcolm.

'Yep,' replied Charlie. 'When he retired to run the Neptune, I'd wager Murdoch became his top police contact, secretly keeping an eye on things from the inside.'

'I can see how that would work,' Viv said, looking round at Sue for her approval. 'In return for a cut he could feed Frank police intel. Tip him off about rivals or raids. Help keep things running with minimal interference from the law.'

'Exactly,' said Charlie.

'If it was so lucrative, why would Craig suddenly kill him?' asked Sue. Absorbed in the moment, she'd stopped shelling pistachios and was all ears.

'Good question,' said Charlie. 'My guess is a mixture of greed, ambition and sheer happenstance.'

'How do you mean?' asked Viv.

'I think that the higher Murdoch rose, both in the police force and the criminal underworld, the more he had to lose,' said Charlie. 'Meanwhile, Frank was becoming reckless. Maybe as his kids flew the nest, he grew increasingly frustrated by being in the closet. Maybe he was struggling with getting older. Some sort of midlife crisis.'

'Hence the wig and woodland hook-ups,' said Malcolm.

'That's what I figured,' agreed Charlie. 'His sex life was becoming chaotic. Indiscreet. Murdoch might've been worried it would compromise him. So one fateful night, he followed Frank to the woods.'

'And saw him with Shane Carter?' asked Viv with a sad sigh.

Charlie nodded. 'We can safely assume so. Except their tryst went pear-shaped. Frank had swapped wigs to look younger, maybe to match his dating-app profile. But it might have meant that Shane recognized him as his abuser from back when he'd been in care.'

'Oh, how awful,' said Sue, clutching her face with both hands. 'Shane must've been in a right old state.'

'It seems so,' agreed Charlie. 'Who knows in what order it all happened, but Shane had a visceral reaction and threw up . . .'

'See those three pools of vomit at the crime scene,' said Tess.

Charlie let that one slide out of sheer embarrassment.

Nobody needed to know that two of them were his. 'And then Shane attacked him,' he continued. 'Probably picked up a nearby log. In his fury, he hit Frank hard enough to knock him to the ground, dazed and semi-conscious.'

'Shane didn't kill him, though?' asked Viv, sounding relieved.

'No,' said Charlie, pleased to assert Shane's innocence. 'He wasn't lying when he insisted he wasn't guilty. That brief flash of anger aside, Shane hated violence. As a drug dealer, he carried a knife for protection – ever since his teenage conviction, which was self-defence in another flash of temper – but never used it. I'd hazard a guess that he pulled it out when Frank was sitting there at his mercy but Shane couldn't go through with stabbing him.'

'So what did he do?' asked Malcolm.

Through the window, the autumn night had closed in. It was completely dark in a way it only can be outside urban areas. The candlelit room felt atmospheric, almost like they were telling each other ghost stories. Only these ones were all too real.

'Panicked, dropped the knife and fled,' replied Charlie. 'Enter Craig Murdoch, who'd been watching all this unfold from a short distance away in the trees.'

'Where we think a fabric-conditioning sheet fell out of his clothing without him noticing,' said Tess, pointing at Charlie's sketch on the board and looking pleased with herself.

'That could have been now or later, but yes,' agreed Charlie. 'Either way, Murdoch saw that Frank was indeed compromised. He'd just been attacked by one of their own drug dealers, who now knew for sure that Frank was on hook-up apps. Murdoch spotted a chance to finish off Frank while he was incapacitated, pin his murder on Shane and take over as top dog.'

There was silence while everyone took this in. Charlie and Tess swapped satisfied looks across the table. Malcolm stretched and blew his cheeks out at the enormity of it all. Sue patted Viv's hand and gave her a reassuring smile.

'So it was Murdoch who actually killed him?' asked Viv at last.

'Yes,' said Charlie, indicating his still life of a knife. He felt hammy and theatrical, a little like he was watching a whodunnit. It wasn't an unpleasant sensation. 'He must've seen Shane drop the knife. It was relatively easy to pick it up and stab Frank where he was sitting.'

'But that would've left fingerprints,' said Malcolm.

'Not necessarily,' pointed out Charlie. 'As an experienced detective, Murdoch probably carried gloves and plastic bags with him.'

'He does seem pretty fastidious,' said Tess with a disdainful curl of the lip.

'I refer you to the tumble dryer sheets,' agreed Charlie. 'I imagine he put on gloves before picking up the knife, then popped it in a plastic bag afterwards, preserving it as evidence. He might need it later to help frame Shane, whereupon it could be magically discovered.'

'What an evil swine,' said Viv. Nobody argued.

'So when Anjali gets the lab results back on the knife, you reckon they'll find Frank's blood on the blade and Shane's prints on the handle but nothing else?' said Tess.

'I'd stake money on it,' said Charlie.

'How about those red fibres we kept hearing about?' asked Sue, pointing at Charlie's illustration of a football scarf. 'If

Shane wasn't wearing his scarf and didn't stab Frank, why were they found on his body?'

'Good question,' said Viv, turning expectantly to Charlie for the answer.

'Ah, interesting,' said Charlie. 'My guess is that Murdoch wanted to make the case against Shane even stronger. He knew Shane wore a signature scarf but didn't realize he only wore it on match days. He probably broke into Shane's flat and stole it that night. Or even early the next morning.'

'Wouldn't that be risky?' asked Malcolm. 'What if Shane had caught him in the act?'

'Shane was badly shaken up.' Charlie shrugged. 'He could've run off somewhere to chemically calm himself down or be in a drug stupor in bed.'

'And Murdoch planted fibres from it?' asked Viv.

'Yes, I'd say so,' said Charlie. 'I mean, all this is still just a hunch, but I'm confident it hangs together. We'd still need proof or a confession.'

'When do you reckon he did the planting?' asked Sue.

'After I found Frank's body, Murdoch was first on the scene, remember? He examined the body and called out to Anjali that it was "one of ours", so she must've been out of sight while he did it. I remember it bugging me that nobody seemed terribly surprised at finding Frank Courtney dead. Presumably Anjali knew he was a wrong 'un, playing risky games . . .'

'And Murdoch wasn't surprised because, well, he'd killed him,' added Tess, torn between horror at the deed and happiness that they'd worked it all out.

'So why did he murder poor Shane?' asked Malcolm with

a rare frown. 'He'd already set him up for murder. Wasn't that enough?'

'I was just coming to that,' said Charlie. 'Although I might need another drink first.'

85

What a Piece of Work

'I've got just the thing,' said Sue, leaping to her feet and scurrying over to their drinks cabinet. 'We developed a bit of a taste for this on holiday in Bilbao last year, so we brought a couple of bottles back.'

With a flourish, she produced a bottle of orujo. Round the table, there were looks of bafflement from everyone but Viv.

'It's a herbal liqueur,' explained Viv, as Sue rooted out five shot glasses. 'A traditional after-dinner tipple over there. Pretty strong but it's supposed to aid digestion.'

Tess grinned. 'Sounds good to me.' She took a swig and winced. 'Hoochie mama. That'll put hairs on your chest, Malcolm.'

'I wax,' said Malcolm. 'As well you know.'

Without saying so, everyone welcomed the release of tension as they momentarily put their investigations on pause. They took tentative sips of orujo, grazed contemplatively at the leftover food, rearranging their numb legs and popping to the bathroom.

When everyone was settled back at the table, the mood turned serious again.

'So where were we?' asked Charlie.

'You were about to tell us why Murdoch killed Shane,' said Tess. 'And don't pretend you didn't know that, Lieutenant Columbo. Just one more thing indeed. You'll be wearing a crumpled raincoat and waving a cigar around next.'

'Well, Anjali can confirm this, but I imagine Murdoch subtly steered the investigation round to Shane becoming prime suspect for Frank's murder. He had a previous conviction for knife crime, of course, so would have been on the police's radar already.'

'And then there was his very public bust-up with Rob Thompson shortly before he was attacked,' said Tess.

'Which just happened to be yards from where Frank's body was found,' added Sue. She shook her head sadly. 'It wouldn't have looked good for poor Shane.'

You could sense mixed feelings round the table – quiet outrage on Shane Carter's behalf, mixed with growing loathing for Craig Murdoch.

Charlie nodded. 'Absolutely. After that, it was a matter of Murdoch drip-feeding further evidence to incriminate Shane and pacing the police inquiry so it looked like they'd gradually rooted out the culprit, rather than been handed him on a plate.'

'I assume that's where planting the fibres came in?' said Viv.

'I mean, world's smallest violin and all that, but I imagine it must have been frustrating for Murdoch,' said Charlie. 'Going through the motions of waiting for forensic tests and phone data to come back, when he knew full well what they'd say. Waiting for the bloodied knife to be miraculously found with Shane's prints all over it.'

'So he ran out of patience and murdered him instead?' asked Malcolm.

'Yes and no,' said Charlie. 'Maybe he thought the case against Shane would be more watertight than it was. Maybe he hoped Shane would confess that he'd met Frank in the woods that night and even that he'd attacked him. But this wasn't Shane's first police grilling. He relied on the classic "no comment" defence and because Anjali plays things by the book, she let him go.'

'And Shane walking free spooked Murdoch?' asked Tess.

'I guess so,' said Charlie. 'Maybe he suspected that Shane knew it was him who'd done it really – or at least knew that he was in cahoots with Frank Courtney. Maybe Shane had seen them together or heard something on the drug grapevine. Maybe Murdoch worried that under police pressure, Shane would expose Frank's drug operation and it would lead back to him.'

'And he killed Shane for his silence?' said Viv, her eyebrows crinkling with concern.

'So it seems,' said Charlie. He exhaled sorrowfully and sipped his drink to compose himself. 'He could've met him at the beach to make sure he'd keep schtum. Perhaps Shane refused and they argued. Either way, Murdoch ended up forcibly drowning him.'

Everyone considered that for a second. What an awful death it must have been.

'At which point the football scarf came in handy again?' said Sue, after a few audible ticks of the mantelpiece clock. Her mouth was set in a disapproving frown.

'Murdoch kept it as further insurance,' said Charlie, nodding. 'He's a calculating so-and-so. He realized he could tie it round Shane's neck and strengthen the case against him for Frank's murder. Further down the line, the knife would seal the deal. A dead man is fitted up for murder and can't say anything different.'

'Oh, lordy,' muttered Malcolm, his eyes downcast, before looking up and asking, 'How about Shane's own death? What did Murdoch think would happen with that?'

'It would either look like suicide or a gangland thing,' said Charlie. 'Shane had tried to take his own life before. It might look like he was consumed by guilt over killing Frank. Since he was a known drug dealer and now an alleged killer, Murdoch probably assumed nobody would look into it too hard. Police resources are stretched. They'd prioritize Frank's murder.'

'Poor, poor Shane,' said Sue. Viv put her arm round her and gave her shoulders a rub. Malcolm looked damp-eyed but gave Tess and Charlie a brave smile.

'So when did you work all this out?' asked Viv, being the one to break the silence again. 'And how?'

'It's been slowly percolating over the past week, but looking at Sue's evidence board is what sealed it.' Charlie glanced at her gratefully and she beamed with pride. 'I realized that it all fits. A bent copper taking over from Frank seemed likely. If it wasn't Rob Thompson, who could it be? Spotting Murdoch in that old police photo got my cogs whirring. The rest clicked into place.'

'He was always telling us pesky dogwalkers to mind our own beeswax too,' said Tess. 'He didn't know who he was dealing with.'

Charlie nodded. 'I reckon he also revisited the crime scene to check on it and retrieve the knife from its hiding place. Except I kept disturbing him as he lurked among the trees, so he'd escape to try another time.'

'So it was Murdoch who sent you those sinister warnings?' asked Malcolm. He shook his head in disbelief.

'The more we poked around, the worse the warnings got,' said Charlie, his mouth downturning as he considered the threats. 'The first toy dog on my doorstep told me to keep my nose out. When that didn't do the trick, he lured Ruby away – let's face it, fairly easy if you use treats – to imply that harm would come to her.'

'Hang on, though,' interjected Viv. 'Murdoch joined the search for Ruby in the woods, remember?'

'Yes, but funny how he happened to be on the spot, wasn't it?' said Charlie. 'My guess is he left Ruby somewhere nearby, maybe in his car, then nipped back to help out and throw us off the scent. Then came the death-threat letter, which rather backfired.'

'How so?' asked Viv.

'It was supposed to imply that my mum would be next,' said Charlie. 'Actually, it confirmed that Frank and Shane were killed by the same person – namely whoever sent the note. It also led to the car headlights clue.'

'Whoa, Nelly,' said Tess, holding up her palm. 'Rewind. What car headlights clue?'

'Sorry.' Charlie chuckled. 'Maybe I just thought about that one, rather than saying it out loud. Remember I saw the drug smugglers at the beach flashing their headlights? When Murdoch drove away from our house the other night, the sweep of his headlights rang a bell. I also heard a car door slam when he dropped off Ruby and heard a car rounding the corner after Coastal's window was smashed.'

'Not his most serious crime,' said Tess bitterly 'But I won't forgive or forget.'

Nobody doubted her. Tess was an excellent grudge-bearer.

'It didn't have to be the same car, sure –' Charlie shrugged – 'but it all connected in my head. Murdoch had also seen up close how much Polly and Ruby mean to me. That's why he knew threatening them would make me back off.'

'And how much I mean to you too, right?' said Tess, only half joking. 'Hence the brick through my window.'

'Yes, he might have overestimated my feelings there,' teased Charlie.

She stuck out her tongue at him.

'And you think that the dogs digging up the murder weapon was some kind of threat too?' asked Sue.

'Rob Thompson worked that one out actually,' said Craig. 'Well, sort of. He led me to it anyway. Murdoch knew me and Anjali were old mates, which he didn't like one bit. Probably saw it as a threat to him. I'd guess he followed her one time and saw her meet me on the bench for a chat, so he stashed the knife there as an extra warning to stop talking. I reckon he buried it deliberately shallow, close to the surface, increasing the likelihood of it being found. Our dogs duly obliged.'

'Very thorough,' said Malcolm, smiling. 'I'm impressed, Agatha Boardy. Anything else in your bulging dossier?'

'I think that's covered everything,' said Charlie, rolling his shoulders and stretching his neck to release the tension. 'Which is a relief because I've got a very dry mouth.' He took a swig of orujo and pulled a face. It was hard work, this deduction business.

'So what's the next step, chief?' asked Viv.

'Telling Anjali, I suppose,' said Charlie. He gave a wry grin. 'Although I fear she'll take some persuading.'

Laying out his theory in detail, seeing it all slot together, had been satisfying. Charlie felt physically shattered and mentally invigorated at the same time. It was a nice feeling, reminiscent of a post-match glow during his sporting days. He had the Framstone killer firmly in his sights. After the tragic demise of Shane and the threats to Charlie's family, this had grown personal. Now it was time to put his hypothesis to the test and bring his opponent down.

86

Strike First, Ask Questions Later

Leaving the others to gossip over a less cosmopolitan nightcap, Charlie said his goodnights and slipped out. Feeling guilty about leaving Polly and Ruby on their own, he was keen to get back to them.

As he walked away from Viv and Sue's house, the cosy glow of their porch light fading behind him, Charlie took his phone out of his coat pocket. He'd been so busy playing the grandstanding sleuth that he'd forgotten to check it for the past couple of hours.

What he saw on the home screen caused his stomach to do a somersault. He'd missed three calls from Polly but there were no voicemails or texts to suggest why. Oh no.

He quickened his stride, trying Polly's mobile as he hurried along beneath the street lights. Nothing. It rang out. Next he tried the house landline. Again it kept ringing. Charlie had a bad feeling. He broke into a run.

As he pounded and panted through the streets of Framstone, Charlie fought the urge to catastrophize but couldn't help himself. His mind raced with horrible possibilities. Had Murdoch escalated from woodland lurking to home invasion? Had he abducted Polly, like he had Ruby? Had he even made good on his threat in that note and visited with murder in mind? Charlie picked up the pace.

By now his lungs were burning and his knees were protesting. His shins ached from the impact of dashing down concrete pavements, but he didn't care. If his mother had come to any harm, he'd never forgive himself.

Realizing he was just a few blocks away now, Charlie put on a spurt. The safety of Polly and Ruby were his priority. Anything else, he could deal with. Make sure they're OK. Protect them first. Anything else could wait.

If he saw Murdoch, he decided as he rounded the corner, he'd hit him first and ask questions later. What was it Mike Tyson used to say? Everyone has a plan until they get punched in the face.

The house was dark. Not even the hall light was on. Gasping for breath, Charlie fumbled and fiddled, struggling to get his keys in the lock. After what seemed an eternity, he burst through the front door.

'Mum!' he called, frantically looking into all the rooms on the ground floor. 'Ruby!' Everywhere was empty, including Ruby's basket in the kitchen. The silence was deafening.

He took the stairs two at a time. By now his chest was heaving with panic. He flung each door open as he passed it. Every room was exactly as he'd left it a few hours ago. There was no sign of Polly or Ruby.

One door left. As he headed for Polly's bedroom door, his pulse hammering and heart in his mouth, Charlie feared what he might find behind it.

He reached for the handle with a clammy palm, then gave a sudden start. Someone was turning the handle and opening it from the inside. Charlie balled his fists and braced himself. Murdoch was in for the surprise of his life.

'There you are,' said a familiar voice. A voice he loved.

Polly appeared round the door, putting her arms into her dressing gown. The smile on her face turned to concern when she saw Charlie's expression.

'What's the matter, dear?' she asked. 'You look like you've seen a ghost.'

'I think I have,' wheezed Charlie. 'Are you and Ruby OK?'

'Of course we are,' she said. 'Aren't we, Rube?'

Over her shoulder, Charlie saw Ruby, curled up on Polly's bed with a guilty look on her face. Her tail thumped against the quilt when she heard who it was.

'It's just that I missed some calls from you and I thought . . . Well, I don't know what I thought,' said Charlie.

'Oh, I didn't mean to worry you,' said Polly with a wave of her hand. 'I just called to wish you goodnight. Then I called again to remind you that all the doors were double-locked. Then I called to tell you that Ruby was coming up to bed with me for a change. She'd been missing you, so I thought she could do with the company. And without you around, she was being protective. Didn't leave my side all evening, bless her.'

'Why didn't you leave a voice message saying all this?' he managed to ask through his gulps for air.

'Oh, you know I hate those things,' she said. 'I never know what to say.'

He couldn't help smiling at that. He'd never known his mother to be lost for words. Charlie bent over with his hands on his knees, breathing hard with a blend of exhaustion and relief.

'You didn't run home on my account, did you?'

'Yes, but it's fine,' he said. 'So nobody came round? No more notes? No rings on the doorbell?'

'Not a thing,' said Polly. 'Shall I come down and make you some tea? A cup of cocoa before bed perhaps?'

He smiled again. She often offered him a night-time cocoa, even though he hadn't touched it since he was a boy.

'No, thanks, Mum,' he said. 'You get back to bed. You and Rube look cosy. I'm going to turn in, too. Got a big day tomorrow.'

'OK, dear,' she said, smiling. 'Goodnight. From us both.'

As she closed the door, Charlie glimpsed Ruby giving him one last wag. Now he knew they were safe, his bed was beckoning. Catching the Framstone killer would make the whole town sleep more soundly at night.

87

Our Mutual Friend

He texted Anjali the next morning, suggesting they meet on their usual bench. Charlie didn't care who might be watching any more.

When she replied saying she'd bring his 'new best mate' Murdoch along, Charlie's nerves jangled. He realized with relief that she was joking when she followed it with a winking emoji.

As Charlie and Ruby entered the woods, Rough and Tumble alongside them, he felt almost as creaky as his dear old dog. That's what running halfway across town for a false alarm will do for you. He'd picked up the two usual coffees from Coastal en route. Tess had been swamped with customers but mouthed 'Good luck' as she handed him Rough and Tumble's leads.

'Your usual, madam,' he said, proffering Anjali her cup with a slight bow.

'Why thank you, kind sir.' She grinned gratefully and pretended to fan herself like a Regency lady.

As Rough and Tumble disappeared into the bushes, Ruby snuffling along behind, they sat down and sipped their drinks, enjoying the shot of warmth on a chilly autumn day when you could see your breath in front of your face.

'So what's on your mind, Boardy Boy?' asked Anjali. 'Judging by the look on your face, it's something big.'

She always had been able to read him like a book. He remembered trying to charm her at school, before she cut him off with: 'Cut to the chase, Champagne Charlie. Which piece of homework is it you want to copy?'

This time was different. He was about to accuse her closest colleague and trusted partner not just of being a corrupt copper but a double murderer, too.

He took a deep breath and dived in. Trying to stay cool and logical, keeping emotion out of his voice, Charlie laid it all out for her the best he could from start to finish. No evidence board this time but he could still visualize it in his mind.

He explained how they strongly suspected that Frank Courtney had run a drug and money laundering racket, first as a corrupt policeman and later as a publican. How he spent the dirty money on private-school fees and Portuguese property purchased in cash. How he potentially used abuse and coercive control of vulnerable young men, probably including Shane Carter, to recruit them and assert dominance. How he was likely to have groomed junior officers like Craig Murdoch to do his bidding. How the dogwalkers had deduced that Murdoch eventually spotted his chance to stab Frank, pin it on Shane and take over the operation. And finally how Murdoch had been rattled by Shane's release from custody and probably drowned him to ensure his silence.

When he'd finished, Charlie took a sip of his coffee, which was now tepid, got his breath back and prepared for Anjali's response. He still had no idea what to expect.

'This is a lot to process, Charlie,' she said eventually.

'A hell of a lot. If it was anyone else sharing their unproven theories, I'd tell them where to go. But it's you, so I'm listening, at least. I'm not saying I believe you – but I'm not saying I don't, if that makes sense.'

'Sort of,' said Charlie, smiling. 'Does any of it have the ring of truth to you?'

Anjali sighed and gazed into the trees before turning to face him. 'Some of it. I've long had my suspicions that Frank Courtney had been a bent copper, then became even dodgier after he retired. You hear and see things, you know?'

'I'm sure you do,' said Charlie. 'What about our mutual friend Murdoch?'

'That's a different story,' said Anjali. 'Craig is a good mate and a good copper. He's earned my trust and vice versa. I'll back him until proven otherwise.'

'I can respect that,' said Charlie gently, sensing her resistance to the idea and trying not to antagonize her. 'Does he have links to the old guard, though?'

'Craig's a different generation,' said Anjali firmly. 'Corruption does seem to have been pretty systemic in the bad old days, more's the pity. It was like the Wild West once upon a time. All police forces have cleaned up their act since then. That includes Framstone's.'

He nodded. 'I'm sure it has.' He knew at least one copper he could trust and she was sitting right next to him. 'What about Murdoch's role in the two murder investigations? Anything strike you?'

Anjali's brows knitted and she licked her lips. 'Hmm, well,' she began, choosing her words carefully, 'what I will say is that Craig was definitely the driving force behind certain aspects of the inquiry in its early stages.'

'Which aspects?' pushed Charlie.

'Don't assume this means you're right,' she warned, 'but matching the red fibres on Frank Courtney's body to Shane Carter's football scarf. It was also Craig who worked out that the murder weapon was the same type of knife used in Shane's previous offence.'

'That tracks,' said Charlie. 'Did he push for Shane to be charged, even when you didn't have enough proof?'

'He did,' admitted Anjali. 'But that's not unusual in and of itself. Coppers take pride in their work. We want results. Nobody likes letting a prime suspect walk free or seeing their hard graft wasted.'

'I'll bet he was behind bringing me in for questioning, too,' said Charlie. 'Maybe thought it would make us dog-walkers back off again?'

'You were a person of interest.' Anjali shrugged. 'Nobody would deny that. Not even you, surely.'

Charlie smiled, conceding the point. 'Fair enough. Has anything else about him raised alarm bells? Or even eyebrows?'

'Not hugely,' she said. 'He's always seemed pretty boring and vanilla to me.'

'That could be a deliberate cover,' said Charlie. 'Presenting as normal to hide in plain sight. How about money? Does he seem better off than someone of his rank?'

'Well, I don't think he has any holiday villas or expensively educated children,' she said. 'He drives a nice newish car . . .'

'Not a dark-coloured BMW, perchance?' asked Charlie, recalling the one he'd seen flashing its headlights on the beach.

'Yes, a metallic grey Beamer,' said Anjali. 'How did you know?'

'Just a hunch,' said Charlie. 'Anything else?'

'I suppose he takes pride in his appearance. His suits and shoes are a bit smarter than the average detective's, but I wouldn't know how expensive they are.'

'Subtly luxurious tailoring, I'd bet,' said Charlie. 'Hence the tumble dryer sheets and dry-cleaning smell. What about comms? Does he have two phones or often slope off to take personal calls?'

'I haven't seen a second phone,' said Anjali. 'He steps outside to make calls sometimes but I assumed it was women. Coppers are a nosy, gossipy bunch. I wouldn't blame him for keeping his dating life on the downlow.'

'But it might be drug suppliers or criminal contacts rather than girlfriends, right?' nudged Charlie.

'Do you have any evidence?' Anjali asked, bridling slightly. 'Proper, actual evidence? Because accusing a fellow officer of corruption – let alone double murder – isn't something we do lightly, let me tell you.'

'I would've thought it was all pretty compelling, wasn't it?' protested Charlie. 'Surely you can check his bank accounts, call logs, search his house . . .'

'It's my career on the line here,' Anjali said, her voice steely. 'I can't go around getting warrants and investigating colleagues on a whim. What you've told me begs some questions, sure, but it's all circumstantial and speculative. And let's not forget that the two key witnesses are now dead.'

'Aren't you interested in the truth?' urged Charlie. 'In an innocent young man being framed for murder, then killed himself?'

'Shane Carter was hardly a paragon of virtue,' argued Anjali. 'To an outsider this looks like a conspiracy theory cooked up by some nosy dogwalkers and a bereaved mother.

If you're accusing Frank Courtney of recruiting colleagues, you're questioning the integrity of a whole generation of officers who worked with him. That's a helluva hornets' nest to stir up.'

'Yes, but –' protested Charlie, before Anjali cut him off with a raise of her hand.

'And don't dare accuse me of not caring,' she said, her tone hardening. 'I've been working all hours for the last two months, trying to bring a killer to justice. Every time we make progress, something else happens – an assault, vandalism, threats, another death – to complicate the case further.'

'Tell me about it,' said Charlie, trying to placate her. 'We've been going round in circles too.'

Anjali sighed with exasperation. 'The big difference is that my entire career is built around law and order. Punishing criminals and keeping the public safe. It's not just a hobby for me, like it is for you and your mates.'

'I think you're afraid of rocking the boat,' said Charlie petulantly and immediately regretting it. 'Closing ranks like your lot usually do.'

'Think what you like,' said Anjali, standing up and throwing her coffee cup in the recycling bin with more force than usual. 'It's easy to be an idealist. To be anti-police and cynical about our motives. I happen to live in the real world.'

'So you're not even going to look into Murdoch?' asked Charlie in disbelief.

'Not until you can bring me something more concrete,' said Anjali, giving the pooches a brief pat before turning to leave. 'Pardon the pun, but wake up and smell the coffee.'

88

Caught in the Crossfire

By the time he got back to Coastal with the wolf pack, the full war cabinet had assembled. Eagerly awaiting news, the dogwalkers' mood was soon deflated.

'And you told her everything we'd worked out?' asked an aghast Viv.

Charlie nodded. 'Everything. She said it was all either circumstantial or based on hearsay.'

'We can't do the police's job for them,' said Malcolm in exasperation. 'Surely we just take them our suspicions, then they try to prove it?'

'Afraid it doesn't work like that,' admitted Sue. 'Anjali's right. There's not enough evidence to go around pointing fingers.'

'Yet,' chipped in Tess. 'Not enough evidence *yet*. Come on, is there anything we might've missed? Another thread that Anjali could pull on to unravel the whole thing?'

Except for the odd clinking coffee cup or snoring canine, all was quiet around the table as they racked their brains.

'I wondered if Rob was a factor,' said Charlie at last. 'Anjali said something about us questioning the integrity of a whole generation who'd worked with Frank. That would include her own husband, right?'

'Right,' agreed Tess. 'No wonder she became defensive.'

'She must be terrified of feeling stupid,' said Viv. 'Imagine if she failed to notice that her own partner was corrupt. Maybe her husband too. That it was happening right in front of her eyes.'

'Wouldn't make her much of a detective, would it?' said Malcolm. 'Perhaps that's why Anjali didn't want to hear it.'

'Professional investigators are rarely good detectives in their own lives,' said Charlie. 'We've all watched enough movies to know that.'

'I tell you who else wouldn't make much of a detective,' said Sue. 'Whoever was supposed to be keeping Shane Carter under surveillance when he was released from police custody.'

Tess nodded. 'You're right. Instead they let him slip the net, go to the beach and get murdered.'

'Could be time I had another man-to-man chat with Sergeant Rob Thompson,' said Charlie. He'd been their prime suspect for a while. It was quite a turnaround but now Charlie wondered if Rob could be the key to unlocking everything.

'Anything else we've forgotten?' asked Tess.

'If it could potentially be traced back to Craig Murdoch, that would be a bonus,' added Charlie. 'Frank Courtney's corruption was no great surprise to Anjali. I think she knew already, deep down. It's Murdoch's involvement that we really need to sell to her.'

As they fell silent again, the only sound was the low rumble of traffic outside. Charlie closed his eyes and cast his mind back to Sue's evidence board. A semi-formed memory was gnawing away at him. He pictured the objects he'd sketched out. The wigs. The bloodied knife. The football scarf. The tumble dryer sheet. There was something else.

He suddenly sat forward, startling the dogs under the table. 'Sorry, gang,' he said. Ruby lazily wagged her tail as if to tell him it was fine. 'What about the vape and the cuddly toy?'

'Sounds like you're listing prizes on *The Generation Game* conveyor belt,' said Malcolm with a smirk. 'Vape, Teasmade, fondue set, cuddly toy. Didn't he do well?'

Sue chortled. 'Good game, good game.'

'I know what you mean,' said Tess eagerly. 'The police found Shane's purple vape near where Frank was discovered.'

'Exactly,' said Charlie, smiling. 'Or one that matched it, at least. But I don't remember seeing it at the time, do you?'

'You think it might have been planted?' asked Sue.

'It seems terribly handy, don't you think?' replied Charlie. 'Too handy maybe.'

'And what was that about cuddly toys?' said Malcolm. 'Come on, Anthea, give us a twirl.'

'Don't start that again,' warned Viv, although a sly smirk suggested she was amused really.

'It was after I found that first toy dog on our doorstep,' said Charlie. 'I remember Murdoch telling Anjali that he'd make enquiries at local shops. But if he was the one who was warning me off . . .'

'He'd hardly have investigated himself,' said Tess, finishing his sentence. 'What are the odds he conveniently forgot?'

'Maybe a conversation with both Thompsons is in order,' concluded Charlie. 'Although probably not together. I wouldn't want to get caught in the crossfire.'

89

Targeted Dog Walking

He knew the best way to corner Rob Thompson for a chat was over a drink. Pubs were where Charlie always seemed to run into the sozzled sergeant. Beer also loosened his tongue. Probably best if it wasn't in the Neptune, though. Too close to home. Hard stares from behind the bar, courtesy of Jackie and Luke Courtney, wouldn't exactly help either. No, best to make it another pub. But how?

The solution was Malcolm's brainwave. 'There's five of us and Framstone's a small town,' he reasoned. 'So let's carve it up.'

'Carve it up how?' asked Viv.

'We'll each take an area and innocently walk our dogs around the streets, checking each pub en route for signs of the fragrant Sergeant Thompson,' said Malcolm. 'Whoever finds him texts Charlie and voila! He can happen to pop in for a quiet pint. "Oh, look who it is. Fancy seeing you here, Rob. What are the chances? Let me buy you a drink." Good idea or what?'

Much as it pained them, everyone admitted that it was a cunning plan. The next evening, targeted dog walking commenced.

After an hour or so, Charlie and Ruby began to lose heart. Well, Charlie did anyway. Ruby was enjoying some new lamp posts to sniff. He was on the verge of popping into the next pub for a pint, regardless of Rob Thompson's whereabouts, when a text alert pinged.

It was from Sue, who'd been walking the Professor slowly around the streets, his back wheels bumping over the kerbstones. RT in situ at F's Arms. Eyes on. Over. Charlie smiled as he set off in the direction of the Fisherman's Arms.

Typical Sue. She was clearly enjoying the chance to deploy some lingo, with the Professor as her faithful sidekick, like a wheely Dr Watson. Sherlock Bones and Dogtor Watson perhaps? Charlie shook his head in shame. All this time spent with pun princess Tess was taking its toll.

The Fisherman's happened to be one of the pubs nearest Framstone police station. The chances are that Rob had finished his shift and gone straight for a pint. With its tatty sign and gloomy windows, it was the sort of boozer you wouldn't look twice at from the street.

Once inside, though, it was a little more homely, with a squishy red carpet, fixtures of dimpled brass and maritime memorabilia on the walls. The near-black wooden furniture was more battered than the Neptune's and the ceiling lower. There was a lingering aroma of cigarette smoke, even though the indoor smoking ban came in over a decade ago. None of the tables or stools seemed quite stable. They rocked unnervingly, threatening a drink spill at any moment.

Not the place for an entire night out, in short, but for a hardened drinker like Rob a handy stop-off for a quick stiffener.

As Charlie led Ruby through the doors – it was a

pet-friendly pub, on account of its old-man-and-his-dog clientele – he spotted their quarry immediately. Not difficult, since there were only a handful of punters – and one of them was a geriatric lady who seemed to be fast asleep. Rob Thompson was sitting at the bar with his back to them, clutching an empty pint glass and gesturing at the barman for a refill.

Charlie casually sauntered up to the bar, a few stools along from Rob, and ordered a pint and a bowl of water for Ruby. As he turned away to find a table, Charlie feigned surprise at seeing a familiar face – not too hammy, he thought, just natural enough.

'Rob!' he said. 'Fancy seeing you here.' He winced inwardly, aware he was parroting Malcolm's theoretical greeting. 'We were just treating ourselves to a post-walk drink. Here, let me get you one.'

'Cheers, Charlie, you can buy me this pint,' said Rob. He looked Charlie up and down appraisingly. 'Bit off the beaten track, aren't you?'

'Not really,' said Charlie, suddenly self-conscious of how fake he sounded. 'We like to mix it up with our walks, don't we, Rube?' She wagged her tail obligingly. 'Please, join us,' said Charlie, setting her water bowl down by a corner table. 'It'll stop me having to talk to the dog like a madman.'

They settled down with their drinks. Ruby lapped at her water, then happily fell asleep at Charlie's feet. He'd been so focused on finding Rob, he realized, that he hadn't really planned what to say. In the absence of any better ideas, he settled for generic small talk.

'So have you just got off work?' asked Charlie.

'You know full well I have,' replied Rob evenly. 'And don't

pretend it's a coincidence that you ran into me. I wasn't born yesterday and I've never seen you in here before. So, go on.'

Charlie was stunned. Had he really been that obvious? He supposed that as a policeman, Rob was probably accustomed to seeing through people's lies.

'G-go on what?' he stammered in reply.

'Ask what you came here to ask me,' said Rob, staring at him challengingly.

Wrong-footed by his frankness, Charlie didn't know what else to say but the truth. 'OK,' he said with a shrug. 'Was Frank Courtney a bent copper? And are you?'

There was a pause that seemed to last forever, punctuated only by Ruby's contented snores.

Eventually Rob took a gulp of his pint. 'I wondered how long it would take.' He smiled ruefully. 'I'll answer your questions, Boardy Boy. But I'm going to need another drink first.'

9 0

Not My Story to Tell

Once he'd been set up with another pint and a whisky chaser, Rob Thompson seemed only too happy to talk. This wasn't the way Charlie had expected their meeting to pan out but he rolled with it anyway.

'So you and Frank did work together for a while?' he asked.

'Only for about a year or so,' said Rob. 'I lied when I told you we didn't overlap at all. But it really didn't seem that long. When I was a rookie constable, Frank was my section sergeant. A bloody good one, too.'

'But he was on the take?'

Rob nodded. 'I didn't clock it for a few months,' he said, nibbling his bottom lip as he thought back. 'Then I started to pick up little signs. Certain offenders would be let go, others would get roughed up. Envelopes changed hands. Confiscated drugs wouldn't make it as far as the evidence room. That kind of thing.'

'What did you do about it?' asked Charlie gently, trying not put him on the defensive.

'Nothing.' Rob shrugged matter-of-factly. 'He was my boss. My mentor. Call me naive but I assumed he was doing it for the right reasons.'

'Did Frank know that you knew?'

'I think so,' said Rob. 'He soon brought me into it – maybe to make me complicit. Before long, he had me working on his little rackets too.'

'Doing what?'

Rob sighed. 'We'd take bribes and backhanders. Seize drugs from one dealer and sell them to another. Look the other way on certain offences. Tip people off when CID were on to them. It seemed like lots of low-level little things but it all added up.'

'Then what happened?' prodded Charlie.

'Then I realized what Frank was really like,' said Rob. He paused to knock back his whisky and looked at Charlie meaningfully. He took the cue and ordered them a refill.

'It was one night after a retirement do,' recalled Rob, once he'd sipped some Dutch courage. 'In the Neptune, funnily enough, before Frank bought it and did it up. A whole bunch of us took over the pub and got stuck in.'

Charlie wondered whether it was the same night out he'd seen in the photograph. It certainly sounded like it.

'We went to a nightclub after closing time, then on to some seedy strip club along the seafront that Frank knew. Gradually the crowd thinned out until it was just me and him. That's when he tried it on.'

Charlie didn't know what to say, so he said nothing. Rob soon filled the silence.

'We'd gone back to mine for a nightcap,' said Rob. 'He was giving it all this flannel about how I was his top man, his number two, his protégé and heir. I was flattered, until he turned physical. He squeezed my leg affectionately and left his hand there. He edged closer to me on the sofa. Before I knew it, he was on top of me.'

'Oh, Rob, I'm so sorry,' said Charlie.

'Ancient history now,' scoffed Rob unconvincingly. 'Even through my drunken haze, I was shocked. I pushed him off and threw him out, despite his threats.'

'Threats?'

'He was slurring about how it was all part of trusting each other. It would seal our partnership, he said. Bind us together. When I stood my ground, he flipped. Started spouting off about how he'd make me pay. How I'd regret it and come crawling back.'

'Jeez,' said Charlie. 'Sorry, Rob, that sounds horrible.'

'I didn't think much of it.' Rob sighed. 'Dismissed it as drunken ranting. Anyway, back at work, I stopped doing what he told me. I didn't want any part of his dirty tricks, but Frank started cutting me out anyway. Blanking me. Giving me the shifts nobody else wanted. Sending me on wild goose chases. He started grooming a replacement for me almost immediately.'

'And who was that?' asked Charlie a tad too eagerly.

'Not my story to tell,' said Rob firmly. 'I'm many things, Charlie, but I'm not a grass. Not of living people anyway.'

Charlie tried to conceal his frustration. 'Fair play. Did you consider reporting Frank?'

'I thought long and hard about it but I'd painted myself into a corner. How could I when I'd been part of it? Frank would've either silenced me or taken me down with him. He was vengeful like that.'

'Surely you could've got immunity in return?' said Charlie.

'Maybe, but I couldn't blow the whistle,' Rob said firmly. 'My career would be over. Maybe my life, too. Instead I watched the corruption carry on, which I hated. That was when I started hitting the bottle too hard. By day, I was ostracized by Frank's cronies. By night, I felt guilty just looking at Anjali. She's as straight as an arrow, but you knew that already. So instead of informing on Frank, I started trying to stop him.'

'How do you mean?' asked Charlie, feeling his cheeks flush slightly at the mention of Anjali.

'I'd quietly warn people. If I saw colleagues getting recruited or civilians being roped in, I'd advise them not to get mixed up in it. I'd tell them that Frank and his inner circle were bad people and it wouldn't end well. Actually, I think you spotted me trying to scare off one of the local dealers at the beach last week. I have a little word whenever I can, just to hammer the message home. If I can make them think twice, maybe realize it's more risky than it's worth, I've done my bit. I always hope the next time I meet them won't be in an official capacity.' He took a sad sip of his pint. 'Unfortunately it usually is.'

Charlie had a moment of realization. 'Is that why you argued with Shane Carter that night in the Neppy?'

Rob nodded. 'I saw him dealing and knew it'd be for Frank's old crew, even if Shane didn't know that himself. Frank was careful about keeping his name out of the frame. He was always one step removed. But I guess I was in my cups. I went about it the wrong way and Shane kicked off.'

'You were never part of the drug-dealing yourself?'

'No way,' insisted Rob. 'Not knowingly anyway. Frank gave me free drinks, though. To keep me sweet and probably so he could keep an eye on me. Once he left the force, it made sense to drop the hostility. He became hospitable instead.'

Charlie sat back and blew his cheeks out. This was a lot to absorb at once. On the other hand, Rob looked oddly relaxed, as if it were a weight off his shoulders.

'Cheers for listening, Charlie,' he said brightly. 'One last drink for the road?'

'Sure,' said Charlie, still taking it all in. 'But there was one more thing I wanted to ask.'

'Fire away, Columbo,' said Rob. 'Just make it quick. I'm parched.'

'How come your uniformed colleagues lost track of Shane the night he was murdered?' asked Charlie.

'Yeah, that was another little lie,' admitted Rob. 'I felt bad about that one, too. Might as well get it off my chest now, I suppose. Shane didn't really slip the net. Someone called off the surveillance long enough to let him.'

'Who?' prompted Charlie.

Rob Thompson stood up to get the drinks with a knowing smile. 'Like I said, I'm not a grass. But I'll look forward to you finding out.'

91

Prepare to Fight

Typical. As Charlie and Ruby left the Fisherman's Arms to head home, it started to rain. Just spits and spots at first but gradually building into a proper downpour. It was soon coming down in sheets.

Charlie zipped up his coat and apologized to Ruby. She was looking up at him with doleful eyes, as if to say, 'Can't we go back to that cosy pub?' He shook his head sadly and picked up the pace.

After a few yards, Charlie became aware of a car creeping up behind them. Its headlights glistened on the rain-slicked road and were getting closer. The engine was barely audible as it crawled along the kerb. They were being followed, although it was hardly subtle.

His heart started hammering as thoughts boinged around in Charlie's head. It couldn't be Rob Thompson, who he'd left in the pub, surely far too drunk to drive anyway. Had he rattled someone else's cage with his enquiries? Could it be Craig Murdoch – or, if he really was straight like Anjali said, whoever the mysterious bent copper was who'd taken over Frank Courtney's operation? The hooded figure or mystery assailant from the woods?

Charlie felt a prickle of fear but another sensation too. It was frustration. Defiance. He was fed up with having to look over his shoulder. The sooner he could bring this all to an end, the better. Right there in the rain, he resolved that much.

Still, first things first. He mentally scrolled through his options. He couldn't run, as Ruby couldn't keep pace and he wouldn't abandon her. He was tired of running anyway. Should he turn and confront them? Duck into the next pub or late-night shop they passed, hoping his pursuer would get the message and give up? Call home and warn Polly? Text the dogwalkers group chat for help from whoever was nearest? Or perhaps none of the above. Perhaps he should prepare to fight.

As Charlie's muscles tensed, he could see in his peripheral vision that the car was drawing up alongside them. He heard the window glide down and prepared to take evasive action. When the noise came, he nearly jumped out of his skin.

'Oi, Boardy Boy,' called a voice. 'Need a lift?'

Relief flooded his body as he turned to see Anjali leaning across to pop open the passenger door. 'I was just heading home after finishing my shift and I thought that was you.'

'You gave me the fright of my life,' said Charlie, his breathing slowly returning to normal.

'Sorry about that.' She smiled unrepentantly. 'Hurry up, hop in. This weather's grotty and I know Ruby hates the rain. Don't you, Duchess?'

Ruby trotted towards the car, pulling on her lead and looking round hopefully at Charlie. 'Go on then,' he said with a chuckle, letting her on to the back seat and climbing in the front himself. 'Thanks, Anjali. You're an angel. Even your name sounds like it.'

'Flattery will get you nowhere,' she said, checking her mirror and pulling away. 'OK, maybe somewhere. Heading home, I assume?'

'Yeah, thanks,' said Charlie, looking over his shoulder to check on Ruby. She sniffed around the back seat for any stray crumbs of food, before curling up and instantly falling asleep, lulled by the warmth and motion of the car.

'It actually means "divine offering" in Sanskrit,' she said. 'My name, I mean.'

Charlie smiled. 'Very apt. I'm glad I ran into you. Or rather, glad you ran into me.'

'Me too,' she said, not taking her eyes off the road. 'I didn't like how we left it yesterday. I stand by what I said. Just not the way I said some of it.'

'No worries,' said Charlie. 'I understood what you meant. You were sticking up for your colleague. For your entire profession. It's admirable.' He snuck a sideways look at her. 'Even if it was annoying, too.'

Anjali laughed. 'Admirable but annoying. I'll accept that.'

'Besides,' continued Charlie. 'I might have that something more concrete that you requested.'

She smirked. 'I figured you might. You were never one to give up easily.'

Charlie realized they were turning on to his street already.

'Let me pull over at your place and you can tell me about it before going inside,' said Anjali. 'Judging by that racket, Ruby will be OK for five minutes.'

As she parked and turned off the engine, Charlie realized

just how loudly his dog was snoring in the back. It was even louder than the rain drumming on the car roof. Hopefully what he was about to tell Anjali wouldn't be quite so snooze-inducing.

92

Strictly Police Business

They turned to face each other in the orangey glow of the street light. In different circumstances it might even have been romantic. However, Charlie was sopping wet, they could barely hear each other above Ruby's snores and this was strictly business.

'What have you got for me, then?' asked Anjali.

'Three things actually,' said Charlie. 'I'll leave it to you to decide which takes priority.'

'Very generous of you,' she said with a sarcastic smile. 'Fire away with thing one. As Doctor Seuss might say.'

'Shane Carter always smoked a purple vape, right?' began Charlie.

'Right.' Anjali nodded. 'Purple bottle-shaped thing. We found one at the first crime scene.'

'That's exactly it,' said Charlie. 'We think it was planted there. Probably by Murdoch, probably at the same time he planted the red fibres to incriminate Shane.'

'How would you know that?' asked Anjali.

'Well, I don't know for sure,' admitted Charlie. 'But me and Tess had a nose around before you and Murdoch arrived – naughty us – but neither of us remember seeing it. And it's kind of distinctive.'

'You know full well you shouldn't have contaminated the crime scene,' said Anjali sternly.

'I know, I know,' said Charlie. 'But we're pretty sure there was no purple vape.'

Anjali frowned. 'I'll check the evidence locker and take another look at the forensic photos. How about that?'

'Sounds reasonable,' agreed Charlie. 'The second thing was the butchered toy dog left on our doorstep.'

'Ah yes,' said Anjali. 'The keep-your-nose-out warning. What about it?'

'Murdoch told you that he'd ask around the Framstone toy shops, in case it was bought locally, remember?'

'In that case I'm sure he did,' said Anjali.

'But what if it was him who left it there, as I suspect?' asked Charlie. 'I'll bet he didn't make those enquiries at all.'

Anjali sighed. 'I reckon you're clutching at straws, but I can find a way to check. And the third thing?'

'With Shane under police surveillance after you let him go, didn't you wonder how he managed to go to the beach and get murdered?'

'Not our proudest moment,' acknowledged Anjali. 'He managed to give us the slip when it got dark.'

'That was the excuse I heard,' Charlie said, nodding. 'But apparently someone on the force called off the surveillance shortly before Shane died. Which is kind of convenient, don't you think?'

'Who told you this?' she said, narrowing her eyes.

Charlie had feared she'd ask that. He didn't want to cause

any more marital discord, especially when Rob had been so forthcoming, so figured it was only fair not to drop him in it.

'I'd rather not reveal my source,' he said, sounding like something he'd seen on TV.

'Hmm,' said Anjali with pursed lips. 'I'd prefer to know how reliable the intel was, but I guess I'll respect that. OK, I'll look into that too.'

Charlie breathed out with relief. He'd hate to be a home-wrecker.

Anjali gave him a sideways look as he reached for the car door. 'Although judging by the pub smell on you, I think I might have a vague notion. Boys will be boys. Am I right, Ruby?'

As Charlie and Ruby hurried up the path to get out of the unrelenting rain, Charlie glanced back at Anjali. Behind those squeaking windscreen wipers, she looked lost in thought.

93

Something He Shouldn't
Have Seen

Why wasn't he being licked back into consciousness? That was Charlie's usual wake-up call when he slept in. Since Ruby got old and creaky, she wasn't able to freely hop up on to the furniture like before. Polly had put a little footstool next to both their beds, so she could do it in two stages. Watching her unsteadily climb the step melted Charlie's heart, like seeing a sweet old lady with a walking stick.

After last night's drinks with Rob Thompson, followed by a drenching and a late-night tête-à-tête with Anjali, Charlie had been pretty bushed. He'd woken up an hour or two later than usual. By now Ruby would usually be eagerly reminding him of his walking duties via the medium of a slobbery tongue. He stretched, yawned and wondered why she wasn't.

As Charlie padded downstairs in pyjama bottoms and T-shirt, he realized what had distracted her. There were voices coming from the kitchen. It sounded like Polly had a visitor. Attention from strangers always tended to keep Ruby occupied.

As he entered the kitchen, Charlie saw exactly how occupied

she was. Polly was sitting at the table with pots of tea and coffee. Ruby was busy being cooed at and stroked by Karen Carter, who was clearly as smitten as her son had been.

Polly beamed. 'Here comes Sleeping Beauty at last. Madam here has been enjoying herself too much to come up and wake you.'

'I can see that,' said Charlie. 'Ruby looks like she's in seventh heaven. Thanks for that, Karen. And hello again.'

'Morning, Charlie,' said Karen with a shy smile. 'Sorry to impose on your breakfast. I was chatting to your mum on the phone last night and she invited me round for a morning cuppa. Except I've been a bit waylaid by this gorgeous girl.'

Ruby wagged her tail happily, knowing full well that she was being talked about.

'Not at all,' Charlie insisted. 'I'm glad you're here. Not least because it allowed me a bit of a lie-in.'

As he helped himself to coffee and popped on some toast, he looked over at the two women nattering away. They were at ease in one another's company. He was pleased that his mum had made a new friend – or, rather, reconnected with an old one – even if it was in tragic circumstances.

Charlie was about to go back upstairs and eat his breakfast, leaving the ladies to it, when Polly spotted his escape plan. She'd always been eagle-eyed like that.

'Sit down for a minute, would you, love?' she said, patting the chair next to her. 'Karen wanted to talk to you.'

'Don't look so scared, Charlie.' Karen chuckled. 'It's nothing dramatic. There was just something else that I remembered about my Shane which I thought might interest you.'

'Of course,' said Charlie, taking a seat. 'I'm always happy to hear memories of Shane.'

'You're very kind,' said Karen, glancing at Polly. 'You both are. I can see why Shane took a shine to you.'

'The feeling was mutual,' said Charlie. 'What was it that you remembered?'

'Well, it might be nothing,' began Karen. 'Or so vague that it's useless. But the day before Shane died, he mentioned something.'

'Oh yes?' prodded Charlie gently.

'I noticed that he was more jittery than usual,' said Karen. 'He'd always been a nervous lad, ever since he came out of care the first time. Each stint after that seemed to make him worse. But he seemed particularly on edge that day, so I asked what the matter was.'

'Poor old Shane,' said Charlie.

Karen sighed. 'I know. Anyway, it took me a few attempts to prise it out of him but he eventually told me. Well, in a way.'

Polly, who'd clearly already heard this story, glanced at Charlie knowingly before returning her attention to Karen.

'Shane said that he'd seen something that he shouldn't have done,' said Karen. 'And that somebody knew it and he was scared.'

Charlie sat forward. 'Nothing more specific than that? Did he say anything else at all?'

'Not really,' said Karen. 'I tried asking what he'd seen and who he was frightened of, but he clammed up. Whenever I mentioned it again, he told me to leave it. Sorry, I realize that must be frustrating.'

'Please don't apologize,' said Charlie, patting her hand. 'You weren't to know how significant it might turn out to be. Besides, it could be more useful than you think.'

'Really?' said Karen, visibly brightening. 'Oh good.'

'I told you, Karen, didn't I?' Polly smiled. 'It was worth sharing just on the off chance. Isn't that right, love?'

'That's right, Mum,' said Charlie. 'Now if you'll excuse me, I need to scoff this, get dressed and take a certain someone out for a stroll.'

'I think he means you,' Karen whispered, rubbing Ruby's ears. 'Thanks again, Charlie. The police won't listen to me, but Polly says you're looking into it and that you have detective friends. I know you'll do all you can for my Shane.'

'That's a promise, Karen,' said Charlie and she smiled gratefully.

He shuffled back upstairs, meditatively chewing his toast and marmalade. He had an inkling of what Shane might have seen. And he knew just the person to tell.

94

Not His First Rodeo

'I hoped I'd find you here,' said Anjali the next morning at Coastal, smiling down at Charlie.

'I hoped you'd find me here too,' said Charlie in reply, grinning.

Across the table, Tess rolled her eyes. 'Please, Anjali, join us,' she said. 'I'll get my fragrant companion to rustle you up an oat latte.' She waved over at Leon, who gave a thumbs-up from behind the coffee machine. At Charlie's feet Ruby raised her head, gave a solitary tail wag at Anjali's arrival, then fell straight back to sleep.

Once Leon had placed three fresh drinks in front of them, Anjali took a deep breath. 'Right, well –'

'Actually, do you mind if I go first?' interrupted Charlie. 'There's some new intel which might affect what you're about to say. If that makes sense. Sorry. Blame the caffeine.'

'Go on then, Boardy Boy.' Anjali smiled patiently. 'Say your piece first.'

She arched an eyebrow at Tess, as if to say, 'Men, eh? Always need to get the first and last word.' Charlie chose to ignore this.

He'd already told Tess about his chat with Karen Carter.

Now he filled in Anjali too. As always, she diligently took notes but soon closed her pad when it became apparent that he'd finished.

'Look, I know it's not much,' said Charlie. 'Just bear with me for a minute. We think Shane dropped his knife in the woods and fled without using it, right?'

'Not we,' corrected Anjali. 'You think that. I'm keeping an open mind.'

'Yep, yep,' said Charlie impatiently. 'This wasn't Shane's first time in custody, though. He'd not only committed knife crime years before, albeit in self-defence, but he was a habitual criminal. And he certainly wasn't an idiot.'

'I'd argue the two go hand in hand,' said Anjali, 'but do continue.'

'He would've soon realized that leaving a knife covered in his fingerprints at a crime scene wasn't the brightest idea,' said Charlie. 'OK, it wasn't a murder scene, not yet. Not as far as he knew. But with Shane's record even carrying a blade would be seen as a serious offence. So he went back to retrieve it.'

'This is all unfounded speculation, of course,' said Anjali. 'You're suggesting that Shane returned in time to witness the actual murder take place with his own knife?'

'Exactly.' Charlie nodded. 'He came back and saw our mate Murdoch stabbing Frank. Hence seeing something that he shouldn't have done.'

'Good, eh?' said Tess eagerly. 'It all fits.'

'Not quite,' said Anjali, taking a thoughtful sip of coffee. 'Why did Shane say that somebody knew what he'd seen?'

'Ah,' said Charlie. 'I guessed you'd ask that. This is where it gets tricky. Maybe Shane made a noise – gasped in horror, stood on a twig or whatever – and Murdoch spotted him. He knew that he knew.'

'That's a lot of maybes,' said Anjali.

'I did have another idea but I'd need your help with this one,' said Charlie. 'The two of them, Shane and Murdoch, soon came face-to-face again, right?'

'Yes, when we interviewed him,' said Anjali.

'What if it was something said during that interview?' asked Charlie. 'Maybe Shane let something slip that meant Murdoch guessed what he'd seen.'

'Nice try but no,' said Anjali firmly. 'Carter did the old "no comment" routine. Every detective's worst nightmare.'

'I'm sure he did,' agreed Charlie. 'Although what if there was some other tell? Either before Shane began with the no-comments or during the introductory chit-chat. Even just with his body language. You probably wouldn't have spotted it at the time because you weren't looking for it. Quite the opposite, in fact. You were looking for Shane to implicate himself, not the man sitting right next to you. But it still might have been there.'

'It sounds like a reach,' said Anjali sceptically.

'I know it's a long shot,' said Charlie. 'Just indulge us, please. You film all your interviews, right? Go back and rewatch the tape with fresh eyes. See if anything jumps out.'

Anjali sighed. 'You're lucky that I like you, Charlie Boardman,' she said eventually. 'You've already had me running around like a headless chicken. OK, I'll take a look.'

Charlie grinned. 'You're my hero, DI Thompson.'

Anjali took a deep breath again. 'Now, about your other so-called lines of enquiry . . .'

95

Not the Average Civilians

Charlie glanced at Tess hopefully. He also smiled inwardly at Ruby's sleep noises down by his feet – she whimpered and whinnied in a doggy dream, doubtless about chasing squirrels – before turning his full attention to Anjali.

'I did some digging about a few things,' she said at last. 'It's not exactly normal procedure to covertly investigate a colleague based on the say-so of civilians but, well, you're not the average civilians.'

Charlie and Tess found themselves inordinately thrilled by this, as if it were the highest compliment.

'Thanks, Anjali,' said Charlie. 'Seriously. I know it must have been a leap of faith.'

'More like a leap of lunacy.' She smirked, opening out her notebook. 'Anyway, let's look at the list one by one.'

'Yes, let's,' said Tess eagerly, before immediately biting her lip.

'First, the surveillance on Shane Carter,' said Anjali methodically. 'How did our officers manage to let him out of their sight long enough for him to go to the beach?'

'With fatal consequences,' added Tess, who immediately

looked annoyed with herself and did a 'lock my lips and throw away the key' gesture.

Charlie shrugged apologetically at Anjali.

'It turns out that a call was received by the officers in our unmarked car near Framstone Rec,' Anjali continued. 'It took some work to squeeze this out of them – they were worried they'd be in trouble, so had agreed to keep schtum – but a colleague rang to say he was relieving them and they could clock off for the night.'

'Right.' Charlie nodded. 'Who was this colleague, may we ask?'

'You can,' said Anjali. 'And you'll probably enjoy the answer. One of them is pretty sure the call came from DS Murdoch.'

Charlie exhaled with relief. He didn't realize he'd been holding his breath.

'Why only one of them?' asked Tess, ever the stickler for detail.

'Only one of them spoke to him on the phone,' explained Anjali. 'The other was so thrilled to be let off work early, he didn't ask many questions.'

'Makes you proud,' said Charlie. 'What do the phone records say?'

'The call came from an unrecognized number, presumably a burner,' said Anjali. 'We're still working on that.'

'What's the betting it matches a number used in the drug operation?' asked Tess. 'Maybe one of the phones that Shane texted?'

'We'll soon see,' said Anjali. 'Now, my next avenue was the toy dog. Charlie, you asked if DS Murdoch had followed it up with local shops, like he promised he would.'

'Yep.' Charlie nodded. 'I clearly remember him saying he'd do it while you visited Rob in hospital.'

'Me too,' said Anjali. 'Well, he told me that it had come to nothing. All very casual. Naturally I didn't question it. But thanks to you, now I did.'

'Are we going to enjoy this answer too?' chipped in Tess.

'No spoilers,' said Anjali enigmatically. 'I surreptitiously checked DS Murdoch's notebook and he had diligently recorded visits to a handful of toy and gift shops.'

'Oh,' said Charlie, a little deflated. 'I was hoping you'd say the opposite.'

'Hold your horses,' said Anjali. 'The thoroughness of the notes made me suspicious. He's not often that organized, so I thought I'd pay a visit to the shops myself. And guess what?'

'This is more like it,' said Charlie eagerly.

'None of them recalled a visit from a dour detective about a cuddly dog,' said Anjali. 'Which, let's face it, is the sort of thing you'd probably remember.'

She tried to force a smile but Charlie saw her heart wasn't in it. The case and the pressure from above had taken its toll. Anjali had lost a little of her twinkle. Having to investigate one of her own must have been extra stressful.

'So you were right,' she continued with a deep sigh. 'He hadn't followed up, but falsified his notes instead.'

'Sly but not sly enough,' said Tess.

'That's not all,' said Anjali. 'One of the shops did recall a man buying a brown toy dog. Partly because he later came back and bought another one just like it. Apparently he said his nephew had loved it but then lost it and was very upset.'

'That's big of him,' said Tess.

Anjali nodded. 'I know. I got a description of the man

and it does sound like a certain someone. I'm hoping to verify that with a formal identification.'

'And presumably Murdoch doesn't have a nephew?' asked Charlie wryly. 'Upset or otherwise.'

'He's certainly never mentioned one,' said Anjali. 'But there's more. When the mystery man purchased the second toy, he also bought a set of glow-in-the-dark pens.'

Charlie felt a mixture of elation and faint nausea. He reached down to give Ruby a reassuring stroke. As he did so, he felt a surge of sympathy for Anjali. Her partner, her trusted colleague on this case since the start, had betrayed her. Who could blame her for not being her usual sparky self?

'Without raising any alarm bells,' continued Anjali, 'I also checked his whereabouts on certain dates you gave me – when threats were left, when you saw shady figures in the woods or dodgy deals at the beach.'

'And?' asked Charlie optimistically.

'Every time, he was either off duty or working alone,' said Anjali meaningfully.

'That's it then,' said Tess triumphantly. 'We've got him bang to rights, surely? Case closed, your honour.'

'Steady on,' warned Anjali. 'Fake phone calls, falsified notes and threatening behaviour. That's all we've got. They're all maybes and even some of that's a stretch.'

'What are you saying?' asked Charlie, his brow furrowing. 'We haven't got him at all?'

'Sadly not,' said Anjali. Her tone had become thick with a mix of frustration and simmering fury. 'And that's even before I come on to item three.'

Charlie's heart sank again. He wanted so much for it all to be over. This sounded worryingly like it was far from it.

96

Fluttering Red Flags

'Uh-oh,' said Charlie. 'This sounds ominous.'

As Anjali turned a page in her notebook, Tess gestured at Leon for another round of drinks. It looked like she and Charlie might need them.

'The purple vape,' said Anjali. 'You thought it might have been planted at the scene of Frank Courtney's murder to incriminate Shane Carter, who smoked a similar one?'

'That's right,' said Charlie. 'We didn't remember seeing it originally, then it conveniently appeared nearby.'

'Well,' said Anjali, 'I looked back at our forensic photographer's pictures, like I promised. I'm afraid to say the vape is present and correct near the base of a tree, tossed on top of some drug baggies.'

'Oh f-f-fiddlesticks,' said Tess, narrowly resisting the urge to swear. 'I was certain I would've noticed that. I've been partial to a bit of purple ever since my Prince phase during my teens.'

'We all had one of those,' said Anjali. 'I genuinely considered buying a raspberry beret at one point. But no, the vape was definitely there, so you can strike that off your conspiracy list.'

'Dammit,' said Charlie. 'I could've sworn it hadn't been there. Sorry to send you on a wild goose chase.' It still didn't quite track for him, but he sensed it was time to cut Anjali some slack.

'No problem.' Anjali shrugged. 'It was fairly straightforward to check.'

'Does that mean we still haven't got enough on Murdoch?' asked Tess.

'I fear so,' said Anjali. 'Look, off the record, I agree with you. There are some big fluttering red flags here. DS Murdoch might well be corrupt or compromised. He might well be complicit with local drug dealers in some way, still to be established. But a murderer? Maybe a multiple murderer? To accuse a fellow officer of that . . . it's serious stuff.'

'I get that –' Charlie nodded – 'but it all points to him.'

'Maybe it does,' admitted Anjali. 'There's plenty of room for doubt, though. That's all a lawyer would need. Besides, consider the optics.'

'How do you mean?' asked Tess.

'To put it in blunt terms –' Anjali sighed – 'I'd be an Asian female officer accusing a white male officer. An ambitious woman accusing a well-liked man. You can imagine the toxic nonsense that might stir up. Especially in the police force. Especially in a town like Framstone.'

'I'm so sorry,' said Charlie. 'I hadn't thought of it like that.'

'Why would you?' said Anjali. 'Trust me, it would become a factor, especially in the hands of a defence lawyer.' She sounded world-weary, like she'd run all the possible scenarios through her mind and none of them had played out well.

'Sometimes I despair,' muttered Tess. 'But I hear you, Anjali.'

They stared into their coffees, absorbed in their own thoughts. The only sound was the hissing coffee machine. Ruby shifted position beneath the table and snorted to herself. With all the steam inside and cold weather outside, Tess's shiny new shop window was misting up with condensation.

Suddenly she perked up. 'Wait up,' Tess said excitedly, fishing her phone out of the front pocket of her apron. 'I might have something.'

'Really?' asked Charlie. 'How come?'

'Remember when I rushed down to the woods after you'd found Frank?' she said. 'I hunted around for clues but you took the mickey and called me "Tess Marple"?'

'That sounds like Boardy Boy,' said Anjali, managing a small smile.

'Yeah, all right,' conceded Charlie, 'guilty as charged. What about it?'

'I seem to recall taking a few pics,' she said, opening up her photo gallery. 'Maybe one of them will include the base of that tree.'

Charlie peered over at her screen as Tess scrolled back through her photos. Lots of Rough and Tumble pics. Some latte art. Tess saw him peeking and pressed her phone to her chest. He could've sworn her cheeks reddened.

'Not all these are for public consumption,' she said. 'Avert your eyes.'

'What could you possibly have on there that I can't . . .' said Charlie before it dawned. 'Oh, I see.'

'A girl's allowed some secrets,' teased Tess. 'Consenting adults and all that.'

Charlie's interest was piqued but he tried not to show it. 'You're a dark horse, Tess Cheong. Carry on.'

As Tess kept swiping, Anjali and Charlie glanced at each other impatiently, as if to ask, 'How many photos can one woman take?'

'Aha!' cried Tess. 'Here we go. Now, I'm no forensic snapper, but let's have a look-see.' She tapped the screen, zoomed in and squinted at the screen.

'This is the tree in question, right?' she asked, holding up her phone to show Anjali.

'Looks like it,' agreed Anjali, leaning in for a closer inspection. 'Yes, I'm pretty sure that's it.'

'Well, look down at the ground,' said Tess. 'No sign of anything purple, let alone a vape.'

Anjali took the phone from her, zoomed in some more and studied the screen.

Charlie glanced at Tess as they waited. Her eyes shone confidently.

'You're right,' agreed Anjali eventually. 'No purple vape.'

'So you agree that it was placed there later?' asked Tess. 'Very probably when Murdoch arrived at the scene? At the same time as he planted the red fibres?'

Anjali was still looking at the phone screen. Now she slowly raised her head, looking first at Tess, then at Charlie. Almost reluctantly she gave a nod.

'So you'll get Murdoch in for questioning?' asked Charlie excitedly.

Anjali's expression melted from deep thought into decisiveness. 'I can do better than that,' she said, reaching for her radio. 'I can issue a warrant for his arrest.'

97

Emergency Stop

After Anjali said her hurried goodbyes and marched off purposefully to follow up on the arrest warrant, Tess had been keen to celebrate. Charlie warned her not to be premature – cue X-rated jokes naturally. When Murdoch had been charged and put behind bars – that was the time for backslapping. Until then, two bereaved families won't have seen justice. Charlie felt a bit self-righteous saying it but knew deep down that he was right. Tess had reluctantly agreed, albeit with several eye-rolls in the direction of the dogs, as if they were on her side. Judging by their wagging tails, perhaps they were.

Walking Ruby through the woods early the next morning in a bid to clear his head, Charlie mentally rewound through the crime and corruption which had rocked his home town. It was seven weeks ago but suddenly felt like a long time since he'd found Frank Courtney's body in these very woods. He prayed they had enough on Murdoch – or that Anjali could unearth it.

He wanted Polly and Ruby out of danger. He wanted the people of Framstone to feel safe again. And he wanted Shane Carter's name to be cleared of murder. Hopefully it would bring poor, grieving Karen some peace.

They were so close but there was still something about the case which niggled away at him. Some detail he'd overlooked. He was probably being paranoid. He couldn't switch off his buzzing brain.

As they moseyed along, Ruby padding happily along the paths they knew so well, Charlie allowed his mind to drift. It felt like the investigation was all he'd thought about lately – especially when it became a matter of his mum and his dog's security. Now he might have to find something else to occupy his brain.

Work harder at building up the design business, that was the sensible option. He was already doing some new menus for Monty's. Attempt to build more of a social life. His fellow dogwalkers had reminded him of the value of friendship. Maybe even find a girlfriend. It had been a while. Charlie smiled at his own daft daydreaming.

Suddenly he almost ran into the back of Ruby, who'd come to a dead halt in front of him. He nearly tripped over her – a hazard that he sometimes worried about with Polly at home – but managed to keep his balance.

'Whoa there, Rube,' he said. 'Why the emergency stop?'

He saw that her ears had pricked up and her nostrils were flaring. He was never sure how much Ruby could actually see nowadays but her brown eyes were fixed firmly on the bushes off to their left.

'What is it, girl?' he whispered. 'Noisy birds? Squirrels getting up to mischief?'

Staying stock-still, Ruby's head turned slightly. He followed her gaze and spotted what had spooked her. There was faint but perceptible motion out there between the trees. And this wasn't wildlife. It was human-shaped.

It was a sinister sight yet an oddly familiar one. A hooded figure moved furtively through the woods parallel to the path. Despite treading softly and deliberately, leaves crunched gently underfoot as they went. Hard to tell at this distance, but from its size and movements, it looked male – and like the same woodland stalker as before.

Charlie's breath quickened and his eyes widened, alert and focused. He took in his old adversary and wondered what was coming next. Only he realized there was something different this time. The hooded man was moving forward purposefully through the trees, while Charlie and Ruby remained on the same spot. For once the figure didn't seem to be following them.

Charlie's rush of relief was followed by a mounting hum of alarm. What if the mystery man was Murdoch or one of his criminal cronies? And if he wasn't chasing Charlie this time, who was he after? It occurred to Charlie that the Framstone killer could be about to strike again.

What if there was a potential victim in need of saving? Charlie had been too late to help Frank or Shane. He might get a chance this time. He instinctively knew what to do. Probably an unwise idea but an irresistible one. This time, he could try covertly pursuing them. The hunter could become the hunted.

As Charlie began to move off the path to the left, Ruby looked up at him quizzically. He put a finger to his lips and whispered, 'Stay.' She cocked her head, one ear folding over, but otherwise didn't move. He thought she understood but couldn't be sure. Besides, he had other things on his mind.

Ducking down, he hurried after the figure, his eyes fixed on his retreating back. As he closed the gap, Charlie told himself that he was just observing, nothing more. *Get within twenty metres or so. See what they're up to. Call the police if necessary.*

As he moved, Charlie's hand went to his pocket. He glanced down at his phone screen. Typical. No signal. He shoved the phone back impatiently and carried on.

What he didn't know was that Anjali had been repeatedly calling to warn him that the police still hadn't located DS Craig Murdoch. In dog-walking parlance, he'd slipped the leash. As of this morning, the suspect remained at large.

Mobile reception was often patchy in Framstone, especially in the woods, so she couldn't get through. Her calls went straight to voicemail. The messages wouldn't be picked up until he was back in range, by which time it might be too late.

As Charlie watched from behind a bush, the hooded figure stopped, methodically put on a pair of latex gloves and reached into a hollow tree trunk. What on earth was he up to?

Charlie gave a start as the man withdrew his hand. It was now holding a knife. And not just any old knife. It looked exactly like the one that killed Frank.

Charlie's heart galloped as he stared at it. The man looked down at it too, before turning in Charlie's direction and slowly raising his head. It was him. It was Murdoch. And he was looking straight at Charlie.

98

Ready, Get Set, Go

Their eyes locked. DS Craig Murdoch looked strangely calm, as if he'd been expecting this. He gazed back at Charlie, his mouth set in a frown, his eyes cold. Charlie realized in horror that Murdoch had been following him after all – before taking a detour to retrieve the weapon.

Charlie's mind raced. It couldn't be the same knife surely? That would be down at the police station under lock and key. Murdoch probably had access to the evidence room but he wouldn't have taken it from there. Too risky.

No, thought Charlie, it was just a lookalike knife. *Just?* Who was he kidding? It was still a deadly weapon. What's more, he knew that the man wielding it was fully prepared to use it.

Charlie seemed to leave his body momentarily. In a flash he guessed what Murdoch's game was. He was going to stab Charlie, leave him to die here like Frank Courtney and deliberately plant the knife nearby to be found. It would suggest the same killer was still out there somewhere.

Murdoch would presumably hand himself in straight away, with a handy alibi for his whereabouts that morning. He was wearing gloves. Nobody had seen him. There was nothing to connect him to this latest murder. It was a desperate move but Murdoch was a desperate man. What did he have to lose? With a warrant already out for his arrest, not much.

Now Charlie knew what was happening, he suddenly felt calm too. Time seemed to slow down. He might be in mortal danger but at least this time he knew who his opponent was. It was just the two of them. Murdoch was armed, sure, but Charlie had an advantage too. There was around twenty yards between them and he knew these woods better than anyone. Well, except Ruby.

Talking of Ruby, he wondered where she was. Still standing on the path, he hoped, loyally waiting, out of harm's way. He was reluctant to leave her behind but he didn't have a choice. Besides, as long as Murdoch was pursuing Charlie, she would be safe.

Charlie realized that his heart rate had elevated, adrenaline pumping around his body. He tried to regulate his breathing in readiness. As he stared back at Murdoch, whose face was half shadowed by his hood, he could swear the other man's frown had turned into a cruel smirk.

Charlie didn't want to give him a warning. He needed every bit of a head start he could get. It took willpower not to twitch a muscle in readiness, nor let his eyes stray from Murdoch's to survey their surroundings.

Ready, get set . . . go. Exploding into action, Charlie took off running, heading deeper into the trees. He didn't dare look round. It would only slow him down. Anyway, he didn't need to. Behind him, he could hear Murdoch giving chase.

99

Chasing Thin Air

It might have been Charlie's imagination but Murdoch was gaining on him. Scrub that. Murdoch was definitely gaining on him.

Charlie silently cursed himself for not keeping fitter. Daily dog walks clearly weren't cutting it. Murdoch was the type who probably ran regularly. Charlie could imagine him being a right bore about it, boasting about his 10K times, logging his routes on running apps and extolling the virtues of sweat-wicking fabrics.

Charlie needed to use whatever advantage he had. He suddenly altered course, veering off to the right, vaulting a fallen tree trunk and accelerating. It seemed to have worked. Taken by surprise, Murdoch took a beat or two to change direction. Not by much but the gap had widened.

Lungs bursting and legs aching, Charlie realized he couldn't keep up this pace much longer. Judging from the sounds behind him and the odd glance over his shoulder, Murdoch wasn't flagging at all. It wouldn't be long before he started gaining on him again.

Even at speed, Charlie knew exactly where he was – near where Rob Thompson had been jumped and also where he'd hidden that night when somebody followed him. Had his late-night stalker been Murdoch as well? He guessed so. But it meant the hollowed-out tree trunk was nearby.

He changed direction towards it, trying not to make it obvious. *Nearer. Nearer. Now.* He stuck out a hand, grabbed a nearby tree to help him screech to a halt and propelled himself inside the hollowed trunk. With any luck, it would take Murdoch a second or two to notice, then he'd have no clue where his prey had gone.

Charlie was desperate to gulp for air but didn't want to make a sound. He stood, breathing through his nose, taking in the mouldy smell of damp timber, and listened. The rhythm of Murdoch's feet hitting the ground didn't seem to have slowed. It got louder and louder, closer and closer. Charlie bunched his fists, ready to fight for his life.

Wait. Murdoch should have reached him by now. Charlie listened. The footsteps seemed to be getting further away again.

Charlie edged out, almost imperceptibly, and peeked round the edge of the tree bark. With a surge of relief, he saw Murdoch dashing away from him, his back disappearing among the trees ahead, the knife still in his hand. As Charlie had hoped, he'd run straight past.

He needed to move fast, before Murdoch realized. Charlie emerged from the trunk, turned back in the direction they'd come and took off again. For now, they were running in opposite directions but he didn't expect that to last.

As he picked up speed, Charlie glanced over his shoulder. This proved a mistake. He should have learned the lesson from his rugby days. Keep your eyes on the try line, their coach used to say, not the incoming tackler. Suddenly Charlie was flying through the air. Not looking where he was going, he'd tripped over a tree root. He managed to get his arms out in front to break the fall but he hit the ground hard, winding himself as he went sprawling to the turf.

Leaves fluttered through the air. A startled bird flapped off. As Charlie laboured back to his feet with a groan, he saw Murdoch heading back his way at speed. If he hadn't noticed before that he was chasing thin air, he certainly had now. The sound of Charlie's fall had alerted him. He was closing in fast.

Even if he shook off the impact instantly, it would take Charlie precious time to get back up to full speed. He needed to hide again. Run for a few seconds, then find another bolt-hole.

This time, it seemed to take forever to accelerate. His muscles screamed in pain and his legs felt heavy but somehow sheer adrenaline took Charlie up through the gears. It was nowhere near quick enough – he could hear Murdoch hurtling towards him – but sufficient to find somewhere.

Charlie spotted a honeysuckle bush up ahead and to the left. There was a hollow dip on the other side, he seemed to recall. He could leap into that, tuck himself down low and hope that momentum took Murdoch past again.

He feinted to run round the bush, before diving into the hollow and ducking down as far as he could. Charlie held his breath. Had it worked?

He gasped in shock as he felt an impact on his back. He didn't know what being stabbed felt like, but was that it? Dizzy and disorientated, it took Charlie a moment to get his bearings, then he heard unmistakable panting sounds. It wasn't Murdoch who'd found him. It was Ruby.

Doubling back on himself had enabled her to catch up, even at her stately pace. Normally he'd be delighted to see her. Not now. He desperately tried to shush her, rubbing her ears in a way that normally placated her, but Ruby was too excited by their reunion. With Charlie down at ground level, she thought it was a game. She snuffled at him loudly, her tail thwacking against the shrubbery.

Charlie pressed his face to Ruby's forehead, making comforting 'ssh' sounds. As he did so, he slowly looked up between her ears. Murdoch was standing over them with a nasty smile on his face – and an even nastier knife in his hand.

100

Fight an Uphill Battle

Charlie gently pushed Ruby aside, gave her a last loving ear rub and straightened up. If there was going to be a knife fight, he wanted his dog out of the way. He also wanted it to be on level ground. Fighting uphill, he knew from history lessons, was a recipe for disaster.

He stepped out of the hollow and took a few steps to the side. Murdoch turned as he went, knife held ready, his eyes following Charlie's every move. The cruel smirk and the nasty grin had gone now. They'd been replaced by a determined set of the mouth and eyes full of hate.

The time for running was over. Charlie prepared to fight for his life. He settled his feet at shoulder width and bent his knees slightly, ready to move. He turned one shoulder towards Murdoch and raised his hands, adopting a defensive position. He began to circle round him, occasionally feinting to move forward, then retreating again. They were moves that Charlie half remembered from judo and boxing at school. If he was about to be stabbed, he wasn't going to make it easy.

Murdoch wasn't used to this, he guessed. The two people he'd already killed were an incapacitated old man and an unsuspecting gentle soul. Let's see how he fared against someone roughly his own age and size. Someone ready to scrap for survival.

He lunged with the knife but Charlie saw it coming. He sprang aside and turned to face him again. Murdoch's face contorted into a snarl and he readied himself again. *This time*, thought Charlie, *I'll try to knock the knife out of his hand. It's my only hope.*

Murdoch pushed forward and slashed again, backhand this time. There was a ripping, rending sound, which seemed to startle them both. Charlie looked down to see his jacket torn and flapping, the lining exposed. That was close. And the knife was sharp. He gulped, raised his eyes and got ready again.

Murdoch glanced at the ground off to one side. Charlie instinctively followed his eyes and took a step in that direction, assuming he was about to target Ruby.

It was a bluff. While Charlie was distracted, Murdoch thrust forward again, this time with more intent and power. It was all Charlie could do to evade the blade. Now it was Murdoch's turn to be off balance. Charlie saw his chance and grabbed his arm, desperately trying to reach the knife.

They struggled and grappled, both grunting with effort. Their bodies were too close together. Arms entwined, neither could get quite enough leverage. Charlie couldn't get to the knife hand. Murdoch couldn't manoeuvre the blade into position to use it.

For a second it was stalemate. The two men were locked together. They could feel the hot, gasping breath on one another's faces. Charlie remembered what Polly had said about Murdoch always smelling freshly laundered. He did even now. Detergent with top notes of sweat and fear.

Suddenly Ruby gave a soft bark. Charlie couldn't help glancing over at her. It was all the opportunity Murdoch needed. With an almighty effort and a guttural roar, he pushed Charlie away. Still half bent over with the effort, he plunged the knife forward. There was a strange squelching sound, like a butcher hacking up meat.

Charlie staggered backwards and looked down at his leg. Through a slit in his jeans he could see a gaping wound already pouring blood. It didn't hurt, not yet anyway, but he felt sick and fuzzy-headed. He felt a tree against his back and slid down it into a sitting position.

Slumped and woozy on the ground, he looked upwards. Murdoch loomed over him, that mean leer back on his face. With a flash of clarity, Charlie realized this was almost exactly how he'd found Frank Courtney. Now he was about to suffer the same fate.

Without taking his eyes off Charlie's, Murdoch adjusted the knife in his hand and advanced to deliver the killer blow.

101

How Death Is Supposed to Feel

This wasn't how Charlie expected death to feel. It was strangely pleasant. Even slightly . . . what was the word . . . ? Ticklish. Yes, ticklish.

Having drifted out of consciousness for a fleeting moment, it dawned on him what was happening. He was still slumped at the base of a tree, bleeding profusely from that stab wound in his thigh. Murdoch was still looming over him, ready to finish him off. And Ruby was licking Charlie's face.

Her paws were on his shoulders as she lapped at him lovingly. Normally Charlie would have laughed. Eventually he'd have gently pushed her away with a fond cry of 'Gerroff!' Right now, though, he didn't feel like laughing or getting her off. He just savoured the moment while he still could.

Murdoch was confused for a moment. He had his blade poised, ready to plunge into Charlie's chest, just like he'd done to Frank Courtney in an eerily similar position. What he hadn't expected was a stocky Staffy to be suddenly blocking his path.

He tried to get round one side of Ruby, then the other.

Each time he moved forward with the knife, she seemed to alter her position on Charlie's shoulders and obstruct him. Becoming exasperated, Murdoch tried to shove her aside with his other hand but Ruby was heavier than she looked. She was also far too devoted to be easily removed from Charlie.

That was when Charlie heard it. He couldn't see what but something was definitely crashing through the bushes towards them. Ruby stopped the frantic licking, turned her head back towards Murdoch and gave another bark.

Murdoch took a wary step back and hesitated. He looked towards the trees where the racket was coming from, then back at Charlie and Ruby. The weapon was still in his hand but a panicked expression crossed his face. His eyes darted around, then he seemed to make a decision. Murdoch shoved the knife into his pocket, turned and fled.

At the same time the source of the noise arrived on the other side of the clearing. Bursting through the trees came the dogwalkers, led by Tess with a determined look on her face. Viv, Sue and Malcolm were just behind. At their heels were Rough, Tumble and Humphrey the accident-prone Labrador. Bringing up the rear was the Professor. His new back wheels might be designed for this off-road business but his front legs weren't.

Now Charlie realized what Ruby had been barking at. It wasn't Murdoch at all. Her other senses made even more acute by her sight loss, she must have heard her friends in the distance or even smelled them.

'Clever girl,' whispered Charlie into her velvety ear. Her intervention had bought him precious time, delaying Murdoch's final attack long enough for the others to arrive on the scene.

Ruby had saved his life. The dogwalkers had arrived in the nick of time to scare off Murdoch. Charlie experienced a brief burst of euphoria. His relief was short-lived when it dawned on him that Murdoch was getting away.

102

Vicious Hellhound

Everyone arrived just in time to see Murdoch making his escape. As Tess and Malcolm helped Charlie to his feet, he instinctively took a step in the same direction as Murdoch. The two of them chasing each other seemed to be ingrained now.

His injury immediately let him know that running wasn't an option. A searing pain took Charlie's breath away. It was all he could do to not let his leg buckle beneath him.

'Whoa there, mister,' said Tess, trying not to let the worry show in her voice. 'Let him go.' She turned to Malcolm and Sue and said, 'Quick! Scarves!'

Both hastily took off their scarves, which Tess used as improvised tourniquets. She swiftly tied Malcolm's polka-dotted silk scarf above the wound and Sue's home-knitted woollen one below it, pulling them as tight as she could, while Charlie gritted his teeth.

Over Tess's shoulder, he could still see Murdoch running away. Knowing that nobody was chasing, he was now moving at more of a jog than a sprint. He almost looked casual. Presumably this was deliberate. Someone fleeing at full pelt might look suspicious and attract unwanted attention. Nobody would look twice at someone sedately jogging through the woods.

Malcolm was already reaching into his bag. He always carried a rather natty tote on walks, invariably emblazoned with the logo of a chic fashion label or arty bookshop. Well, there was stuff to lug around – leads, poo bags, dog treats and the like – and Malcolm wasn't the type for bulging pockets or, shock horror, some kind of bum bag.

'You were a sporting hero once upon a time, weren't you?' said Malcolm. 'Go on. Prove you've still got it.'

With due reverence and a knowing wink, he handed Charlie an orange rubber ball. It was Ted's favourite, they all knew that. Usually only Malcolm was allowed to throw it. For anyone else it was a rare honour.

Charlie weighed the heavy ball in his hand. He winced slightly as he turned towards the retreating back of Murdoch and rotated his shoulders side-on, like he'd always done when making a long throw. He glanced at Malcolm, who smiled back encouragingly.

Charlie returned his focus to the target, drew back his arm, then flung it forward with a whiplash action.

Everyone held their breath, their eyes fixed on the ball's path through the air. Seemingly in slow motion, it flew in a low arc, then began to descend, straight and true, homing in on Murdoch like a tracer bullet.

As he jogged away, his hood bounced behind him. He appeared not to have a care in the world, little suspecting that an orange missile was whistling towards him. Charlie gasped in satisfaction. As soon as the ball left his hand, he knew he'd judged it perfectly. The ball hit Murdoch flush on his spine, between the shoulders. Even from this distance they all heard the impact. A thump followed by a grunt from Murdoch.

He stumbled, staggered for a few steps and began to fall forward. Charlie smiled as he watched Murdoch flail, taken by surprise. They all waited for him to hit the deck – but somehow he didn't. Murdoch miraculously managed to recover his equilibrium and stay on his feet. He looked back over his shoulder with a face like thunder and kept on running.

The dogwalkers watched him go, feeling deflated. That is, until they noticed that Murdoch wasn't the only one running. Like a silvery-blue blur, something was streaking after him. What's more, it was closing in fast.

'Go on, boy,' murmured Malcolm, somewhere near Charlie's shoulder. That's when he realized with a slow-spreading smile that it was Ted the greyhound, chasing after his favourite orange ball. And Ted was so speedy he was already about to reach it.

In full flight he was graceful and perfectly balanced. Eyes locked on his target, Ted's paws barely seemed to touch the ground as he sprinted at express pace.

Having hit Murdoch's back and bounced to the ground, the ball was still bobbling around on the uneven path. Upon it in a flash, Ted was going too fast to catch it cleanly in his mouth. Instead it ricocheted off his snout as he dipped his head to pick it up. This only propelled the ball further along the path, towards the fugitive detective. Clearly relishing the game, Ted gave chase again.

Everyone held their breath as Ted streaked along, rapidly gaining on the fleeing figure. Suddenly he caught up. His momentum unstoppable, Ted barrelled straight into Murdoch's legs from behind.

He really did hit the deck this time. Feet wiped out from

underneath him, Murdoch flew through the air, his arms windmilling, before crashing painfully to the ground.

The dogwalkers were already running. As soon as they'd realized what was happening, they had set off after Ted and Murdoch.

With a surprisingly sporty turn of pace, still wearing her Coastal Coffee apron, Tess led the way. Malcolm was somehow in second place, despite looking like he was hardly making any effort, let alone breaking a sweat. Viv was just behind, with Humphrey, Rough and Tumble milling around her feet.

Sue huffed and puffed, trying to keep up but faintly annoyed that her partner was outrunning her. Ruby, enjoying all the excitement, was next. Charlie, limping badly, improvised bandages fluttering behind him, brought up the rear with the Professor.

By the time they reached Ted and Murdoch, it was an almost comical sight. Murdoch was rolling on the ground, grovelling and panicking as Ted pranced around him, darting in and out. Arms covering his face, Murdoch breathlessly cried for help. He clearly thought he was being attacked by a vicious hellhound. In reality, gentle Ted was merely trying to get at the orange ball, which was trapped underneath Murdoch.

The dogwalkers looked at each other and nodded. No words were needed. Charlie stepped forward, sank down heavily and simply sat on Murdoch's chest. The corrupt copper looked surprised by this turn of events. Charlie grinned down at him, relishing his bafflement.

Tess kneeled down by Murdoch's head and pinned his arms to the ground. He grunted and struggled, trying to free himself and push Charlie off, but he wasn't quite strong enough. At the other end Malcolm held down Murdoch's legs so he couldn't kick out. With three of them bearing down on him at once, the captive was badly outnumbered.

Meanwhile, Viv and Sue set about tying Murdoch's hands and feet with dog leads. Between them all, they had plenty. Leather ones, rope ones, canvas-webbing ones. All pretty much unbreakable. Well, unless you were Ruby as a puppy, when she had a habit of gnawing at them until she could burst free. Still, they made more than decent temporary restraints. Murdoch quickly exhausted himself by thrashing about to no avail. As the dogwalkers stood up and got their breath back, he soon ran out of steam and lay there looking up at them, his lip curled into a sneer.

There was still one final indignity to come. Ruby waddled over and licked Murdoch's cheek. As he tried in vain to turn away, she lapped away at his face enthusiastically, her tail wagging.

Charlie chuckled. He could hear wailing sirens.

103

Tied Up and Gift-Wrapped

Charlie and Tess sat on a park bench and watched the pandemonium unfold around them.

'Do you think we're in danger of becoming voyeurs?' he asked. 'Always rubbernecking at crime scenes?'

'At least this particular crime scene is your fault,' she said. 'Otherwise you would officially be a pervert, yes.'

'That's reassuring,' he replied, sipping his coffee and looking down at his torn jacket, pondering whether the knife slash was mendable.

'I don't make the rules,' Tess said with a shrug. 'Hang on. Actually, I do.'

Tess had filled him in on events elsewhere, while he'd been locked in combat with Murdoch. Anjali had phoned Coastal Coffee when she was unable to get hold of him. She had warned Tess that the rogue detective was still on the loose but Charlie wasn't picking up. Knowing the patchy reception all too well, Tess had alerted the others, who happened to be at their usual table.

They'd hurriedly scooped up the dogs and dashed to the woods. They hadn't known where to start their search but luckily the dogs did. As soon as they were let off their leads,

Rough and Tumble had plunged into the bushes in the right direction, with the rest in hot pursuit. Or tepid pursuit in the Professor's case.

Once Murdoch has been trussed up, Tess had called Leon at Coastal and asked him to bring five drinks down to the woods. The whole gang's usual orders. There had to be some perks to being the boss. He was even allowed to close the shop temporarily while he did so. Leon looked disappointed when it became clear that Tess expected him to head back and open up again afterwards.

It had been a weird sight as Anjali arrived to arrest Murdoch. It must have been even weirder for her, taking her erstwhile police partner into custody. Charlie hoped it wouldn't reflect badly on her. Craig Murdoch was just the latest in a long line of corrupt cops in the Framstone force. Who knew how high up it went? Murdoch had fooled everyone for a long time. Who better to commit crime and get away with murder than an experienced police officer?

Anjali had smiled, coming over to talk to him. 'Still full of surprises after all these years, Boardy Boy. You didn't just catch him. You tied him up and gift-wrapped him for me.'

'Not just me,' said Charlie. 'Everyone played their part. Even the dogs. Especially the dogs.'

'Well, I'm grateful,' she said. 'What's the prognosis on your leg?'

Charlie glanced down. The scarves had been swapped for a bandage, applied by paramedics who'd arrived shortly after the police. Charlie refused to miss Murdoch being led away, so they'd patched him up and given him painkillers on the understanding that he'd come to the hospital later for proper treatment.

'I'll live,' he said. 'Although it might affect my modelling career.'

Tess nodded sympathetically. 'He'll have to concentrate on face and torso work from now on. No more leggy stuff, so that's the swimming trunk and underwear contracts gone.'

'How will your many fans worldwide cope?' Anjali grinned. 'Now, if you'll excuse me, it looks like we're ready to go.'

Her police colleagues had done their work. Two scenes – the sites of Charlie's stabbing and Murdoch's capture – had been taped off. Photographs had been taken of both locations and even of Murdoch as he lay there, still trussed up. He'd been particularly unamused by that.

The dog leads had now been untied and swapped for handcuffs. Two uniformed officers flanked Murdoch as he stood. They looked low-key furious at the actions of one of their own. Charlie suspected they were secretly willing Murdoch to attempt another escape, just so they could use maximum force taking him down.

Other officers busied themselves taking statements. Forensics bagged and labelled Murdoch's gloves and the bloodied knife. Charlie had requested that they leave the orange ball behind. Ted was still lying near the path, the ball between his front paws, contentedly chomping on it. Any evidence on it was surely long gone. Anjali had nodded her assent.

She'd been patiently waiting for this moment and it was time. Anjali walked up to Murdoch and stood staring at him until he raised his head and met her eye. In an authoritative tone with an edge of anger, she read him his rights.

'You do not have to say anything but it may harm your defence if you do not mention when questioned something which you later rely on in court. Anything you do say may be given in evidence.'

Murdoch didn't reply or even nod; he just gazed back at her arrogantly.

Anjali wasn't intimidated. She glanced at the two uniformed officers and they marched Murdoch towards the entrance to the woods, where several police vehicles were waiting.

Anjali walked behind, briefly looking over her shoulder at Charlie and Tess. They smiled back until the last of the police officers were out of sight. At which point, all the dog-walkers descended on Ted and made a huge fuss of him.

Exhausted but happy, Ted waited patiently for the hubbub to die down, then went back to chewing his orange ball. A just reward for the hero of the hour.

104

Wounded Warrior

He was moving at the same rate as Ruby nowadays. For the first time in years, Charlie didn't need to deliberately slow his pace or wait patiently for her to catch up. It might be painful but at least they were in sync.

A few days after Murdoch's arrest, Charlie's leg was starting to heal. When he'd belatedly gone to hospital, they'd cleaned out the wound again, put in a few stitches and redressed it. Charlie was put on courses of painkillers and antibiotics. He'd have a scar but he didn't mind. He planned on telling people it was a shark bite.

He still had a slight limp but that would sort itself out in time. In the meantime he was secretly enjoying it. It made him feel like a war hero or gangster. Possibly even a pirate.

Ruby also seemed to like the new slower Charlie. She looked proud to be walking at his heel. He couldn't escape quite so easily when she wanted to lick him either.

It took longer than usual but at last they arrived at Coastal Coffee. Charlie had been looking forward to a cup of Tess's finest. She'd been visiting to help walk Ruby and bring him takeaways while he'd been laid up recovering but it wasn't the same. Not least because Polly was forever fussing, bringing in home-made cakes or biscuits for Tess, painkillers or extra cushions for Charlie. He knew his mum meant well. She was a caring, attentive nurse but he wasn't the best patient. Or indeed the most patient patient.

The dogwalkers greeted him with a cheer. There were hugs and backslaps for Charlie, treats and tickles for Ruby. Now it was Tess's turn to fuss over him, pulling up a chair, positioning it carefully and sitting Charlie down in it gently. He was beginning to feel less like a battle-scarred pirate, more like a hobbling pensioner. He consoled himself by leaning under the table and saying hi to Ted – to his mind the real hero here.

By the time Charlie was settled with a hot drink, Ruby flopped at his feet as usual, everyone had started chatting among themselves. Viv and Sue were bickering affectionately about the merits of some true-crime podcast. Malcolm and Tess were exchanging innuendoes about a handsome new staff member in the nearby DIY shop. It stocked things like ballcocks and screws, so you can imagine where they were going with this. Charlie sipped his Americano happily and half listened. Everything seemed back to normal, for now at least. He wouldn't have it any other way.

He snapped out of his pleased-to-be-back reverie when he suddenly realized that the others had gone quiet.

'Well?' said Viv.

Charlie looked round at their enquiring faces. He'd clearly been asked something but hadn't heard. 'Well what?'

She chuckled. 'I knew you were daydreaming. We were just saying, look at us, yakking away, forgetting we'd not seen you for a few days. How's the leg?'

'Healing nicely, thanks,' said Charlie. 'Although I got

overtaken by an asthmatic snail on the way here. Now, give me all the gossip. What have I missed?'

'Just the regular giddy roller coaster of dog walks, debauchery and glamour,' said Malcolm.

'And Sue finished a new scarf, didn't you?' added Tess.

'The previous one got blood-stained –' she shrugged – 'and then sealed in an evidence bag.'

Charlie grimaced. 'Sorry about that. And about your silky number too, Malcs.'

'No need, darling,' said Malcolm, waving him away. 'Plenty more where that came from. My favourite legal client is welcome.'

'So come on,' said Viv. 'Debrief us. Dish all the juicy details from before we arrived in the woods.'

'Actually,' said Charlie, draining his coffee and putting the cup down meaningfully, 'I hoped we might celebrate with something a bit stronger.'

'Say no more,' said Tess, leaping to her feet. 'I'll fetch my emergency bottle from under the counter.'

'Wait a minute,' said Charlie. 'I was thinking maybe somewhere with a wider range of drinks? Like, you know, an actual pub? No offence, Tess. But with my mum insisting on healthy food and non-stop soup, I haven't had a proper drink in days. I feel like we've earned it.'

'In that case, the pub it is,' declared Tess. 'It's Leon's day off, so I'll close early.'

'Are you OK, sweetheart?' asked Malcolm, faux-concerned. 'Have you suffered a blow to the head?'

'Yeah, you never shut up shop,' said Sue. 'Not even on your birthday.'

'It's a special occasion,' said Tess firmly. 'It's not every day that a wounded warrior walks – well, limps – back into town after catching a killer. Where you were thinking, Hopalong Cassidy?'

'How about the Neptune?' replied Charlie.

It seemed only apt, after all. He was intrigued to see what sort of welcome they'd get – and whether catching Frank's killer had brought the Courtney family peace at last.

105

Canine Company

'That's thrown a spanner in the works,' huffed Tess. 'I genuinely had no idea it wasn't dog-friendly. Then again, we've only ever been here in the evenings, *sans des chiens*.'

They stood outside the Neptune, staring in bafflement at the NO DOGS ALLOWED sign in the window. Who knew?

'And it's not like we're smuggling in one,' said Viv, looking round at Ruby, Rough, Tumble and Ted. 'We've got a whole pack in tow.'

'Ah well,' said Charlie. 'It was a nice idea, poorly researched.'

'Story of your life,' said Tess. 'Does that work? Still a gag in progress, that one.'

They were about to head elsewhere when the pub door was flung open.

'Where are you lot off to?' cried Jackie Courtney, who'd presumably spotted them from behind the bar. She beamed. 'Come on, don't make me drag you in off the street.'

'Sorry, Jackie,' said Charlie, nodding towards the sign. 'We didn't realize our four-legged friends weren't allowed. We'll come back another time without them.'

'What?' said Jackie. 'Oh, that old thing. Frank put it up

years ago, the grumpy git. I'd forgotten it was there, to be honest. Would this change your minds?'

She hurried back inside, gave them a regal wave through the window and unpeeled the sign, before ostentatiously screwing it up and throwing it to the floor.

'How about now?' said Jackie, reappearing in the doorway with a broad grin. 'Starting today, the Neptune is officially dog-friendly. Pedigree pals not just welcome but actively encouraged. Perhaps you can design me some new signs, Charlie? And forget about mates' rates. I'll pay you full whack.'

Charlie chuckled. 'It would be my pleasure. If you're sure? We wouldn't want to force a policy change on you without due process.'

'One hundred per cent sure,' said Jackie. 'Especially if it means two of my favourites can come in.' She squatted down to make a fuss of Ruby, who she already knew, and Ted, who she'd clearly heard all about. 'No offence, you two,' she added, fondly greeting Rough and Tumble too.

As she ushered them all inside, Jackie gave a soft whistle. There was a noise like an armchair falling down some stairs and Bobby the bulldog waddled out from behind the bar, his stumpy tail wagging with giddy excitement.

'He'll be glad of some canine company for a change,' said Jackie as he sniffed hello to Ruby and the rest. 'Bobby gets tired of us boring old humans. Now, please, sit down here. Best seats in the house.'

She waved them over to a table by the open fire, helped limping Charlie into his seat and gestured over to her daughters. 'Drinks are on me, of course. But first let's toast you all with something fizzy. Proper champagne naturally. None of your Prosecco nonsense.'

Malcolm smiled approvingly. 'A woman after my own heart.'

An ice bucket, bottle and flutes duly arrived with impressive speed. Once Jackie had expertly popped the cork and poured them all a drink, she solemnly cleared her throat.

'To the people – and the dogs, of course – who helped find my Frank's killer,' she said, her voice briefly quavering with emotion. She raised her glass and looked round at them all. 'Here's to the Dogwalkers' Detective Agency.'

'If only Wagatha Christie hadn't already been taken,' added Tess.

As everyone laughed and took a sip, Viv turned to Sue and said, 'The Dogwalkers' Detective Agency? You know, I think that could catch on.'

106

A Family Affair

It soon became a family affair. As the carousing continued and the drinks flowed, Jackie beckoned over the bar staff. 'Now you might know each other by sight already, so forgive me,' she announced to the table, 'but meet our – sorry, *my* – three children.'

She turned to the two smiling young women and the strapping barman, who looked rather less impressed to be summoned. 'These are my daughters, Grace and Ruth.'

'What lovely biblical names,' noted Malcolm, ever the smoothie.

'Well, we're a very devout family,' said Jackie with a wink. 'And this is my son Luke. Another godly name, I suppose. We all owe you a debt of gratitude, don't we?'

Grace and Ruth grinned in agreement. Luke begrudgingly nodded.

Charlie was struck by how warm and welcoming the Courtney family were being. He felt conflicted, knowing what he knew about Frank. He saw no reason to add to their grief by telling them exactly what sort of man he was, or why and how he was killed. That wasn't Charlie's place. Better to leave them with whatever image they had of Frank before he died.

He gingerly stood up and said his hellos. As he shook Luke's hand – trying not to wince at his vice-like grip – he took the opportunity to glance down at his knuckles. They were pretty much healed but he could still detect some faint marks on the skin.

'Nice to meet you again, Luke,' said Charlie. 'Sorry once more for your loss. I hope you can find some peace now.'

'Maybe,' said Luke in a low voice. 'And look, mate, I'm sorry I got you wrong. You did right by my father after all.'

Charlie was about to ask what he meant but Luke was already turning away, returning to his duties behind the bar. Which mainly seemed to involve fulfilling his mother's requests for more freebies for the dogwalkers.

Soon the gang were on their feet, mingling merrily with Grace, Ruth and the Neptune's other punters, who gradually drifted over, attracted by rumours of drinks on the house.

Charlie's leg was stiffening, so he stayed seated, sipped his beer and looked on, letting his mind wander. He wasn't sure why, but something about their investigation and its resolution still bothered him.

'Penny for your thoughts, Charlie,' said a voice in his ear.

He turned to see Jackie plonking herself down next to him. A few celebratory drinks had suited her. Her cheeks were flushed and she smiled at him fondly.

'Oh, I was just thinking about something Luke said,' said Charlie casually.

'Oh yes?' Jackie raised her eyebrows in amusement. 'He tends not to say much, my son, so you've already done well there. What did he say?'

'That he was sorry for getting me wrong. Any idea what he meant?' probed Charlie gently.

'I think so,' said Jackie, sighing. 'He was a bit of a daddy's boy, was our Luke. A man's man. Good at sport, which Frank always liked. Apple of his father's eye. Frank's death has hit him hard.'

'I'm sure,' said Charlie sympathetically. 'What does that have to do with me?'

'I'm coming to that,' said Jackie. 'He's very protective of his father's name and reputation. With a man like Frank, that's quite the full-time job. Luke doesn't know the half of it, of course. I'm not sure I do either. I suspect I don't want to know. But Luke has never liked people bad-mouthing Frank. Even more so since he passed.'

'Right,' said Charlie. 'So he thinks I was disrespecting his dad's memory?'

Jackie nodded. 'Afraid so. There was one night in here when you were asking all sorts of questions. Whether Frank was a bent copper, on the take, that sort of thing. Luke overheard you and didn't take kindly to it at all.'

'I'm sorry,' said Charlie, meaning it. 'I was only trying to work out who might have a motive to murder him.'

'I know that, darling, but Luke didn't,' said Jackie. 'The red mist descended. Luke has always been quick with his fists. Another quality he inherited from his father. He was badly bullied when he was little, but since his growth spurt he tends to get his retaliation in first.'

'Wait, so it was Luke who followed me into the woods that night?' asked Charlie. 'I'd assumed it was Craig Murdoch, especially with what we now know about him.'

'Understandable,' said Jackie. 'But no, it was Luke. When you left the pub that night, he stormed off after you. I tried to talk him out of it, but there was no reasoning with him in that mood. At least there was no harm done, eh?'

'True.' Charlie smiled. 'Although he gave me one helluva fright.'

'In that case accept my apologies too,' said Jackie kindly. 'He admitted the next day that you'd disappeared before his very eyes. Like some sort of ninja, he said. I think he was secretly impressed.'

Charlie chuckled, looking down at his leg. 'Oh, I'm no ninja. Especially not at the moment. I just know Framstone Woods better than most, that's all.'

'Well, I'm glad you do,' said Jackie, smiling. 'I know how badly Luke can rough people up when he's riled.'

Charlie put two and two together. 'You mean Rob Thompson?'

Jackie nodded. 'Yes, I feel awful about that,' she said sadly. 'Rob's a liability but he didn't deserve that much of a kicking. Drink had loosened his tongue. He was saying all sorts about Frank and not exactly being discreet about it. His death was still recent then, still raw, so Luke lost it. I didn't twig until it was too late.'

'What made you realize?'

'His hands were in a terrible state the morning after,' said Jackie. 'He claimed he'd cut them on a broken bottle. I didn't believe him for a second but patched them up for him anyway. Later, doing the laundry, there was blood down his shirt. When I heard Rob had been hospitalized, it wasn't hard to work out what had happened.'

'Does Rob know it was Luke?' asked Charlie. For a while he'd wondered if Rob thought Shane had attacked him as a result of their pub bust-up. When Shane was murdered soon after Rob was discharged from hospital, Charlie had suspected a revenge killing. Now he knew better.

'I reckon so,' said Jackie. 'Although when you're a bad drunk like that, you tend to rub people up the wrong way. Rob's got almost as many enemies as my Frank did.'

'I wonder why Rob didn't report him,' mused Charlie.

'My guess is he didn't want Anjali to know he'd been throwing accusations around. Better to paint himself as the innocent victim. Rob's on thin ice already, marriage-wise, but then you know that.'

For the second time that evening Charlie was about to ask a member of the Courtney family what they meant – but Jackie was already rising to her feet.

'Listen to me, gossiping away while you've got an empty glass.' She smiled. 'Same again, Charlie?'

107

Just the Bubbles Talking

As Jackie tottered off towards the bar, Tess slid into her seat and gave Charlie a knowing look.

'Do tell,' she said, leaning in conspiratorially. 'What was that all about, you old flirt?'

'Less of that,' said Charlie. 'Don't judge everyone by your standards, Tess Cheong. It turns out that it was golden boy Luke who gave Rob Thompson a kicking. Furious about him casting aspersions on his dodgy dad's name apparently.'

'I knew it,' said Tess. 'Told you when I spotted his hand injury, didn't I?'

'That's not quite how I recall it,' said Charlie, laughing. 'But fine. It was also Luke who followed me into the woods after closing time. He was planning to dish out the same punishment, but I managed to escape.'

Tess smiled. 'Lucky you did. You've already got enough battle scars.'

'Exactly,' said Charlie. 'Anyway, all seems forgiven now. Luke sort of apologized in a grunting macho kind of way.'

'Grunting and macho,' said Tess. 'Two qualities I like in a man.'

'Better make yourself scarce again,' muttered Charlie.

'Jackie's coming back and I want to see what else I can squeeze out of her.'

'I bet you do,' teased Tess. 'Good luck.' She and Jackie exchanged friendly grins as they passed each other.

'I do like that Tess,' she said, putting another pint in front of him. 'I think she's sweet on you as well, Charlie Boardman.'

'We're just mates,' scoffed Charlie. 'Wait, as well as who?'

'Anjali Thompson, of course,' said Jackie. 'Don't tell me you hadn't noticed.'

'Not really,' said Charlie, suddenly feeling hot-faced. 'Anyway, where were we? Oh yeah. I was going to ask what you meant when you said that Luke didn't know the half of it about Frank?'

'Probably just the bubbles talking,' said Jackie, waving her hand. 'I just meant that Frank was a complicated man. There's nothing to be gained by Luke knowing exactly how complicated.'

'If you don't mind me asking,' said Charlie, trying to put it tactfully, 'how much did you know about what Frank got up to?'

'Normally I'd tell you to mind your own business –' Jackie sighed – 'but I suppose it doesn't matter now. Besides, you caught his killer. We owe you.' She paused. 'I knew bits. Not all, by any means, but bits of it.'

'You knew he was on the take when he was a policeman?'

'Not in so many words, but yes,' she admitted.

'And you knew he was involved in drug-dealing?'

'I guessed,' she said sadly. 'He was out at odd hours with odd people. The money had to come from somewhere. But I never asked him straight out. It was a case of least said, soonest mended.'

'He was never violent towards you, was he?' asked Charlie, suddenly concerned.

'My Frank?' She gave a brittle laugh. 'No way. I wouldn't have stood for any of that nonsense, don't you worry. But as I've said, Frank had a rough old start in life. I think it messed up his sense of right and wrong.'

This chimed with Charlie's own thinking. If he'd suffered abuse himself, Frank might well have grown up with a distorted understanding of morality and a lack of boundaries. Living with shame and hiding his sexuality would have warped it even more, leading him to continue the cycle. That can be the tragic legacy of childhood trauma.

Charlie looked at Jackie. He wondered if she knew about Frank's abuse and control of young men. He suspected that deep down, she did. But some things are just too painful to confront.

'And the money?' he asked, deciding to change the subject.

'I always saw it as family money.' She shrugged. 'School fees and nice holidays were what the rest of us got in return for Frank . . . well, being Frank.'

She was a mother who made a pragmatic decision, thought Charlie. Even if it was a deal with the devil.

'So what are your plans now?'

'Moving on with our lives, I suppose,' said Jackie. 'And putting my own stamp on the all-new dog-friendly Neptune. Keep it thriving. Not let it get sold off and turned into flats, like far too many pubs nowadays.'

'Why did Frank put up that sign?' asked Charlie. 'I mean, you had Bobby so he was clearly a dog lover.'

'I suppose he didn't want to attract old men with their

dogs,' she said. 'He wanted a younger crowd. They drink more and spend more.'

And they're more likely to buy drugs, thought Charlie. He also wondered if banning pooches meant the police couldn't sneak in an undercover sniffer dog. It occurred to him that the Neptune's location, looking out to sea, would have enabled Frank to keep an eye out for shipments arriving by boat.

Jackie sighed again and said quietly, 'What happened to Frank is awfully sad, especially for the kids. But between you and me, there's a sense of relief, too. You'd understand that, surely, Charlie?'

'How do you mean?'

'Tell me if I'm wrong or prying, but there's daddy issues in your family too, right?' She tilted her head to one side, a kind look in her eyes.

'I guess so,' said Charlie, frowning at the memory. He hated to put his own father in the same bracket as Frank Courtney, but he knew what she meant. 'I certainly felt some relief when he left.'

'And your mum?' asked Jackie gently.

'I think so,' mused Charlie. 'Although I do sometimes wonder if she knows more about my dad's departure than she lets on.'

'Wives of men like that usually do,' said Jackie sympathetically. 'Believe me. Didn't your brother leave Framstone, too? There might be more of a story there than you know.'

Charlie stared into his pint and pondered. He realized he was thoughtfully rubbing his finger again. He'd hate to upset Polly but perhaps the next family he needed to investigate was his own.

108

Contacts on the Inside

'You're being very mysterious, young man,' said Polly with a smile. 'Why all the secrecy?'

'That would be telling, wouldn't it?' said Charlie. 'But bless you for calling me young.'

It wasn't often these days that Polly joined him on dog walks, but this was a special occasion. Not that he'd explained why. Ruby had looked equally confused as he turned in the other direction upon leaving the house, away from her usual beat in the woods or on the beach. Instead they arrived at Framstone Rec.

While Ruby busied herself taking in the different smells, Polly tried to probe Charlie about why he'd insisted on coming here and why today. He refused to be drawn and instead told her to be patient.

'Aha, here's our surprise special guest,' said Charlie.

Ruby gave a wag of her tail and Polly turned to see who was coming down the path.

'Karen!' she cried. 'What are you doing here?'

Karen Carter smiled. 'I was about to ask you the same thing. We've clearly been set up by this son of yours.'

She looked brighter than when Charlie had last seen her.

Still slightly sad around the eyes but less tired and troubled. Hopefully Shane's name being cleared had helped. 'Hi, Karen,' he said. 'Thanks for coming. Sorry to be enigmatic.'

'I'll let you off,' she said. 'As long as there's a cup of tea and maybe a cake in it.'

Charlie laughed. 'I predicted you'd say that.' He patted the satchel slung over his shoulder. 'I came prepared. Now, if you ladies will step this way, please. That includes you, Rube.'

Taking his time – well, both Ruby and Polly moved at a stately pace nowadays – he led the two women and one dog on a lap of the children's playground towards a cluster of benches.

'I thought we might stop here for a cuppa,' he said, gesturing towards one of the seats.

Charlie opened his bag, solemnly took out three plastic mugs, handing one each to Polly and Karen. He opened a flask and, with due ceremony, poured steaming-hot tea for them all.

'I don't suppose –' began Karen.

'Milk and sugar?' Charlie interrupted. 'Of course.' He fished a small bottle, some sachets and teaspoons out of his bag.

'You really have come prepared.' Polly grinned. 'My little boy scout.'

'Dib-dib-dob-dob,' said Charlie.

The three of them stood sipping their drinks for a moment.

'Where are my manners?' said Charlie suddenly. 'Sit down, ladies, please.'

As Polly and Karen went to sit, he whipped out a hand-kerchief. 'Just let me make sure it's clean.'

Polly looked at him quizzically as Charlie ran the cloth around the slatted bench, wiping away any residual dirt or raindrops.

'And let's give the plaque a little polish while we're at it,' he added.

He buffed a small brass plate on the back of the bench and glanced round at Polly and Karen, beckoning them forward. Both leaned in for a closer look.

Karen gave a gasp. 'Oh!' she said, her hand going to her mouth. 'What is . . . ? How did . . . ?'

Charlie stood back proudly as Polly read aloud. '*In loving memory of Shane Carter, 2004–2025. Happiest in nature and with animals. Framstone FC forever.*'

'It's perfect,' said Karen, clutching Charlie in a tight hug. 'Thank you. Shane would thank you too.'

Ruby seemed to sense something was afoot, coming over to rub herself affectionately against Karen's legs.

She turned to Polly with a quizzical expression. 'Did you know about this?'

'It's a surprise to me too,' said Polly, smiling. 'How did you organize this, son? I heard there was a council waiting list for memorial benches.'

'Contacts on the inside,' said Charlie, tapping his nose. 'Well, Malcolm's contacts.'

'That's Charlie's friend,' Polly told Karen. 'He seems to know everyone.'

'Just don't ask how,' joked Charlie. 'Anyway, I'm glad you like it, Karen. I thought you might like to sit here sometimes to remember. In fact, no time like the present.'

As Polly and Karen proudly plonked themselves down, turning to look at the shining bronze plaque again, he produced the final flourish from his satchel: a Victoria sponge cake, expertly baked by Leon from Coastal Coffee.

'I'd say "Shall I be mother?"', said Charlie, chuckling, 'but there are two mothers sitting right in front of me.'

The women beamed at each other as he cut three generous slices.

109

The Cops Are Coming

Surprise guests on dog walks seemed to have become Charlie's new thing.

While tramping through Framstone Woods the next day with the full crew – Tess, Malcolm, Viv, Sue and a crowd of dogs almost in double figures – Charlie suddenly leaped off the path and into the bushes, with a stage-whispered 'Quick, hide! The cops are coming!'

'Very droll,' said Malcolm, who'd already spotted Anjali heading down the path towards them.

'I had you for a moment, though, right?' said Charlie, turning to the three women.

They all shook their heads and rolled their eyes in unison, which was a skill. Even Ruby looked distinctly unimpressed by his prank. Charlie shrugged sheepishly and walked ahead to greet Anjali.

She grinned. 'Here we see the native Boardy Boy in his natural habitat. How's the war wound?'

He smiled back. 'Healing up nicely, thanks for asking.' It was indeed. You wouldn't notice his limp now unless you were looking for it. Which naturally, Tess usually was. She'd taken to calling him 'Verbal Kint', 'Dr House' or 'Herr Flick'.

'Carry on walking, please,' said Anjali, turning to the group. 'I hope you don't mind me gatecrashing. I told Charlie I'd tag along and update you on the case. By way of thanks really. We couldn't have got this far without you all.'

Everyone looked quietly proud as they fell into step behind Anjali and Charlie. He could've sworn Viv even blushed, not that she'd ever admit it.

'This is exciting,' said Charlie. 'Like a proper police debriefing. Will there be coffee and doughnuts?'

'You'd be lucky,' said Anjali. 'The best we get at the station is from the vending machine. You could probably sue for calling it coffee.'

'Coastal is always happy for your custom,' said Tess, never one to miss an opportunity. 'Discounts offered for our favourite detective.'

'Thanks, I'll bear it in mind,' said Anjali, grinning. 'Now, the main news is . . . Drumroll, please . . .'

Charlie did his best impersonation of a snare drum, which momentarily startled the dogs.

'Former Detective Sergeant Craig Murdoch has been charged on two counts of murder, with other charges pending.'

Everyone gave a cheer, which startled the dogs again.

'That's great news,' said Charlie. 'Except for him, I guess.'

'It is indeed,' agreed Anjali. 'There are still loose ends to tie up, but we've passed the evidence threshold, so I'm pretty confident of a conviction.'

'Only pretty confident?' asked Sue in a worried tone.

'These things are rarely cut and dried,' explained Anjali. 'We already had a fair bit on him, mainly thanks to you guys. The fact that he was carrying a knife which matched the weapon used in Frank Courtney's murder only strengthens the case against him. As does the attack on you, of course, Charlie.'

'Happy to help, officer,' he said, glancing down at his leg. 'Have you found out much more about how it all went down?'

'Well, the first murder happened largely as you'd deduced,' she said. 'Murdoch was in an organized crime group with Frank but became worried that he was either being indiscreet or cutting some sort of side deal. Murdoch followed Frank to his assignation here in the woods. When he saw Shane Carter hit him, drop his knife and flee, Murdoch spotted his chance to get rid of Frank and set up Shane for killing him.'

'What a douche bag,' muttered Tess.

'How about killing poor Shane?' asked Charlie. 'What was his motive there?'

Anjali gave a sympathetic frown. She knew the gang, Charlie in particular, had a soft spot for Shane Carter.

'Killed for his silence,' she said. 'Shane's death ensured he couldn't blow the whistle on the local drugs trade, let alone accuse Murdoch of being the real murderer. Putting Shane's football scarf back round his neck post-mortem helped keep him in the frame for Frank Courtney, considering the fibres found at the scene. It diverted our attention in the wrong direction.'

'I'll say it again,' repeated Tess. 'What a douche bag.'

'Quite,' agreed Anjali.

'Hang on,' said Charlie. 'So Shane definitely did suspect Murdoch of killing Frank? And Murdoch knew he did?'

'Ah yes,' said Anjali. 'I was coming to that. Let's sit down for a minute while I explain. I'm worried about your leg, not to mention mine. I'm not used to all this yomping about.'

She plonked herself down on a bench. As everyone gathered round, Charlie wished there really was coffee and doughnuts. All this amateur detecting was making him peckish.

110

A Fatal Escalation

'I hate to give you any credit, as you know,' said Anjali, looking up at Charlie, 'but you were right.'

He smiled. 'It happens occasionally. What specifically was I right about?'

'You wondered if something said during Shane Carter's interview hinted that he knew the real killer's identity,' said Anjali. 'Something I might not notice unless I was looking for it. Well, I went back and rewatched the tape.'

'Don't leave us hanging,' said Tess. 'Or that coffee discount might disappear.'

'It was just ambiguous enough,' said Anjali almost admiringly. 'Before he started "no comment"-ing, Shane said something with a double meaning. Murdoch accused him of stabbing Frank, to which Shane replied, "You know I didn't."'

'Is that it?' asked Viv incredulously.

Anjali smiled. 'It was the way he said it. The emphasis wasn't so much on the denial as the "you".'

'Aha,' said Charlie. 'If I'm interpreting this correctly, Shane said it like "*You* know I didn't do it". Meaning that of all people, Murdoch would know because he'd done it himself.'

'Exactly,' said Anjali. 'I've replayed it a dozen times. The way

Shane says it and Murdoch's body language in response – he bristles slightly – made me pretty certain. Shane was smarter than some might assume.'

'Funny how one change of emphasis can seal someone's fate,' said Charlie sadly.

'Indeed,' said Anjali. 'Murdoch has now admitted that's when he knew that Shane was on to him and partly why he drowned him.'

'Only partly?' asked Malcolm.

'I think there's more to it,' said Anjali. 'My educated guess would be that they had a dispute. Murdoch called off the surveillance so he could meet Shane. Maybe he tried to pay him off to leave town. Maybe he tried to change the terms of their drug deals. When Shane wouldn't play ball, it escalated.'

'Tragically for Shane, it escalated fatally,' said Tess.

'Afraid so,' said Anjali. 'I'm still hoping to get more answers.'

'There's still stuff to come out?' asked Malcolm. 'Was Jack the Ripper involved? Lord Lucan riding Shergar the racehorse? The mind boggles.'

'Big cases like this take time,' Anjali explained. 'There are details to nail down. Triangulated signals from burner phones. The positive ID from the shop worker who sold Murdoch the toy dogs and glow-in-the-dark pens. Sounds laborious but it all helps build a watertight case. Besides, the interviews are proving quite a long process.'

'How come?' asked Charlie. 'I never had our mate Craig down as chatty.'

'Well,' said Anjali, smiling again, 'that's the other piece of good news I came to tell you.'

III

No Honour Among Thieves

'Corruption rarely happens in a vacuum,' said Anjali gnomically. 'Sometimes it's isolated, sure, but often it's a network. Other times it's institutionalized.'

'All right, Confucius,' said Viv. 'Can we do words of one syllable, please?'

'What she's trying to say,' chipped in Charlie, glancing at Anjali for her assent, 'is that Murdoch wasn't the only rotten apple in the Framstone Police barrel.'

'Well put, my learned friend,' said Anjali. 'In that regard, Mr Murdoch is proving rather more useful in disgrace than he ever was on duty. In the hope of reducing his sentence and, let's say, more lenient custody arrangements . . .'

'Because coppers have a tough time in prison,' said Sue as a knowing aside.

'Mr Murdoch is being pleasingly forthcoming with intel,' continued Anjali.

'Quite right too,' said Malcolm. 'Singing like the proverbial canary is the least he can do after all the grief he's caused.'

'Are further arrests imminent, then?' asked Tess.

'Again, still to be finalized,' said Anjali, ever the professional. 'Patience and planning are required. But with what he's given us, we're hoping to bring down the drugs ring operating in Framstone.'

'The whole shebang?' asked Viv delightedly.

'The traffickers bringing it ashore. The distributors packaging it up. The dealers selling it on the streets. It's all a chain, but thanks to Murdoch's leads, we've got a way in,' said Anjali.

'Thank goodness there's no honour among thieves,' said Sue.

'And what about all that vacuum stuff?' said Viv. 'I'm assuming there were other bent coppers with their hands in the sweetie jar?'

'I think that's a fair assumption,' said Anjali. 'Let's say we're investigating all police involvement in the local drugs trade.' She glanced at Charlie. 'The two officers who dropped the surveillance on Shane that night are on my hit list, incidentally.'

'So what was Murdoch doing with his ill-gotten gains?' asked Tess. 'We know Frank spent his on school fees and holiday homes.'

'Well, as Charlie deduced, he had nice cars and nice clothes,' replied Anjali, 'but not flash enough to draw undue attention. He was also bankrolling his elderly grandmother's care. She pretty much raised him. It seems he was repaying her by stumping up for a five-star care home, which would be beyond the means of a regular copper.'

'It would almost be admirable if it wasn't dirty money and he wasn't a murderer,' said Tess.

As everyone thought about that, Charlie bent down to give Ruby some attention. She'd earned it by being so patient as the humans did all their talking.

'There is one other aspect of all this that we shouldn't

forget,' he said, straightening up to look at Anjali. 'The alleged abuse by Frank Courtney.'

'I couldn't agree more,' said Sue, suddenly impassioned. 'He shouldn't have been able to get away with it.'

'Is that being investigated now too?' asked Malcolm.

'Absolutely,' Anjali assured them. 'Don't worry, we haven't overlooked that. An internal inquiry has been launched into historical abuse. Specifically how Frank – and potentially others – might have exploited their position of authority to groom and take advantage of vulnerable young men.'

'Good,' said the dogwalkers almost in unison.

'In many ways that's the most serious crime of all in this. It might be belated but we're on the case.' Anjali sighed. 'Now, I think we're all sufficiently rested. Shall we carry on walking? If we could be heading vaguely in the direction of civilization, that would be a bonus.'

It might have been Charlie's imagination but as they set off again he was sure the sun burst through the clouds, as if signalling brighter times ahead.

112

Above and Beyond the Call of Duty

Suddenly Charlie was walking alongside Anjali at the head of the dog pack. He glanced behind at the others and Malcolm gave him a saucy wink. Charlie got the feeling they were being clumsily set up.

'Thanks for sharing all that with us,' he said. 'I know it's above and beyond the call of duty to be so open with members of the public. It's appreciated. Truly.'

'Well, you're not just any members of the public, are you?' said Anjali, giving him a nudge in the ribs. 'You're not only an old friend but you lot solved this case as much as I did. Probably more. It's appreciated. Truly.'

'Sounds like we're square,' said Charlie. 'Otherwise it could have been awkward.'

'Oh, it's always awkward,' she replied.

They walked on for a while in contented silence, Ruby trotting alongside them, before Charlie asked, 'How's Rob doing?'

'Good actually,' said Anjali, sounding mildly surprised. 'He's delighted we've got Murdoch bang to rights for both murders.'

'Good,' said Charlie. 'Although I got the distinct impression there was no love lost between Rob and Frank Courtney either.'

'Rob was shooting his mouth off, huh?' said Anjali with an eye-roll. 'Yes, there was some animosity there. Boys will be boys, I guess. All in the past now.'

Charlie wondered whether Anjali had ever deemed her husband a murder suspect – and how much she knew about his involvement with Frank's activities years ago. Thankfully it was all academic now. Although there was a chance Rob's name might still come up during the inquiry into Framstone Police corruption. Talk about awkwardness.

'Shooting his mouth off might be less of a problem from now on, though,' added Anjali.

'How do you mean?' asked Charlie. 'Had his lips sewn together, has he? Joined an order of monks and taken a vow of silence?'

She laughed. 'I wish. No, I just meant that Rob seems to have turned a corner when it comes to his drinking.'

'Oh really?'

'He's not touched a drop in a week and counting,' she said. Charlie thought he detected a note of something in Anjali's voice. Pride? Relief?

'Well done him,' said Charlie, trying to sound upbeat despite feeling conflicted.

'We've even been talking about him going to AA,' she continued. 'He's never been open to it before. Tended to get defensive if I tried to discuss it.'

'That definitely sounds like progress then,' said Charlie encouragingly.

'Yes, it is,' she said. 'Although we'd need to find him the

right group. He's worried local ones will be full of either fellow coppers or criminals he's nicked over the years. Not to mention his drinking buddies from the pubs and clubs of Framstone.'

'Don't worry too much about that,' said Charlie. 'The clue's in the name. Alcoholics Anonymous. There's a pledge of confidentiality. Besides, anyone gossiping would have to admit they'd been there too.'

'True,' said Anjali, giving him a curious sideways look as they walked. 'You seem to know a lot about it.'

'Oh, you know,' said Charlie vaguely. 'I read a lot and watch too much TV drama, that's all.'

'It's baby steps but at least they're in the right direction,' she said. 'I didn't give him an ultimatum or say it in so many words, but if Rob had carried on the way he was going, it would have been hard to stay together.'

'Did you seriously consider leaving him?'

'At times I'd started thinking about it,' admitted Anjali. 'But for now we're back on track.'

'I'm pleased,' he said.

'OK, this is me,' said Anjali, coming to a halt. They'd reached the entrance to the woods. 'Are you heading my way or are you carrying on walking?'

'Carrying on for a bit, I think,' said Charlie, looking around. The others were lagging quite a long way behind.

'Thanks again then, Boardy Boy,' said Anjali, leaning in for a quick hug. Her hair smelled clean and coconutty. 'I'll keep you informed. Wish me luck.'

'Good luck!' he called at her retreating back.

As Charlie watched her go, he reflected on his mixed feelings about the Rob Thompson news. It was good that he was tackling his drinking. Of course it was. But had Charlie been secretly hoping they might split up eventually? Subconsciously had Rob gone from a prime suspect to something of a rival for Anjali's affections?

Charlie shook his head, as if to banish such thoughts, and turned back towards the others.

113

Sweet Sorrow

'Have you two been rent asunder?' said Malcolm. '*Parting is such sweet sorrow.*'

'Don't quote *Romeo and Juliet* at me,' said Charlie, chuckling. 'I bite my thumb at you, sir. Besides, she's a married woman.'

'*O rude unthankfulness,*' said Malcolm in faux-outrage. 'So what now, you lot? Another lap of the woods to tire out these reprobates?'

'Go on then,' said Viv. 'Charlie can tell us what he and DI Thompson were talking about. Unless it's classified, of course?'

'Just chit-chat.' He shrugged. 'Nothing juicy, I'm afraid.' Might as well start the whole anonymous thing now, he figured.

'One more lap it is, then back to Coastal,' Tess said, nodding. 'The coffees are on me. Just don't get used to it.'

It was a beautiful autumnal day for a walk. Bright and bracing, all brown leaves and birdsong. Christmas was gradually heaving into view but the cold hadn't yet begun to truly bite.

As they rambled down the path, everyone cheerfully

chatting away and dogs milling around, Charlie was preoccupied. Partly by Anjali and Rob Thompson's rocky marriage getting back on an even keel. Partly by Craig Murdoch and his confession. Something else was gnawing away at him too.

He found himself walking behind Sue. That's when it caught his eye. Slung over one shoulder was her trademark knitting bag. As she walked along the path, it bobbed up and down, directly in Charlie's eyeline. A knitting needle was poking out, with a piece of yarn wrapped round it.

The wool's shade of red looked familiar. It reminded Charlie of the fluff he'd found on the leg of his jeans after having his wound bandaged with Sue's scarf. Wait. Wasn't it also the same colour as the wool fibres found on Frank Courtney's body, purportedly from Shane Carter's Framstone Rovers scarf?

Another image flashed into his mind, like a snapshot. The supper at Viv and Sue's house. As she'd walked to the head of the table to improvise an evidence board, Sue had paused and nudged her knitting bag with her foot. She'd subtly pushed it under the sideboard out of sight.

Charlie's head spun. Physically he seemed to be moving in slow motion but his mind raced. Thoughts cascaded and fell into position. It felt like he'd floated up out of his own body and was looking down at a wider view. No, it was impossible. Or if not impossible, highly improbable. Come on. It couldn't be . . . could it?

He snapped back into the present. Strolling through the woods on this lovely crisp day, Sue was still right in front of him. He could reach out and touch her.

Without breaking stride, he tapped Sue gently on her shoulder. When she turned round, Charlie briefly put his finger to his lips, then beckoned her, indicating that they should drop behind the others for a one-to-one chat.

Sue looked fleetingly confused, then nodded in understanding. They both slowed their walking pace until a gap opened up between them and the others.

'I'm not sure how to say this, Sue . . .' began Charlie.

'Shush, it's fine,' Sue reassured him softly. 'I wondered how long it would take you to work it out.'

114

It Had Already Happened

'What you've got to understand,' said Sue in a quietly steely tone, 'is what a malign, toxic man he was.'

'We're talking about Frank Courtney, right?' asked Charlie. He knew. He just had to check.

'I can barely bring myself to say his name,' said Sue through gritted teeth. 'But yes, of course. Frank bloody Courtney.'

'Oh, Sue, I'm so sorry,' said Charlie. 'Do you want to talk about it? What he did to you?'

'It wasn't me,' said Sue. 'It was my brother Ian. My big brother. My late big brother.' Tears welled in her eyes.

As they walked, Charlie put his arm round her and gave her a squeeze.

'But I'm fine to talk about it,' said Sue when she'd composed herself. 'I need to explain what happened. It would probably do me good.'

'If you're sure,' said Charlie gently. 'In your own time.'

Sue took a deep breath and gathered herself. A few steps later, she began to talk.

'Ian was three years older than me,' she said wistfully. 'We were so tight growing up. A real team, you know? When we got into our teens, sure, we grew apart a bit, but that's what kids do – especially a boy and a girl with an age gap. You develop at different rates. You find your own friends. Girlfriends, too. But I still worshipped Ian. We were still great mates.'

'He sounds lovely,' said Charlie, ruefully thinking how he'd once been tight like that with Danny, his own elder sibling.

'He was.' Sue smiled gratefully. 'One of the good 'uns. He was a good footballer, was our Ian. He played for local teams and went through all the age groups from primary school onwards. He was in his early teens when Courtney became the team coach.'

'OK,' said Charlie. He thought he knew what was coming and didn't want to push too hard.

'The upshot is that Courtney groomed Ian and . . . well, abused him.' Sue's voice wobbled and she took another deep breath. 'We only found this out later, of course, otherwise we'd have done something. But it explained a lot. It explained everything actually.'

'I'm so sorry,' said Charlie. 'No child should have to go through that.'

'I know, right? Because he was a child. Ian might have been a strapping sporty lad, but he was still a kid. Courtney took advantage. It was shortly afterwards that Ian began going off the rails. He got into drinking at fourteen, drugs at fifteen. Started staying out at all hours. Wouldn't say where he'd been. His schoolwork suffered. My parents just figured it was normal teenage rebellion stuff.'

'But it wasn't,' said Charlie.

'No, it wasn't,' said Sue. 'Not only did Courtney get him into taking drugs. He got him into dealing, too. But because he was a policeman and Ian's football coach, we never suspected a thing. He played the avuncular authority figure role to a tee. Underneath he was a predator.'

'So what happened?' asked Charlie softly.

'Ian was never the same again,' said Sue. 'He'd been a promising footballer, a promising student, but he fell into this life of drugs and crime. He left home and moved into a grotty little flat in town. I imagine Courtney sorted it for him. He liked people being in debt to him. Once Ian wasn't under the family roof, it became harder to work out what was happening and how to help him.'

'I'm sure you all tried,' said Charlie. 'Please don't blame yourself.'

'I did for a long time,' admitted Sue. 'Until I realized Courtney was the one to blame. You might have heard but when I was seventeen, Ian took his own life. It devastated us.'

Charlie stopped and turned to give her proper hug. They stood like that for a moment, before Sue nodded towards the others up ahead and indicated they should keep going. She patted Charlie's arm gratefully as they walked.

'It completely blew up my family, as you can imagine,' she continued. 'I was planning to go to university, but I couldn't leave my parents in that state. Not in an empty house with both their children gone, albeit in very different ways. But it's hard for a marriage to survive a tragedy like that. They split up a few years later.'

'Oh, man,' muttered Charlie. 'I feel for you all, I really do.'

'Thanks, mate.'

'If you don't mind me asking, how did you find out about Courtney's role in all this?'

'It was something that Ian wrote in his suicide note,' said Sue. 'Nothing clear, just a mention, almost as an aside. *You*

449

don't know what happened to me a few years ago, I think it was. Decades later, I heard rumours about Courtney. He'd always given me the creeps, so I did some digging and put two and two together. Somehow, deep down, I just knew I was right.'

Charlie sighed. 'Sadly, it sounds like you probably were.'

'When we met Shane Carter that day on the beach, that confirmed it for me,' said Sue. 'There was something about poor Shane that reminded me of Ian. A look in his eye. His body language. Broken in a way. That was what Courtney did to young men who crossed his path.'

'And that convinced you that your suspicions were correct?'

'Yes, but it had already happened by then,' said Sue, turning to look Charlie in the eye. 'I'd already killed him.'

115

Only One Deadly Option

It was like somebody had pressed a mute button. The background twitter of birds fell away. The sounds of dogs snuffling and barking switched to silent. Even the chatter of Tess, Viv and Malcolm up ahead was suddenly inaudible to Charlie. All he could hear was his own heartbeat and the rushing of blood in his ears.

It took him a few metres to gather himself and return to the moment.

'You . . .' He couldn't believe he was asking this. 'You killed Frank Courtney?'

'Yes,' said Sue firmly. 'I'm pretty sure I did. You can't imagine what a relief it is to finally tell somebody that.'

'Viv doesn't know?' said Charlie incredulously.

'No,' said Sue. 'Not yet anyway. I dread her finding out. I don't know how she'll react. But we'll cross that bridge when we come to it.'

'But what . . . ? How did . . . ?' Charlie couldn't get his words out.

Sue briefly touched his hand. 'Let me tell it from the start,' she said. 'I was on a dog walk with Viv here in the woods with a couple of our regulars. Weren't we, Prof?'

She looked down at the Professor, who was squeaking alongside them on his wheels. He gave a small wag at the mention of his name.

'Anyway, Humphrey disappeared into the bushes,' continued Sue. 'You know what he's like. Labradors are nutty enough anyway, let alone when they've caught the scent of something. Viv walked on with the other dogs, while I went after Humphrey. That's when I found him.'

'You found Frank?' asked Charlie. He had a flashback to how he'd chanced across him in similar fashion.

Sue nodded. 'Yep. Or Humphrey did, strictly speaking. He didn't know what to do, bless him. He must have sensed something was up because he was just standing there, staring at Courtney and quietly whining.'

'Frank was still alive?' asked Charlie, suddenly aware that he was asking lots of dumb questions.

'Just about, yes,' said Sue. 'He was slumped against a tree with a nasty head wound – courtesy of Shane, it later transpired – and an even nastier stab wound, courtesy of Murdoch.'

'How did you know he was alive?' said Charlie. 'Did you check his pulse?'

'No need,' said Sue. 'I assumed he was dead at first but when I went for a closer look, I saw his chest was still rising and falling. Gave me the fright of my life.'

Charlie understood that. He'd half expected to leap back in a jump scare himself if Frank had shown signs of life.

'Did you think about calling for help?'

'Good question.' Sue sighed, thinking back. 'Very briefly, yes. I was about to shout to Viv, but then I realized who he was and what he'd done. It seemed to me that there was only one option.'

'Which was?' said Charlie, a note of fear in his voice.

Not fear of Sue. Not his friend. Not dear, quiet, gentle Sue. Fear of what she was about to say.

'Finish him off,' she said. 'I'd fantasized about justice or payback ever since I worked out what he'd done to Ian years ago. And now here was Courtney, right in front of me, helpless and vulnerable. At my mercy. Nearly dead but not quite.'

'So what did you do?'

'I looked around but there was no sign of a weapon,' she said. 'Murdoch took the knife with him, as we now know. That's when I realized I had one on me already.'

She patted her trusty bag. Always on her shoulder. Such a fixture that Charlie had stopped noticing it until today. He gulped.

'I took out a knitting needle and pushed it into the wound that was already there,' she said quietly. 'It was strangely easy. It slid in so serenely.'

Charlie could picture the scene all too vividly. The dead man's face floated into his mind's eye.

'Oh, God, I feel sick,' said Sue. She clutched her hand to her mouth, remembering the physicality of it. She bent over with her hands on her knees. Charlie patted her back until she gasped down some air and straightened up.

'I think it's passed,' she said. 'Let's walk on before anyone notices.'

'Did he say anything? Scream out or something?'

'Not a sound,' said Sue, shaking her head. 'It was almost like nothing was happening at all. Although I swear I saw a look of surprise cross his face. I whispered, "That's for Ian" and by the time I looked down, his chest had stopped moving. I pulled out the needle, wiped it on the ground and got away from there as fast as I could.'

'And what then? Didn't Viv ask where you'd been?'

'Nope,' she said. 'I caught up with her, a little out of breath. She assumed I'd been chasing Humphrey around. Which I sort of had. So I just carried on like nothing had happened. Like I said, it almost felt like nothing had.'

'Except you left some fibres behind,' said Charlie.

'Apparently so –' Sue shrugged – 'but Murdoch was so keen to frame Shane for it, everyone assumed they were from his football scarf. Lucky for me, I suppose.'

'But unlucky for poor Shane,' said Charlie.

'Yes,' said Sue with a deep sigh. 'I wanted to talk to you about that.'

116

Bad Dreams and Bleeding Hearts

Charlie decided to stay quiet and let Sue speak. She clearly wanted to offload. He could tell she was upset by the thickness in her voice.

'Shane is who keeps me awake at night,' she said. 'I have bad dreams about him. I mean, I didn't harm him myself but maybe indirectly I did. And I feel so terribly guilty.'

'You don't feel guilty about Frank?' asked Charlie.

'I don't actually,' she said firmly. 'To be honest, I mainly feel a sense of relief. Closure, if you like. He was an evil man who wrecked a lot of lives, my family's included.'

'Yes, but . . .'

'I know, I know,' she said. 'You shouldn't take the law into your own hands. But he'd got away with it for decades. Look at Ian. Look at Shane. Heaven knows how many boys over how many years.'

'Talking of Shane . . .'

'Shane, yes,' said Sue, keen to unburden herself. 'Like I say, I feel horrible about that poor lad. I keep thinking that if I hadn't done what I did, there might have been no red fibres left on Courtney's body. Shane might not have become prime suspect. And Murdoch might not have ended up killing him for his silence.'

'That's a lot of maybes,' pointed out Charlie.

'It is,' she agreed. 'Murdoch would've framed Shane anyway, right? And once he knew Shane was on to him, he probably wouldn't have let him live. Football scarf or no football scarf. Fibres or no fibres.'

It sounded like she was convincing herself, thought Charlie. Maybe that's the only way she could live with it.

'How do you feel about Murdoch taking the fall for Frank's murder?'

'I'm pretty much at peace with that,' said Sue. 'Murdoch tried to kill Courtney. He thought he had. He still does. He's a murderer and a corrupt copper anyway. He kidnapped Ruby and tried to kill you. My heart doesn't exactly bleed. Pardon the pun.'

He smiled ruefully. 'That was worthy of Tess.'

'Besides, Courtney would probably have died there anyway,' added Sue. 'He couldn't move. He was bleeding out from wounds that had nothing to do with me. All I did was hasten it along, so to speak.'

'I suppose,' said Charlie. 'Don't think the police would see it like that, though.'

'Probably not.' She sighed. 'Are you going to tell Anjali? I mean, I wouldn't blame you if you did.'

Charlie's head was still reeling. He hadn't got as far as deciding what to do next. 'Oh, Sue,' he said. 'I really wish I wasn't in this position.'

'I know and I'm sorry,' she said. 'Just weigh it up. That's all I ask. Frank Courtney is the real monster here and he's dead. Craig Murdoch is the real killer and he's been caught. It sounds like he'll take some bent coppers and drug traffickers down with him. What's to be gained by turning me in, too?'

'I'll need to think about that,' said Charlie, already mulling it over.

Sue nodded, tacitly accepting that her fate lay in his hands. They walked on in silence, quickening their stride to catch up with the others before their absence became a talking point.

117

Thick as Thieves

As they strode along, the dogs milled around their feet, occasionally crashing into the bushes, squabbling over a stick or chasing each other around like giddy children.

Despite his mind being elsewhere, Charlie couldn't help smiling at their antics. Ruby seemed to sense it. She turned her head and looked back at him lovingly with her big brown eyes.

Charlie realized how happy he was – here in Framstone, here in the woods, with the dogs and his fellow dogwalkers. He hadn't known what to expect when he moved back from London to his faded home town. At first he'd felt like a bit of a loner. The only member of his generation left here. Apart from Anjali, it turned out.

With the dogwalkers, he'd found his tribe. He'd found friendship. A feeling of home and family, alongside what he and Polly had. Ruby wagged her tail at him as if to say, 'Oi, don't forget about me.' He grinned back at her. Yes. Charlie was content now. He couldn't have imagined that a few years ago.

Rounding the corner, they saw Tess, Viv and Malcolm up ahead, waiting by the entrance to the woods.

'Hurry up, slowcoaches,' called Malcolm. 'I'm gasping for my complimentary coffee.'

'Keep your voice down,' whispered Tess, glancing around. 'Everybody will want one.'

'You two have been as thick as thieves,' said Viv. 'What have you been bending his ear about, babe?'

'True crime mainly,' said Sue. She wasn't entirely lying.

'And knitting,' added Charlie. He wasn't entirely lying either.

They glanced quickly at each other. Sue had a hopeful expression in her eyes.

'Poor you,' said Viv, laughing. 'Now you feel my pain, Charlie.'

As everyone put pooches on leads and turned towards the gates in unison, Charlie reached down. He took Sue's hand and gave it a supportive squeeze. She smiled up at him gratefully. No words were needed.

Soon they were all back round their familiar table at Coastal Coffee. Dogs flopped at their feet, either snoozing or on the lookout for stray crumbs. Tess brought over a tray of steaming cups and sat down to join them. Everyone helped themselves, took a sip and sighed with satisfaction. You can't beat a hot drink after a long bracing walk.

As Charlie raised his strong white Americano to his lips, he caught Sue's eye across the table. He subtly raised his cup to her in a silent toast and mouthed 'To Ian'. She beamed back at him, mirrored the gesture and added a 'thank you'.

Charlie had decided to keep her confession strictly between them. To his mind, Sue's actions hadn't changed any outcomes. Frank Courtney would still have died there in the woods. Craig Murdoch would still have tried to frame Shane Carter for murder, then kill him for his silence. Murdoch would still have come after Charlie and Ruby as he tried to cover up his crimes. Reporting Sue's role might let Murdoch partially off the hook, which was the last thing Charlie wanted.

Sue was right. There was little to be gained by turning her in. She'd achieved some closure by speeding up Frank's death, that's all. No point wrecking her life and Viv's. Or, for that matter, the Courtney family's. They weren't to blame for Frank's vile abuse, which would all come out in a police inquiry.

Poor Shane remained on his mind, though. Charlie wondered if somehow, without revealing her motivations, Sue could make amends to Karen Carter. It might help both of them.

He had a light-bulb moment. Maybe Nuts About Mutts could take on Karen as a part-time dogwalker. An extra pair of hands when they needed help or holiday cover. Charlie grinned, thrilled with his own idea. Karen loved dogs as much as her son. Wherever he was now, Shane would surely approve. Charlie would suggest it to Sue the next time they were on their own. He knew she'd agree.

As conversation turned to local gossip – not local crime for the first time in a while – Charlie finished his coffee and glanced down. Ruby lay at his feet, looking content but exhausted. That extra lap meant their walk had been longer than usual. Charlie realized he was feeling it too, especially in his injured leg.

As he stood up to say his goodbyes, the others were hatching plans for another drink at the Neptune.

'You've just got a taste for free beverages,' said Charlie with a laugh. 'Jackie's hospitality might soon run out on that score.'

'Not if you bat those long eyelashes at her again,' teased Tess.

'Maybe I'll bat mine at her too,' said Viv. She cast an impish sidelong glance at Sue, who rolled her eyes.

'A merry widow with her own pub?' said Malcolm. 'I doubt she'll stay single for long. Get in there while you can, that's what I say.'

As they all started gossiping again, Charlie's farewells got drowned in the hubbub. He headed for the door with a wry chuckle. Even before recent events, the dogwalkers had very much been a gang. Now they were bonded even tighter by what they'd been through – and by the secrets they kept.

Charlie and Ruby headed home at a leisurely pace. He decided to stop off at Malcolm's friend the fishmonger. Polly would appreciate fresh fish for supper. He'd pop into the butcher's and get Ruby something special, too. She'd earned it.

After all the excitement of recent weeks, a cosy dinner for three was just the ticket. Charlie was already looking forward to slumping on the sofa afterwards to watch TV, with Polly in her favourite armchair and Ruby curled up in a crescent shape, snoring in her basket.

No crime dramas tonight, though. He'd had enough of those. For now anyway.

Acknowledgements

First of all, I'd like to thank you, the reader, for picking up this novel and making it to the end. I'm new to this author lark, so it's appreciated more than you know.

Getting a novel written, published and into your hands takes a village. When it's a debut novel, it takes a small town. Perhaps one a little like Framstone, in fact. So there are many to thank. Please bear with me as I come over a bit like weepy Gwyneth Paltrow at the Oscars (pink Ralph Lauren frock to be confirmed).

Thanks to my magnificent agent, Juliet Pickering, who has championed and supported me tirelessly, along with Finlay Charlesworth and everyone at Blake Friedmann. Juliet has been instrumental in this project growing from a paragraph-long pitch in early 2023 to an actual proper book in late 2025. It wouldn't exist without her hard work, wisdom and good humour.

Thanks to my editor, the brilliant Grace Long, whose observations and ideas improved the book no end, and the entire team at Penguin Michael Joseph. Deputy editor Emily Van Blanken, publicity director Gaby Young, press officer Lily Evans, marketing assistant Jack Hallam, cover designer Nina Elstad, production manager Serena Nazareth, editorial manager Nick Lowndes – total dudes, one and all. It's genuinely such a thrill to have that iconic aquatic bird in the corner of something I've written. A childhood dream fulfilled.

Thanks to my copy-editor Jennie Roman and proofreader

Jill Cole for their sage advice, skilful work and for saving my blushes. I owe you a large drink or several down the Neptune. And to Claiborne Hancock at my US publisher Pegasus. Another ambition ticked off.

Thanks to my journalistic mentors over the years, first from my magazine days and then my freelance writing era. That means you, Fiona Gibson, Marie O'Riordan, Mark Ellen, Kath Brown, Phil Hilton, Serena Davies and Barry McIlheney. The latter is sadly no longer with us but I hear his voice in my head daily, usually saying something hugely inappropriate but hilarious. He, Lola, Frankie and Mary were also generous enough to let us share ownership of their dog Roxie, which set me on this pooch-populated path.

Thanks and soppy love to our own dogs, the much-missed Betty and her successor Ivy – both rescue Staffies, both the best of girls. They were adopted from the Dogs Trust, which does incredible work rehoming dogs and helping owners. Please support them if you can.

Thanks to Polly and Max the Schnauzer – my first ever dog-walking 'client', back in my early teens. And to all the dogs I've walked or strolled alongside since. The likes of Pepsi, Rafi, Pablo, Albie, Sam, Dave, Bramble, Sparrow, Trixie, Biff, Stanley, McNulty, Tuppence, Steve, Josh, Rosie, Lottie, Chocolate, Hugo, Dublin, Pearl, Inca, Gizmo, Mabel, Barney, Gracie, Bailey, Cookie, Otter, Sylvie and Scamp. Your humans aren't half bad either.

Thanks to my dear friends the Boardmans, who let me borrow their surname and much else besides.

Thanks to the friends and fellow writers who've given me encouragement and advice: Lucy Mangan, Sali Hughes, Julia Raeside, Jess Ruston, Mhairi McFarlane and more. These include the mighty Jilly Cooper, who offered kind words and sent me a signed copy of her glorious dog-walking memoir, *The Common Years*, when I needed a welly boot up the backside.

Thanks to all the locations that inspired the settings in the novel and the people who live in them. The fictional town of Framstone is partly based on Felixstowe, where I grew up. Framstone Woods has a strong flavour of Abney Park, near where I now live in North London. There's also a touch of Taunton, where I spend a lot of time, along with coastal towns like Whitstable, Minehead, Margate, Brean, Whitley Bay, Dunwich, Southwold and Blue Anchor.

Thanks to my mum Valerie for, well, pretty much everything. And my stepfather Pat, brother Patrick and sister-in-law Lins for their understanding and patience. Thanks to my in-laws, the Sanderses, both those still with us and those dearly departed. They've become my extended family, a constant source of support and laughter.

Lastly and mostly, thanks to Alex, the love of my life, our amazing daughter Kitty and the other Charlie, who is missed and loved always.

On a station platform, with nothing to read,
and a four-hour train journey stretching ahead of him...

That's where the story began for Penguin founder Allen Lane.
With only 'shabby reprints of shoddy novels' on offer,
he resolved to make better books for readers everywhere.

By the time his train pulled into London, the idea was formed.
He would bring the best writing, in stylish and affordable
formats, to everyone. His books would be sold in bookstores,
stationers and tobacconists, for no more than the price
of a ten-pack of cigarettes.

And on every book would be a Penguin, a bird with a certain
'dignified flippancy', and a friendly invitation to anyone who
wished to spend their time reading.

In 1935, the first ten Penguin paperbacks were published.
Just a year later, three million Penguins had made their
way onto our shelves.

Reading was changed forever.

—

A lot has changed since 1935, including Penguin, but in the
most important ways we're still the same. We still believe that
books and reading are for everyone. And we still believe that
whether you're seeking an afternoon's escape, a vigorous debate
or a soothing bedtime story, all possibilities open with a book.

Whoever you are, whatever you're looking for,
you can find it with Penguin.